## Acknowledgments

The first on my list of thanks will always be the love of my life. I might not have been as pouty this time around about criticism, but I'm sure I had my moments. And the support is always there regardless, as it is from my family who I thank from the bottom of my heart. Special thanks to my great friend Pat from across the pond. Your help with cleaning up the manuscript and being available so that I could bounce opinions off you is appreciated more than you know. Once again, many, many thanks to my editor, Benee Knauer and her way of working her magic on me. Her wise advice made When White Fades to Black a much better novel. And thanks to my editor, Michael Carr. All I have to say is that you are a genius.

GW00643037

To the countless women and men who have suffered the senseless and undeserved consequences of racism and prejudice

**Foreword**

I have only one reason for including a foreword with this novel. I would like to offer my sincere apologies to anyone who might be offended by the racial slurs used in When White Fades to Black. They appear for no other reason than authenticity in the interest of the arts and to express just how ugly and abhorrent they can be.

**Prologue**

The percussion of the blast was enough to blow out the eardrums of any living creature within half a mile. The urea nitrate explosive planted at the base of the Washington Monument had strewn every imaginable body part—arms, legs, fingers, feet, noses, eyes, even internal organs of some very important people— over the area of a football field. Anguished wails from those unlucky enough to survive penetrated the thick, smoky air, then were drowned out by the approaching sirens from scores of emergency vehicles. The long, slender fingers of fire flickered skyward, charring the heavens with toxic black plumes where the towering monolith had stood seconds ago. Flames flared in patches on either side of the Reflecting Pool, burning grass and flesh alike.

The morning had begun peacefully enough. Some hard-core spectators had been allowed to camp out overnight to secure a spot for the festivities, though Secret Service surveillance was heavy. The remainder of the crowd started to gather just before seven a.m. for the long-anticipated repeat of the Million Man March of 1963. It was a beautiful day in the nation's capital, not a cloud in the sky, with a forecast high of seventy degrees—balmy weather for this time of year. The purpose of the gathering: to celebrate the progress made by African Americans since the first march. Many high-profile guests, black and white, were scheduled to give speeches. The keynote was to be delivered by none other than the newly elected president of the United States, Benjamin Cooper, the second African American to hold the most powerful position on the planet.

Many celebrities were expected to attend and perform, including superstar recording artist and Academy Award winner Thelma Brown. Thelma was a true rags-to-riches story—a metaphor, synthesis, and personification of all that the event represented. She had been raised by a single mother who had four other little ones to look after in the slums of Los Angeles County. In Compton, even the young girls found it difficult to avoid the influence of the gangs, and Thelma Brown, sucked into that world at the tender age of 13 by her 16-year-old boyfriend, was no exception. Once you were in, giving up your membership was hardly an option. Thelma realized her mistake from the outset. Her initiation alone included gang rape and beatings. She was forced to do drugs and commit crimes, including theft and aggravated assault with a deadly weapon, all before her fourteenth birthday.

If not for her amazing singing talent, she might never have escaped. Random luck or fate—however one tends to evaluate such things—shone on her one day when she was 15. Thelma didn't even know she was being watched. She generally didn't like to sing in front of strangers. Forced by gang leaders in preparation for an ultimate inside burglary job, she had gotten part-time work as a clerk at Murdock's video rental store, not far from her home. Her only colleague on that particular day, at that exact moment, had stepped out to grab a bite to eat. Thelma was in the process of replacing some tapes on the shelves when, unbeknownst to her, not just any customer walked into the store.

One of the leading African-American record producers had been unsuccessfully trying to get his stubborn dad to move out of Compton for twenty years. Every Sunday, his visits to his aging father's home included popcorn and a rented movie from Mr. Murdock's store. While placing the film *Spellcaster* between *Sleepwalkers* and *Stepfather III,* Thelma broke out into a Mariah Carey song, and the rest was history. Within a month, she had a record deal with a major production company. Her days as a gang member on the streets of

Compton were over. Thelma became an overnight sensation. Since her debut CD, she had twenty-one *Billboard* number one hits and eight number one albums. Besides her Oscar for best supporting actress in her second film, she had fourteen miniature gramophones in her trophy case, for Grammies won in her twenty-two years as a pop artist. Perhaps her best work was her tireless effort to clean up the streets of America and end gang violence. She had contributed countless hours and millions of dollars to the cause.

Thelma had gotten her invitation to the Million Man March from the president himself, who was going to deliver his speech upon completion of her performance. He would be waiting in the wings as she finished her last song. Then she would introduce him. But she would never get that chance. Nor would she ever again delight a crowd with her unparalleled five-octave singing voice. The stage was set up within feet of the George Washington Memorial monolith. In the last minute of her first encore, the explosion that rocked the world set the entire stage and everything on it ablaze. One second, she was singing the song that had kick-started her amazing career; the next, she was dead.

**Chapter 1**

*Four months earlier*

The chirping sounds of medical machinery echoed off the walls of the small alcove in the intensive care unit at Jackson Memorial Hospital in Miami, Florida. Registered nurse Donna Ortiz was seated at a desk at the foot of her patient's bed. She was paying as close attention to the monitors assessing her patient's condition as her powers of concentration would allow. Keeping her focus was proving difficult, and by health-care industry standards, it probably wasn't very safe. For the past several hours, she had been seriously considering requesting the rest of the day off, before she killed someone else. Her previous shift was one she would not forget for the rest of her life.

Two nights ago, not long after the start of her shift, United States Senator Alvin Fitch was admitted to the hospital for a simple cardiac procedure. He had come to Miami for a political fund-raising event at the Convention Center on South Beach. As special guest speaker, the senator had just finished his dinner and was about to address a large group of senior citizens when he suddenly felt crushing and debilitating chest pain. His team, fearing he was having a heart attack, called 911. The responding ambulance rushed the senator to Jackson Memorial, where he underwent a battery of tests to determine whether there had been any damage to heart tissue. The initial results were negative. To cover all the bases, the cardiologist on call, Dr. Alan Freeman, ordered that his patient undergo an angiogram first thing in the morning. The senator was placed in the cardiac ICU, where he was to receive one-on-one care from the unit's most experienced nurse, Donna Ortiz.

By the middle of the night, Senator Fitch was hanging on to life by a thread. He had taken a turn for the worse just hours before his scheduled procedure. In an attempt to pinpoint the reason for his deteriorating condition, more blood tests were ordered, ultimately revealing severe liver and kidney malfunction. Before the lab ever delivered those results, the senator's heart monitor flatlined, and Nurse Ortiz was forced to call a code blue. A team of eight nurses and two docs worked for more than an hour to save the life of one of the nation's most esteemed senators, to no avail. Dr. Freeman made the decision to terminate the code, and at 5:27 a.m., he pronounced Senator Alvin Fitch dead.

The Dade County chief medical examiner performed the autopsy later that morning. The cause of death was identified as an overdose of insulin, a medication not in the protocol for a nondiabetic cardiac patient. A relative certainty of foul play was later discovered by FBI Special Agent Daniel Falcone while conducting the preliminary inquiry into the senator's death. He determined that the lethal medication had not been prescribed by any of the treating physicians. An official investigation into the assassination of a U.S. government official was launched immediately thereafter.

Daniel already had a prime suspect. One of the senator's three bodyguards, James Crane, had disappeared off the face of the earth before Fitch was transferred to intensive care. Crane was last seen by the two other plainclothes Capitol Police officers hired to protect Fitch. They told Daniel that Crane had left to get lunch for the security team and never returned.

The chief medical examiner estimated that the insulin was injected about fifteen minutes before cardiac arrest. After an exhaustive review of all the medical records, Agent Falcone concluded that the only person who had contact with the senator during the window of opportunity was Nurse Donna Ortiz. In fact, she was the only health-care provider in the unit to administer *any* medication after midnight.

Until Nurse Ortiz reported to work this morning, two days after the senator's ordeal, she hadn't known that his death was the result of foul play. When the unit supervisor advised her that the FBI had just called to notify the hospital that she was wanted for questioning, finishing her shift was no longer an option.

* * *

Ominous black storm clouds filled the southeastern sky, blocking the rising sun. Annie Bryan thanked her lucky stars that she had decided to go to the office early and avoid rush-hour traffic. She despised driving in South Florida thunderstorms. Visibility was often not more than ten feet. Inevitably, there was an accident on the slick, dangerous roads. Leaving her condo at six thirty a.m. had saved her from all that and the accompanying gridlock.

She scrambled to switch on the lights in the lobby of her new law office. Though she had made great progress toward healing, just a few short seconds spent in the stark blackness of an unlit room almost always brought on a crippling panic attack. She had spent nearly two weeks in terror-charged darkness after being kidnapped by the FBI's most wanted—and still at large—serial killer. Shortly after her rescue, she had resigned from her position as executive VP of security with King Cruise Lines. She had given it her best effort to dissociate the job from her horrifying experience. In the end, she decided that a clean break was her only option if she wanted to achieve some semblance of a healthy, functional psyche.

Annie had initially met her abductor during one of her routine work-related visits to the *Diamond,* a cruise liner owned by her company. At the time, he was employed on the ship as a security officer, under the alias Damien Drysdale. The instant he laid eyes on her, he had suffered a fatal attraction of the most malignant variety. As a direct consequence of his obsession, he murdered and dismembered her beloved neighbor, then massacred the wife and in-laws of her closest friend, Daniel Falcone. Annie was raped and tortured repeatedly while held in captivity. By the grace of God, as well as an extraordinary act of courage on her part, she was rescued by Agent Falcone. Unfortunately for her and the rest of the world, the monster got away.

After resigning her position with King, Annie was forced to take an extended leave to recover from the tragedy and undergo intensive therapy. She refused the FBI's offer to give her anonymity through the Witness Protection Program. With the psychopathic maniac still at large, it may not have been the wisest decision. Depression and apathy had set in, and she found it impossible to muster up the energy to care about anything—not even her own safety. Only after countless sessions with her psychologist, and an initial regimen of antidepressive and antianxiety medication, did she begin to think again about her hopes and dreams.

Annie had studied criminal justice at George Washington University. She received her bachelor's degree, then continued her education at Harvard School of Law, graduating number one in her class. It was always her ambition to establish her own law firm as a criminal defense attorney, practice for ten years, then enter politics. But when they offered her the lucrative position at King, it was an offer she couldn't refuse. Having saved a lot of money during her time with her former employer and feeling emotionally stable, she knew that it was time to open her new law office.

So far, things weren't going exactly as planned. She knew that the first few years would be rough. She had never dreamed that after six months, she would have a grand total of five clients. Something had to give.

* * *

At 9:15 a.m., Annie's secretary, Kelly Olsen, poked her head into the office to tell her that a Mr. Julio Ortiz was asking to speak to her in reference to the Fitch assassination. Annie picked up the phone before Kelly could complete her sentence.

"Hello, Mr. Ortiz. This is Annie Bryan. How can I help you?"

"Good morning, Ms. Bryan. I'm Donna Ortiz's father. I'm sure you must have heard about her in the news?"

"Can't really avoid it. It's been dominating the airwaves since the assassination. What can I do for you?"

"I was wondering if maybe we could schedule an appointment to see you sometime today. The FBI asked her to come in for questioning tomorrow morning. How they can possibly suspect my daughter is a mystery to me. She's the sweetest, most caring person I've ever met in my life. I decided to call you because I read you opened up your own practice. I followed the whole story about the kidnapping. Anyone who could survive something like that, I want on my side. I have to admit, uh . . . I thought it might help that you're a good friend of the investigating agent."

Annie hesitated a moment before replying. This case could put her on the map. On the other hand, as an officer of the court, her personal relationship with the investigating officer could potentially be considered a conflict of interest. The Florida Bar's rules of ethics would disqualify her in that event. After doing a quick calculus in her head, she decided to give it a shot.

Though Annie had absolutely nothing on her schedule this afternoon, she preferred not to publicize it.

"Excuse me, Mr. Ortiz, let me check with my secretary to see if I can fit you in today." She held the phone down for several seconds then raised the receiver back up to her ear and said, "It looks like you're in luck. I can see you and your daughter at one p.m."

He agreed to the time, and Annie ended the conversation, then turned to her computer to do a search of Internet articles on the Fitch assassination. She watched the reports on the nightly news but wasn't that familiar with the details of the investigation that the FBI had allowed to leak out to the press. If she were to be retained by Ms. Ortiz, she would obtain the Bureau's investigative file. For the moment, she wanted to know all the facts as reported by the media.

In the past two days, thousands of articles had been published on the subject. Annie narrowed her search to the major national newspapers such as the *New York Times, Miami Herald, Wall Street Journal, USA Today,* and *Washington Post.* She was totally unaware of a potentially damaging statement by Ortiz until she read a report from the *Times* headlined, "Nurse Ortiz admits to shift supervisor that Senator Fitch never left her sight in ICU." The piece went on to make the inference, "An exclusive Times investigation revealed that the insulin was injected just fifteen minutes before Senator Fitch went into cardiac arrest. It stands to reason that Nurse Ortiz either witnessed the insertion of the insulin-filled syringe into the intravenous port or injected it herself."

If these statements were accurate, it was entirely possible that Annie's potential client's fingerprints had been found on the syringe.

Clifton Harris, a reporter Annie knew from her ordeal with the serial murderer, had written an article on Alvin Fitch in the *Miami Herald*. Annie scanned the parts from the story that helped her get a genuine understanding of the senator's work and character.

"Alvin Fitch began his first term in the United States Senate in the early 1970s. A native of Fort Lauderdale, Florida, he represented the state in some political capacity from the time he graduated from the University of Florida law school in 1964. He was a champion of civil rights, acclaimed for taking the side of the underdog. The senator was a stalwart proponent of affirmative action and credited as the single most influential politician in the passing of the Americans with Disabilities Act in 1990. His latest efforts were directed toward passing a fair and just federal immigration law."

After reading just about everything written on the assassination in the five major national newspapers, Annie came to the conclusion that the FBI probably didn't have enough to indict Ortiz. If they did, they would have already done it. There was no reported connection between her and the missing bodyguard, James Crane. Motive was totally absent. The most difficult task Annie might have to face would be to controvert any evidence that Ortiz injected the insulin. It was way too early in the process to come to any solid judgments. Annie felt it would be a while before Daniel felt secure enough to formally charge her client, if he even had the evidence to do so.

14

Despite her lack of trial experience, Annie felt capable of advising Donna Ortiz in the preindictment phase. If she was officially charged, Annie would decide whether to seek assistance from a more seasoned veteran.

A rumble in her stomach reminded her it was time for lunch. Feeling as if her luck was taking a turn for the better, she invited Kelly to join her at Il Mulino for a small celebration.

* * *

The South Florida summer sun beat down on the black pavement of the parking lot of the Sea Gate Plaza office building, bringing the surface temperature above 100 degrees. A nervous Donna Ortiz got out of the passenger seat of her father's Mercedes Benz E-class sedan. She was a tall, thickset woman, slightly overweight, of Costa Rican descent. Her bright green eyes were a striking contrast against her olive skin and jet-black hair. Beads of perspiration formed on her forehead as she made her way to the building's entrance. When she walked through the door held open by her dad, she was relieved by the fresh cool, dehumidified atmosphere of the air-conditioned lobby. After checking in with the building's receptionist, Donna and Julio Ortiz took the elevator to Annie Bryan's office on the third floor.

The reception area of the Bryan law firm was furnished with an antique colonial sofa and four Early American wingback chairs. Traditional cherrywood end tables and wrought-iron floor lamps stood on either side of the sofa. Walnut hardwood floors supported the provincial theme Annie was after. A Lt. Moses Willard candlelight chandelier hung from the center of an American tin ceiling.

15

Annie had spared no expense in decorating her office. Although the fancy digs had not yet rendered results, once business picked up, it would be important for the decor to reflect success.

The Ortizes were ten minutes early. Kelly offered them their choice of a soft drink, coffee, or tea, then notified Annie that they had arrived. Annie instructed Kelly to escort them to the library, where she joined them at one o'clock sharp.

"Good Afternoon, Ms. Ortiz, Mr. Ortiz. I'm Annie Bryan. Please stay seated." Annie took a seat at the head of the conference table, which ran most of the length of the room. Donna was in the chair to her right, and Mr. Ortiz was directly across from his daughter.

After the initial greetings, Julio spoke first. "Like I told you on the phone, Ms. Bryan, Donna was asked to appear at the FBI's Miami Field Office tomorrow to answer questions about her care of Senator Fitch. From what we've heard on the news, she seems to be one of their prime suspects. We figured it would be best to retain a lawyer. We were wondering if you would be available."

"I'll take your case, Ms. Ortiz. And my first advice to you is, you are not attending the meeting with the FBI tomorrow morning."

"But won't she be arrested if she doesn't show up?" Mr. Ortiz asked.

"Dad, I can speak for myself," Donna complained. "I'm very happy you're here to support me, but please let me handle this."

"I'm sorry, honey. I'll keep my mouth shut."

"You can contribute. But I'm a big girl now. I can speak for myself. Can you explain, Ms. Bryan?"

"To answer your dad's question, no, they won't arrest you. It's your right to plead the Fifth Amendment. They would be violating the United States

Constitution if they put you in jail for refusing to talk to them. If they want to drop you from the list of suspects, then by all means, have at it. Tell them everything you know. For now, it's my advice that you remain silent. That obviously doesn't mean I don't want to hear your side of the story. We might as well get straight to it. I'll help you through the details by asking questions along the way. I'm also going to tape the interview for future reference. Do I have your permission to do so?"

Donna Ortiz agreed, and Annie turned on her handheld recorder.

"Okay, the beginning is always a good place to start. Tell me when you first became aware Senator Fitch was a patient in your hospital."

"News and gossip travel fast at Jackson Memorial. Senator Fitch's visit caused an immediate buzz. I think I first heard about it when I went to the cafeteria to grab a cup of coffee around nine. Alice, the cashier, told me. I didn't hear any specifics about why he was at the hospital until much later. The cardiac ICU charge nurse, Wendy Pierce, got a call from the emergency room at about one thirty a.m. They told her Senator Fitch was being transferred to the unit. I happened to be approaching the nurse's station as she was ending her conversation. After she hung up, she told me Senator Fitch was scheduled for a cardiac catheterization in the morning, and asked if I wouldn't mind taking him as my patient. Ordinarily, I take care of patients fresh out of open-heart surgery. Since we weren't anticipating having any surgical patients that night, Wendy thought it best that I take care of the senator. He was a VIP, and I was the most experienced cardiac nurse in the unit."

"Did you have any contact with the patient before he was transferred to Intensive Care?" inquired Annie.

"No, I prepared the room and spoke with the emergency room nurse to get a report on the patient's symptoms, treatment, and meds. I didn't actually meet him until the orderlies brought him up."

"Can you tell me the details of her report to the best of your recollection?"

Nurse Ortiz described the symptoms recorded and tests performed during Fitch's first hours at the hospital. She finished with an explanation of the treatment prescribed and the physician's conclusions.

"He was given nitroglycerin spray under the tongue, aspirin, and a clot-buster drug. Senator Fitch spent a total of six hours under observation in the emergency room. The cardiologist's diagnosis was gastritis. To rule out cardiac disease, he scheduled the senator for a catheterization the next morning."

"Was Senator Fitch experiencing any symptoms when he was transferred up to the cardiac intensive care unit?"

"When a patient is suffering from chest pain, we ask them to rate its intensity between one and ten, ten being the most severe. The first time he was asked that night, he rated it a nine. The nitroglycerin didn't seem to give him any relief. That was another indication he probably wasn't suffering from any heart-related anomalies. By the time he was transferred to the unit, the pain was almost completely gone."

"When exactly did he arrive at the unit?"

"The records would reflect the exact time. I think it was around two o'clock in the morning."

"Did you have any other patients that night?"

"No. It was a slow night, plus the brass at the hospital wanted him to have one-on-one care. Senator Fitch was my only patient."

"I assume you had a conversation with the senator. Can you tell me everything that was said as best you can recall?"

"When he was brought into the unit, I introduced myself and told him I would be his nurse until morning. I asked him about his chest pain. I let him know, if he needed anything during the night, I would be setting up a makeshift desk with his over-bed table right outside the entrance of his room. I would hear him if he called my name in a normal voice. I explained that the doctor prescribed a sedative for him to sleep. He said he was very tired and would like to take it right away. So I gave it to him. Within ten minutes, he was out."

"How many other nurses were working in the unit that night?"

"Since we weren't that busy, several floated to the floor. It was just me, the charge nurse, Wendy, and one other ICU nurse, Tara Licek. The unit secretary was also there."

"Did the senator ever wake up before he went into cardiac arrest?"

"No, he was asleep the entire time."

"Did anyone, including hospital personnel, visit the unit while Senator Fitch was a patient there?"

"The phlebotomists came periodically to draw blood. I believe it was Selma Thatcher that night. The pharmacy also delivered some medication, but I can't remember who it was. Two bodyguards came into the unit to see how many points of access there were. When they were satisfied that the only entrance was through the front doors, they set up their post just outside. The charge nurse felt it was best for the senator and other patients that the bodyguards weren't in the unit."

"Did you know any of the bodyguards who accompanied Senator Fitch to the hospital?"

"No, I never met or saw any of them before they introduced themselves that night. The one bodyguard had already disappeared by the time Senator Fitch was transferred to the unit."

"Did you have any conversation with James Crane before that evening?"

"No, I never heard of the man or saw him ever in my entire life."

"Did you administer any medication to Senator Fitch through the IV port?"

"Yes, I did. He had a history of allergic reactions to dye, so the doctor ordered an IV push of fifty milligrams of Benadryl and a hundred and twenty-five milligrams of Solu-Medrol three hours before the procedure, then again just before he was transferred to the cath lab. Obviously, I never had the opportunity to give him the second dose."

"What's an IV push?"

"Oh, that's when you inject the medication straight through the IV port into the vein."

"Do you remember exactly what time you gave him those medications?"

"Uh . . . it would've been some time just before four in the morning."

"Just before the senator took a turn for the worse?"

"Yes, that's true."

"Where did you get the medication from? Is it delivered to you from the pharmacy, or do you keep those drugs in the unit?"

"There's a room just behind the nurse's station where we keep all the medications for our patients. It's always locked. A pharmacy tech usually delivers them in the morning and then again in the evening. If I remember correctly, since the senator was a late admission, some of his meds weren't delivered until after midnight."

"Did you give this information to the investigating agent? Is Agent Falcone aware there was a late delivery?"

"I'm not sure. He did ask me some initial questions the night of the incident, but I don't remember if we talked about that. I'm sure he interviewed the other nurses, the lab techs, and maybe even the pharmacy techs. There would also be a record of the delivery. I assumed he was going to be getting into much more detail at the meeting tomorrow."

"Well, there won't be a meeting. I'll be chatting with him. I'm gonna need to know the name of the pharmacy tech who delivered the medication, and any other techs who were on duty that day. Eventually, I'll get that information directly from the hospital or through the FBI records. But I want to start preparing a defense right away. If you can get it to me ASAP, it would help. Is it true what I've read: the senator was never out of your sight before he coded?"

"He was only in the unit for two hours when he went into cardiac arrest. I didn't take a bathroom break. I went to the medication room to get the Benadryl and Solu-Medrol. The senator's room was directly across from the pharmacy, and I left the door open so I could keep an eye on him. I guess the answer to your question is yes. I never lost sight of him."

"Now, why don't you tell me, in as much detail as you can, what happened when Senator Fitch's condition started to go downhill? I want to know who was involved and all measures taken to save his life."

Donna Ortiz recounted the events that ultimately led to the senator's death. When she was through, Annie had her sign a formal contract of representation and told her she would be contacting Agent Falcone later that afternoon. The FBI would have many loose ends to resolve before they could formally charge her with the murder of Senator Fitch, if they were even contemplating it. Annie expressed her opinion that Agent Falcone was a capable investigator who would probably make the right decision in the end. Annie promised that if, by chance, he was considering Donna as a suspect, she would do everything in her power to make sure no charges were filed.

* * *

"Boys, Boys! Settle down! Finish your breakfast! You're gonna be late for tennis camp." Daniel Falcone gave his two young sons a look. He had the sole responsibility of raising Dale and Timmy since his wife of nine years was murdered by the serial killer he now referred to as "Nameless." Since the massacre, Daniel had made it his mission in life to capture the psycho. Over the past year, he hadn't uncovered any significant leads, but certainly not through lack of effort. At least, the killer had not come back into their lives, although Daniel never let his guard down when it came to protecting his boys.

"Dad, Dale won't stop saying Katelyn's my girlfriend," said Timmy. "I don't even like her."

"Timmy, it's not a bad thing to have a girl as a friend—or to have a girlfriend. Your brother probably wishes he had one."

"I *do* have one," retorted Dale.

"You do? And how is it that I know nothing about this?" Daniel asked.

"We just started going out a couple of days ago. She's the number one player on the girls' high school tennis team. I meant to tell you but I forgot."

"Convenient memory loss. You're only fourteen years old, Dale. Don't you think you're a little young to have a girlfriend?"

22

"I'm gonna be fifteen this year. All my friends have girlfriends, Dad. Stop being so old-fashioned! How old were you when you had your first girlfriend?"

"That's beside the point. Times have changed. How old is she?"

"Fourteen and a half."

"Does her mother know about you?"

"Yes, I've been over to her house. Her mom likes me a lot."

"Well, I want to talk more about this later. We don't have time right now. You've got to get to camp, and I've got to get to work, so finish up and let's get movin'."

"But, Dad, Katelyn's not my girlfriend," Timmy repeated.

"Stop teasing your brother, Dale. He won't say it anymore, Timmy. Both of you, go get your gear!"

Fifteen minutes later, Daniel dropped the boys off at the American Heritage Summer Day Camp in Plantation, then took I-95 South toward North Miami and the FBI field office. Although the capture of the Nameless serial murderer was always first on his list, he was currently lead investigator for one of the biggest cases ever assigned to him. He had worked many important crimes during his career with the FBI, earning both national and international accolades. The Fitch murder would put him in contact with some of the most powerful people in the world—an experience that never lost its thrill or, more importantly, its value.

As Daniel drove patiently through the stop-and-go rush-hour traffic, he planned his day and organized his thoughts on the assassination investigation. He was blessed with exceptionally keen intuitive skills. His initial impression of Donna Ortiz was that she had played no role in the murder of Senator Fitch.

Making her a suspect was more a media creation than any decision he had made as chief investigating agent. Either way, her involvement would have to be ruled out since it was clear that she administered the fatal dose of insulin into the IV port. The syringe was covered in her, and only her, fingerprints. That was more than enough to implicate her, at least for now. The only explanation that would possibly exculpate her would be if someone had tampered with the medication. This morning, Special Agent Christopher Frye, who was working the case with Daniel, would be visiting Jackson Memorial Hospital to pursue that more probable line of reasoning. Daniel would spend most of his morning preparing for the Donna Ortiz statement and would join Frye in the afternoon to help interview hospital personnel.

The FBI field office was in North Miami Beach, in a white two-story federal building. Just over five years ago, Daniel was appointed the thirty-fourth special agent in charge of the South Florida Division. Not a year into his administration, he was framed and convicted for the murder of his wife and in-laws by the Nameless serial killer, and spent almost a year in prison. When he was finally exonerated, he returned to the North Miami Field Office. He rejected the FBI's offer to resume the position of special agent in charge, his preference being to solve crimes out in the field. Above all, he wanted to be able to honor his commitment to his children and himself to capture the psychopath who had murdered his wife.

In his cramped ten-by-fifteen-foot cubicle, Daniel worked most of the morning and part of the afternoon reviewing the Fitch file. He wasn't pleased when, shortly after his lunch break, he received the telephone call from Annie Bryan notifying him that Ms. Ortiz wouldn't be attending the meeting.

24

"Annie, you can't be serious," he grumped. "You shouldn't believe everything you read. The media is blowing things out of proportion. We need her statement."

"Are you telling me she's off your list of suspects?"

"You know I can't make that promise right now. But I can tell you I have no intention of arresting her."

"That's not good enough. You went to law school, Daniel. You know as well as I do that I would be committing malpractice if I let the investigating agent interview my client."

"I never was very good at winning arguments with you," he said. "I shouldn't give up so easily, but I guess you gotta do what you gotta do. I think us having her statement will help more than hurt her chances." He wasn't about to waste much time trying to change Annie's mind. He knew her well enough to realize it wasn't going to happen. As Ortiz's defense attorney, she was doing the right thing, anyway.

"Well, maybe if you spend more time investigating the pharmacy, you'll get your answer. I think the medication sent up to the ICU for Senator Fitch was tampered with."

"And what makes you believe that?"

"Nice try, Daniel. You guys just need to concentrate on finding out how insulin got into his antiallergy medication vials. That's how you'll solve this crime. In the meantime, so long as my client is a suspect, she won't be available for questioning."

## Chapter 2

His legs and lower back were as stiff as an overstarched dress shirt. Spasms ran up and down his spine, sending pins and needles to the tips of his toes. Billy Ray Johnson let out a heavy sigh of relief as he pulled into the driveway of his home in Jackson, Mississippi. He had made the fourteen-hour trip from Miami straight through the night, stopping only for gas. He refused to eat at restaurants, not even fast food, and especially not a fried-chicken joint. One never knew who was handling the food, whether it was some filthy black cooking and sweating into his meal, or an oily, stinking wetback dishwasher pawing his silverware. Then there was always the chance some diseased faggot was serving. Billy Ray would just as soon eat roadkill as food touched by one of those freaks. After five days away from home, he was looking forward to grabbing something to eat and then finally stretching out on his own king-size bed. Approaching the front door, he thought about how proud of him his father was going to be. Billy Ray hoped he was still awake, but it was already well past midnight.

The Johnson men were the direct descendants of a long line of who's who in the world of white supremacy. Billy Ray's Dad, Emmett Johnson, was the presiding officer of the Jackson Chapter of the Ku Klux Klan. Billy Ray had hopes to follow in his footsteps and even go further, with the ultimate goal of one day being named grand wizard of the entire organization. With his sights set on horizons well beyond Mississippi, he was already well respected nationally by the Klan and was vice president of the southeastern division of the Neo-Nazi Skinheads. Lately, he had been working a new project on a much grander scale. He was planning to form a right-wing paramilitary group spanning from coast to coast. In his opinion, it was high time for something to be done about the coons, spics, and Jews taking over a country that rightfully belonged to the white man. The writers of the Constitution were no doubt turning over in their graves.

He quietly unlocked and opened the front door of his parents' whitewashed and white-trimmed palatial antebellum plantation estate, located in Jackson's Capital/River Region. In stark contrast, the house was pitch black inside except for a night-light in the library, which barely illuminated the foyer. Billy Ray made a beeline for the refrigerator, his growling stomach overtaking any thoughts of physical discomfort from the drive. Since his parents' bedroom door led straight into the kitchen, he made his way to the refrigerator without flipping on the light switch. As he felt his way along the black granite countertop, his hand brushed against a glass vase, sending it crashing to the floor in a thousand pieces. He swore under his breath, still hoping he hadn't woken his parents. That idea was quickly dashed when the recessed overhead lamps filled the room with light, and Billy Ray found himself looking down the barrel of a Remington Model 870 pump-action shotgun.

"Whoa, Dad. It's just me."

Emmett Johnson had switched on the lights to see his son with his hands up in the air, standing in a puddle of glass shards. Petals from the dozen red roses he had given his wife for their thirtieth wedding anniversary were strewn across the floor in a neat line toward the bedroom.

"What the hell is goin' on, Billy Ray? I could've blown your head off!"

"I just got back from Miami. I was starvin' and wanted to get somethin' to eat. I didn't want to turn the lights on and disturb you guys. Ended up wakin' you up anyway."

"Not a big deal. I figured you might be gettin' back sometime tonight. I wanted to wait up for you. I fell asleep on the couch, and your mom made me go to bed. I couldn't be more proud of you, son. Job well done!"

"Thanks, Dad. It wasn't easy. I had a few close calls. I'll tell you all about it in the mornin'."

"We probably shouldn't be talkin' about it inside the house, anyway. You never know who could be listenin'. I can't wait to hear the story. I always knew my son would do great things for his country. You'll go down in history as a great American patriot, as sure as God made little green apples. Your mother's very proud of you, too, by the way."

"Thanks, Dad. Mom awake?"

"I don't think so. That woman could sleep through the droppin' of an atomic bomb."

"Well, you go get some rest. I'm sorry I woke you up. After I eat, I'm goin' straight to bed myself."

"Don't worry about it, son. You go ahead and make yourself a feast if you want. You deserve it. I'll see you in the morning."

Billy Ray fixed himself two ham sandwiches with good old American cheese and mustard, put them on a paper plate, poured himself a tall glass of Coca-Cola, and carried his meal upstairs to his bedroom. He devoured the sandwiches and the Coke in minutes. With a full stomach and the fatigue from the long-distance drive settling in, he should have no difficulty falling asleep. He couldn't have been more mistaken. The minute his head hit the pillow, instead of drifting into slumber, he began to replay in his head the events of the past couple of days.

* * *

Seventy-two hours earlier, Billy Ray Johnson had checked into the Ritz-Carlton South Beach under the alias Harrison Butler. The concept for the plot to assassinate the liberal pig, Senator Alvin Fitch, was his from the outset. It was the proudest moment of his life when the Klan chose him to devise and execute the plan. At the age of 28, Billy Ray was considered quite young to have any influence on decisions made by the organization. He was an exception to the rule, though, and had shown much promise from the time he was an adolescent. His genealogy played no small role in the clout he had.

Billy Ray created a very detailed and organized strategy for the growth of the Ku Klux Klan. He had a vision. Its members would consist of a new breed. They would break through the molds of their ancient stereotypes. America would no longer see them as a demented bunch of Southern hicks. Their people would be smart, educated, well respected, and widespread.

It was the consensus of most of Billy Ray's peers that it was time for them to act. They had taken a backseat and allowed the situation in their country to get out of control. Through his leadership, the Klan would reemerge as strong and influential as ever. He argued to the Klan's directors that Senator Fitch's expulsion from the Senate was taking way too long. The traitor to the Caucasian race was gift-wrapping our beloved country for the mud race from Latin America. Billy Ray predicted that within twenty years, if the Klan sat back and let bleeding-heart liberals like Senator Fitch give away our country, the official language of the United States would become Spanish. In a rousing speech he gave at a national Klan gathering, he blasted the senator, accusing him of opening up our borders to all kinds of trash. "It's no wonder they blew up the World Trade Center and

Pentagon," he contended. "It was only a matter of dumb luck and incompetence that the Middle Eastern terrorists didn't get the White House."

Already, through Billy Ray's hard work and perseverance, the Klan's membership was up 25 percent. The key, in his opinion, was to expand the Klan's borders beyond the South. Through his intelligent use of Internet social media, he had already recruited new members from states as far afield as Illinois, New York, Florida, and the land of liberals, California. And he had no plans to stop there. His sights were set on much loftier goals. It was his life's mission to restore order to the country and take back what rightfully belonged to the true-blooded citizens who made up the real United States of America.

The network he was establishing had helped facilitate the execution of his latest assignment. He didn't have to pay a cent for his stay at the Ritz. The manager, Karl Simmons, was one of Billy Ray's more recent recruits. Not only was his stay comped, but there was no record that he ever spent a night at the hotel. Karl erased the fictitious name, Harrison Butler, from the computer database the day Billy Ray checked out. The only reason he had to make a reservation in the first place was to prevent corporate headquarters from booking the room to some random caller.

The plan to assassinate Senator Fitch had been conceived over a year ago when the extreme leftist Democrat was appointed to chair the Senate Judiciary Subcommittee on Immigration, Refugees and Border Security. The subcommittee had jurisdiction over immigration, citizenship, and refugee laws, and oversight responsibilities for the Department of Homeland Security, U.S. Citizenship and Immigration Services. The senator was very outspoken about his ultraliberal policies concerning immigration. He was ready to give every illegal alien who had lived in the United States for more than five years a free ticket to American citizenship.

The chief administrators of the Klan agreed with Billy Ray that chairmanship of the subcommittee was too powerful a position to be in the hands of such a radical latitudinarian. Close attention was paid to the minutest details during the many months over which strategy was devised. When Senator Fitch announced his schedule indicating that he would be appearing in Miami, the Klan leadership, including Billy Ray, felt that the plot had its best chance for success in that city. The grand dragon for the state of Florida, Willis Zachary, lived there and had already developed a far-reaching network of professionals in various lines of business. A lifetime member of the Klan was the manager responsible for booking and overseeing events at the Miami Beach Convention Center—the senator's choice. That alone had played a huge part in their decision-making process. Having control of that major function was everything. From there, many aspects of the plan could easily be manipulated. Billy Ray's recruiting efforts only added to making the most populous city of the Sunshine State the ideal site for an assassination.

Although Billy Ray had made his best effort to leave no stone unturned, he never anticipated that the senator would be staying at the Ritz. Fitch's team of plainclothes Capitol Police officers acting as bodyguards had made last-minute arrangements at the hotel—a customary precaution. When Simmons notified Billy Ray that the liberal prick had checked into the hotel, he had no choice but to do his best to avoid Fitch and his entourage. There was no question that the bodyguards would see him at the Convention Center; he couldn't afford to be recognized at the hotel, too.

Fortunately for Billy Ray, senators weren't protected by the army of Secret Service agents normally provided to the president or the vice president of the United States. His preparatory research revealed that the federal government did not provide bodyguard services to U.S. senators. Those who required protection typically hired off-duty Capitol Police officers. Billy Ray knew for a fact that Alvin Fitch never went anywhere without at least one bodyguard, James Crane. And he often hired extras. The hotel would also provide him with security personnel, but they wouldn't be at the Convention Center or the hospital.

Billy Ray had the benefit of a professionally designed disguise created by a former television makeup artist and long-standing Klan member. As a waiter at the Convention Center, he would shave his full beard, slick back his naturally blond hair, and sport the navy blue tuxedo with white shirt and red bow tie required for waiters serving at the banquet. At the hospital, he would wear a fat suit, blue scrubs, a black wig, and a false goatee. With the help of his friends at the Convention Center and the hospital, he didn't expect to encounter too many bumps in the road. He would quickly learn a valuable lesson about taking things for granted when planning to assassinate a United States senator.

Unbeknownst to Billy Ray, on the night before the fund-raising event, Fitch's personal bodyguard, James Crane, had made a special effort to give Billy Ray the once-over, though his motive for doing so had nothing to do with protection. Whenever Billy Ray was away from home for an extended time, he bought all his food from a nearby supermarket only after scoping out its employees. Waiting until late that evening, he had decided to hail a taxi to pick up some provisions at the twenty-four-hour grocery store on Sixth Street. At the same time, the senator, who was suffering from a migraine headache, had asked James to fetch him a bottle of Excedrin Migraine from the pharmacy next door to the hotel. Though he kept it a secret in his professional life, James was gay, with a preference for blonds. When he walked out of the elevator into the lobby, he couldn't help but notice the tall, handsome, fit, fair-haired man coming out of the opposite elevator. Billy Ray, who kept his head down to avoid eye contact with people, had no clue that Senator Fitch's bodyguard was checking him out.

\* \* \*

On the day of the political rally, Billy Ray spent most of the morning reviewing his plan and each building's layout and escape routes, then contacting his coconspirators. The event would take place in the Convention Center's ten-thousand-square-foot Meeting Hall A. The vast room was arranged in banquet style with more than a hundred dining ten-tops. A master of ceremonies table was set up on a dais, where Senator Fitch would be seated. The lifetime Klan member and manager for the Convention Center, John Dobson, chose himself to oversee the fund-raising affair. As a part of the job, it was his responsibility to hire the catering company. His choice was American Gourmet, whose owner, Richard Kraft, was a member of the Klan's Miami chapter.

After touching base with both men, Billy Ray called Andrew Lansbury, the pharmacy director at Jackson Memorial Hospital. Lansbury was another of Willis Zachary's men, and an ex-member of the Florida Neo-Nazi Skinheads. He had two sons who were currently affiliated with the Skinheads, and postulants for membership in the Klan. They had helped with preparations for the mission and would contribute significantly to its execution.

Billy Ray's task at the hospital would be the most complicated. Since the doctor assigned to the senator would not be a part of the assassination plot, there was no guaranteeing what course of treatment would be prescribed or what department he would be admitted to. Based on consultation with Klan physicians, Billy Ray had a good idea what was likely to occur, though they warned him that a portion of the plan might require some improvisation.

The chosen drug he would put in Fitch's iced tea was an antidiuretic medication known as vasopressin. It would mimic the symptoms of a heart attack long enough for doctors to hospitalize the patient for further testing. The drug's normal function was to reduce the excretion of urine from the body. In larger doses, it would cause chest pain and an increase in blood pressure and perspiration. It was colorless and odorless and would be processed through the body in twenty minutes. There wasn't a chance it would be traceable in subsequent blood analyses.

Lansbury had manipulated the schedule so that his best friend and pharmacy supervisor, Doug Simms, would be on duty that evening. He had been a member of the Klan's Miami chapter for more than five years. Because most department supervisors had keys to the drug dispensary, there was no assurance Doug Simms and Billy Ray would have exclusive access. When the actual medications to be prescribed were ultimately determined, Simms would give Billy Ray the appropriate vials to make the switch. If he and Simms were the only people in the pharmacy, they would conduct the exchange there. Otherwise, they would find a secluded place either inside or outside the hospital. Simms would then deliver the vials substituted with insulin to the unit where the senator was admitted.

Satisfied that everything was in place, Billy Ray had opted for a bit of entertainment to relax his mind. He picked up the TV remote from the lower shelf of the cherrywood armoire and scanned the available pay-per-view movies offered by the hotel. When he found *Mississippi Burning* as one of the choices, he considered it an ideal source of inspiration for the mission he was about to embark on. The movie was, in part, based on true events from 1964 involving the Ku Klux Klan and members of his own family. Although it exaggerated the taking down of Klan leaders, the story it told was accurate in its depiction of the weakening of the Klan and the turning tides contributing to its downfall. As he daydreamed through the initial credits, he came to the conclusion that this day would be the birth date of a defining moment in American history and for the resurgence of Ku Klux Klan. He would do whatever it took to correct the mistakes of the past.

When the movie was over, Billy Ray slapped several thick slabs of fresh turkey from the local market on two slices of Wonder bread. By the time he swallowed the last bite, there was no time to waste in preparing for the night's work. The wait staff was required to report to the Convention Center by five in the evening. More than three thousand guests were expected, and a lot of prep work would be necessary. The liberal pig senator had demanded a culturally diverse staff. Billy Ray would be forced to work side by side with a bunch of low-life spics and spades. He would do everything in his power to avoid touching any of them. Nevertheless, when all was said and done, he'd be sure to take a nice, long, hot shower to scrub off any germs and scum that polluted his body.

\* \* \*

The Ritz-Carlton was just a half mile from the Convention Center. Nevertheless, Billy Ray refused to walk the short distance dressed in a three-piece tuxedo. The Florida heat and humidity was far too oppressive, and he could sweat with the best of them. He had the hotel valet hail a taxi and took the two-minute ride in air-conditioned comfort. The Pakistani cab driver made his annoyance about the minuscule fare quite obvious with a deep sigh, a roll of his eyes, and mumbling under his breath. In response, when he arrived at his destination, Billy Ray paid the amount reflected on the meter, then handed the cabbie a single penny. The cabbie tried to return the coin and aggressively explain what he thought of the tip, only to have Billy Ray flip him the bird, step out of the taxi, and slam the door behind him.

The Miami Beach Convention Center spanned a distance of four city blocks, its gross area exceeding half a million square feet. The colorless front facade was designed in the typical art deco style of South Beach. It was the site of several historic events, including Muhammad Ali's first heavyweight championship, the Republican National Convention of 1968, and the Democratic National Convention of 1974. Billy Ray couldn't care less that the loud mouthpiece of heathen horseshit had fought at this venue, nor was he impressed that it was crawling with bleeding-heart liberals in 1974. His grandfather had attended the Republican National Convention on behalf of the State of Mississippi, and he was a man whose footsteps were worth retracing.

Billy Ray walked through the doors and into the huge lobby of the Convention Center. The back of his shirt was soaked with perspiration in defiance of his efforts to avoid it. He removed his jacket and took a moment to stand under an air-conditioning vent. He had only a couple of minutes to kill before he was due to check in with the caterers. He was just seconds from making his way to the banquet hall when James Crane and one of Senator Fitch's other bodyguards entered the building. They had come to conduct their final pre-event security inspection. The first thing that attracted Crane's attention after walking through the doors was the blond man in the tuxedo standing alone in the lobby. Crane instantly recognized him as the man he had seen coming out of the Ritz Carlton elevator last evening.

"Joe," he said, "I think I recognize that guy standing over there by the ticket office. I saw him last night at the hotel. Over there . . . tuxedo."

"You sure it's the same guy?"

"I'm not a hundred percent sure, but I'm not far from it. He was leaving the hotel when I went down to pick up some aspirin for the senator."

"I guess it couldn't hurt go over there and ask him a few questions."

"No—better safe than sorry."

Billy Ray had some of his buddies in the D.C. chapter of the Klan tail Fitch to observe his security procedures in a public setting. They were paid to take photos of the senator and his escorts. Billy Ray was well aware that one of the two men in black suits approaching him was James Crane. He did his best to act nonchalant. Crane spoke first.

"Sir, I'm James Crane, with the United States Capitol Police. We're conducting random security checks since Senator Fitch will be speaking tonight at a dinner engagement. Are you working the party?"

"Yes, sir, I'm serving."

"Can I see your identification?"

Billy Ray had figured that at some point he might have to pass through a security check at the Convention Center. He was well prepared with a license he had gotten weeks ago from the Florida Drivers' License Bureau, using a fraudulent birth certificate. The name on the license was Christopher Reilly. He presented it to Officer Crane.

"Is this a current address, Mr. Reilly?" Officer Crane asked.

"Yes, sir."

"Is your home located in the South Beach area?"

"Yes, it is."

"Were you at the Ritz Carlton last night?"

"Actually, yes. I was visiting a friend who's staying there."

"Can you tell me his name?"

"Yes, sir. Harrison Butler. He's a friend of mine from high school. He's in town from New York on business. Is there a problem?"

"No, we just have to be extra cautious. I happened to see you last night at the Ritz. Do you mind waiting here while we confirm that Mr. Butler is a guest at the hotel?"

"Not at all. I totally understand. You can't be too security conscious these days."

\* \* \*

Crane handed the driver's license to Officer Joe Clerici, who stepped outside to run a search. After ascertaining its validity, he removed his cell phone from its case on his belt and phoned the front desk at the Ritz-Carlton.

Clerici introduced himself to the clerk, then made his request.

"I need to confirm that a Harrison Butler is a guest in the hotel. Can you do that for me?"

"Please hold, Officer Clerici. I'll put you through to Mr. Simmons."

The manager, Karl Simmons, had instructed all clerks to transfer calls involving Senator Fitch's security team to him. The front desk clerk complied with his orders after giving Simmons a brief description of the conversation.

"Officer Clerici, this is Karl Simmons. What can I do for you?"

"Yes, Mr. Simmons. I'd like to verify that a Mr. Harrison Butler is a guest at the hotel. If so, I need to know when he checked in."

Karl tensed at the mention of Billy Ray's alias. How in the world had they come across the name? He hoped Billy Ray wasn't in any kind of trouble.

"Yes, sir, he's a guest in the hotel. He checked in yesterday afternoon. Is there some issue I should be aware of?"

"No, not at all. Just a routine security check. Thank you for your help."

"You're welcome. If you have any other questions or you need anything, you can just call me directly. My cell phone number is 212-555-3777."

After ending the call, Agent Clerici reentered the building and had a quick conversation with James Crane. They decided it was safe to return the driver's license to Mr. Butler and let him proceed to the banquet hall.

\* \* \*

Billy Ray couldn't believe his bad luck. He had managed to talk his way out of this particular situation. To avoid similar problems at the hospital, he would have to be extra careful. He was designated to deliver the laced glass of iced tea at the dinner. Not only was it his guarantee that the job would be done correctly, but he also wanted to bask in the glory that came with killing such a powerful enemy. It would be a bitter disappointment if any more mishaps obliged him to turn over his duties to preselected alternates. He should be thankful they hadn't searched him, for they would have found the chest pain-inducing drug in his inside jacket pocket. Maybe he wasn't so unlucky after all.

## Chapter 3

The sign pointing to the fund-raising event led Billy Ray down a long, deserted hallway. When he turned right at the end of the corridor, he saw up ahead a group of mostly undeserving men and women dressed in the colors of the American flag. They were standing outside the door to what he assumed was the banquet hall. As soon as the clock struck the hour, a Convention Center staff member arrived with the keys.

The hall was lavishly decorated with sheer white curtains covering the temporary partition walls and lining the dais. Long, narrow red, white, and blue drapes hung from ceiling to floor throughout the hall. Round dining tables, covered by tablecloths in the same color scheme, filled the room. Each table had a centerpiece of white calla lilies, blue celosia, and red billy buttons. Baskets of the same flowers were placed on top of the many tall columns decorating the vast open space.

For the next two hours, Billy Ray helped the other servers set the tables and lay out the condiments. He had spent six weeks rehearsing his serving skills for fine dining at a Jackson, Mississippi, Klan member's high-end steak restaurant. During the political fund-raising dinner, he was assigned to the guest of honor's table. His practice was about to pay prodigious dividends.

At 6:45, the guests were admitted to the room, to be seated at their reserved tables. Senator Fitch entered the hall from a private entrance, directly onto the dais, at exactly seven o'clock, flanked by his bodyguards. James Crane positioned himself directly behind the senator's seat while the two other officers took their posts at either side of the dais.

Like many people from the South, Senator Fitch was fond of unsweetened iced tea. Billy Ray made sure his glass was never empty. After the entrée was served, while dessert was being prepared, Billy Ray stepped into the kitchen's walk-in refrigerator with a pitcher of tea and a glass of ice. He closed the door behind him, poured a new glass of iced tea for the senator, then took one of the two small vials out of his pocket and poured forty units of vasopressin into the drink. He thoroughly stirred the mixture together and set it on his serving tray with a pitcher of water. Balancing the tray on his right hand, he pushed the door open with his left and exited the refrigerator. With only one spare dose of the drug, if he should drop the tray or tip over the senator's glass of tea, he would have only one other chance to complete his mission.

From the kitchen's exit, he had to walk the length of the room and climb six steps to the dais. Twice during his trek to the honored guests' table, Billy Ray fumbled with the tray, though not because he was nervous. The thrill of anticipation made it almost impossible to keep his hand steady. He breathed a sigh of relief when he finally made it to the senator's table without incident. He took Fitch's empty glass and replaced it with the drugged tea, then filled the glasses of those guests at the table who requested water.

According to the experts, the vasopressin should take less than five minutes to take effect. Billy Ray lingered at the table as he refilled the water glasses and began to clear the dinnerware. He stacked the used plates and utensils on his tray, moving as slowly as possible to be sure the senator drank his tea. By the time Billy Ray collected as many dishes as he could fit on the tray, the senator had downed three-quarters of the drugged beverage. He refilled the glass and noticed that beads of sweat were already forming on the man's forehead. Shortly, Fitch would inject a bit of unexpected drama into the night's festivities.

Before returning to the kitchen, Billy Ray made a quick detour to the restroom located immediately outside the banquet hall entrance. Just inside the restroom door was a small lobby with a pay phone. Instead of using it, he pulled his cell phone out of his pant pocket and dialed the number for Troy Lansbury stored under "ambulance driver." He let the phone ring twice, hung up, then repeated the process. The code was Troy's warning that a call from the Miami Convention Center for an ambulance was imminent.

Troy Lansbury, son of Andrew Lansbury, was a 22-year-old EMT who had worked for the Miami Fire Department Rescue Service since high school. In his junior year at Killian High in South Miami, he signed up for the school's vocational training program. The day he graduated, he received his license to practice as an emergency medical technician. In his five years with the fire department, he had worked his way up to the position of supervisor of ambulance drivers. In the assassination plot, it was Troy's responsibility to assign himself to drive the ambulance that would respond to the call for Senator Fitch. He would see to it that the patient was taken to Jackson Memorial Hospital.

When Billy Ray reentered the banquet room, all hell had broken loose. The senator was surrounded by his bodyguards and the other guests at his table. He was hunched over in his chair, clutching his chest. There were screams and shouts, and a few women were crying. One of the bodyguards announced that everyone should remain calm, then asked if there was a doctor in the house. A heavyset Asian woman at one of the tables nearest the stage raised her hand and immediately proceeded up the steps to the senator's table.

Billy Ray made an abrupt about-face and turned back toward the kitchen. He burst through the double doors to find that all cooks and servers had left their stations due to the commotion in the banquet hall. Avoiding appliances, pots, and pans as he shucked off his jacket and tie, he hurried across the room and into a private office. He checked the desk drawer where Simmons had left him a blue button-down dress shirt. He put it on, stashing the used one in the drawer with the jacket and tie. Simmons would dispose of them later. It was time to move on to phase two of the plan.

* * *

Back in the kitchen, Billy Ray peered through the windows of the double doors leading out into the corridor. He waited several seconds for two men to disappear around a corner, then walked out. When he arrived at the lobby, he slowed his pace. He left the building, trying his best to be casual in his manner and stride. Outside, he picked up his speed once again and jogged the half mile back to the hotel.

He was perspiring from every pore of his body as he slid the key card into the slot, unlocking the door to his room at the Ritz. With no way of knowing exactly when he would be needed at the hospital, a shower was out of the question. He quickly stripped to his underwear and dried himself off with a bath towel.

The fat suit he would wear underneath his scrubs was laid out on the king-size bed. He struggled to pull the heavy silicone-filled nylon over his legs and torso. As sweat continued to pour from his chin and soak his underarms, he slipped into the blue scrubs draped over the desk chair, and stepped into a pair of tennis shoes. Then, using his cell phone, he called the driver of the limousine that would be taking him to Jackson Memorial Hospital. The chauffeur reported that he was already downstairs, waiting under the hotel porte cochere.

Billy Ray bonded the false goatee to his face and generously applied liquid-tape silicone adhesive to the top and sides of his head. He retrieved the black wig from his suitcase and carefully placed it over his scalp. After looking in the mirror to be sure it was on straight, he pressed down on the areas where he had applied the glue. Satisfied with his new look, he took the zippered leather bag with the insulin from the safe, placed it in his backpack, and rushed out the door.

Andrew's eldest son, Kyle Lansbury, was standing outside the limousine, anticipating Billy Ray's exit from the hotel. Playing his role as chauffeur, Kyle held the back door open for his client, then quickly hopped behind the wheel to drive the ten-minute route to Jackson Memorial. Their specific destination was an employees' entrance on the west side of the medical center. As they pulled into the driveway, Kyle's father was leaning against the pale white exterior wall of the building and smoking a cigarette. With a quick scan of the area to ensure that they were alone, Andrew stamped out his Camel nonfilter, unlocked the door, and held it open for Billy Ray.

Just inside the west entrance, they took an elevator to the third floor and got out directly across from Andrew's office. Kyle would remain with the limousine in the hospital parking lot in the event a fast getaway was necessary. If everything went according to plan, he was to take Billy Ray back to the hotel after the deed was done. Billy Ray cringed when the doors to the elevator sprang open and the one passenger, a black housekeeper, barged past him. He did his best not to make himself conspicuous though even the slightest touch was almost more than he could bear.

Senator Fitch had been in the emergency room for twenty minutes at the time Billy Ray sat in Lansbury's swivel chair and put his feet up on the desk. Might as well make himself at home. The exact hour when he would need to act was an unknown variable. He would be in this office until the moment was right to make the insulin switch. It could take anywhere from forty-five minutes to several hours. Andrew planned to call Billy Ray every half hour with updates. When Senator Fitch was settled in for the night and all his medications were determined, Andrew would find a way to discretely escort Billy Ray to the pharmacy.

Billy Ray had packed his iPod, expecting that he would likely be spending hours rather than minutes waiting for his moment. Listening to music helped soothe his nerves and keep him on an even keel. He took the tiny music player from his backpack, placed the headset over his ears, and listened to Lee Greenwood's latest CD. Forty-five minutes later, he was startled awake by his cell phone's ring tone: "I wish I was in Dixie . . ." It was Andrew.

"Hey, Andrew, what's up?"

"What the hell, Billy Ray? Were you asleep?"

"Yeah, I musta dozed off. What's up?"

"You need to try to stay awake—that's what's up. I'm taking some really big risks here. When the time comes, you need to act fast and get the hell outta here. I had to call you three times before you finally answered."

"All right, Andrew. Chill out! I won't fall asleep again. You have anything I can take to make sure I stay awake? It's not too easy sitting in this little office with absolutely nothing to do. I'm not used to sitting still."

"I'll bring you up some coffee. In the meantime, Senator Fitch is still in the ER. They haven't sent any orders down to the pharmacy yet. I'm hoping to get them within the hour. I'll be up there with the coffee in about ten minutes."

Billy Ray ended the call and stood up to stretch. Andrew was right: he really couldn't afford to fall asleep again. The less time spent at the hospital, the better.

Five minutes later, Andrew appeared with a pot of coffee and poured them each a tall Styrofoam cupful. He told Billy Ray that the cardiologist had completed his assessment and had written orders, meaning that Billy Ray was on deck and would be up to bat shortly. Andrew expected the prescription to come down to the pharmacy within the hour. He finished his cup of coffee, wished Billy Ray good luck, and left the office.

Billy Ray downed a second cup of coffee, only to regret it a short time later when nature called. It would be risky to go out into the hallway. For a moment, he considered urinating into the Styrofoam cup, then decided it might not be big enough. Eventually, it was no longer a matter of choice: either chance it and go to the restroom, or piss in his pants. Choosing the former, he opened the door just enough to peek out into the corridor. Seeing no one, he opened it the rest of the way, stepped out, and closed it firmly behind him. He didn't know which way to go, and looked to either side for a restroom sign.

He was so distracted by the urgency of his search, the ring of the elevator bell didn't register until too late. There was no time to turn around and go back into the office. For the second time in as many days, Billy Ray found himself face to face with Senator Fitch's bodyguard coming out of an elevator.

* * *

At first, James Crane didn't allow his look to linger for more than a second. The fat man in scrubs wasn't much to look at, after all. If not for his training in protecting human beings, he might not have taken a second look. This time, he looked directly into the heavyset man's face. It took Crane an instant to realize that except for the hospital employee's bulky size, he looked just like the handsome blond at the hotel last night—and again at the Convention Center earlier this evening. Those limpid blue eyes were the giveaway. Instead of continuing on his way to the cafeteria, he turned around to examine the man more closely.

* * *

Billy Ray could hear the footsteps of the bodyguard, who had changed direction to follow him into the restroom. A shiver of nervous tension ran down his spine. He wiped away an annoying droplet of sweat from the tip of his nose and reprimanded himself. Now was not the time to show any sign of agitation or stress. When he entered the restroom a hundred feet down the hall from Andrew's office, he went directly into a stall and locked it behind him. The anxiety of the moment had temporarily abated the urgency to urinate. Rather than do his business right then, he peeked through the crack between the door and the stall.

The bodyguard was rinsing his hands at the sink. It was obvious to Billy Ray that Crane hadn't come into the restroom to wash up. He was glancing into the mirror, toward Billy Ray's stall, every two or three seconds. Billy Ray considered having a seat on the toilet and waiting it out. As seconds that felt like minutes passed, and a jumble of conflicting ideas raced through his head, he finally decided it would be suspicious if he stayed much longer. If Crane had seen through the disguise, he probably wouldn't be leaving anytime soon anyway. Billy Ray went ahead and relieved himself, then left the stall. Despite the bodyguard's attempt to be surreptitious, Billy Ray knew that he was being observed.

Crane was now certain that this was the man he suspected. He recognized his gestures and the expressions of his face. Soon, he would also recognize his voice.

"You work at the hospital?" he asked.

"Yeah. What about you?"

"Bullshit. I'm taking you downstairs with me. Turn around and face the wall."

"Whoa! What the fuck! Who the fuck are you?"

"You know damn well who I am, so cut the shit. Now, either you can do this the easy way or I can make you do it. Your choice, but make it now."

"I ain't doin' nothin' wrong. Since when is taking a piss a crime? I'm not just gonna walk outta here with you. How do I know who the hell you are? Show me your badge, and I'll do what you want."

"You're going to play it like that, huh? Okay, I'll show you my badge. Then no more bullshit. If you don't cooperate, there's always this." Crane lifted the lapel of his jacket to reveal his holster and handgun.

Still standing next to the hand dryer, with his left hand holding his jacket open, he reached into the inside pocket with his right hand to pull out his badge. Billy Ray had deliberately created this opportunity to make his move. Although Crane was well muscled and skilled in physical combat, he was no match for Billy Ray. From the time he was four years old, Billy Ray had trained in several styles of martial arts and hand-to-hand combat. In spite of the fat suit, he moved with

48

amazing dexterity and swiftness. He also held the advantage of surprise for the split second he needed.

Before Crane could react, Billy Ray rushed him and put him in a bear hug. Without hesitating for an instant, Billy Ray lifted the bodyguard off his feet and swung him sideways, smashing his head against the stone wall. Crane was dazed, allowing Billy Ray to temporarily release his hold. Crane slumped to the floor in a half-seated position, arms behind him, hands on the floor to support his weight, legs stretched outward, slightly bent at the knee. Billy Ray acted immediately, grabbing Crane's head and slamming it against the granite countertop. When he was absolutely sure that his victim was unconscious, he approached him from behind, sat him up, placed his hands on both sides of his drooping head, and twisted violently to the left. The cracking sound of the cervical vertebrae assured Billy Ray that he had severed the spine. He waited several seconds, then checked for a pulse and found none.

* * *

The dead weight of a six-foot-two, 210-pound body would be a heavy load even for a fit man. Not for Billy Ray Johnson. He was in superior shape, at the gym at least five times a week, two to three hours per session. He had won several bench-pressing competitions as a teenager and could lift up to 400 pounds at his strongest. It was a cinch dragging the corpse of James Crane into one of the stalls and propping him up on the toilet seat.

So far, no one else had entered the restroom. There was a lock on the door, but Billy Ray chose not to use it. He didn't want to raise any further suspicions. The bodyguard would be safe for the moment where he was. He called Andrew Lansbury on his cell phone.

"Hey, Billy Ray, what now?"

"We've got a bit of a complication on our hands—dead body in the third-floor restroom. We need to get rid of it. Can you get a stretcher up here?"

"What the fuck are you talking about? What the hell happened? What the fuck did you do, Billy Ray?"

"Don't get your panties in a bunch. I can get Troy to come back to the hospital with the ambulance. We just need to get the body to the transport area. Then I'll have it taken up to Davie. I have a cousin who owns a ranch up there."

"What are you talking about? What body?"

"Had some bad luck. I had to take a piss from the coffee. No sooner did I walk out the door of your office, Fitch's fuckin' bodyguard appeared out of nowhere. Motherfucker recognized me from the banquet. I had no choice. He was taking me downstairs for questioning."

"Come on. You're shittin' me, right?"

"No, I ain't shittin' you. Now, get your act together and let's get rid of this asshole."

"Holy . . . I can't believe this. You promised this would go smooth. What the fuck am I supposed to do? Where's the body? Is there blood?"

"Stop cryin' like a little girl. I'm telling you what to do. It'll be okay. There's no blood. I snapped his neck. He's in a stall in the restroom. Just get a stretcher up here. We can make it look like we're transporting a patient. We'll need an ambulance. We gotta hurry before they come looking for him."

"In a *stall*? Are you kidding? What if someone uses the restroom? This a huge fuck-up."

"I'm gonna say this once. If you speak to me that way again, you're gonna end up sittin' on the same toilet, with your insides spilling out—and not from your asshole. I don't have time for this shit. Now, put Kyle in some scrubs and send him up here with a stretcher. Then get Troy to come back with the ambulance as fast as he can get here. Do it now."

Andrew didn't have to be told a second time to back off. He had heard that vicious tone in Billy Ray's voice before. His threats were rarely idle. "Okay, Billy Ray. No problem. I'll get it taken care of."

"Tell Kyle to leave the stretcher outside the restroom. That way, we can make sure there's no one in the hallway before we carry the body out. Luckily, it's late and there's not that much activity up here. And don't worry, everything will be taken care of. You won't have any problems."

"Actually, the cafeteria's closed, so there shouldn't be any traffic up there at all. Has anyone come into the restroom since it happened?"

"No. I've got his stall locked and I'm gonna wait till Kyle gets here. If someone comes in, I'll handle it."

"No more bodies, please. I'll get Kyle up there right away."

"All right . . . Actually, it'll probably be faster and easier if I call Troy while you take care of that. Just make it quick."

Billy Ray hung up the phone and immediately dialed Troy Lansbury's cell phone. He cursed under his breath when the call went directly to voice mail. While he was leaving a message, Troy called back.

"Fuck, man, I thought I wasn't gonna get a hold of you. I hope you're available. We have a small emergency at the hospital. Do you have access to an ambulance?"

"It's been a pretty slow night. Why? What's goin' on? Why do you need the ambulance again?"

"I need to haul a dead body to my cousin's cattle ranch up in Davie. Think you can handle it?"

"Shit, Billy Ray, what happened?"

"I really don't have the time to explain now. Let's just say this person tried to get in the way of the mission, and I wasn't gonna let that happen. Can you help me out?"

"Yeah, man. I'll just take my lunch break now. I can get one of the guys to keep an eye on things while I'm gone. When do you need me there?"

"Ten minutes ago."

"I'll be there in fifteen."

"I'll take it. By that time, we should be able to meet you at the employees' entrance on the west side of the hospital. Give us a call when you get there, to let us know whether the coast is clear. And thanks a lot, Troy. I'll remember this."

"You bet. Glad to help. White power, man!"

* * *

The rest of the mission went off without a hitch. Shortly after Troy left the hospital with James Crane's body, Billy Ray returned to Andrew's office and received the call that Senator Fitch's cardiologist had prescribed antiallergenic medication to be administered intravenously several hours before his procedure the next morning. Since Doug Simms was the only employee assigned to work in the pharmacy overnight, Billy Ray could make the switch at the dispensary while

Simms served as lookout. Billy Ray replaced the vials of Benadryl and Solu-Medrol with enough insulin to kill three adult humans, then wiped them clean of any fingerprints.

He was burying the ashes of James Crane deep in the woods behind his cousin's ranch when Simms delivered the insulin to the cardiac intensive care unit well after midnight. Troy had arrived with the ambulance in the time he had promised. Billy Ray and Kyle were able to load James Crane's corpse onto a gurney Andrew had snatched from a deserted hallway. They wheeled the body, covered from head to toe with a white sheet, to the west employees' entrance, Andrew leading the way to be sure they didn't attract any unwanted attention.

Billy Ray had no trouble getting his cousin Travis's approval for the plan to dispose of the body. Travis gave him access to an incinerator used to burn steer carcasses after they were stripped of their meat. In the early-morning hours of the following day, the 1,800-degree heat of the cattle furnace reduced James Crane's mortal remains to a heap of ash.

After waking from a three-hour nap in the comfortable king-size bed in his cousin's guest bedroom, Billy Ray got the news that Senator Alvin Fitch had died. Refreshed and ecstatic, he grabbed a cup of steaming-hot coffee freshly brewed by Travis's wife, hopped into his Ford Expedition, and began the fourteen-hour trek back to his home state of Mississippi.

**Chapter 4**

The bane of any detective in criminal investigation is a dead end. And for Special Agent Daniel Falcone, they were appearing around every corner that he turned in his attempts to follow leads on the Senator Alvin Fitch investigation road map. He was getting a hundred calls a day from the ever-present nutcases who either confessed to the murder or claimed they had significant information that could result in the assassin's capture. This type of call didn't qualify as a lead, though the end result was no better or worse than from any other clue he had come across in the first few weeks after the senator's murder. So far, he had exactly zip.

Daniel had arrived at headquarters early that Friday morning to read and analyze some new information about the investigation that he considered the pariah of all dead ends: the case of the Nameless serial killer. Never in all his years with the FBI had he pursued a case more riddled with roadblocks. His absence from the field office over the past few days had kept him from getting to reports that reached his desk yesterday morning. At his request, one member or another of his research team had been checking the Violent Criminal Apprehension Program (ViCAP) every day for three years, with a target of recurring gruesome murders. After reading the first few lines of his researcher's summary, Daniel sat up, fully alert. Over the past few weeks, three female corpses had been found in the Laurentian Mountains in Quebec, Canada. At first, these murders didn't catch the research assistant's interest. They didn't match Damien Drysdale's MO, mainly because no body parts were missing.

They became relevant when he ran across a case in Southern Quebec that was originally deemed a ski accident and only later judged a murder. The cause of death was a blunt-force blow to the head. It was initially assumed that the woman lost control while skiing and crashed headfirst into a white oak tree. She was found in the woods skirting one of the more dangerous runs. Her skis were detached from her boots, only the tips peeking out from the deep snow on the slope. By the time a ski park ranger located her body, she was missing several fingers and toes. The authorities assumed they were nibbled off by animals.

The medical examiner who conducted the autopsy was inexperienced, made too many false assumptions, and didn't do the most thorough job. If not for a sharp Montreal detective who was investigating the other murders, this one would have slipped past, right under their noses. While reviewing the autopsy photographs, he noticed that some of the cuts at the amputation sites were a bit too uniform to be caused by teeth. He had the body exhumed for a repeat autopsy by an experienced, reputable pathologist. Two days ago, the new medical examiner's closer examination of the flesh surrounding the wounds revealed that a serrated blade had been used to remove the digits.

Delving deeper, Daniel's research assistant discovered a second murder that had occurred the same day as the autopsy. The owner of a tenement building in Montreal was found dead in one of her tenants' apartment. The killer had performed a crude partial decapitation. Later that day, the researcher contacted the investigating law enforcement agency. After a series of calls, he was ultimately directed to the original detective from Montreal. The detective was glad to provide an update. The medical examiner had compared the wound from the decapitation to that of the victim whose fingers and toes were amputated. The weapon used in both instances was the same serrated knife.

After completing his read, Daniel immediately called the cell phone number for the detective in Montreal. He said who he was and described his relentless three-year search for the Nameless killer. He offered his help, which was promptly accepted. Daniel requested copies of the files, intending to have the Nameless case profiler, Special Agent Frazier, review them. Based on the information he had so far, Daniel was leaning toward the idea that they had located the recent whereabouts of the serial murderer. The fact that no fingerprints were found at either crime scene fit the theory.

Despite having uncovered the first lead in three years, Daniel found it impossible to feel any real excitement. He had been close too many times to get optimistic or feel more than a faint glimmer of hope. True, it was something rather than nothing, and he would take it. One of these days, the road would lead beyond a dead end. Eventually, the nightmare had to come to a conclusion.

Turning his attention to his more current caseload, Daniel flipped through the Alvin Fitch file. Though the evidence developed so far had led to no significant results, it was way too early to get discouraged. They were developing a foundation and perhaps even ruling out suspects. Everything indicated that Nurse Ortiz was squeaky clean. An NCIC criminal background check reflected that she had never been arrested or convicted of a felony or misdemeanor in the United States. The research team assigned to the assassination had discovered nothing of any relevance when they contacted the international policing agency Interpol. Family, friends, and colleagues, both current and former, were tracked down and interviewed. Employment and educational records were pored over. Her fingerprints were compared to the broad IAFIS database. After all that, not one iota of evidence established a connection between Nurse Ortiz and James

Crane or Senator Fitch. Absolutely no proof was uncovered that demonstrated motive.

Daniel had decided that he would waste no more time investigating any theories identifying Ortiz as assassin or coconspirator unless some other form of proof arose from the ashes. He directed the task force to focus on the premise that someone had tampered with the medication prescribed by the cardiologist. Logically, the next most likely suspect was the bodyguard, James Crane. Just the fact that he had disappeared hours before Senator Fitch went into cardiac arrest was enough to place him at the top of the suspect list. To the surprise of most members of the task force, including Daniel, that line of reasoning hadn't helped advance the investigation as much as they had hoped. Grounds for motive were just as elusive for Crane as for Nurse Ortiz. Everything Daniel had learned about Crane led him to believe that the man was devoted to his job and the senator. No documentation, witness testimony, or physical evidence suggested any feelings of animosity toward Fitch.

Crane had begun working for the senator as a plainclothes bodyguard shortly after he signed on with the United States Capitol Police at 21 years of age. He was now 35. Every Fitch staff member indicated in their statements that the senator and Crane had a very close relationship. The senator considered him more of a son than an employee. By all accounts, Crane felt the same bond with Fitch. His fellow officers, including the two other bodyguards hired to protect the senator the night he was killed, had only good things to say about him. They both went to great lengths to convince Daniel that Crane could not possibly have anything to do with the assassination. In fact, they were very concerned about what became of him. They felt that Crane had gotten himself into a predicament—a "wrong place at the wrong time" situation.

Daniel had the task force using all FBI index systems available, including ViCAP, to compare Crane's physical characteristics to any unidentified murder victims. So far, the search had borne no fruit. So long as Crane remained at large, Daniel had to consider him a suspect. This was especially important since, in the great majority of murder cases, the perpetrator and victim had a close relationship.

The pharmacy employee Doug Simms was second on Daniel's short list of potential assassins. If the medicine was switched, it had most likely happened between the time it was prescribed and the time of delivery to the cardiac intensive care unit. That presumption was not foolproof, since the emergency-room physician had not yet been completely cleared as a coconspirator. The cardiologist's participation would be the only way the insulin could have ended up in the appropriate vials before the actual medications were prescribed. Daniel considered the doctor about as likely a suspect as the nurse. A thorough background search bore the same results as for Ortiz: he wasn't likely the guy.

She and Simms were the only two people to touch the medication after the cardiologist wrote his orders. In his sworn statement, Simms claimed he received the prescription from the doctor, then gathered the medications from the pharmacy shelf. Immediately thereafter, he took them to the unit without making any stops along the way. Assuming he was being truthful, Daniel could safely deduce that no one else had touched the vials in that time period.

At the moment, there was no reason to suspect Simms over any other potential subject, for a variety of reasons. According to hospital management, many employees had access to the pharmacy. There was no way to prove exactly when the switch was made. The records reflected that after the prescription was issued, Simms left the pharmacy eight times to make deliveries. Anyone with keys to the pharmacy could have entered during his absence. To throw further doubt on Simms's status as a possible suspect, the pharmacy manager, Andrew Lansbury, vouched for him, saying he was an honest and loyal employee.

Daniel had given some thought to conceivable locations for the exchange for each person on the list of plausible assassins. The switch could have been made while the medicine was in the ICU's pharmacy rather than in the hospital apothecary. Every nurse who worked in cardiac intensive care had access to the room where all medications to be disbursed to unit patients were stored. The only staff members who admitted having gone into the room the evening in question were Donna Ortiz and the other unit nurse, Tara Licek. They both were confident they would have seen anyone else who entered the unit pharmacy. Unless either Ortiz or Licek was mistaken or involved in the murder, this hypothesis at least did not identify any additional suspects.

Neither Daniel nor the task force investigative team had yet uncovered any physical evidence to support a tampering theory, though test results were still pending. The only fingerprints found on the vials of the antiallergenic medicines were those of Doug Simms and Donna Ortiz. No one could provide any eyewitness testimony concerning strange or suspicious characters in the hospital that evening. Indeed, once it was determined that the senator would be admitted to the hospital, visitation had actually been suspended for security purposes.

The hospital staff conducted an audit of all the insulin stored at Jackson Memorial, to determine whether any of the diabetic medication was missing. The audit was repeated three times with the same result. The insulin that killed

Senator Fitch could not have come from the hospital supply. The staff could account for every unit.

The more Daniel worked the Fitch assassination, the clearer it became that a break in the investigation was not going to come from evidence or testimony procured through the hospital or its employees. The bulk of his efforts had revolved around them without producing any real results. It was time to take a different approach. The members of the investigative team all agreed that much time and detail had gone into the preparation and planning of the senator's assassination. It was time to start at the beginning—more specifically, at the fund-raising banquet. To create the opportunity to inject the fatal dose of medication, the assassins had to get their victim to the hospital first. Although no drugs other than the insulin and those prescribed earlier in the evening were found in the senator's postmortem toxicology reports, it stood to reason that the illness was brought on by something he ingested during the dinner. Certainly, it could have been as simple as the placing of some type of rapidly metabolizing, chest pain-eliciting drug in Fitch's food or drink by his bodyguard or someone else. Whatever the case, it was time to focus more attention on the personnel at the Miami Beach Convention Center.

* * *

The crutches were getting to be a huge annoyance for Tabitha Freemont, now on them for the third day after spraining her right ankle. Still, she should be counting her lucky stars she hadn't broken her neck when her fiancé, Kyle Lansbury, threw her down the stairs. This wasn't the first time she had pulled up lame because of the son of a bitch. In fact, she couldn't count all the scars and bruises on her body from the beatings he had given her. And every time, afterward, Kyle would be full of apologies and pleas for forgiveness. With each injury came a new piece of jewelry or an expensive item of clothing. Every time, Tabitha fell for his act. Not this time, she told herself. She had had it with the mean bastard. This time, she was going straight to the police—at least, she'd be on her way as soon as she got off these damn crutches.

Kyle had been so sweet in the beginning of their relationship. Back then, he was loving and generous and never hit her. They met at a Ku Klux Klan gathering in Georgia, when Tabitha was just 17 years old and Kyle was 21. Tabitha's dad was a member of the Klan since she could remember. As a child in Alaculsy, Georgia, she had bought into the teachings of the Klan. Now that she was 23 years old and had a mind of her own, her opinions were evolving. She had met enough men of the Klan to realize that they were a bunch of closed-minded, bullheaded, aggressive bastards with major unresolved issues from childhood. Her own dad was no exception to the rule. Although Tabitha never actually witnessed her father beating her mother, she heard every one of his thrashings and couldn't help but notice the broken bones, the bumps, and the bruises.

Four nights ago, Kyle had come home plastered after a night out with the boys. When he drank, he could become either the sweetest man in the world or a raving maniac. That night, he was the latter. Tabitha had spent the evening working a party for Richard Kraft's company, American Catering. She was dead on her feet when she got home afterward. She decided to take a quick hot shower and go directly to bed. Several hours later, she woke from a deep sleep to hear Kyle screaming her name and ordering her to get her ass downstairs and fix him something to eat.

Telling him to fuck off was an impolitic choice of words when he was in that kind of mood. Tabitha couldn't help herself. The next thing she knew, the lunatic had yanked her out of bed by her hair, dragged her to the top of the steps, and tossed her down the staircase. Besides spraining her ankle, she had suffered a concussion from banging her head on the tile floor at the end of her fall. The impact knocked her unconscious. She woke up three hours later, still lying in the position she had landed in. Meanwhile, Kyle was asleep in their bed, snoring and grunting like a hog.

Though her head was pounding and her ankle was swollen to three times its size, she drove herself to the emergency room and spent the rest of the night, into the morning hours, waiting to be treated. When asked how the injury occurred, she told the nurse she accidentally fell down the steps. The doctor recommended that she be admitted for observation due to the severe concussion. Tabitha refused. She knew she would be in bigger trouble if she wasn't home to make Kyle's breakfast when he woke up. How she was going to manage it on crutches, she would figure out later.

Now that Tabitha had had almost four days to think about this latest incident, she decided she was sick and tired of Kyle's drunken rages. There was a lot she could tell the police that could put the bastard away for many years— probably the rest of his life. Kyle Lansbury was going to be sorry he ever laid a hand on her.

\* \* \*

On Monday, the phone had been ringing off the hook all morning long. Special Agent Daniel Falcone had half a mind to unplug it for some peace and get some

62

real investigative work done. Up to that point, he had received calls from the special agent in charge of the Miami Field Office, Spencer Hoffman, from Assistant Director Howard Evans, and from the director of the FBI himself, Christopher Ryan. All were calling under the pretense of requesting an update on the Senator Alvin Fitch case. Daniel knew the real reason: to light a fire under his butt. They wanted progress, and they wanted it fast. The unrelenting phone calls were also preventing him from setting up interviews with several people he had contacted from the list of political banquet employees and guests. He was waiting on callbacks from potential witnesses. Pulling the plug on the phone would not be a wise choice. He would have to put up with the barrage of calls from confessing nut jobs that were still coming in every hour or two. He hoped that after a month they would decrease somewhat.

Now that some significant lab test results had come in over the weekend, Daniel was seriously considering officially striking Donna Ortiz from the list of suspects. It wasn't an issue that she had injected the deadly dose into the IV port. That alone wasn't enough. The vials from which she drew the insulin were marked with the names of the medications prescribed by the cardiologist. Analysis of what remained inside them showed traces of both insulin and the antiallergenic medications. A thorough audit of the pharmacy was repeated twice, confirming that the vials had been taken from the hospital's supply that evening. The tampering theory was becoming increasingly more viable, if not a certainty. Those findings, combined with the lack of connection between Ortiz and bodyguard James Crane, helped justify Daniel's pending decision.

Daniel's desire to interview the senator's nurse was another excellent reason for declaring her free of guilt. He hoped that ultimately, she might help shed light on how the switch was made. He wasn't ready to take the leap just yet.

It was a calculated risk, though he was increasingly confident that the numbers were heavily on his side.

He desperately wanted to talk to Annie about the case. She was the brightest human being he knew. Normally, he wouldn't be able to get such a well-informed opinion. She represented a material witness and was conducting an exhaustive investigation of her own. He needn't worry about not being able to reveal secret FBI information about the case—she probably had more than he did. Annie's insight usually proved invaluable. The time had come to try a different approach to solicit her assistance. He picked up the phone and dialed her office number. After engaging in some idle chitchat with Kelly, he got around to why he was calling.

"What's Annie up to?"

"She's finally been very busy," Kelly said. "Ever since she took on Donna Ortiz as a client, the phone hasn't stopped ringing. We've gone from five clients to fifty in a matter of a month. And we could have many more, but with only one lawyer in the office, Annie had to limit the number she accepted. She's actually thinking about hiring a young associate."

"That's great news!" Daniel said. "I'm happy for you guys. Is she available?"

"I'll check. She just got back from a hearing at the courthouse and has a client waiting out in the lobby. I'll tell her you're on the phone."

Barely twenty seconds passed before Annie picked up.

"Good morning, Annie. I haven't spoken to you in a few weeks, so I thought I'd give you a call. I hear you're a busy woman these days."

"Yes, I am. Swamped, actually. Want to come work for me?"

"Uh . . . no, thanks. I think I'll stick with the good guys."

"What's that supposed to mean? Are you saying I'm a bad guy?"

"Take it the way you want. You know I was born to put criminals away, not try to keep them out on the streets. I'm just sayin'."

"Yeah, you're always just sayin'. Someone has to protect the wrongly accused. Anyway, we're wasting time here. I've got a full schedule today. Actually, I've got a full schedule every day for the next several months. If I know you, you weren't calling just to chat."

"You know me too well. Really, I was just hoping to get together, maybe have dinner sometime soon. Do you think you can fit me into your busy schedule?"

"Sure, I'd love to get together. One does have to eat. When did you have in mind? Are you gonna bring the kids?"

"No, I thought it would just be the two of us. You tell me when. You're the one who's swamped."

"How does this Saturday night sound? And I hope you don't plan on pumping me for information on the Fitch case."

"Now, how could you accuse me of such a thing? I'm hurt."

"Yeah, right. How does eight sound?"

"Sounds great. I'll pick you up at your place. Think about where you want to eat."

* * *

The familiar thumping of her heart at a pace approaching tachycardia persisted as Annie hung up the phone after her conversation with Daniel. In a no-holds-barred rebellion against her efforts to quash her feelings for him—especially since his release from prison—Annie's love for her former college sweetheart had not diminished one iota. To the contrary, it had grown. Beginning in their second year at George Washington University, through their graduation from Harvard Law School, they were involved in a serious romance. Years after their breakup, just before Deborah's murder, Annie had confessed to Daniel that she was still carrying a torch for him. When those feelings, along with her misguided persistence to get him into bed, caused trouble in Daniel's marriage, they both agreed it would be best to discontinue any form of contact. Since Annie's kidnapping, their friendship had become stronger than ever. Up to now, neither of them broached the subject of taking what they shared to another level. Annie didn't dare make the first move, out of respect for his wife's memory. Her despicable behavior had helped cause Daniel's separation in the first place. He seemed to be holding back for the same reasons.

Annie tried her best to sweep all thoughts of Daniel from her mind. She had an overloaded schedule and no time for daydreaming. She picked up the phone to let Kelly know she was ready to meet with her new client, and instructed her to escort him to the conference room. The man was charged with felony possession of marijuana. She glanced at his file to remind herself of his name: Kyle Lansbury.

Tabitha and Kyle were not the most media-conscious people in the world. Neither had the least desire to keep up with current events, nor had they ever heard of Annie Bryan. Kyle had left it to Tabitha to schedule the appointment. He was completely ignorant of the fact that she had selected the attorney representing a suspect in the Senator Fitch assassination. If one were to ask Kyle, there was another fact about Tabitha's choice that he would consider even more repugnant. When Annie entered the conference room, he was seated at the head of the table. She extended her hand to introduce herself, then withdrew it when he didn't reciprocate. With a look of disgust on his face, he said, "*You're* the lawyer?"

Having an idea but not really knowing what he meant by the question, she answered in the best professional manner she could muster, "Yes, Mr. Lansbury. Is there a problem?"

"Yes, there's a fuckin' problem. I don't do business with niggers." And with that, he got up from his seat and stormed out of the office. Annie was so shocked, she stood frozen in place for several seconds.

Kelly came running into the conference room to find her employer in openmouthed silence. "What happened?"

"That asshole just told me that he doesn't 'do business with niggers.'"

"You've got to be kidding! What a bastard. I hope he's still out in the parking lot . . ." Kelly made a move for the exit, only to be stopped by her boss.

"No, Kelly. That behavior doesn't deserve a response. You would think he'd do some research before he scheduled an appointment with a lawyer."

"That racist pig? He probably would if he could read. I'm so sorry, Annie. Maybe I should come up with some kind of a screening process for morons like that."

"It's not your fault, Kelly. Things may be getting better, but there are still way too many haters out there. It's not as if you can ask a caller, 'By the way, are you a bigoted moron?'"

"Yeah, I guess you're right. It just bugs the hell out of me. It's disgusting!"

"Well, we've already given it more time than it deserves. We've got plenty to do today. Let's get back to work."

## Chapter 5

The deserted country road was lined with hundreds of southern bald cypress trees. Thick Spanish moss hung from as high as thirty-five feet, forming a tunnel that reminded Billy Ray of long, unkempt, hag hair. A scene that most people found charming about the South had always frightened him as a child. The flowing moss, blowing in the soft southerly breeze, blocked out most of the late-afternoon sunlight and still managed to give him the creeps.

Billy Ray and his dad were on their way to Savannah, for what they were publicly calling a "hunters' convention"—especially if asked by anyone at the resort. In fact, it was a strategy meeting of twenty-three of the most influential leaders of the Ku Klux Klan. Billy Ray had spent much of his time over the past month preparing the presentation he would give on Sunday night to the highest-ranking members of the organization. He was hoping to convince them that the time had come to begin executing his long-term plan to reclaim America.

The Klan was mightily impressed with his management of the Fitch assassination. The FBI still had no real leads on who had committed the crime. The members Billy Ray had recruited to assist in the assassination all proved to be loyal. Thus far, there was no suggestion that the Klan was even remotely suspected. Several other radical groups had already tried to take credit for the deed. That was fine with Billy Ray and the elders, for it took the attention away from them. They felt it was essential they remain under the radar for the time being. Too many important plans in the works could be compromised otherwise. Billy Ray felt that pride was half the reason why the Muslim terrorists weren't more effective in their campaigns against the United States and its allies. Their arrogance often got in the way—they were always too eager to take credit for their work. He would not make the same mistake. The opportunity to take credit would come in due time, and those who counted already knew.

The twenty-three elite were meeting at the Westin Savannah Harbor Golf Resort and Spa. They would spend Saturday night at the hotel and enjoy its amenities through Monday. A friendly golf competition was scheduled for Sunday morning and early afternoon, partly for their entertainment but more for a diversion. After the tournament, the men would temporarily relocate the meeting to Lake Warren State Park in South Carolina, just twenty-five miles outside Savannah. The topics of discussion had to be well out of the auditory range of eavesdroppers. Most of the elite group of leaders were the subjects of covert government surveillance, either currently or at some point in the past. They were forced to educate themselves on the most efficient ways to avoid the watchful eye of Uncle Sam.

It was approaching seven when Billy Ray and his Dad arrived at the hotel. By 7:30, they had settled into their room. Emmett, who was not as obsessive as his son about being served food by people of color, had scheduled a late dinner with some of his Klan buddies at the Aqua Star, the Westin's signature restaurant. He encouraged Billy Ray to join him.

"Son, I think it might be a good idea for you to socialize with these men," he said. "After all, each has an equal vote when it comes to ratifying the plans you're promoting for the next year."

"Dad, you know I can't stand to eat at a restaurant. It would be worse if I vomited into my dinner plate in front of them. Besides, it's not like we're gonna be able to discuss anything of substance at the table, anyway. And I just ate a sandwich not too long ago and I'm not that hungry."

"We don't always convince people to do what we want them to by the substance of our arguments. People have much more of a tendency to agree with you if they know and like you. That's Basic Human Nature One-o-one. We're gonna need a unanimous vote to do some of the things you're suggesting. It's your decision, son. A little bit of socializing can work wonders. Yes, you know a lot of these guys, and most of them hold you in very high esteem. There are still a couple we don't know all that well—and, worse, some that crave more power within the Klan. John Christy and Willis Zachary are two of those people, and they're joining us for dinner."

"I suppose you have a point, Dad. I'll have plenty of time to socialize and get to know people tomorrow during the golf competition. I'll make sure I pay some extra attention to John. Thanks for the invitation, but I gotta pass."

"Suit yourself. It was just a suggestion. I'm proud of you no matter what."

\* \* \*

Tabitha felt like celebrating when, after two weeks of struggling with the crutches, she could finally bear weight on her ankle. She didn't realize how much such a simple limitation could affect one's entire daily routine. Getting anything done was a complicated ordeal. Fortunately, Kyle had been as sweet as tupelo honey while she was laid up. He waited on her hand and foot, took all her shifts at the catering company, brought her fresh flowers every day, and had bought her a Tiffany's charm bracelet. He even let her off easy about the black lawyer she had picked at random out of the telephone book. That was a giant step in the right direction. She had high hopes that he was really turning the corner this time.

Tabitha had convinced herself yet again that maybe she was being a little rash when she decided to report him to the police. She was madder than a wet hen the night she woke up at the bottom of the stairs and had to take herself to the hospital. As usual, time and Kyle's wonderful behavior changed her attitude. She made him promise he wasn't going to drink anymore—not that it was the first time she had made that request. She told him that if she even smelled a hint of beer on his breath, she would pack her bags and go home to Georgia. This go-around, he had gone thirteen full days without a drink. That was a record. It was another sizable step in the right direction because there was a much more important reason why Tabitha was considering giving Kyle another chance. Tomorrow, she would be three weeks late with her period. Just an hour ago, she had bought a home pregnancy test, and it popped positive. She was planning to go to the local Planned Parenthood office and get an official test later this afternoon.

Setting her reservations about Kyle aside, she was thrilled at the prospect of being pregnant. Tabitha felt that her purpose in life was motherhood. She wanted a child more than anything else in the world. The thought that she would be a mother in less than forty weeks was enough to put her in a forgiving mood. She would work hard on Kyle and make sure he didn't relapse.

Her mama had always told her, people could change. Mama would tell the story of Uncle Teddy, her brother, who was an alcoholic and a heroin addict. After spending twenty-five years in prison for voluntary manslaughter, he had gone back to school and gotten a master's degree in business administration. Now he was a successful building contractor, humanitarian, and major contributor to the cause for abused children. Mama might have clung to that story for a few too many years, in Tabitha's opinion. Her only salvation from Dad's beatings was his death. Tabitha wasn't going to repeat the same mistake. She would give Kyle a chance to change, but this was the last time for sure.

* * *

After arriving at Savannah's international airport behind schedule, John Christy made a mad dash for the Avis Rent-a-Car office to pick up the car he had reserved for his stay. He had about forty minutes to make it to the dinner he couldn't afford to miss, for fear of raising suspicions. Something huge was about to unfold. All his hard work and the tremendous risks he had taken over the past several years were about to pay off.

Since the Timothy McVeigh Oklahoma City bombing, Christy had been working undercover for the FBI in its national security task force concentrating on paramilitary groups and homeland violence. Because of growing concerns over the resurgence of the Ku Klux Klan and other white-supremacist groups, four years ago he was assigned to infiltrate the organization. His role had increased in importance after the nomination of a second African American for the presidency of the United States, and then his election last November.

Much like Billy Ray Johnson's, Christy's rise in the ranks of the Klan over the past four years was meteoric. But unlike Johnson, having no familial connections, he had to rely solely on his own accomplishments. This necessitated his being involved in many activities that could never be revealed to the American public. Sometimes, small sacrifices were necessary for the greater good.

There had been little discussion about the details of the meeting. Christy knew that an agenda would be presented to the group and voted on.

Beyond that, he was mostly in the dark. For security purposes, the Klan made it a practice to keep the subject matter of these secret gatherings close to the vest, revealed only to those in the highest positions. His instincts told him that big things were coming down the pike.

For reasons beyond his comprehension, the Johnson kid had a lot of influence over the elders. Christy wasn't impressed with the man's intelligence, although he was a hard worker and extremely motivated. Billy Ray exemplified every principle the Klan embodied—a racist and white supremacist to the core. He would be doing most of the talking tomorrow night. Christy had tried to get more information about the content of his presentation. A head start on the information-gathering process could give the FBI's support team an advantage when it came time to act. He worked hard on getting close with several of the elders, trying to get anyone to reveal even the smallest tidbit. Either they were unwilling to talk, or the Johnsons weren't sharing.

Christy had met Billy Ray on several occasions at various Klan meetings. In spite of his many attempts, he could never get the Johnson boy to warm to him. His closest Klan contact, Willis Zachary, from Miami, had told him the Johnsons perceived him as a threat. As the Klan grew to proportions never attained in its entire history, the Johnsons wanted to make sure no power struggles developed. According to Zachary, they were concerned about John's rapid rise. Christy was disappointed he couldn't forge a better relationship with them. The Johnsons clearly possessed great power in the Klan. Now that Christy was invited to one of the most important meetings of the year, he would finally be in on their best-kept secrets.

Christy's superiors were anxious to get some results after all the time and money allocated to this investigation. The Klan's mobilization had been a concern to the powers that be, for quite some time. The racist organization had been putting out ever-increasing efforts to fortify its numbers, and continued to do so at alarming rates. By early Monday morning, the FBI would finally be in a position to take some action and reverse the momentum the Klan was gathering.

When Christy arrived at the Avis counter, he was second in line. It took less than five minutes to sign the paperwork. A shuttle bus took him to the rental car garage, where he located the Ford Taurus he had chosen for the weekend. Seated behind the wheel, he programmed his GPS phone app for directions to the Westin resort. Ten minutes before the dinner was scheduled to begin, he handed the rental car's key to the hotel valet. Registration was a breeze, leaving him just enough time to race up to his room for a quick change, run a comb through his hair, then rush downstairs to join the others at the restaurant.

The hostess at the Aqua Star notified him that his party was already seated. She escorted him to the table, where seven of the KKK's most influential members were already in deep conversation. Emmett Johnson had taken one of the head positions of the table, and Christy's closest confidant, Willis Zachary, had claimed the other. The only empty place remaining was to Zachary's right. Seated to the left of the empty chair was the grand dragon for the state of Georgia. Continuing counterclockwise around the eight-top, excluding the head chairs, were the grand dragons for the states of Alabama, Ohio, Virginia, Massachusetts, and Texas. The grand wizard, Austin Dobson, who presided over the entire Klan, was not attending the dinner. He wouldn't be joining the group until Sunday night's secret meeting.

Before sitting down in the place reserved for him, Christy circled the table to greet each of the men with a handshake. When he encountered Johnson, he took an extra few minutes to ask about him and his family. Everyone was energized, the discussion animated. It never ceased to amaze Christy that Klan members were loud, proud, and public about their hatred of other races and that the topic was so prevalent in every conversation. "Nigger," "spic," and "kike" were flung about as casually as "hello," "good-bye," and "thank you," coming up in every other sentence. Where they were or who was around was of no consequence. The display was especially shocking coming from little white-haired men in the twilight of their lives. Christy had become an expert at hiding his embarrassment and repugnance from his supposed colleagues. Though he was obliged to sling racial slurs to avoid raising eyebrows, he would never get used to it. The day he got to put these assholes, whatever their age, behind bars would be one of the highlights of his life. If he played his cards right, that time should be coming in less than forty-eight hours.

The dinner lasted until just before midnight. When it was finally adjourned, he and Emmett entered the same hotel elevator. As they approached their rooms on the second floor, they discovered they were actually next-door neighbors. In a last-ditch effort to get ahead of the game, Christy asked Emmett whether he and his son would like to come over for a nightcap. The old man politely declined.

After Christy entered his room, he decided he wasn't going to deprive himself of a drink to wind down just because the Johnsons wouldn't join him. He checked the ice bucket and saw that it was empty. He preferred his scotch on the rocks, so he threw on a T-shirt, grabbed the bucket, and headed for the ice machine.

Several steps into the hallway, he saw Billy Ray Johnson coming out of the elevator and heading directly toward him. Christy extended his hand.

"Hey there, buddy, it's nice to see you. Sorry you couldn't make dinner."

"Hi, John," Billy Ray replied in his normal cool tone. "Eating at restaurants isn't my thing."

"I'm looking forward to your speech tomorrow night. It's an honor to be a part of it."

"I hope for your support. We've got a lot of work to do this year."

"I don't see a problem with that. When is your tee time in the morning?"

"Not till nine thirty. I suppose I'll see you out there. I've got some more work to do tonight."

Almost as soon as the conversation had started, it ended. Billy Ray mumbled something inaudible and continued on his way toward his room.

\* \* \*

After placing the key card in the slot, Billy Ray turned to watch Christy walk away. He was about thirty feet from the ice machine room when a small rectangular object resembling a business card slipped out the bottom of his right pant leg. When Christy kept walking, Billy Ray assumed he hadn't noticed. As the electronic keypad's green light flashed to indicate that the door was unlocked, Billy Ray considered ignoring the dropped item. Then curiosity got the better part of him. He had never liked Christy much—didn't appreciate his aggressive efforts to achieve power within the Klan, or his phony attempts to curry favor with Billy Ray and his dad.

The moment Christy entered the small vending-machine alcove next to the elevators, Billy Ray moved quickly to where the card lay on the plush, multicolored woven carpet. To save time, he stuck it in his pocket and hurried back to his room. The grinding of the ice machine's motor acted as the perfect buffer to prevent Christy from hearing approaching footsteps. Billy Ray was inside his room before Christy reappeared in the hallway with his full bucket of ice.

Once the door was closed behind him, Billy Ray pulled the card out of his pocket. His initial reaction after reading it was shock, which almost instantly evolved into intense disgust and rage. On the card was an FBI logo with the name "Assistant Special Agent in Charge Michael Gerard." On the reverse side, scribbled in pen, were the words "Cell phone in case of emergency," with the number 810-555-1752.

**Chapter 6**

Saturday night had at last arrived. Annie Bryan was looking forward to finally granting herself some leisure time. Who would have thought, just one short month ago, that she would be craving a break from work? Since business started to pick up, she hadn't done anything that could remotely be considered fun. She was working seven days a week and a minimum of ten hours a day. By the time she forced herself to leave the office in the evening, she had enough time to drive home and fix something quick for dinner before she nodded off in front of the TV.

After pouring herself a glass of zinfandel, she took a moment to enjoy the beautiful sunset from the office of her beachfront condo facing the Intracoastal Waterway. There wasn't a cloud in the sky to obstruct her view of the blazing fireball as it took its slow plunge beneath the marshes of the Florida Everglades. Despite the lack of color due to the absence of clouds, the sight was nevertheless awe inspiring. Beautiful red-yellow rays of light emanated in every direction until darkness extinguished the spectacle, spreading like spilled black ink across the sky of the western horizon.

The ring of her cell phone woke her from her reverie. Unable to recall where she had put it, she listened intently for direction. The muffled ring seemed to be coming from somewhere in the kitchen. By the time she found it at the bottom of her purse, she had missed the call. Seeing that it was Daniel, she pressed the callback option.

"Hello, Annie. Just wanted to let you know I'm on my way. I should be there in about fifteen minutes."

"Sorry, I missed the call," she said. "The phone was buried at the bottom of my purse. These damn cell phones never seem to ring long enough. I'm always getting to it a split second too late. But I'm babbling. I'm ready."

"Have you decided yet where you'd like to eat? It's my treat."

"Daniel, you don't have to do that. I can pay for myself. After all, I am the senior partner in a law firm."

"That may be the case, but I invited you, and I insist on paying. End of discussion."

"All right, I won't argue. I hope you can afford my taste, though. I'm in the mood for a nice steak tonight. What do you think about the Capital Grille? You can't get a better piece of meat anywhere, at least according to the *Sun Sentinel*. Oops, I didn't mean it that way." She giggled to mask her embarrassment. "It's really expensive, though," she fumbled. "You're sure you don't want me to pay for my dinner?"

"I thought you weren't gonna argue. I'm positive I want to treat. I'm not exactly in the poorhouse. I was actually considering suggesting it. I just wanted the choice to be totally yours."

"Wow, you're really buttering me up. I'm gettin' the feeling you want something."

"Again, you hurt my feelings. How much can a man bear?"

"Yeah, we'll see. I better call the restaurant to make sure we can be seated. I'll be downstairs in ten minutes. See you then."

A quick call to the Capital Grille from her home phone confirmed that plenty of tables were available. She reserved one just in case. Before leaving the apartment, she checked herself in the mirror and saw that a retouch of lip gloss was in order. She made the correction, then grabbed her purse and walked to the elevators.

Annie lived on the penthouse floor of the Maya Marca Condominium, on Fort Lauderdale Beach. Only two apartments were on that level, and the other had been vacant for the past three years. She missed her rides down to the lobby with her neighbor and dear friend, Hannah Richards. Since her murder, the condo association thought it best to place additional security in the building. Not only was the serial murderer still at large, but at the time her neighbor was killed, he had developed an obsession with Annie and was stalking her.

When the elevator door swung open, she was greeted by the condominium's valet and security officer, Benny Rivera. He had a license to carry a firearm and would accompany women to their car or taxi if requested. It was only recently that Annie felt comfortable enough to forgo an escort to the parking garage to retrieve her BMW, or was willing to wait for a ride alone outside the condominium entrance. This was a tremendous advancement in her psychological recovery from the intense torture she had suffered over several weeks. Traumatized by the inhuman beatings, bleedings, and rape, she had barely left her apartment for months after her rescue. It required almost a year of intensive psychotherapy before she finally began to live like a normal human being, though any intimate contact with men was still out of the question.

In less than five minutes, Daniel pulled into the driveway in his government-issued Crown Victoria. As he approached the portico, he noticed that Annie was wearing an elegant strapless black cocktail dress—further evidence of progress in her healing process. It had been a while since she wore a form-fitting garment that exposed every curve of her athletic body. He couldn't help but admire the stunning beauty of the woman whom, once upon a time, he had asked to marry him. She hadn't lost a thing in all the years he had known her.

Daniel stopped the car and was about to hop out to open the passenger door for Annie, but she waved him off. He should have known better, he mused. Annie was never one to accept special treatment simply because of her gender. It wasn't a case of being a women's rights activist, nor did she have anything against chivalry. She was a very independent person, and it seemed ludicrous to have a man go out of his way to do something for her that she was perfectly capable of doing herself.

A light sprinkle began to fall as Annie stepped into the car. Confused, she scanned above them, wondering where the rain was coming from. There didn't seem to be a cloud in the sky. As Daniel flicked on the windshield wipers, she said, "Where the heck did this rain come from? It was perfectly clear when I was watching the sunset just ten minutes ago."

"Don't worry. I'm sure it's just a temporary shower. Besides, I have an umbrella in the backseat if you need it later. Your hair is safe. You look great in that dress, by the way. Did you reserve a table at the Capital Grille?"

"Thank you, Daniel. That's sweet. And yes. They're not busy at all."

"Great. Expensive steak and wine it is, then."

Daniel pulled into the parking lot of the Galleria Mall, where Fort Lauderdale's version of the Capital Grille was located. This time, he didn't bother to go around to Annie's door to let her out. They walked into the restaurant at exactly 8:00 and were immediately escorted to their table.

Discretion being the better part of valor, Daniel had carefully thought out his plan for raising the subject of Donna Ortiz. He had experience in these matters. Though it was a little trite and certainly underhanded, he would let Annie drink a glass or two of wine. She would likely see through this ploy. In fact, it was a foregone conclusion. Regardless, the wine would loosen her up. He would deal with the consequences later.

Knowing full well she could never refuse the offer of a fine French wine, he suggested a red: Chateau Beau Soleil Bordeaux. Annie's rapid nod of the head, risking a neck sprain, signaled her agreement with his selection and let him know he was scoring points. It was going to put a dent in his pocketbook. Fortunately, money wasn't an issue for him anymore. He had received a nice little settlement from the United States government for his wrongful imprisonment. Also, although it was money he hated to collect, his wife, Deborah, and her parents had quite a bit of life insurance. Since Deborah was her parents' sole heir, and Daniel and the children were the same for Deborah, he had received the benefits of three large insurance policies.

By the time their appetizers were served, Annie was on her second glass of wine and already showing signs of giddiness. Daniel's initial response was typical. He should have known he wasn't going to get away with a plot to pump her for information without guilt rearing its ugly head. If his devotion to his job, and his tremendous sense of responsibility to it were not such a driving force, he might have abandoned the idea.

"I'm so happy things have finally taken off at your office, Annie," he said. "I'm very proud of you."

"I guess I just got lucky. Sometimes that's all it takes. Obviously, everything started after Donna Ortiz walked through my door."

"Well, I'm sure, with your talent, eventually you would have been just as successful. I'm a firm believer that we make our luck. Speaking of Miss Ortiz . . ."

Annie cut him off in mid-sentence with a speech she had already prepared. "Daniel Falcone! Have you no shame? Is that what this is all about? The fine restaurant, the wine? You're trying to get me tipsy, aren't you? And here I thought you were after my body. How insulting! I have half a mind to call a taxi and end this right here and now." She couldn't help breaking into a wry smile.

"Oh, Annie, come on. You can cut the drama. You knew all along I was gonna talk about the Fitch case. Still, it hurts me that you would suggest it's the only reason I asked you out. But since my cover is blown, how about giving me a little something you know that I don't? I'm sure, pro that you are, you've done a thorough investigation—probably better than mine."

"Flattery will get you everywhere."

"I know," Daniel replied, a big, irresistible grin on his face.

"Okay, maybe I'm being a little bit dramatic. Regardless, I'm not going to violate my responsibility to my client by turning over confidential information to you."

"All right, if I can't get something specific, at least give me your thoughts about who could've done this. There isn't anyone else in the world whose opinion I respect more, and I mean that. You're operating on more information than I am, which sucks. I know it's early, but I'm spinning my wheels. Well, maybe that's an exaggeration . . . Things just need to move faster. You can imagine how much pressure's coming from above to get it resolved. I'm sure there's some small tidbit you can throw my way to help. I know you want to get this case solved just as much as I do."

"Well, you're right about that. But it wouldn't hurt, as a show of good faith, for you to remove my client from your list of suspects. You know she's innocent. Why not just make it official?"

"I'm sure that'll happen sometime not too far down the road. With all the heat I'm catching from as high up as the director and the *president,* I can't afford to make any rash decisions. What do you say? Will you help me out?"

"As far as my investigation is concerned, I can't tell you I've considered any more suspects than you. What I can tell you, though . . . I've been doing a lot of thinking about motive. There's a total lack of evidence to prove it was either of your suspects. I decided to focus more on the victim and who might want him dead. Something strange happened at my office the other day that got me thinking . . ."Annie proceeded to describe the incident involving Kyle Lansbury. Afterward, she continued, "It made me realize how much racism is still alive and well in America. Yeah, things are better than they were forty years ago, but there are still plenty of extremist groups out there right here in the United States. Maybe even your next-door neighbor."

"I think I see where you're going."

"I'm not giving you any new information by telling you motive is a big key to solving any murder. When you ask yourself who would want to eliminate Senator Fitch, you have to consider the racism factor. He was one of the most liberal senators in the country. He was a champion of the civil rights cause. Who stood up for minorities more outspokenly than Alvin Fitch? He was heading the Senate Judiciary Subcommittee on Immigration, Refugees and Border Security. Lots of changes were on the agenda. He was aggressively pushing for a very liberal immigration law. If his proposal is passed, millions of illegal aliens will become citizens of the United States. You know that has to piss off the extreme right-wingers and white-supremacists. I would seriously be considering organizations like the skinheads, neo-Nazis, paramilitary groups, and even the

84

Ku Klux Klan. From what I've read, the Klan has been making a resurgence. That's a scary thing."

Daniel was impressed, and happy, to be hearing the same analysis he had brought up in the task force think tank on Wednesday morning.

"So, we're thinking along the same lines, then. Good. Chris and I were just talking about where to start. We have some ideas."

"Such as?"

"Now, you know I can't tell you, Annie. First of all, I can't reveal specifics about the investigation. Second, you represent a material witness and potential suspect."

"What the hell? Wipe that smirk off your face! Is this tit for tat? Doesn't seem very fair."

"You just gave me a theory. I didn't get any details. All kidding aside, I really wanted to hear what you had to say. I would have preferred some solid information as well, but your opinion means a lot, and it helps."

"Okay, well, next time you want to hear any of my theories, you can just ask. They're free. Now, can we get back to enjoying our dinner?"

"Sure thing. How about another bottle of wine?"

## Chapter 7

Moonlight reflected off the sleek surface of the historic Savannah River, and the scent of honeysuckle wafted on the warm late-summer breeze. The city had gone to sleep. The only sounds were those of an occasional car passing on Hutchinson Island Road, and the crickets and frogs along the water's edge. The night may have been peaceful, but it was no help to Billy Ray. For him, falling asleep was about as likely as snow in Miami. He stood out on the balcony of his room, looking out at the river as he analyzed his predicament. He had not yet told his dad about his discovery. The news might make him want to postpone tomorrow night's meeting, and that was the last thing Billy Ray wanted. He didn't know whom else to trust. On the one hand, it could serve him well to notify the other elders so they could help strategize how to respond. Then there was always the possibility that others were working with Christy. Handling the situation on his own was probably the best option.

When he finally made his decision to go solo, his first order of business was to determine whether Christy did, in fact, have any allies. The plans to be revealed tomorrow night could not be allowed to fall into the wrong hands. He doubted that any other members of the elite group were helping the snitch. All of them had been faithful to the Klan for more than forty years. Christy was the only relative newcomer. But Billy Ray didn't want to rely on assumptions, if there was a better way. At the very least, he would try to get the information from Christy himself.

Now that he had made the decision to act alone, sleep was out of the question. He couldn't afford any mistakes—delay would only add to the risk. He would deal with Christy before daybreak. If he waited for the sun to rise, he would lose his advantage. Postponing it until after his presentation wasn't possible, either. He didn't want Christy to have an opportunity to report to the FBI.

As Billy Ray closed the door on his doubts about when to proceed, a brilliant idea struck him. Writing always helped him organize his thoughts. He quietly walked back into the bedroom and grabbed a pen and notepad, then returned to the balcony, sat down on the lounge chair, and began to compose.

\* \* \*

John Christy searched every nook and cranny of his room looking for ASAC Michael Gerard's business card. For the life of him, he couldn't recall whether he had gotten rid of it at the airport. He had meant to immediately after his second-to-last conversation in the terminal with Gerard. The trash can he had chosen was only a few feet from the rental car counter. He had taken a few steps toward it as soon as he hit the cell phone's "end" button. But then Gerard had called back to report a last-minute change—a support team member he had forgotten to mention. Now Christy couldn't remember whether he had actually torn up the card and placed the bits in various bins. The whole incident came to mind after he called Gerard from the hotel room before retiring for the night. Reaching into his pocket for the card, he had found nothing but a huge hole. Panicked, he retraced his steps to the vending machine room, the restaurant, and his car, with no luck. It wasn't in his suitcase, either, not that he expected it to be there. On a whim and a prayer, he asked the attendant at the front desk if anyone had turned it in, specifically requesting that she check with the Aqua Star staff. After a quick inquiry, the clerk called back to say they didn't have it.

He wouldn't have needed the business card in the first place if his supervisor, Ed Harding, weren't on vacation. Before leaving California, Agent Gerard, who was substituting as special agent in charge during Harding's absence, had handed Christy the card with his cell phone number. Christy had thought about committing the number to memory rather than keeping the card, but quickly rejected the idea—he had terrible recall for numbers. His alternative plan was to store it in his cell phone under a fictitious name and throw the card away. Before Gerard called the first time, he had managed to get step one done. He hoped to God he had also completed step two.

His other grave mistake arose from the fact that he had unknowingly put on a pair of trousers with a hole in the pocket this morning. The issue was whether he had inadvertently put the card back in his pocket, and, if so, at what point he lost it. The possibility that one of the Klan members could have seen it fall and picked it up was unthinkable. The last time he was sure he had the card was just before he intended to dispose of it at the Savannah airport. If he had failed to do so, he could have lost it anywhere between there and the hotel.

Christy tried to convince himself that it wasn't a sure thing the card had fallen into the wrong hands. The normal human reaction after seeing someone drop something was to notify them immediately. Obviously, that hadn't happened. Even if a Klan member eventually picked it up, if they hadn't seen it fall from his pants, there was no way they could link it to him. This line of reasoning made him feel a little better.

After spending the past hour and a half searching frantically, Christy had worked himself into a healthy state of fatigue. There was nothing more he could do tonight anyway. If he was busted by a Klan member, he would most likely find out soon enough. He undressed, put on a pair of pajama bottoms, put his Glock 22 handgun in the nightstand drawer, and climbed into bed. If he needed his weapon at any point during the night, it would be well within reach.

The loss of Gerard's card had no effect on Christy's ability to fall asleep. Normally, putting his head on the pillow and closing his eyes was enough to put him in a relaxed, semiconscious state. This time was no exception. Less than an hour later, just as he was drifting into the fifth and final stage of slumber, a light tapping came from the door. The sound lifted him into a less profound rest, giving him the impression it was a dream. When the knock got louder, it woke him to full alertness. He looked over at the alarm clock on the nightstand and saw that it was after one o'clock. His heart rate quickened. This could have something to do with the business card. He slipped on a T-shirt and holster harness, then shoved the Glock into its receptacle. To conceal the weapon, he threw on an Anaheim Ducks windbreaker, then switched on the light, went to the door, and engaged the bar lock before opening it a crack. After his eyes adjusted to the light, he was surprised to be looking into the eyes of Billy Ray Johnson.

This could mean nothing good. Before thinking about letting Billy Ray in the room, Christy looked down at his visitor's hands and scanned his body for any sign of weapons. Seeing nothing, knowing he had his Glock close to his chest, Christy removed the bar lock and opened the door.

"Come on in, Billy Ray. Something wrong?"

"I'm sorry to bother you at this time of night, John. I really need to talk to you, and I didn't want anyone else to know about it. I wanted to make sure everyone was asleep before I came over."

"What's up? What can I do for you?"

"Before I start, let me say I'm not here to cause you any problems. Actually, I want to help any way I can."

"I have no clue what you're talking about. Is everything okay? You feelin' all right?"

Billy Ray pulled Gerard's business card out of his pocket and handed it to Christy.

"I found this out in the hallway when I saw you earlier this evening. It dropped out of your pant leg. I was going to take it to you in the ice machine room. When I saw what it was, it threw me. Are you an FBI agent?"

Christy didn't respond immediately. Was this attempt to befriend him an act, or was the kid for real?

"No, I don't work with the FBI. This agent approached me in California. He's an asshole. He's been trying to get me to cooperate with him."

Christy immediately regretted his comment. It was weak. Billy Ray would have to be a moron to believe that he had rejected the agent's overtures. If so, why would he have kept the card?

"He's called me several times and even showed up outside where I work. I've told him to fuck off every time. Last time, when he handed me his card, I just shoved it in my pocket. I was going to tell you guys about it at the meeting."

Christy was right—Billy Ray wasn't fooled. Billy Ray put on his best scared-shitless face and turned to flee the room. His acting skills weren't as good as he might have hoped. Christy grabbed him by the shoulder to prevent him from leaving.

"Wait, Billy Ray. Where you going?"

"Let me go. I gotta get outta here. I'm a dead man."

"You're confusing the hell out of me. What in God's name are you talking about?"

"Doesn't matter. I gotta go. I fucked up royally."

Christy was now holding on to Billy Ray's arm. It looked as though each man knew that the other was lying through his teeth. Christy's cover was blown. The question was how to handle it. Could he get any valuable information from Billy Ray while Billy Ray was engaging in this obvious ploy? What was Billy Ray hoping to accomplish? Should Christy throw in the towel and call his support team to get him out of there? These were the thoughts competing for answers in his head. With no real time to analyze the situation and come to a conclusion, he decided to play along. The delay would give him a moment to think. And he always had his insurance policy inside his holster vest.

"All right, Billy Ray, I'll admit it. Lately, I haven't been all that happy with the Klan, either. I lied. I've been cooperating with the FBI. I just wasn't sure I could trust you."

"You're *serious*? You're not just feeding me a line of shit to buy time so you can tell the grand dragons I'm a traitor?"

"I'm telling you the God's honest truth. I can even call the guy if you want."

"You're for real? Shit. What the fuck! Who cares? I'm heading straight outta here anyway if you're bullshittin' me. I'm done with the Klan. Go ahead, call him."

"I promise I will. If not, you can run. I just want to explain. I want to be sure we're not bothering him in the middle of the night without a good reason. I haven't been all that much help to the agent, because I'm not really in the loop. No one tells me important Klan secrets. This weekend's the first time I've been part of anything confidential. What is it that you have?"

"Hell, I can tell you things that would blow your mind. Some big things are in the works. I can help them put a lot of people away before they do any more damage. But I ain't sayin' shit unless you call that number."

\* \* \*

Billy Ray's hopes of finding out whether anyone else was working with Christy and the FBI were on the verge of being dashed. It became clearer to him as the conversation progressed that Christy was onto him. He could sense the deceit in the man's body language and smell it in his sweat. Billy Ray was going to have to rely on his instincts that no one else was involved in the snitch. He would get no answers tonight.

Christy was standing beside the desk chair opposite the bed, beside the armoire that housed a forty-two-inch flat-screen television. Billy Ray was facing him, standing at the foot of the bed. Christy spun around to pick up the business card he had placed on the desk next to the telephone. His next move was set in his mind. Just like Billy Ray, Christy knew that to persist on this tack was a waste of time and downright dangerous. When he turned to address Billy Ray, he would have his firearm drawn and be ready to put the conversation to an end.

As Christy moved toward the card and lifted his hand to place it inside his jacket, Billy Ray pulled out the wire fishing leader from his pant pocket. In the blink of an eye, he advanced one step, whipped the wire around Christy's throat, and pulled it tight.

The shock of having his air supply abruptly cut off resulted in a fatal delay in Christy's counterattack. Seeing Christy's hand move for the gun, Billy

Ray released the line with his right hand, grabbed the brass lamp on the desk, and smashed its heavy metal base into the back of Christy's head. Christy had managed to unholster the gun before he was struck, but the force of the blow knocked him nearly unconscious. He and his weapon fell to the floor.

Having thwarted Christy's only real means of self-defense, Billy Ray looped the wire leader around his neck and applied twice as much tension as before. As he continued to cut off the blood supply to his brain, hundreds of capillaries in Christy's bulging eyes burst, painting the sclera an eerie deep crimson. Christy, dazed from the clout to the temple, could do nothing but weakly flail his arms for the several seconds he remained conscious. In the final instant of his life, a sea of white light passed before his field of vision, then faded to black.

**Chapter 8**

The cacophonous din of frogs performing their nightly serenade along the riverbank drowned out the sounds of Kenny Jones's footsteps in the courtyard beneath the balcony of John Christy's hotel room. Kenny had been waiting in the Westin parking lot for the past hour for Billy Ray Johnson's call that the deed was done.

Kenny and Billy Ray had been friends and next-door neighbors since the age of 4. For Kenny, the term "friend" in relation to Billy Ray applied only in its loosest form. They were close through most of their childhood and adolescence but hadn't had much contact since Kenny went off to college. He lived in Savannah now, where he practiced since graduating from the school of law at Mississippi State University. Kenny knew he was in trouble when, earlier tonight, he got the call from his old friend. Billy Ray told him he needed to call in a favor. Kenny's first thought was that "favor" wasn't the word for the situation. It was more like blackmail. The only question remaining was how deep the trouble would be.

Like the Johnsons, the Jones family men had been members of the Ku Klux Klan for generations. When he came of age, Kenny had been initiated into the Klan like his father and grandfather before him. The difference for Kenny was that his heart wasn't in it. He had been brought up by parents who despised people simply for the color of their skin, their sexual preference, or the religion they practiced. From a very young age, Kenny had never bought into the whole hate thing. Perhaps as an act of rebellion, in his teens he had secretly dated a black girl from his high school, by the name of Harriet Brown. When he knocked her up, he made the huge mistake of going to his friend Billy Ray for help. At the time, he hadn't realized how much the error would cost him.

Harriet refused to have an abortion and warned Kenny that she expected him to support the child. Kenny's parents would literally kill him if they ever found out he had impregnated a black girl. Fearing for his life, one afternoon shortly after he learned of the pregnancy, he recounted the whole story to Billy Ray as they were driving home from school. Although Billy Ray was totally disgusted that Kenny had done it with a black girl, he was well aware that men sometimes had strange sexual desires. He knew of plenty of Klan members who forced black women to have sex with them. He convinced himself Kenny probably had done the same, and decided to help his friend.

Both Kenny and Billy Ray were just 17 years old at the time. Harriet had already turned eighteen and wouldn't need permission from her parents to abort the baby. Billy Ray was totally against terminating a pregnancy under normal circumstances. This prohibition didn't apply here, since he didn't consider a black child a human being. He recommended to Kenny that they do anything necessary to convince Harriet to agree to an abortion. Kenny committed his first fatal error in not asking what Billy Ray meant by "anything." His second mistake was in allowing Billy Ray to make the decisions about the methods they would employ to convince her.

Billy Ray wasn't shy about taking over management of the problem. He ordered Kenny to set up a meeting with Harriet. Kenny would offer to pick her up after one of her shifts at McDonald's. Once they had her in the car, Billy Ray would do all the talking. Kenny had an inkling Billy Ray was going to use some aggressive tactics to change her mind about the baby. Ordinarily, he wouldn't condone such methods, but he was desperate. He had already been accepted at

95

Ole Miss to study political science. It was his career plan to take the bar exam, work for the public defender's office, then eventually open a criminal defense practice at some point later in life. He could count on being cut off from all financial support if his parents ever discovered his secret. Not that he should be worried about money. More likely, he wouldn't be alive to attend college in the fall. He had no doubt whatever that his dad would put a bullet in his head if he ever discovered the scandal.

Jasper Jones, Kenny's father, was a callous, cruel man with few redeeming qualities. He was overly strict in raising his children and didn't hesitate to take them out to the woodshed for a serious hiding if the circumstances called for it. Historically, the circumstances had called for it quite often. Most beatings involved either a razor strop or a spiked paddle. That was his mild side. Jasper Jones was a cold-blooded killer.

In the early 1960's, he had participated in his share of lynchings. To this day, he bragged about setting fire to several black churches, including one in which eight children burned to death. What frightened Kenny even more was his dad's total lack of feelings for his own father, whom he had murdered in a dispute over money. He was never convicted of that crime, because the body was never found. No one ever discovered exactly how Kenny's grandfather died.

Jasper made sure each of his children was aware of what he had done. Kenny knew that if Jasper could kill his own next of kin over such a ridiculous issue, no one was safe from his wrath. Kenny had no doubt that if Jasper discovered he was about to be the grandfather of a mixed-blood baby, several people would die—Kenny, the baby, and its mother, for starters.

Billy Ray's motive for scheduling the meeting with Harriet on neutral ground would become clear to Kenny later. When he called her to schedule it, he offered to discuss the future of the baby and how they would handle custody and support. The reason for the get-together was another of Billy Ray's suggestions. Harriet gladly agreed.

* * *

Born to a heroin-addicted mother and a deadbeat father, Harriet, the oldest of five children, had become the caretaker and financial support for her four younger brothers when barely an adolescent herself. She carried out her responsibilities without complaint. Indoctrinated with religion at a very early age by her maternal grandmother, Harriet was a devout Christian and attended her local Baptist church on both Saturdays and Sundays. She believed in a Father in heaven with all her being and was certain he had a plan for her.

She had prayed incessantly for weeks after she sinned with the white boy. She promised God she would never do it again until after she took her vows, if only he would spare her child. A month and a half later, she learned that she was indeed pregnant, and cried the entire afternoon and evening. The next day, she accepted her fate as God's will and started looking for a second job. Her plans to attend night college classes after graduating from high school would have to be put on hold. Still her faith in God's plan did not waver. With the resolve of a mature adult, she set out to make the situation work.

She thanked God that Kenny had finally come to his senses. The idea of an abortion had never entered her thoughts until the day he demanded she have one. There was no way that Harriet Brown was going to condemn her soul to Hades for all eternity. If she had to take care of the baby without the assistance of its father, then so be it. But she was relieved it was no longer a worry. It seemed as if Kenny was ready to accept his responsibility. Just maybe she wouldn't have to bear the burden on her own.

On a stormy Thursday night in September 2005, Kenny and Billy Ray were waiting outside the McDonald's on Montgomery Street, where Harriet worked. Heavy, cold rain fell in buckets, soaking her hair and uniform as she approached Kenny's Ford Mustang.

Harriet was not happy to see Kenny's backseat passenger. She was too Christian to hate, but if she were ever to have those feelings for another human being, they would be directed at Billy Ray Johnson and his entire family. It was common knowledge that the Johnsons were members of the Ku Klux Klan. Harriet was sure that Emmett Johnson himself was responsible for hanging her maternal grandfather. As far as she was concerned, Billy Ray was worse than his father. She shuddered to think what he might be capable of.

When she reached the passenger door, she signaled Kenny to roll the window down. After he complied, she poked her head in the car and said, "Kenny, what's Billy Ray doin' here? I thought we were gonna have a private conversation."

"Don't worry about it. I just saw Billy Ray coming out of the lumber store on Forty-fourth and pulled over to talk to him. Turns out, he needed a ride home. I'm just gonna drop him off. Now, get in before you get yourself sick. You're in no condition to be standin' out in the rain."

Harriet considered telling Kenny to come back and get her afterward. Rather than get the discussion off to a rocky start, she decided to get into the car. She politely said hello to Billy Ray and couldn't believe he actually responded with a nod of the head. Before that moment, he had never even acknowledged her existence. Kenny pulled out of the parking space and turned south on

Montgomery Street. For the first few minutes of the ride, no one spoke a word, until Harriet realized they were heading in the wrong direction to go to the Johnson estate.

"Kenny, you went the wrong way," she said. "You should have turned left on Montgomery."

"Actually, we're not going to my house," said Billy Ray. "The three of us are going to have a nice little chat."

"No way, Kenny. There's no way I'm talking about my personal life with Billy Ray. You might as well take me home right now."

"No, Harriet. You're gonna listen to what I have to—"

Harriet cut Billy Ray off mid-sentence. "You can go to hell for all I care, Billy Ray! God, forgive me. Now, Kenny, turn this car around and take me home. The nerve of you to share our business with him! This was supposed to be a private conversation between me and you. What does he have to do with this, anyway?"

Before Kenny had the opportunity to respond to Harriet's question, Billy Ray grabbed a fistful of her hair and forced her head back. Then he reached around with his right hand and put the sharp tip of a big pocketknife against her throat.

"Now, you're gonna listen to me, you nigger bitch, and you're gonna do exactly what I tell you to do," Billy Ray bellowed. "Do you understand what I'm saying?"

Harriet was not a woman to take crap from anyone. But she was smart enough to know when discretion was the better part of valor. This was certainly one of those times. Billy Ray wouldn't have a problem using the knife. "Yes," she said.

"That was a good decision. Now, I'm gonna take this knife away from your throat. Don't you doubt for a second I'll use it if I have to. So no funny business. We're gonna be taking a little ride out to a friend's house. Kenny, take I-fifty-five north. You know the way to Ridgemont?"

"Yeah, Billy Ray. Why are we going out there?" Kenny asked.

"You'll find out soon enough. Once we get out that way, I'll give you the directions to my friend's house. In the meantime, it'll give me a chance to have a nice chat with this nigger slut."

Harriet didn't like the idea of being taken to the house of a friend of Billy Ray's. Nothing positive was going to come of that. In a trembling voice, she asked, "What are you gonna do to me?"

"So long as we can reach an understanding, you won't get hurt. I'm not here to answer your questions. Now, you know Kenny asked you nicely not to have this baby. He's even willing to pay for any medical expenses for an abortion. You don't get to make the decisions here. We're gonna take care of things right now. It's all arranged. You just do as we say and shut your ugly, monkey mouth."

"I'm not gonna shut up! There's no way I'm gonna do what you say. You're a monster. I don't care if you kill me."

"You may or may not care if I kill you, but I bet it's a different story if I cut your filthy little snot-nosed brothers' throats. And it won't be a quick and easy death, either. I'll make 'em suffer. They'll wish they were never born."

"You better not lay a hand on my brothers. I'll kill you, you evil motherfucker." Though Harriet couldn't believe she had uttered those words, she could handle whatever Billy Ray had to dish out. His threat to harm her brothers had gone too far.

100

"That'll be a nice trick from six feet under. Use that language with me again and there won't be a need for an abortion."

"Please, Billy Ray, you can't be that cruel. Don't make me do this. This has nothing to do with my brothers. Please leave them out of it." A stream of tears began to spill from Harriet's eyes. Her thick, unsteady voice had made her words barely comprehensible.

"I don't know what African language you're speaking. I don't care. It's your choice. Do what we're askin', keep your mouth shut, and everyone'll be fine."

Harriet's tears, stained with mascara, faded into the coal-colored skin of her cheeks. She couldn't believe the predicament she had gotten herself into. She agonized over why God was throwing one trial after another at her without respite. She had no idea what she had done to deserve it. She considered enlisting Kenny's assistance, but she knew he was just as helpless to control Billy Ray. There wasn't a doubt in her mind Billy Ray would at least kill her, and for spite, he would probably murder her brothers. If she could be sure he wouldn't harm them, she didn't care what happened to her.

Even if she were to get to the authorities unscathed, the Johnsons owned half of Jackson and practically the entire police department. The realization that she was actually going to have to concede made her heart feel as though it would break into a million pieces. A pressure was building below her breasts, as if they were supporting a thousand-pound barbell. She bowed her head and began to sob uncontrollably.

"You better quit your bawlin'. I want your answer now. By the way, I've got to blindfold you. The good doctor doesn't want you knowing where he lives, or seeing his face."

When she composed herself enough to be able to speak, she said, "Billy Ray, are you sure this doctor friend of yours knows what he's doing? I've heard lots of horror stories. How about if I agree to go to a licensed clinic?"

"Not a chance. It's happening tonight. The man's a surgeon. He operates on people every day. Hell, I don't know why I'm justifying things with you. You fuckin' do it tonight, or you and your brothers are dead."

"All right," she whimpered. "I'll do it."

\* \* \*

The light was fading over the western banks of the Mississippi river as Kenny led the blindfolded Harriet into the medical offices of Dr. Clayton Saxon. Dr. Saxon wasn't *exactly* a surgeon. The closest he had ever gotten to an operating room was to assist in a tonsillectomy or two, and that was in the outpatient ward of the hospital. He was only thirty-four years old and had been practicing medicine for less than five years. After completing his residency in internal medicine at a Savannah hospital, he had opened up a private family practice in Vicksburg. He was originally from Jackson, where his entire family now lived.

As an intern, he had had the opportunity to observe two abortions while studying under the tutelage of a gynecologist. He had neither performed nor assisted in the procedure. Undeterred by his inexperience, he had an overabundance of self-confidence. Truth be told, his career choice had arisen more from a greed for prestige than from any real passion for healing people. The nurses at Promise Hospital of Vicksburg mockingly referred to him as "God," but only behind his back. On the minute chance that something seriously went awry, one less darkie was no great loss to him. Saxon had no doubt that Billy

102

Ray had every angle covered. In fact, Dr. Saxon had received a personal guarantee.

When Billy Ray called with the request, Saxon was happy to oblige. His Klan membership was more important to him than his license to practice medicine. Any opportunity to augment his status within the organization was welcome. Billy Ray was young, but he was already developing a powerful reputation, and a favor of this magnitude for the Johnson family would most assuredly be remembered.

Conveniently, Billy Ray reached him while he was doing rounds at the hospital. Physicians at the medical center performed abortions exclusively in emergency situations. The instrumentation required was tucked away in a storage room in a seldom-frequented hallway. Before leaving the facility later that evening, Dr. Saxon had collected everything he would need for the procedure. He grabbed some sterilizing products and surgical tools from the OR supply closet, then made his way to storage to pick up the vacuum. To avoid the attention of any nosy onlookers, he placed the machine in a large medical equipment bag with the rest of the gear.

Dr. Saxon greeted Billy Ray and his company at the side entrance to his office. He had Kenny lead Harriet into one of his larger examining rooms, where there was a table with stirrups. Since agreeing to the abortion, Harriet had not spoken a word. The only evidence that she wasn't in some catatonic state was the apparent steady stream of tears dampening the blindfold. She offered no resistance as she was disrobed from the waist down, she got on the table, and put her feet in the stirrups. Billy Ray and Kenny, having no desire to observe the operation, left the room to wait in the lobby area.

The sterilized tools were organized on a steel tray next to the examining table. After scrubbing, Dr. Saxon picked up the syringe with a local anesthetic, warned Harriet she would feel a slight pinch in the genital area, then injected the numbing medicine. Harriet made no indication that she heard what the doctor was saying. He used a second needle to administer the drug that would dilate her cervix.

The main instrument used to perform the procedure was known as a suction curette. It was a hollow tube with a knife-edged tip that would be inserted into the womb. The opposite end was connected to a vacuum machine said to be twenty-nine times more powerful than a household vacuum cleaner. Before using the curette, Dr. Saxon generously applied Betadine over the entire genital area, upper thighs, and lower stomach. Satisfied that the surgical site was as clean as possible, he inserted the curette with his right hand into her vaginal canal, through the cervix, and into the womb.

As he reached with his left hand to pull the switch that engaged the vacuum, his right hand slipped ever so slightly, causing the knife of the curette to cut through the uterine wall. Dr. Saxon knew something was terribly wrong when copious amounts of blood were being sucked through the transparent tube of the vacuum. He immediately switched off the machine, to no avail. Blood continued to flow at an alarming rate from Harriet's vagina. In an attempt to stop the bleeding, Dr. Saxon applied pressure to the lower abdomen and stuffed sterile towels against her groin area. The measures he employed had no effect at all. The bleeding was internal. There was nothing he could do in his small, unstaffed medical office to stop it.

With his stethoscope, he listened to Harriet's heartbeat. It was barely audible. He reached for her wrist to take her pulse and couldn't find one. Covered in blood from the middle of his chest to his upper thighs, he calmly walked out into the lobby to notify the boys that Harriet had suffered a fatal injury. When Kenny saw all the blood, he rushed into the examining room to check on Harriet. Seeing her lying unconscious if not dead, he screamed, "What the fuck happened in here!"

"Hey, whoa, hold on there," said Dr. Saxon. "There are potential complications for every procedure. I explained them to Billy Ray. There must have been some internal bleeding caused by the curette. There's no way to stop it. She's going to bleed to death if she hasn't already. These things happen. What's the big deal, anyway? It's not as if she were a white woman."

"I'm calling an ambulance," Kenny said. "I'm not just gonna let her die."

"Are you fuckin' *crazy*?" said Billy Ray. "We'll all end up in prison, and that's if the bitch lives. If she drops dead, then we're facing the electric chair. I don't know about you, but I ain't goin' to jail or getting fried over no jungle bunny. Let the slut die!"

"No worries," said Dr. Saxon, the bloody thumb and forefinger of his right hand on Harriet's wrist. "She's dead."

* * *

What most people never did in a lifetime Kenny Jones was now doing for a second time in less than ten years. The first time was when he and Billy Ray buried Harriet Brown's body in the forest of the Ross Barnett Reservoir in Ridgemont, Mississippi, to avoid a murder rap. Tonight, they would be burying the body of John Christy in the woods just outside Skidaway State Reserve in Savannah.

Billy Ray had the crazy idea to throw the dead body off his second-floor balcony into the courtyard below, where Kenny would be waiting. Luckily, the ground was covered with grass, and obviously, the guy's heart wasn't beating, so there probably wouldn't be too much blood. Their major obstacle was to do it without being seen. It helped that it was three o'clock in the morning and the area was poorly lit. Kenny had nervously scoped the grounds for more than an hour and didn't notice any security guards patrolling the property. He didn't see a guest or employee of the hotel, either.

In spite of the cool breeze coming off the river, Kenny's shirt was soaked with perspiration as if he had taken a dip in the resort's pool. When he was as sure as he could be that the courtyard was deserted, he called Billy Ray's cell phone to tell him the coast was clear. Five seconds later, he saw Billy Ray standing on the balcony, the corpse slung over his shoulder. He motioned for Kenny to stand to one side, then tossed the body over the railing, feet first. When it hit the ground, Kenny thought he heard the cracking sound of bones breaking. He felt a wave of nausea. Fortunately, the body didn't land in an awkward position. If it had, he might not have been able to keep his dinner down.

He looked up toward the balcony, where Billy Ray was giving him a thumbs-up. Kenny didn't see it as the appropriate signal for a situation like this. Then again, he was dealing with Billy Ray Johnson, and the man was anything but appropriate. While Billy Ray made his way downstairs to join him, Kenny started to place the body in the sleeping bag he had brought with him, while keeping an eye out for passersby. His anxiety had reached the breaking point. His revulsion at what he was doing had stirred up a huge migraine. To make matters worse, rigor mortis had set in, and the stiffness of the corpse was almost more than he could bear. Only fear of the consequences from Billy Ray gave him the discipline to keep his stomach from turning.

It took quite a bit of strength to straighten the legs so they would fit in the sleeping bag's opening. He could feel the broken femur grinding under his hand as he applied pressure. By the time Billy Ray arrived, he had managed to get Christy's legs and most of his torso into the bag. Together, they managed to push the body completely inside and pull the zipper closed.

Before they carried their cargo anywhere, Billy Ray ordered Kenny to check the parking lot, to be sure no one was about. Kenny felt that if he had any balls at all, he would hop in his car and leave Billy Ray to do his dirty work on his own. The urge to flee was nearly irresistible.

In less than a minute, he was back, signaling that it was safe to go. Billy Ray grabbed the head end while Kenny held on to the feet. They carried the corpse as quickly and quietly as they could to Kenny's Cadillac Escalade, parked in the most remote corner of the parking lot. After they stuffed the body into the storage space in the rear of the SUV, Kenny started to get in the driver's seat. The flat of Billy Ray's upturned palm let him know that he would be riding shotgun in his own car. Kenny had no objection at all.

As they backed out of the parking space, Kenny was relieved and amazed that they had made it through the entire experience without being seen. It seemed that his old friend had the luck of the devil. Kenny brooded over the possibility of life in prison as they turned east on Highway 26 and set out on the twenty-minute ride to Skidaway State Reserve.

Chapter 9

The deep-blue sky held not a single cloud, as one might expect of the city considered to have the best weather in the nation. The temperature was a perfect seventy-eight degrees, with humidity of less than 20 percent. Regrettably, San Diego Field Office Special Agent in Charge Ed Harding wouldn't get to take advantage of the beautiful day. It was his first morning back at work after a two-week vacation in Miami, where the stifling heat and humidity had forced him to spend most of his holiday indoors. Spending two of his three weeks' vacation time in South Florida during the summer wasn't exactly his preference, but he had been promising his wife for the past five years that he would take her to visit her mother in Miami. It was time to make good on his word.

Harding was happy to finally be back in what he considered paradise. His first order of business for the morning was to be briefed by the assistant special agent in charge, Michael Gerard, about all that had happened during his absence. Harding's main concern was the status of Special Agent John Christy's investigation of the Ku Klux Klan. He knew that Christy was expecting a major breakthrough, and he had gotten news of his agent's disappearance while still in Miami. It was a huge blow to the investigation, to say the least.

According to Gerard, the meeting of the national leaders of the Klan supposedly happened Sunday. Christy was expected to call in that night, but no one had heard from him since he spoke to Gerard Saturday evening. The support team backing Christy was given the order to move in during the late-morning hours of Sunday, after they made several vain attempts to contact him. Half the team searched the woods where the gathering was scheduled to happen. By the time they arrived, the meeting had long since been adjourned.

108

Ashes of a material assumed to be a burned wooden cross were collected, and numerous footprints of various sizes, and a refilled hole were photographed. Later, the Evidence Response Team cast the prints and combed the area for other clues, though nothing of any real significance was found except for traces of an accelerant—probably kerosene.

The other half of Christy's backup squad raced to the Westin Hotel in Savannah to search for their missing colleague. The front desk clerk's computer inquiry revealed that Christy had not yet checked out. After getting a key and directions from the clerk, the four agents took the stairs to the second floor, then entered Christy's room with guns drawn. He wasn't there, though his belongings were strewn about, including surveillance and recording equipment he was supposed to use at the meeting.

Next, they checked the rooms of the known participants of the Klan meeting, only to find them vacant. The beds were unmade, garbage cans had not been emptied, and hotel pamphlets and informational magazines were scattered on desk and dresser tops. It was assumed that the Klan leaders had left in the middle of the night.

That afternoon, the Evidence Response Team did a much more thorough search of Christy's and the Klansmen's rooms. The team was looking for blood trace, fingerprints, or any other evidence that could help them determine what happened to Agent Christy, and who was involved in his disappearance. Visual inspection uncovered nothing of relevance. All the rooms were then sprayed with luminol, a chemical that emitted a bluish glow upon contact with blood. In Christy's room, on the floor near the desk, several droplets of blood registered. They were smeared, as if someone had tried to wipe the carpet clean. The ERT tore up the stained section for testing and also to determine if any blood was underneath. They found nothing appreciable.

Often, the luminol chemicals tended to destroy genetic markers. Such was the case for the drops of blood on the carpet surface. They were rendered useless for later DNA testing. But it was evidence of foul play. It also provided important information about the point of attack if the blood should prove to be Christy's. The luminol test couldn't measure how long the blood had been there, making it impossible to pinpoint the time it was spilled.

The sum of all the circumstances had Hardy seriously concerned that Christy was in major trouble if not already dead. The task force created to combat white-supremacist and paramilitary groups within the United States had met earlier in the morning at the San Diego field office to discuss the predicament. Hardy was presiding, and he ordered the interrogation of every known member of the Klan who was present for the gathering in Savannah. It was too late to worry about blowing the undercover operation. No circumstances imaginable would induce Christy to breach protocol. Everyone agreed, it was time to move in. Two special agents were dispatched to Jackson, Mississippi, to interview the Johnsons. At the same time, teams of two were sent to Florida, California, Texas, Alabama, Georgia, Virginia, Ohio, and Massachusetts to question the other Klansmen known to be guests of the hotel. Another team was sent to California to interrogate Christy's Klan contacts in his home state.

On behalf of the task force, Harding was contacting the FBI field offices around the country to request support for the agents conducting the interrogations. His first call was to the North Miami field office. Normally, he would contact the special agent in charge. Having worked together on several task forces over the years and in the FBI's career advancement program, he and

Daniel Falcone had developed a good working relationship. More importantly, Harding had great respect for the man and his reliability. He picked up the phone and dialed Falcone's cell number. After the initial greetings, Harding got straight to the business at hand.

"I'm calling because we're worried about one of our agents. Do you know John Christy?"

"Can't say I've ever met him."

"Makes sense. He's been working undercover for us for years now." Harding gave Daniel the specifics about Christy's mission, the meeting he was supposed to attend in Savannah, and his disappearance. "We're sending two agents your way to interview a guy by the name of Willis Zachary. Ever heard of him?"

"Sure have. He's one of the richest men in the state. He's big-time in the Republican Party. Contributes a lot of money. He's personal friends with the governor of Florida and our Republican U.S. senator—and a real asshole."

"Yeah, well, he was at that meeting. We need to find out what he knows. You think you guys can make sure my people have some good backup? Hook 'em up with anything they need?"

"You can count on it. I'll talk to my SAC about it. I'm sure he'll have no problem assigning a few guys to keep an eye out for them. I'll do what I can, too. You know, it's really interesting you called me this morning about this. Kinda bizarre, actually. I mean what's going on with Fitch and the investigation." Daniel explained his rationale about white-supremacist organizations and their potential involvement in the assassination. "I'd like to hear a lot more about these guys you're looking into, Ed. Do you think you could share some information with me?"

"Absolutely. Do you want to come out here? We have files on all these guys at the office. This is obviously an undercover operation, and there are other agents out in the field who could be at risk. There's no way I can send them by interoffice mail. And I'm sorry, but I won't be able to give you the names of the investigators."

"No problem. I completely understand. If it gets to the point where I need to talk to one of them, we'll figure it out then. For now, I'll schedule a trip, probably within the week. I'll give you a call when I come up with a date. In the meantime, I hope everything turns out okay with Christy . . . Uh, before I let you go, I'm thinking I might join your men for the Zachary interview. Can you make that happen?"

"I don't see why not."

* * *

The pungent smell of chlorine stung Billy Ray's nose as he swam laps in the Olympic-size pool of his parents' exclusive country club. The burn and the exhilarating stab of the chilly water brought him to full alertness. Swimming was usually a form of relaxation for him. He did it to clear his mind, and it gave him a chance to think without distraction. Some of his best ideas had come to him in this very pool.

At the moment, his thoughts were on the successful trip to Savannah. The Klan meeting had gone better than he could ever have expected. When he returned to the city after burying John Christy's body deep in the woods near Skidaway State Reserve, he had decided not to wait until morning to advise his brethren of John Christy's betrayal. He woke his father up first to tell him about his discovery and his resolution of the problem. Together, they called the other members of the elite group and brought them up to date. They decided then and there to hold the meeting immediately. By sunrise, they all would be well on their way home.

At this time of night, the drive to Lake Warren State Park in South Carolina took less than thirty minutes. The black night sky was cloudless and shot through with a million bright pinpricks. A convoy of six vehicles drove onto the wildlife trails and into the forest. The trees provided a thick, impenetrable canopy, all but blocking out the starlight. The menacing bright high beams slashed through the night, leading them to the predetermined site of the covert gathering.

The younger men unloaded the eight-foot wood cross from the bed of the truck driven by Willis Zachary. In the center of the clearing, Billy Ray began to dig a hole deep enough to secure the structure. When it was anchored and upright, he doused it with a generous amount of kerosene and set it ablaze. The white-hot flames flickered hungrily upward into the dark heavens as the men donned the customary Klan garb and sat in their designated places around the fire. It was already a stifling, humid night without the heat generated by the burning rood. Two flags, the Stars and Stripes and the Stars and Bars, were planted in the ground behind Grand Wizard Austin Dobson.

Dobson was staying at the Westin Hotel under a false name and, for reasons of secrecy, hadn't joined the other men at the dinner, nor would he have participated if the golf tournament had taken place. Once everyone was seated, he began the meeting.

"The burning of the cross is a symbolic act. In ancient times, Scottish clans would use one formed in the shape of an X, known as Saint Andrew's

Cross. It was a beacon to motivate their warriors before battle. In 1915, we adopted the upright Latin version as our symbol, and it has endured more than an entire century. Tonight, it has special significance. We, as a race and as the only true citizens of the United States of America, are facing our most critical struggle. Our country has been overrun and overtaken by the niggers, Jews, and spics as we sat idly by and allowed it to happen. Now our worst fears have been realized. For a second time in a row, a ghetto monkey from Africa has been elected leader of the republic that our forefathers established on our behalf. As I have heard Billy Ray say on numerous occasions, they must be turning over in their graves. Thanks to him, we have grown in strength and numbers. He has mobilized us, not just in the South but from coast to coast. We are more than ready to act and take back the country that is rightfully ours. Billy Ray came up with a detailed design for accomplishing this goal. Tonight, we will vote on our course of action. Billy Ray."

The words of the grand wizard roused the spirits of the other men seated in a circle around the blazing cross. But it was a mere trifle compared to the effect of Billy Ray's passionate speech that night. His plan was adopted unanimously without amendment. He was elected general of the Klan army, charged to gather the forces necessary to execute their agenda, and given full authority to act on their behalf. Billy Ray promised his brethren that the decisions they made that evening would set in motion the dawning of a new era in the history of the United States of America and its beloved organization the Ku Klux Klan.

\* \* \*

Over the past few weeks, mornings weren't Tabitha Freemont's favorite time of the day. When she woke up, she would be famished. Ten minutes after finishing breakfast, she would find herself hugging the toilet bowl. More recently, she had decided to forego her normal first meal of the day, consisting of soft-boiled eggs and a bowl of raisin bran. She had made an ironclad decision that she would not let the intense nausea dampen her spirits over her pregnancy. She was just as excited as ever about having her first baby, in spite of the way she felt or Kyle's reaction to the news. She had been hoping for, and maybe even expecting, a more favorable response from him. At least, he hadn't blown his stack.

At first mention of her pregnancy, he seemed pretty upset. Eventually, he calmed down and pretended to be happy. She considered it encouraging that he hadn't beaten her. Kyle was doing extremely well with his sobriety. This was the longest he had ever gone without a drink. Tabitha was beginning to let herself believe that he had finally kicked the habit. That was good news for both her and the baby.

It was nearly noon, and finally her stomach was showing signs of settling. She was about to head for the kitchen to fix herself something to eat when the doorbell rang. Tabitha wondered who could possibly be calling on her at this time of the day. All her friends were at work, and she had no family in South Florida. Thinking it may be some salesperson trying to push some product on her, she initially chose to ignore the caller. When the knocking persisted, she looked through the peephole and saw a tall, good-looking man in a dark suit standing on the landing. Her curiosity got the better part of her. To be safe, she slipped the chain lock in place, opened the door a crack, and asked, "Who's there?"

The man held up a badge and said, "Good morning, Miss Freemont. I'm Special Agent Daniel Falcone with the FBI. If you don't mind, I'd like to ask you a few questions about the night you worked Senator Alvin Fitch's fund-raiser."

"I already gave my statement to an agent."

"I know, ma'am, but I'd like to go into a little bit more detail with you. May I come in?"

"Well, I don't know. I think I better check with your office first. How do I know you're not some freak rapist or serial killer?"

"Feel free. I'll wait out here."

"My boyfriend doesn't allow me to invite strange men into my house. Maybe you could come back when he visits?"

"This is an extremely important matter, ma'am. I'm going to interview you now, so you have a choice. Either we do it here, or you can come with me to North Miami FBI offices. You pick."

"Hold on, I'll make that call. What was your name again?"

"Daniel Falcone."

Tabitha's hands were trembling so badly, she didn't know whether she'd be able to dial the phone. Kyle wouldn't be happy she was talking to the feds. She thought she was done with them after giving her statement to the young agent the day after the senator's death. The idea that she was going to have to go through it a second time made her feel nauseated all over again. Knowing that if she screwed up, her child would have to live with the stigma of having a convict for a daddy, made her all the more anxious. She considered calling Kyle and asking what she should do, then decided it was a dumb idea. Just last week, she had gotten into big trouble for calling him at work. She picked up the phone, dialed the correct four numbers for free information on the second

116

try, and asked for the telephone number of the North Miami FBI office. Since she was making the guy wait outside, she figured she had better call to confirm he was an agent, even though she didn't really doubt it. She didn't need to create any unnecessary suspicions. In the meantime, it would give her a chance to calm down and get into a better state of mind to think.

After speaking with the squad secretary at the field office, she unlocked the door and let the man in. She directed him to have a seat on the living room sofa while she sat on an easy chair facing him. Concerned that he might notice her shaky hands, she placed them underneath her thighs. She doubted her effort to conceal her stress had worked.

Falcone opened his briefcase and pulled out a yellow legal pad and pen to take notes. He also took out a Dictaphone and notified Tabitha that he would be recording the interview. Tabitha rejected her instinct to offer the agent something to drink, for fear of stumbling and fumbling, maybe even spilling it on him in her anxiety. He made a statement on the tape describing what was to take place, identified the witness, then began the questioning.

"How long have you been employed by American Gourmet?"

"I've worked on and off for them for the past three years. When Mr. Kraft needs me for a job, he calls."

"When did you get the call that you would be working Senator Fitch's fund-raising event at the Miami Beach Convention Center?"

"A couple of weeks before it was scheduled."

"What did he ask you to do?"

"He said it was a big job. He needed help with some of the shopping and food prep. The week before the event, I was supposed to go to American Gourmet's kitchen every day and help the cooks. Then I served that night."

"Did you know Mr. Kraft before you applied for the job?"

This question made Tabitha stiffen with apprehension. She was well aware that Richard was a member of the Ku Klux Klan and had played an integral role in the senator's assassination. Kyle's dad, Andrew Lansbury, had introduced them. The evening she met him, Tabitha was returning a borrowed electric drill to Andrew. Richard happened to be at the house, discussing Klan business with him, when she arrived.

Tabitha astutely realized that she had hesitated before answering the question. In an attempt to conceal her concern, she answered, "Sorry, I was just trying to think back. Three years is a long time." She lied: "I met him for the first time at my interview."

Once again, Tabitha recognized that her delayed response and her tense body language did not escape Daniel's attention.

"Do you have a personal relationship with Mr. Kraft, or is it just professional?"

Tabitha and Kyle had been to several barbecues and parties at the Kraft house. With each falsehood she invented, her heart beat faster, the muscles in her stomach tensed, and her body seemed to overheat. It required a colossal effort just to keep her knees from shaking. She could feel the beginnings of a horrible headache coming on. In spite of it all, she had to behave as if it were just another day. If she screwed up, there would be hell to pay.

"Strictly professional," Tabitha muttered.

She was losing her battle to stay calm. She wondered whether her last answer was even comprehensible. Now, for the third time, the agent must have sensed her anxiety. Just the experience of being questioned by a law enforcement official often made civilians nervous, but this had to be over the top. He seemed to be paying extra close attention to her reaction to his questions.

"Do you know of any ties that Richard Kraft may have with any white-supremacy groups such as the Ku Klux Klan or the Neo-Nazis?"

Tabitha was taken completely off guard. In no uncertain terms, she had been warned that Mr. Kraft's membership with the Klan, and Kyle's connection to the Neo-Nazis were top secret information. She couldn't afford to hesitate. She blurted out, "No way. Mr. Kraft is the sweetest man in the world."

Everything about her delivery was wrong. She practically shouted her answer. It didn't require a trained detective to see that her body language was stiff and her demeanor completely conflicted with her words. Falcone had to be getting suspicious.

"Have you ever been associated with such a group?"

The realization that she was at a precipice motivated Tabitha to act. Either she got herself together, or she was going to be directly responsible for putting the father of her baby in the electric chair. The thought of raising her child as a single mother was sufficient incentive. Instead of continuing to behave like a scared little schoolgirl, she embodied the strong woman she knew she could be. She donned her best offended expression.

"That's insulting. I would never be a part of something like that. I can't stand racists."

"I'm sorry, but it's a question I have to ask. I really don't mean to insult you. You can take time to think about your answers. I don't want you to miss anything . . . Okay, along those lines—meaning the issue of white supremacy—do you know anyone who worked the fund-raising event at the Convention

Center who has ever had any kind of association with the Ku Klux Klan, Neo-Nazis, paramilitary groups, or any sort of racist organization?"

The easy tone of Daniel's words reassured Tabitha that she might not have generated that much suspicion. She fought hard to stay strong. At least, she was now capable of controlling her knocking knees and speaking at a volume that wouldn't break the agent's eardrums. She prayed it wasn't too late to rehabilitate her credibility.

"Not that I'm aware of. Mr. Kraft would never hire anyone like that, and I would never work with them."

For the next fifteen minutes, in response to Falcone's questions, Tabitha specifically described her actions and observations on the night of the incident. When asked to name all the people who had worked the party for American Gourmet that night, she neglected to include Billy Ray Johnson. Not only was she sworn to secrecy, but she was acutely aware that if she revealed his participation to anyone, her life and, more importantly, the life of her baby would be in dire jeopardy. Throughout the remainder of the interview, she managed to present herself in a more reasonable manner.

She wasn't looking forward to later this evening, when Kyle got home from work. She would have no choice but to tell him about the interview. He was going to be furious, especially after hearing that Falcone was fishing for information concerning the Neo-Nazis and the Klan.

An hour and a half after the agent arrived, he announced that he had only one or two more questions. Tabitha felt an immediate sense of relief. The first question put her right back on the hot seat.

"Do you live here alone?"

Tabitha had no doubt how Kyle would want her to answer this question. Due to his many surreptitious and illegal activities, he didn't even want his name on the lease. Certainly, she thought, he wouldn't want an FBI agent breathing down his neck, especially since he was directly involved in the senator's death. It didn't take much reflection to come out with the next of her mounting deceptions.

"Yes, I have no roommates."

"I want you to take your time and think about this final question." Falcone waited a few seconds evidently to allow his instruction to sink in. "Was there anyone—and I'm not limiting this to just the people working for American Gourmet. Was there anyone you saw who was behaving suspiciously that night? Was there anything odd or peculiar about anyone or anything you saw at the Convention Center on the night Senator Fitch was murdered?"

Tabitha took a few minutes to reflect on the question, though she had no uncertainty about what her answer would be. "Not at all. It was just a typical night at work for me, right up until all hell broke loose."

**Chapter 10**

United Airlines flight 1262, arriving from Memphis, touched down at Washington D.C.'s Dulles International Airport at 9:01 p.m., three minutes ahead of schedule. Normally, flying wasn't Billy Ray Johnson's preferred way of traveling. He would much rather be behind the wheel of a good old American-made car than hurtling through the atmosphere at over five hundred miles per hour, seven miles above the earth's surface. He didn't trust any machine that had to generate that much power to get him where he wanted to go. Lately, his schedule dictated his means of transportation. It just wasn't practical or feasible to travel the distances required in the limited time at his disposal.

He would spend the night in D.C., then catch the first plane in the morning to Atlanta. The wheels were set in motion, and only a major blowout could stop the momentum that his game plan was gathering. Tonight's affair wasn't originally part of the overall scheme. It was, however, one of the most important business transactions he would handle to date. He didn't know the true identity of the man he was meeting with. What he did know was the person's value to the mission. The contact was a conduit to one of Washington's most powerful politicians. Billy Ray was scheduled to meet with the man he knew only as Brody at precisely midnight, near the steps of the Supreme Court Building. He was instructed to wear dark blue jeans and a Jacksonville Jaguars football jersey. Brody was described to him as a male in his late forties, about six feet tall, 175 pounds, wearing a black trench coat and a Cleveland Indians baseball cap. After spending most of the evening at the ESPN Zone on Twelfth Street Northwest, Billy Ray arrived at the rendezvous site at exactly 11:57 p.m., following the detailed instructions. When he saw Brody approaching from across

122

the road, Billy Ray walked toward him with the intention of meeting in the middle of the street. As their paths intersected, Brody surreptitiously passed a thick envelope he had hidden under his coat into Billy Ray's left hand. Brody continued walking toward Constitution Avenue while Billy Ray headed toward East Capital Street. Other than the transfer of the package, neither man acknowledged the other's existence.

Ten minutes later, Billy Ray was in his hotel room at the Holiday Inn on C Street Southwest. He set his alarm clock to wake him up at seven a.m. His flight to Atlanta was scheduled at nine thirty. He hoped he wouldn't have any difficulty falling asleep. The cloak-and-dagger activity had caused an increased amount of adrenaline to invade his bloodstream. As it was, if he nodded off immediately, he would get only six and a half hours' sleep.

* * *

Democrat Brandon Atkins was originally elected to the U.S. Senate in his home state of Iowa on an independent platform. Two years ago, the man destined to be the next president of the United States had persuaded him to join the Democratic Party. At the time, Benjamin Cooper was a rookie senator from Michigan who was rapidly rising in popularity and had just announced his candidacy for the presidency. Senator Atkins was enough of a visionary to see that Cooper was going places, and made a strategic decision to ride on his coattails. When Cooper was elected president, Atkins was his first publicly announced appointment to the cabinet, as secretary of defense.

Secretary Atkins was one of the country's most brilliant military minds. Immediately upon graduating from high school, he had enlisted in the Army. He fought in Vietnam, Grenada, and both Gulf Wars. During peacetime, between the wars in Grenada and Iraq, foreseeing the crucial need for peace in the Middle East, he studied Arabic while earning a bachelor's degree in military science. Within a year, he was fluent. He played a major role in leading U.S. troops to victory in Desert Storm and was one of the masterminds of the attack on Iraq in 2003. He retired with the rank of four-star general at the end of that year, after thirty-nine years of loyal service. In 2004, he decided to run for the Senate seat being vacated by his predecessor. He won by a landslide. Other than the president, Atkins was one of the Democratic Party's foremost rising stars.

Tonight, Atkins was scheduled to have dinner with the president and Secretary of Homeland Security Tom Logan to discuss an immigration platform. After Senator Fitch's death, the Senate, as a tribute to him, was instigating a push toward enacting the former lawmaker's proposal for regulating illegal immigration. President Cooper wanted to hear what Atkins and Logan had to say about the issue, in a more intimate setting.

Tom Logan was the Republican former governor for the state of Virginia. His appointment to the cabinet had baffled the political pundits. Offering such an important position to the opposing party was considered a bold move by the Democratic president. It was, in reality, an attempt to bridge the gap between parties in the hope of getting concessions on those issues near and dear to the president's heart. The fact that Cooper and Logan had been roommates during their years at Harvard was definitely a factor.

Atkins knew that Logan's view on immigration was typical of the conservative Republican Party. Logan didn't want to grant automatic citizenship, or any of the rights associated with it, to illegal immigrants simply because they managed to stay unlawfully in the country for a given period of time. For him,

U.S. citizenship was not a right but a privilege that had to be earned. He was also concerned that less stringent rules could open up the borders to Middle Eastern terrorists wanting to do harm to the nation. Although Atkins had become affiliated with the Democratic Party, his views on the issue were not as liberal as his colleagues'. With Logan's help, he thought he might be able to convince the president to exercise his influence over the Senate and adopt a more moderate set of regulations. Both men had the chief executive's ear on a variety of issues. It was widely known in Beltway political circles that Logan and Atkins were two of his most respected advisers.

* * *

Washington, D.C., was Daniel Falcone's favorite city in the world. He had always dreamed of living in the U.S. capital one day, as director of the FBI. Because of recent life experiences, namely his false imprisonment, that dream would have to remain a flight of fancy. He was here now because he was scheduled to meet with the current director, Christopher Ryan, Assistant Director Howard Evans, and President Cooper in the Oval Office of the White House to discuss progress on the Fitch investigation. Normally, when Daniel was meeting with the president of the United States, he was filled with a sense of awe and anticipation. That was not the case today. He wasn't looking forward to the encounter at all. Though he felt that he had taken some small steps toward solving the assassination case, he was sure the men he was meeting with were expecting much more.

After the interview with Tabitha Freemont a week ago, he was sure she hadn't been completely forthcoming. For that reason, he had an agent assigned to temporarily observe her apartment. The decision had borne fruit almost

125

immediately. There was a young male spending a great deal of time in the apartment, most likely her boyfriend. Throughout the four-day stakeout, without exception, the undercover agents observed the man entering Tabitha's home around the dinner hour and not leaving before the next morning. As soon as Daniel was informed of the potential deception, he had the undercover surveillance agent call him the next time the boyfriend made an appearance. The instant he received the warning, Daniel hopped in his Crown Victoria and headed for Tabitha Freemont's residence.

She was obviously shaken when she opened the door for Daniel. Initially, she lied that she was alone. Nettled by her dishonesty, Daniel admonished Tabitha, saying she could be charged with obstruction of justice for withholding information, and threatened to search the apartment. He stood up to do just that when she realized she was out of options, and admitted that Kyle was in the bedroom.

Daniel told her to have him come out for a chat. After forty-five minutes of intense interrogation, Daniel came to the conclusion that the boyfriend was at least as evasive as his mate. For the moment, he didn't have much choice but to file his assessment for future reference. The only valuable information he uncovered was the boyfriend's last name. It immediately raised a red flag as Daniel remembered the pharmacy manager at Jackson Memorial. When asked if he was any relation to Andrew Lansbury, Kyle confessed that the hospital employee was indeed his father.

It didn't take a Sherlock Holmes to conclude that this was no coincidence. Not surprisingly, Kyle denied any involvement with white-supremacist groups or in the assassination of Senator Fitch. Still, Daniel had no legal basis to detain either Kyle or Tabitha for further questioning. On a positive note, they had given him a definite lead that he would set high on his list of priorities. He had the task force research team get on with conducting a thorough background study into their lives and that of Kyle's father.

The day after his talk with Kyle, Daniel made an unannounced visit to Jackson Memorial Hospital. Like his son, Andrew Lansbury denied any involvement in the Alvin Fitch assassination or with any racist organization. Everything about his mannerisms led Daniel to the same conclusion: something was amiss. Daniel planned to place his trip to San Diego at the top of his to-do list. There was the distinct possibility that they had files on these guys. Unfortunately, the detour to D.C. interrupted his work for the moment. Meanwhile, Frye and a team of agents were interviewing friends, neighbors, family members, and fellow employees both past and present for any information they could gather about the Lansbury men and Tabitha Freemont.

The interview with Willis Zachary was nothing less than a farce. He denied being a member of the Ku Klux Klan. When confronted with footage, taken by Christy's backup team, showing him at Klan gatherings, he claimed that either it wasn't him or the film was altered. It was true that some of the video was not of the greatest quality. All Klan meetings occurred after dark, and infrared film didn't always produce the clearest pictures.

The only allegation Zachary was willing to admit was his friendly association with John Christy. He confessed that they had met at a golf tournament in California. Golf was also his stated reason why they were scheduled to get together in Savannah. According to Zachary, the morning he arrived in Georgia, he got a call from Christy saying that something had come up and he had to cancel his trip. Disappointed that his friend couldn't make it,

Zachary decided to head back home the next day. Telephone records confirmed that Zachary had indeed received a call from Christy that Saturday morning.

When asked about his relationship with the other Klan members at the hotel, Zachary acknowledged that he knew they were competing in the tournament. He denied ever seeing them before that weekend. After the questioning agent challenged his veracity, Zachary refused to answer any more questions without the presence of his lawyer. That statement essentially terminated the interview. The results of this interview and those of Tabitha Freemont and Kyle Lansbury were the only updates Daniel had to report at his upcoming meeting. It wasn't much to offer the most powerful man in the world, but it was a lot more than he had just a week ago.

Daniel was staying at the Crowne Plaza Hotel on Fourteenth Street Northwest. Since he had a little extra time before he was expected at the White House, he decided to walk. The sun shone brightly on the National Mall, accentuating the almost glowing marble of the Lincoln Memorial and the Washington Monument. The sites and beautiful weather did nothing to ease Daniel's tension, nor did the incident he was about to witness. While he headed north on foot, away from the sharp, white obelisk and toward 1600 Pennsylvania Avenue Northwest, he noticed a group of protestors gathering on the southwestern corner of the Reflecting Pool. It soon became obvious that the men were more a band of hoodlums than an assembly of peaceful political dissidents. The signs they were carrying all had large swastikas surrounded by a red circle. There didn't appear to be anyone in the bunch over 25 years old, even though not one of them had a single hair on his head.

Freedom of assembly was a precious and cherished right, especially for those who gathered in the nation's capital. On this particular occasion, Daniel

128

saw nothing good coming out of the demonstration. It was just another incident of many around the country confirming the turning tide of prejudice. As he got closer, he could read the messages on their poster boards denigrating the president of the United States and his race, employing words that could incite a riot rather than convey some peaceful message.

Daniel reached for his cell phone. He would have gotten involved himself if he didn't have a pressing appointment with the president of the United States. Before he could dial 911, he saw a group of Secret Service agents sprinting across the Mall toward the rowdy group of skinheads. Since the agents seemed perfectly capable of getting everything under control, Daniel replaced his cell phone in its case and continued on his way. If he had investigated further, he might have recognized a boy who closely resembled Kyle Lansbury, holding a sign that read, "Down with NIGGER Presidents who open up our borders to GREASY WETBACKS."

\* \* \*

First Lady Patricia Cooper sat with her husband as he finished his lunch in the Oval Office's small dining room. Once it was officially confirmed that Alvin Fitch's death was not from natural causes, security in the White House was stepped up in a big way. Mrs. Cooper would visit with her husband while he ate his afternoon meal, to discuss household issues, especially those related to their children's safety. Since both parents had full schedules every day until well into the evening hours, they wanted to make sure the children's needs were covered until the first family met for a late dinner.

The president never let an opportunity go by to tell the story of his romance with the First Lady. For him, it was love at first sight. He had met her in their ninth-grade advanced British Literature course in their hometown of Detroit, Michigan. Patricia initially played hard to get. After two years of bullheaded persistence, Benjamin finally got her to agree to go out on a date with him in their junior year. From that point on, they were essentially bound at the hip. Both were exceptional students and were accepted as undergraduates at Brown University in Providence, Rhode Island. Benjamin studied political science, and Patricia had a double major in African Studies and the Social Sciences. They were especially community minded, and during the time they worked toward their bachelor's degrees, they participated in a number of extracurricular activities, especially those involving charitable causes. Benjamin was very much involved in University politics. In his final two years at Brown, he was elected president of the Student Council. His association with the Democratic Party began early in his sophomore year, when he contributed time every day for a year and a half toward the reelection of President Jimmy Carter.

After receiving his bachelor's degree, Benjamin was accepted at Harvard Law School. By that time, he had proposed marriage to the love of his life. Patricia immediately accepted, and their engagement was formally announced to family and friends just weeks before he started his first year in Cambridge. At the same time, Patricia was admitted into Harvard's master's program in international relations. She insisted that they maintain separate residences. Being from a very religious background, her beliefs and morals prohibited her from cohabiting with the man she loved, until after they were married. Benjamin went on to graduate second in his law school class and was the third African American to be elected president of the *Harvard Law Review.*

130

Two years after his graduation, they were married in a small community church in their hometown, Detroit. It wasn't until seven years later that they decided to start a family. One year after that, their first daughter was born.

During the first seven years of marriage, Benjamin worked for one of the most prestigious law firms in Detroit and was very active in the Democratic Party. His popularity in his home state was rising meteorically. He worked untiringly on cleaning up the slums and helping underprivileged children get the education that every American deserved. After the birth of his daughter and first son, he was elected the first black governor of Michigan. In 2008, when he spoke at the Democratic National Convention upon President Barrack Obama's first nomination, he burst onto the national scene. After he announced his own candidacy for the presidency of the United States eight years later, not many experts in the field of politics were giving him half a chance. His decision to follow in his predecessor's footsteps and employ a campaign strategy requesting contributions from the public rather than the special-interest groups quickly moved him from underdog status to favorite after the first caucuses. Against all odds, he became the second consecutive African American to be elected to the highest office in the country.

He never spoke of it outwardly, yet from the day he announced his candidacy for the presidency, he was concerned for his family's and his own safety. The United States of America had taken great strides toward ending racism, but the president was far too wise to think the problem was a thing of the past. Too many Americans still hated other human beings simply because of the color of their skin, their religion, or where they were born. The security provided to him so far was outstanding. He took the death of Senator Fitch as a reminder that he couldn't afford to get complacent.

The Coopers had three children. The oldest, Jasmine, was an eighth-grader at Hardy Middle School, while their two boys, Troy and Cory, were in fifth and third grade respectively at Stevens Elementary. When the Coopers moved to the White House, the president insisted that his children attend public school. It may have been a good move politically, though it was a nightmare for the Secret Service. After the Fitch assassination, the agents protecting the children tried to convince the president to place the kids in a much more secure private school or, better yet, consider educating them at home. Mrs. Cooper refused to let the assassins believe that their conduct could instill fear in the first family of the United States. The children continued to attend public school while the Secret Service presence was tripled at both learning institutions.

Discussing security issues with his wife over lunch, President Cooper reiterated that they should never let their guard down when it came to their safety and, more importantly, their children's. While keeping that his number one priority, he wasn't about to let the criminals who had assassinated his good friend change the way he governed. It certainly wasn't going to affect his policy decisions. He told Patricia he was going to push for adoption of Alvin Fitch's version of the immigration regulations.

\* \* \*

Senator Tom Logan couldn't believe his ears as he watched CNN's broadcast of the White House Press Secretary's news conference from earlier in the evening. The president had decided to back Fitch's proposal in its entirety. Logan felt that the president was making a big mistake giving thousands of illegal immigrants a free pass to citizenship. He had thought he had the president's ear when he met with him for lunch to discuss the issue. Neither Logan's constituents nor his colleagues in the Republican Party were going to be happy. They were counting on him and his close relationship with the president to put an end to this "lunacy," as they put it. In politics, friendship was a useful commodity that sometimes had its limitations.

Over the years, Logan had developed the relationship into what he was sure the president considered a friendship. "Keep your friends close, your enemies closer" was a mantra drilled into Tom Logan's head by his father since he was a young boy. There was never a doubt in his mind that he would follow in his dad's footsteps and enter the world of politics. Samuel Logan had been a U.S. representative from the state of Kansas for more than thirty-five years. He had brought his son up to love and serve his country, with the unspoken expectation that Tom would run for the presidency one day. Samuel never directly communicated that desire to his boy, though his hopes and dreams were more than obvious. Tom had no intention of disappointing the man he admired most in all the world. It was originally his goal to announce his candidacy for president in 2008. After the incumbent Republican president had made it all but impossible for the party to hold on to the White House, Logan made the strategic decision to put his own presidential hopes on hold.

His major concern was time. It wasn't on his side. He was now 62 years old. If Cooper got reelected in 2020, it would be a hard sell to elect a 70-year-old to a first term of office. His best chance would be for Cooper to have a major screw-up in the next couple of years, so that the Republican Party would have a realistic chance in the 2020 election. The immigration issue could very well be Cooper's big mistake. Whatever the error turned out to be, Logan needed to make clear that he was taking a stand against this most recent decision.

His only other chance for success in 2020 was a taboo notion that he would discuss only with those he trusted implicitly. He was well aware of the growing numbers of white Americans around the country mobilizing against the reality of a second black president of the United States. More assassinations were not out of the question.

Tom Logan had first met Benjamin Cooper in his freshman year at Brown University. They were both political-science majors who were not shy about discussing their career goals. In their first semester, they were classmates in three of their five courses. Up to that point in his young life, Tom had never befriended an African American. In the part of Kansas where he was brought up, meeting a black person was a rare occurrence.

Despite his lack of experience with black people, Tom had seen something in his fellow student that immediately called to mind his father's lesson about enemies. From that moment, Tom had made it a priority to develop a close friendship with his impressive classmate. They became a part of the same study group, and Logan discovered that tennis was a passion of Benjamin Cooper. They played at least once a week. Just before the start of their sophomore year, Tom invited Benjamin to be his roommate, and for the next two school terms they lived together in a fifteen-by-fifteen-foot dormitory room. Their relationship evolved into one that was sometimes contentious but never combative, and the rivalry was always congenial. Besides the competition on the tennis court and their diametrically opposing political views, they had an ongoing contest for the best grades.

After graduating from Brown, they went their separate ways. Tom Logan was accepted at both Harvard and Yale Law Schools. He chose Yale, his father's alma mater, but he always kept in touch with his old college buddy, calling him at least once a month and insisting they visit each other when their busy schedules allowed.

Now they were together once again. The competition was infinitely more pervasive because Cooper was in the way of what Logan had been working toward his entire life. There was no better time to take advantage of his closeness to the president.

* * *

Incompetence was one of Secretary Atkins's pet peeves. He had absolutely no patience for it. As far as he was concerned, any president who was willing to hand thousands of illegal immigrants a free pass to American citizenship without making them earn it was the very embodiment of the ineptitude that irritated him so much. He felt as if he had wasted his breath expressing his opinion on the issue to Cooper. After thirty-nine years of dedicated military service to his country, one would think his opinion might have more value.

He lifted his big six-foot-four frame into the backseat of his limousine, then barked at the driver to take him to his home in Alexandria, Virginia. It had been a long day at the White House. A sense of frustration and resentment overcame him at the idea that he must continue the charade requiring him to behave as though he were a fan of the president. He didn't know how much longer he could keep it up. He had no one to blame but himself. The decision to ride on Cooper's coattails was his own. At this juncture, he was beginning to regret his choice to join the Democratic Party. Though he first ran for office as an independent, many of his views were very conservative, especially those regarding financial issues. The president had deceived Atkins and the entire country, for that matter. Cooper ran for office on a centrist platform. Recently, Atkins had come to realize that the president's claim to be a moderate was a show for the public, to conceal his true extreme left-wing convictions.

Atkins's membership in the cabinet and in the Democratic Party dictated his support of Cooper's positions. It wasn't going to be easy for the secretary of defense to convince people he was in favor of the president's views on immigration. If it were truly up to him, he would round up the whole bunch and have them shipped back to Mexico or whatever Latin American country they came from. He was livid that President Cooper was willing to risk erasing all the progress the United States had made in its fight against terrorism with one brainless decision.

Atkins's personal dedication to protecting the nation from Middle Eastern extremists for most of his life had made the president's decision that much harder to swallow. At their meeting, Atkins had vehemently argued that the immigration amnesty provision alone would legalize scores of terrorists already within our borders. That was just the start of the problem. Fitch's less stringent entry rules for migrant workers from Mexico would open the door for thousands more terrorists seeking to establish cells around the country. Why Cooper thought he knew better than a former four-star general was beyond Atkins's comprehension.

The secretary of defense was absolutely certain about one thing: he wasn't one to sit idly by when it came to the security of the United States of America. His strategy for advancing his political career placed him in a difficult position, but not a hopeless one. He still felt he had made the right move in taking advantage of the president's popularity. Eventually, that decision was going to pay off in a big way.

136

By the time his limousine pulled into the driveway of his mansion in Alexandria, he had made a pledge to himself to do whatever was necessary to further the best interests of his country.

## Chapter 11

Hailstones the size of robin eggs glanced off the conference room windows of Annie's law office. The racket was loud enough to make conversation nearly impossible. Daniel Falcone's interview with Donna Ortiz was scheduled to take place in that very room in a half hour. All parties involved were concerned that the participants wouldn't be able to hear themselves think, much less conduct business, if the storm didn't let up soon.

Kelly asked Annie if she wanted to change the location of the meeting or perhaps postpone it. Annie, who had finally convinced Daniel to officially announce that Donna Ortiz was no longer a suspect in the Fitch assassination, was unwilling to reschedule. They would wait out the downpour.

Just as the hail finally ended its assault on the conference room windows, Annie, Donna, and Daniel sat down at one end of the oversize table to begin the interrogation. Most of the questioning focused on Donna's actions and observations after Senator Fitch was admitted into the cardiac intensive care unit. Her story added little to the information Daniel had already gathered from other sources, including his examination of Nurse Ortiz's colleagues. The more interesting and useful material came from the examinee during her recitation of what she had witnessed before Alvin Fitch ever left the emergency room.

"What time did you arrive at the hospital for duty that night?" Special Agent Falcone asked after he had the witness state her name and address.

"I usually try to arrive at least ten minutes before my shift starts. I would say it was sometime around six fifty."

"What were you doing at the time the senator arrived at the hospital?"

"Not a whole lot. We had very few patients in the unit that night."

"What do you do when you have no patients?"

"Sometimes, I float to one of the other floors, or I can choose to go home. If I'm expecting a patient later in the night, I'll do some paperwork or prepare for their arrival. In this case, I knew I'd be taking care of Senator Fitch when he was admitted to the unit, so I wasn't transferred to another department. There really wasn't much for me to do while I waited. I helped Tara out with her patients, straightened up and got Senator Fitch's room ready, then sat and read a book."

"Did you leave the unit at any point? We're still talking before you had the senator as a patient."

"I took a couple of breaks. I went to the cafeteria to get a cup of coffee, and I went to visit a friend in the cath lab. I remember they were working late that night because of an overbooked schedule."

"So you were never in the emergency room while Senator Fitch was being treated there?"

"No, I didn't meet him until he was brought up to the unit."

"Did you have any contact with his entourage? By that, I mean his bodyguards—again, before the senator was taken to your unit."

"No, not at all."

"From the time you arrived at the hospital until the time Senator Fitch was wheeled into the cardiac intensive care unit, did you see anyone or anything you considered strange or out of the ordinary? Anything of a suspicious nature? Please take your time to think."

Late in the afternoon of their first meeting, Annie and Nurse Ortiz had discussed the occurrence she was about to recount. Ortiz had been racking her brain after leaving Annie's office, trying to remember every detail about her shift the evening Fitch died. When the incident came to mind, she had called Annie at once to describe it. Before this interview, Annie had instructed her client to be sure she worked it into one of her answers.

"There was something that happened that was a little bit unusual. For the first day or so after my patient was murdered, I was more focused on trying to analyze everything that happened *after* he came to the unit. After I met with my lawyer, I thought more about everything that happened that night. I remembered something I definitely thought was strange at the time—still do. When I went to visit my friend in the cath lab, I saw Andrew Lansbury and another man, who I didn't recognize, dressed in scrubs and pushing a gurney out the door at the other end of the hallway. I thought it was odd Andrew would be doing that. He's not a caregiver. There would be no reason for him to transport a patient. He's responsible for the pharmacy. It also didn't make sense they would be going out that exit. It leads out to the parking lot. Once I went through the doors of the cath lab, I didn't give it a second thought. I'm not sure it means anything, but I definitely thought it was out of the ordinary."

"Was anyone on the gurney?"

"It looked like there might have been someone or something on it. I didn't get a good look. The two men were blocking my view. The doors were already open when I noticed Andrew. I'm sure they must have pushed the button on the wall that automatically opens them. Both men were at the head of the gurney, lifting and pushing the back wheels over the threshold."

"You didn't bother to find out what they were doing?"

"It didn't feel like it was my place. I don't remember getting the sense at the time that they were doing something illegal or in violation of hospital rules. I

140

just thought it was weird. I don't like having to speak to Andrew anyway, so I just continued on my way."

"Did you ever ask him about it later?"

"No, I never really thought about it again until just before I spoke to my lawyer about it. That was the day you originally wanted to talk to me."

"How long have you known Andrew Lansbury?"

"I've known him since I started working at Jackson Memorial—seven years."

"When you say you didn't recognize the man he was with, did you get a good look at his face?"

"No, he had his back to me. I could kinda see the side of his face. What I saw, I didn't recognize."

"What color hair did he have?"

"Black."

"He was a Caucasian male?"

"Yes, he was."

"Can you estimate how tall he was, and give a description of his body type?"

"He was taller than Andrew, and Andrew is over six feet. I'd say he was at least six three. He had a goatee. He seemed to be heavyset, almost obese. Offhand, I can't think of anyone who works at the hospital who would match that description."

"Since that night, you've never seen an employee who could have been this unknown man?"

"No, I haven't."

"Getting back to Andrew Lansbury. How well do you know him?"

"I've worked with him a long time. Our relationship is strictly professional. I've never really done anything social with him, except when we've both attended parties sponsored by the hospital. We're cordial with each other. If I see him in the halls of the hospital, I say hi. I've never had any kind of a real conversation with him. He's not very talkative—at least, not when I'm around."

"What do you mean by that?"

"He's very friendly and even flirtatious with just about all the women who work at the hospital—all the white women, anyway. Even when he says hi to me, it seems like he's doing it against his will. I've always wondered whether he had something against Latinos."

"Do you know either of his sons, Kyle or Troy?"

"I see Troy from time to time. He's an ambulance driver. I can't say I know him. I've met Kyle once or twice. He came to a hospital Christmas party once with his dad, and I might have seen him one other time here at the hospital. Again, I don't know anything about him."

"Have you ever met his girlfriend, Tabitha Freemont?"

"No. I didn't even know he had a girlfriend."

"Is there anything else you can tell me about Andrew or his boys, either from your own personal knowledge or from what you've heard from others? For instance, do you know any of their likes and dislikes? If they're members of any clubs or organizations? Anything at all?"

"It embarrasses me to say this. Uh . . . in the past, I overheard Andrew making some racist comments. I heard him use the 'N' word. I considered reporting him to hospital administration. Then I decided against it. I didn't feel like I needed any enemies. It's one of the reasons why I thought he might have a problem with Hispanics. I just get the impression he's prejudiced. That's about it."

"Do you have any knowledge of the relationship between Andrew Lansbury and Doug Simms? I know Mr. Lansbury is Mr. Simms's boss. I'm asking if you know whether they might be friends outside the hospital."

"When I heard Andrew make that derogatory comment about black people, it was Doug he was talking to. From what I've heard, they're good friends. I know their families visit each other. Doug is good friends with Lansbury's sons, too. I think they go hunting together."

"How well do you know Doug Simms?"

"I don't know him well at all. Most of what I know about him or Andrew, I've heard from other hospital employees. I actually see Doug more often than Andrew since he delivers medicine to the pharmacy. He doesn't even say hi to me. I can't say I've ever had a conversation with him other than to discuss pharmacy orders. He's not exactly a warm and fuzzy type of guy."

"What have you heard about him from others?"

"Other than to discuss work, I don't think he talks to anybody at the hospital except Andrew. He hasn't worked here—I mean at Jackson—that long. Maybe a year and a half."

Over the ensuing three hours, Daniel had Nurse Ortiz give a detailed account of everything that happened from the time the senator was admitted to the cardiac ICU until his death. When he announced that the interrogation was over, Annie called Kelly over the office intercom to ask her to escort Donna to the client-attorney meeting room. When Daniel and Annie were left alone, he addressed her first.

"Thanks a lot, Annie. That stuff about Lansbury and the gurney is pretty big. You couldn't have thrown me that bone?"

"Come on, that's not fair. What the hell is this? You trying to pick a fight? It's not my job to investigate your cases for you. I wanted to tell you—even gave you hints. But I wasn't going to lose my license to practice law over it. I knew you'd eventually get there. That wasn't very nice."

Daniel instantly regretted what he had said. The pressure coming from above to get a quick resolution wasn't Annie's fault. He couldn't help getting angry at the situation.

"I'm sorry, Annie. I'm an idiot. I'm pissed off at myself and taking it out on you. If I had listened to you and taken her off the list of suspects, I would've known about it right away. *Damn it!* Well, anyway, I'm gonna have to have another little chat with Andrew Lansbury and Doug Simms. I wonder who the guy was helping Lansbury with the gurney, and what they were up to."

"I wouldn't mind hearing what those guys have to say. I'm sure they were up to no good. I don't know how you're gonna prove it, but it seems like at least Lansbury was mixed up in some shenanigans."

"I don't see any reason to put it off. I'll go pay him a visit right now. Before I leave, what are you doing Saturday night? You have plans?"

"*Really?* After the way you just treated me?"

"I said I was sorry. I was totally wrong. I'll make it up to you, I promise."

"I've been working like a dog. I usually work a full day on Saturdays. I'm wiped out by the time I get home." She grinned in spite of herself. "Oh, hell, what did you have in mind?"

"How about dinner and a movie?"

"Okay, I'm going to make the time. But you're lucky. I'm only letting you off the hook because you've been under a lot of stress."

\* \* \*

Saint Christopher AIM Church on Martin Luther King Boulevard in Savannah, Georgia, was holding its annual carnival on the school grounds situated just behind the church. It was 9-year-old Adalia Jones's favorite event of the year, mainly because it was the only opportunity for her dirt-poor family to enjoy amusement park rides or engage in any form of entertainment requiring cash. Her mother worked as the school janitor, qualifying her for free admission for herself, her daughter, and her two sons; passes for the rides; and three tickets for cotton candy, one for each child. For the past three years, Adalia had counted down the days on her calendar for a full two months before the carnival was scheduled to start.

As a single mother of three young ones, Mrs. Jones had to work two jobs. Her financial condition was the definition of living paycheck to paycheck. What she earned barely covered the cost of supporting her family. To supplement her meager earnings at the church, she cleaned houses and commercial offices for a local housekeeping service. Twelve-hour days were not uncommon. Within forty-five minutes of her arrival home in the evening, she would be in a deep sleep on the living room sofa, in front of the TV. Adalia had to tuck herself into bed most nights. The chance to ride the Tilt-A-Whirl was not the only reason why she looked forward to the fair. It was finally a chance to spend some quality time with her parent.

Adalia would be more annoyed at her mom than usual that Saturday morning. Mrs. Jones was unexpectedly called in to work a double shift when one of her housekeeping colleagues called in sick. Adalia was crushed.

Heartbroken and exasperated to the point of tears, she refused to accept her fate. There was no way on God's green earth that Adalia Marie Jones would miss her once-a-year chance to have some real fun. It wouldn't be the same without Mom, but she was ready to move mountains to make it happen. Happily, she wasn't forced to expend that kind of effort. In fact, the resolution was fairly simple. Her best friend, Caniqua, was planning to meet her at the carnival. Before her mom left for work, Adalia got her permission to ask Caniqua's dad for a ride and escort. She got the affirmative response she wanted from both parties. The only component of the equation that Adalia couldn't solve was her two half-brothers. They would have to miss the carnival. No one was going to take responsibility for two very active and rambunctious 3-year-olds.

Since Caniqua's father had to work half a day, they didn't arrive at the fairgrounds until three o'clock that afternoon. Adalia made herself forget the blow she had suffered earlier in the day, and before long, she was having the time of her life, enjoying the sights, sounds, and smells. They rode the roller coaster five times and, as luck would have it, got stuck at the very top of the Ferris wheel for more than five minutes.

Not an hour and a half into the festivities, her short stretch of good fortune would again take a turn for the worse. Caniqua, while sprinting from the House of Horrors to the Tilt-a-Whirl, tripped and fell over one of the many bulky and poorly secured cables that ran in all directions throughout the grounds. The injury to both wrists was so severe, the ambulance came to take her to Saint Joseph Candler Hospital. Her father, not wanting to leave his panic-stricken daughter alone with the EMTs, insisted on riding in the ambulance. Before they left, he arranged a ride home for Adalia and negotiated with Reverend Agee to care for her until she was picked up.

146

* * *

Reverend Thomas Agee, founder of Saint Christopher's AIM Church, had presided over his congregation for more than forty years. He established the church in honor of his wife and young daughter, who were killed under what he considered very suspicious circumstances. As a young husband and father, Reverend Agee had stood up to George Tipton, the richest man in Savannah and owner of half the city. Tipton had referred to the Reverend's wife as a "dumb nigger" after she bumped into his Cadillac, causing minor damage. Reverend Agee's mistake was to choose a public forum to confront the man who had verbally assaulted his wife. At a town meeting, he referred to Tipton as a shameless racist, demanded a formal apology, and urged all of black Savannah to boycott Tipton's businesses. It wasn't 1960s Georgia, but in the early 1970s, Agee's actions were still quite bold and risky. Many would call them just plain stupid.

The next day, the confrontation was the subject of a front-page article in the *Savannah Morning News*. Two months later, Reverend Agee's wife and daughter were killed in a freak car accident. Police estimated her speed at more than eighty miles per hour when she struck an oak tree head-on. The limit on that particular road was thirty-five. Agee insisted that his wife would never speed to such excess, and definitely not with her young child in the car. He fought desperately to prove that his wife and child were murdered. In the end, the authorities, who were essentially Tipton's lackeys, concluded that it was a tragic accident. Refusing to let the memory of his wife and daughter fade into oblivion, within months Reverend Agee began the project to build Saint Christopher AIM

147

Church. Over the years since, he had become one of the most respected religious leaders in the city.

Seeing the tears streaming down Adalia's cheeks, Reverend Agee decided to take his charge to the rectory for some milk and cookies. Adalia, whose entire day had amounted to a few wild roller coaster rides, looked to have all but lost her enthusiasm for the event. As they headed for his house, she asked Reverend Agee if she could use her tickets to buy cotton candy for herself and her brothers at home. Her simple request changed the course of events to follow. Holding the little girl's hand, he walked across the carnival grounds to the vendor, where Adalia waited in a line behind six other customers to exchange her tickets for the treat. The transaction delayed their entry into the rectory by more than ten minutes.

When they finally arrived at Reverend Agee's residence, he unclipped his keys from his belt, unlocked the front door, and opened it. Once Adalia was settled at the dining room table, he went to the kitchen to get the package of double-stuffed Oreo cookies he always had on hand for such occasions.

The instant he reached into the pantry, an explosive device was remotely detonated with a cell phone operated by one of three men observing the event from across the street. That same man had planted the bomb in the rectory's cabinet under the kitchen sink just six minutes before Reverend Agee and Adalia walked through the front door. The church and rectory exploded into a ball of fire. Later, witnesses would compare the blast to a ferocious, ear-splitting stroke of lightning. The heat from the detonation could be felt from hundreds of yards away. Thirty-three carnival guests unlucky enough to be within a stone's throw of the church were killed either by flying debris or by the shock wave itself.

Mercifully, Reverend Agee and Adalia Jones felt or heard nothing. In a fraction of a second, their bodies were vaporized and turned to ash.

\* \* \*

Frank Hess was in and out of mental institutions for the better part of his adult life. Officially diagnosed with bipolar disorder when he was a teenager, he had tried a dozen times to commit suicide. Most of those attempts occurred after he quit taking his lithium. Without medication, his disease sent him rocketing on amazing highs before plunging him into deep depression. On the brink of death after at least five of those attempts, he still hadn't learned to follow his doctors' advice. He just wasn't willing to give up forever the rush he experienced when in the manic phase of the swing. For a good part of the past year and a half, thanks to his mother's attentiveness, he had been diligent about following his psychiatrist's orders. It wasn't until about two weeks ago that he decided it was time to experience the mania again—though he had some help making that choice.

He had been living most recently with his mother in Brooklyn, New York. Since she had a professional's eye for detecting when he wasn't taking his medication, he was doing his best to avoid seeing her. She worked most of the day as the tailor at the dry cleaner's on 20th Avenue. At night, he would make himself scarce by hanging out with friends. One of those friends was a nurse from the Woodhull Medical and Mental Health Center, where Frank had done his most recent stint after a commitment hearing pursued by Mrs. Hess.

When her son wasn't taking his medicine, he suffered from severe delusions of grandeur. These were typically followed by a bout of incapacitating depression. At the time just before his admission to Woodhull, for several nights in a row he had told his mother he needed the car so he could meet with the president of the United States for a top secret mission to save the world. Knowing that the delusions were often followed by a suicide attempt, his mother immediately called his psychiatrist to begin the commitment proceedings.

\* \* \*

The very first time mental health nurse Keith Peterson met Frank, he knew that the young man's delusions would make him the perfect candidate to execute the mission he and Billy Ray Johnson had so carefully planned. Keith and Billy Ray were the leaders and cofounders of the New York chapter of the Ku Klux Klan. Like Billy Ray, Keith was born and raised in Jackson, Mississippi. His parents were best friends with Mr. and Mrs. Emmett Johnson, and very much involved in the Klan. If anyone could possibly match Billy Ray's intense dedication to the cause, it was Keith Peterson. Keith's hopes and plans for the organization were fierce and complex. He would stop at nothing to pursue his desire to rid America of the filth that invaded and settled within its borders.

Keith's specific purpose for going to nursing school was to work with psychiatric patients. No part of his motivation to choose his career came from a good place. It was a means to make decent money and stick with what he knew. His older brother, Burt, suffered from a debilitating case of paranoid schizophrenia, and Keith was often responsible for his care.

When Keith graduated from nursing school, he and Billy Ray hatched the plan for Keith to pursue his career in the Big Apple so that he could recruit new members and extend the Klan's reach. After Billy Ray described to Keith his current plot for New York City, they took weeks to devise a detailed strategy to accomplish their goal. Keith had learned, through his studies and experience with his older brother, that those with certain psychological disabilities could be easily manipulated. He often used Burt to carry out his dirty work. By tapping into his past experience and formal education, Keith ultimately came up with the idea to engage Frank Hess as their guinea pig. Keith convinced Billy Ray it was foolproof. In the event that Frank became unreliable and revealed the plot to his caretakers or the authorities, the only person he could identify would be Keith. And even then, it would be the word of a crazy person with a long history of telling tall tales.

During Frank's hospital stay, Keith paid special attention to his assigned patient. His goal was to endear himself to Frank and gain his trust. Most evenings, Keith stayed after his shift was over to join Frank in the sitting room, watching TV. He gave Frank his cell phone number, encouraging him to call after hours or on his days off. After Frank's discharge, over two weeks, they spent a good part of Keith's free time together.

By the beginning of Frank's third week out of the hospital, Keith felt it was safe to initiate his plan. The first step was to encourage Frank to stop taking his medication. Keith made the argument that his nursing studies showed that long-term use of the medicine would cause profound brain damage. It was the same argument often used by bipolar patients themselves to justify defying doctor's orders. Frank gladly followed his friend's advice, knowing that he would soon experience the highs that he desperately craved.

After a few short days, Frank was already showing signs of the manic phase of his disease. Keith knew that delusions would manifest soon. Frank didn't disappoint him when he showed up at Keith's apartment less than a week after quitting his medication, telling him about his top secret world-saving mission with the president. At that point, it was a piece of cake to persuade Frank to do the Klan's dirty work.

\* \* \*

One week later, Frank was behind the wheel of a Dodge Grand Caravan, stuck in heavy traffic on the Brooklyn Bridge. He was on his way to the Jacob K. Javits Federal Building in Manhattan. He believed that a group of Middle Eastern terrorists were gathering there to plan an attack on the entire city of New York. Keith was the first to warn him of the plot, and with Keith's help, Frank was able to intercept calls from the outlaws and hear what they were conspiring to do. The meeting with several government agents was one of the high points of Frank's life. He was riding a manic buzz like never before when they elected him to save the day. Now all he could think about was death.

Traffic began to move again, allowing him to pull into the left lane, which was flowing slightly faster than the others. He was already behind schedule. He was supposed to arrive at the building anytime between nine and nine fifteen a.m. It was getting close to nine. Once he could get off the bridge, he expected to make up some time. The congestion should lighten up. At that point, the building would then be less than half a mile away.

He crossed over the northwest side onto Manhattan at 9:03 am. The female voice of his GPS directed him to turn right on Centre Street. The "G-men" wanted him to have the global positioning system in the event that he made a wrong turn, but he was not about to make any mistakes. For every day of the entire past week, he and Keith had done dry runs of the trip—more than thirty-five in all. Frank could do it with his eyes closed.

When he made the turn from Lafayette Street onto Federal Plaza, he saw the Federal Building less than a tenth of a mile ahead. Following the agent's detailed instructions, he waited at the end of the one-way street until the car directly in front of him turned at the next intersection, leaving the entire street before him vacant.

Along the outside of the Javits Federal Building, ten-foot-square concrete columns ran the length of the structure at ten-foot intervals. Frank ignored the incessant honking of the cars behind him as he set the two columns on either side of the front entrance in his sights. He then floored the accelerator, racing the city block's distance to his target. When he arrived at the selected impact point, he turned the wheel abruptly, cleared both columns, and crashed through the glass doors of the building. The instant the van came to a crashing halt, the explosion of the ammonium-nitrate-and-fuel-oil bomb packed next to the wheel well nearest the gas tank caused the vehicle to blow into a billion pieces and a billowing ball of flame.

Frank Hess's body was torn apart and burned to cinders in the bat of an eye. The entire facade of the building facing Federal Plaza was blown to bits, the first four stories destroyed beyond recognition. The offices on those floors were open for business, bringing the immediate death toll to over three hundred. Among the agencies hit hardest was the U.S. Citizenship and Immigration Services, on the third floor.

* * *

153

The all-American running back for the Murphy High School Panthers was the pride of Mobile. There weren't many activities more important to the people of Alabama than college football, and the University of Alabama's Crimson Tide was their state treasure. Jeremiah Fields led the entire nation in rushing yards, all-purpose yards, touchdown receptions, kickoff returns, and rushing touchdowns. He was the number one NCAA football prospect in the country. To the delight of the local fans, he had already committed to playing for their beloved university.

His many football accomplishments extraordinary though they were, weren't the most impressive thing about him. Despite his being brought up in the projects of Mobile and having a father who was an abusive alcoholic, any parent would have been proud to have a child with half his character.

As a preteen, Jeremiah didn't have the tools to avoid being lured into the neighborhood gangs and engaging in the usual low-level criminal acts including theft and drug dealing. If his middle school football coach hadn't recognized his exceptional talent, he might have been lost. Becoming the father Jeremiah never had, the coach turned the boy's life around, encouraging church attendance and emphasizing paying his gift forward.

By the time Jeremiah was a freshman in high school, he had won several awards for his civic-minded acts off the field. On weekends, he contributed his time distributing food and blankets to homeless people. At his church, he was always first to volunteer his services for its various activities to help the poor. He told anyone who would listen that his proudest accomplishments came as a member of the Mobile Big Brother program, through which he had saved several young boys from the rough streets of the city, and certain incarceration.

154

The Saturday after his first football game of the season, Jeremiah participated in the clothing drive sponsored by his parish, Mary Magdalene Baptist Church. Hundreds of boxes of dresses, shirts, pants, and shoes had been donated for the event, filling the entire chapel, which was the site of the charity function. Jeremiah and four of his football buddies were responsible for carrying the boxes and setting the clothes up on racks before the doors opened to the public. At the end of the day, they were to take any leftover boxes of clothing to the Salvation Army. Since they weren't needed until then, the four teenagers spent most of the afternoon, into the evening, watching college football. Just after seven, they got a call from the church secretary telling them the drive had been closed for the night and it was time to box up the remaining clothes and take them away.

The boys arrived at Mary Magdalene a few minutes later. The secretary stayed with them to help. Before any of them had the chance to box a single item of clothing, a blast shook the very foundation of the church and pulverized the wall between the chapel and the larger cathedral building. A chunk of concrete the size of a football hit the secretary in the temple, killing her instantly. At the same time, shards of flying debris sliced through both of Jeremiah's closed eyelids and lodged in his cornea. His three teammates, who were farther from the explosion, managed to stagger out of the wreckage with Jeremiah and rush him to the hospital. He survived the trauma, but the doctors couldn't save his eyes. What remained of them was surgically removed. Jeremiah Fields would never step on a football field again.

* * *

Billy Ray Johnson, Keith Peterson, and Kyle Lansbury looked on as the three black kids wearing high school letter jackets carried one of their own out of the rubble that remained of Mary Magdalene Baptist Church. They stayed to watch their handiwork, as they had done in Savannah at Saint Joseph's AIM Church and the Jacob Javits Federal Building in New York. Billy Ray gave Kyle the honor of engaging the remote detonator this time as a reward for the great work he was doing for the cause.

Something had gone amiss, however, since they had been attempting to set off the bomb for the past forty five minutes. At the time, the church was packed with shoppers. Hiding in the field behind a thicket of bushes more than a hundred yards away, they persisted. Each man tried numerous times to tap in the four number code that would initiate the explosion. Finally, the bomb blew for no apparent reason. The three men were sorely disappointed that so few were killed.

Billy Ray warned his two cohorts there was no time to waste lamenting a small mishap. He noticed that one of the boys had grabbed a cell phone from his pickup truck and was no doubt reporting the incident to the authorities.

Billy Ray, Kyle, and Keith started the two-mile trek through the woods across the road from the church. Their car was parked on a dirt path on the north side of the woods. As they painstakingly made their way through the thick underbrush, they could hear sirens in the distance. Once they were safely in their car and began the three-and-a-half-hour ride back to Jackson, Billy Ray congratulated his coconspirators on a job well-done. He didn't want to show his dissatisfaction with the failure of the bomb. There was still plenty of work to be done, and he wanted his men to maintain a high morale. They were getting much closer to their ultimate goal, and they couldn't let a small glitch cause them

156

frustration. To cheer his colleagues up, he pointed out that at least one black woman was dead and the injured one didn't look as though he was going to make it. A third of the way into their trip, when they discovered the identity of the boy and the nature of his injuries via a radio news report, they planned a real country-white-boy celebration for later that evening.

**Chapter 12**

The North Miami FBI field office's Joint Terrorism Task Force was in hyperdrive. The supervising agent who normally led the division had been temporarily replaced by Daniel Falcone. Daniel successfully made the case to Special Agent in Charge Spencer Hoffman that the rash of racist violence occurring across the country could be related to the assassination of Senator Alvin Fitch. His well-presented argument had just landed him in the largest leadership role in his almost fifteen years with the Bureau. With the approval of Director Christopher Ryan, Daniel was currently managing a team of more than two hundred men from a variety of federal and local agencies based in Georgia, New York, and Alabama. Several more governmental regulatory commissions were now at Daniel's disposal according to Homeland Security's National Response Plan and the U.S. Government Interagency Domestic Terrorism Concept of Operations Plan.

The FBI continued to run the show through Daniel. The Department of Defense was prepared to provide military support if necessary. On-scene commanders were designated for each separate attack site. In an address to the nation, President Cooper, following Daniel's suggestion, strongly urged that local authorities provide additional police protection by increasing their presence in African American neighborhoods and around their churches. He assured everyone, including government employees, that security was being beefed up at all federal buildings. He promised the country that the U.S. government was using every means within its power to bring the matter to a quick resolution.

The teams in each state were conducting an exhaustive in-depth investigation. Local police officers and Bureau agents were reaching out to their informants to gather any information regarding black-market purchases, explosives laboratories, or any other rumors on the street that might help identify the perpetrators. Bomb components, including batteries, tape, vehicle parts, and explosives residue, were recovered at all sites. Some of the fragments were removed from victims. Blood, hair, fingerprints, tire tracks, and footprints were collected amid the rubble and in the surrounding areas. Hundreds of witnesses were interviewed.

Comparison of all the evidence led the task force to the conclusion that the attacks were carried out by the same subject or subjects. Two witnesses in New York City who had seen the driver of the Dodge Caravan came forward. They gave a detailed enough description for the FBI computer graphics artist to create a fairly accurate composite drawing. No identification had yet been made.

The pressure to produce results was as profound and omnipresent as ever. It wasn't just the administration at the Bureau calling for answers. The entire nation was up in arms. The African American community was screaming for justice. While some were protesting in the streets, both peacefully and otherwise, others were terrified to leave their homes or attend religious services. The stock market had suffered its third-worst decline in its 224-year history.

The media were relentless in their coverage of both the Alvin Fitch assassination and the terrorist attacks. Clifton Harris, *Miami Herald* executive reporter and Daniel's old nemesis, had reappeared like a phoenix from the ashes. Harris wasn't going to miss his first opportunity in three years to put Daniel's feet to the fire. To Daniel's chagrin, Harris wasn't the only journalist watching him. All the major networks were joining the party. Guilt over the way they had treated him during the Nameless serial murder case was not in their makeup. They cut him no slack. This sort of hate crime drew millions of viewers.

Racism and the attacks were the main topic of every major news talk show and discussion panel. National interest in the media was at an all-time high and showing no signs of slowing.

Daniel was doing his best to ignore the hullabaloo and direct all his efforts to the investigation. The evidence mounting against the Lansbury family was creating reason for restrained optimism. An extensive background check of Andrew Lansbury turned up information that would be hard to call coincidence. The Jackson Memorial Hospital pharmacy director was a member of the Ku Klux Klan and previously had ties to a Miami-based neo-Nazi organization with links around the country. The research team recovered criminal records, which had been expunged, from Lansbury's teenage years. They showed two arrests: one when he was 14 and another at 16. Both involved hate crimes. The first conviction arose from the beating of a man outside a gay nightclub. The man was thrashed to within an inch of his life. Lansbury was placed on probation since there was no evidence to contradict his story that he had done nothing more than observe.

His other brush with the law was much more serious. As part of a neo-Nazi ritual, he and a group of four other boys had set an elderly black homeless man on fire. This time, witnesses were willing to testify that Lansbury actively participated in dousing the victim with lighter fluid. The old man survived, barely, after suffering second-degree burns over three-quarters of his body. The prosecutor of the case persuaded the judge to try Andrew as an adult. Andrew's parents hired one of the finest defense lawyers in south Florida to represent him. The case was tried, and Andrew was found not guilty, based on conflicting testimony from some of the other participants in the act. The lawyer not only succeeded in having his client acquitted but also convinced the judge to expunge the arrest from his record. The only way the team managed to discover the information about the attempted murder was through a search of old newspaper articles after pulling Lansbury's NCIC rap sheet, which listed his incarceration.

Daniel paid a personal visit to one of Andrew's coconspirators in the human-arson case, currently serving time at Glades Correctional Institution in Belle Glade, Florida. The prisoner, Jake Larson, was more than happy to share information about Andrew Lansbury. Larson, less fortunate than his coconspirator, had gotten thirty years for the attack. Andrew Lansbury offered testimony at Larson's trial, fingering him as the ringleader who threw the match that started the fire. Larson told Daniel that Andrew Lansbury had been very active in the neo-Nazi organization when he was younger. From what he heard from fellow prisoners over the years, his involvement lasted several decades, and to the best of his knowledge, both of Lansbury's boys were members of the party. In no uncertain terms, Larson described Andrew as a racist to the core, and he didn't doubt that the same applied to his sons.

When Daniel confronted Andrew Lansbury with the information gathered against him, Lansbury claimed he was a reformed man. He admitted he had been an angry young boy back in the day. Since then he had cut off all ties with the neo-Nazi organizations.

His explanation of the gurney incident on the night of the senator's death was just another of his growing list of lies. His first reaction to the question was total denial. He claimed to have no idea what Donna Ortiz was talking about. When Daniel challenged him, Lansbury admitted that it was possible, though he didn't recall the episode. During the entire line of questioning, Lansbury was outwardly nervous, fidgety, and talking at an unusually fast pace—all clear signs of deceit. Daniel continued to push him on the issue, inadvertently giving him time to come up with a fairly reasonable explanation. Lansbury claimed that gurneys were used at times to transport heavy objects and machinery from the main hospital building to one of the adjacent outpatient structures. He suggested it was possible that the man Nurse Ortiz saw him with was one of the employees from another building in the complex. Through it all, he maintained that he didn't recall either the occasion or the person he was allegedly assisting. Having no evidence to challenge Lansbury's probable fabrications, Daniel had to file them for the moment.

Doug Simms wasn't any more cooperative. He disavowed any connection with the Klan or the neo-Nazi skinheads. Unlike Lansbury, he had never been arrested, not even as a juvenile. He admitted having a friendly relationship with Andrew Lansbury but denied awareness of any links with white-supremacist organizations. Daniel was sure Simms's responses to his questions were rehearsed. Though he never seemed to get anxious during the interrogation, his answers were immediate and mechanical.

For the moment, Daniel didn't have the hard facts he needed to arrest either Andrew Lansbury or Doug Simms. What he did extrapolate from all the information he had gathered pushed him to investigate further into their lives and the lives of Lansbury's sons. Although much circumstantial evidence pointed to the father's involvement in the plot against Alvin Fitch, Daniel had the feeling that Kyle was much more active in the white-supremacist organizations. As often happened for Daniel, his intuition served him well.

In response to the terrorist attacks of September 11, 2001, Congress enacted the Aviation and Transportation Security Act. It required airlines flying to, from, or over U.S. territory to provide Customs with passenger name record data contained in their reservation and departure-control systems. According to the bill, all pertinent facts were to be transmitted to a centralized database operated by the Customs, Immigration and Naturalization Service. From there, the information could be shared with other federal agencies.

The National Security Branch Analysis Center of the FBI took advantage of the Security Act to create a data-mining system. This tool collected information from the various airlines and other modes of public transportation, hotels, and rental car companies. Materials in its archives included credit card transaction histories from major department stores such as Sears and J.C. Penney. With this knowledge, the Bureau could follow the actions and whereabouts of known terrorists and flag suspicious activities of unknown potential terrorists.

Daniel employed this system and another federal program, the Computer Assisted Passenger Pre-Screening System, or CAPPS II, to collect evidence against Kyle Lansbury. CAPPS II had been a controversial tool proposed by the Transportation Security Administration (TSA) to prevent further hijacking of U.S. jets. It allowed the TSA to gather statistics on airline passengers and categorize them according to their level of threat to other travelers. The program used knowledge procured from government and commercial databases to ascribe a passenger a color-coded score. Green signified that the passenger posed no threat to the safety of the aircraft. Yellow indicated a potential risk and that further security measures should be employed. If a passenger was assigned the color red, it meant imminent danger of a terrorist attack, and boarding of the flight would be prohibited.

Using these tools, Daniel found that Kyle Lansbury had been engaged in some very questionable behavior. He had been a passenger on flights to both Mobile and Savannah on the day before the church bombing in each city.

No sooner was this information discovered than Daniel was on his way to Tabitha Freemont's apartment to have a word with her boyfriend.

* * *

Tabitha Freemont was a nervous wreck. After Agent Falcone's last visit, she had vowed she would never again lie on Kyle's behalf. He had really gotten himself involved in some serious shit. Tabitha did everything she could to convince him to break off his ties with Billy Ray Johnson. From the moment she met Billy Ray, she knew that the guy was bad news. She tried to use the baby as a bargaining chip to convince Kyle that his responsibilities were at home, not doing work for the Klan. In no uncertain terms, Kyle told her to keep her "fucking nose out of my fucking business." Now he was in way over his head and probably couldn't get out even if he wanted to.

The last time she had seen him was more than a week ago. According to his schedule, she probably wasn't going to be seeing him for at least another week. Because of the FBI agent snooping around, Kyle had decided it was best to stay away from Tabitha's apartment even while he wasn't traveling. When he told his associates about the run-in with the FBI, Billy Ray strongly recommended that Kyle make himself scarce. Tabitha knew that it was nothing short of an order. He was basically directing Kyle to move out of her home, and she didn't appreciate it.

Now Falcone was standing on her front porch yet again, waiting for her to open the door. Kyle had given her explicit instructions to tell the FBI agent that they had split up and he had moved out of the house without leaving a forwarding address. She wasn't so sure Falcone would fall for the story. He didn't seem all that easy to con.

Tabitha had learned to be a good liar out of necessity. As the child of an abusive father and then the girlfriend of a batterer, it was second nature. Nevertheless, having to lie to a law enforcement agent made her terribly anxious. Her main objective was to keep a calm exterior; otherwise, he would see right through her, as he evidently had the previous times he questioned her. She would have been better off if Kyle hadn't told her everything he and his buddies were up to, including the address of the hideout they had chosen. She opened the door, cementing onto her face the best smile she could muster.

"Hello, Agent Falcone. It's nice to see you again. Come on in."

"Hello, Ms. Freemont. Thank you." Daniel walked into the apartment and scanned the room before accepting Tabitha's offer to sit.

"So . . . what can I do for you?" Tabitha asked.

"I'm not gonna beat around the bush. I think your fiancé is involved in some very serious criminal activity that could get him into a whole lot of trouble. Do you know where he is? I need you to be straight with me, or you will find yourself facing charges as an accessory. Do you understand?"

While listening to the question, Tabitha employed her tested method to prevent her nerves from affecting her ability to function: she thought about her baby. Then she responded without hesitating, ignoring the knot in the pit of her stomach.

"I haven't seen him for at least two weeks. He's not my fiancé anymore. We broke up. I kicked him out. What did he do?"

"I'm not here to answer your questions. Where is he?"

"I'm sorry. I don't know, and I don't want to. I hope I never see the bastard again. He's a good-for-nothin' asshole."

Falcone's stare was fixed on Tabitha's eyes. She was getting the distinct impression that she was being analyzed by a human lie detector. Avoiding taking any calming deep breaths that could be mistaken for a nervous sigh, she relaxed her posture.

"I'm not buying it."

"The bastard was cheating on me. I came home from work early, walked into my room, and he's screwing some whore in my bed."

"I'm not playing with you anymore. You're lying. You know where he is. I want an address. I have no problem arresting you for obstruction of justice and accessory after the fact."

"I'm telling the truth. I swear I don't know where he is. If he's done anything bad, I hope you catch him and he rots in jail."

"Listen, I don't believe a word you're saying. But, I'm gonna give you a chance to change your mind. Maybe, just maybe, when it sinks in that no man is worth thirty years in prison, you'll come to your senses. I'll give you twenty-four hours. I'll be back tomorrow, same time. Don't even think of not being here. I promise you, if I don't get what I want, you'll be the one rotting in jail."

That said, Daniel stood up and left the apartment, obviously confident that his threat had hit the mark.

\* \* \*

She was rattled. Did Falcone really know what Kyle was involved in, or was it just a bluff? Whatever the case, Tabitha had to get in touch with her fiancé right away, even though doing so without getting caught wasn't going to be easy.

Tabitha Jane Freemont was no fool. Falcone had to be watching every move she made. They probably had her phones tapped, too, so she wouldn't be able to call him from home or her cell phone.

Time was critical. There was always the possibility Kyle could call her. If that happened, she may as well have led them to his door. With the speed at which caller ID traced phone calls these days, the FBI could instantly get the information it needed to swoop right down.

There was one way she could probably get a warning to him without alerting the authorities to his whereabouts. She didn't dare use her phone to call the intermediary she had in mind. She grabbed her purse and keys off the kitchen counter and left the apartment, doing her best to act as if she were on a normal errand.

The Publix store where she shopped for groceries was well within walking distance. Ten minutes later, she strolled through the automatic doors and headed straight for the women's restroom. In a small lounge area between the store and the toilets, attached to the wall, was one of the few remaining pay phones in Broward County. Tabitha prayed it wasn't in use, though her requests for divine help seldom seemed to get the desired results.

This time, she was in luck. Before she picked up the receiver, she checked the stalls and common area to be sure they were vacant. Seeing no one, she quickly reached into her purse for a handkerchief and a tissue. With the tissue covering her right hand and fingers, she placed a quarter in the phone, then dialed her cousin's number at work using her right index finger blanketed by the hankie.

Tabitha could trust Tracy with her life. They were like inseparable sisters. Tracy had lost her parents in an airplane accident when she was a toddler, and was brought up by Tabitha's parents. She subscribed even more devoutly than Tabitha to the Klan's ideals. They always had each other's back. Tracy would never betray her.

When her cousin answered, Tabitha said in a hushed and hurried tone, "Tracy it's Tabitha. This has to be quick. I'm being followed . . ."

Tracy tried to interrupt to ask what was going on, but Tabitha shut her up and continued. "I don't have the time to explain. Please call this number immediately and tell Kyle that under no circumstances should he call me at home or on my cell phone. I'm sure the FBI is going to get my phone records and find out where he's called me from in the last few days, anyway. At least, he'll be warned. Tell him Agent Falcone knows something. Call him right away. I gotta go."

Tabitha hung up the phone and walked out into the grocery store. Standing in front of the door, almost blocking her exit, two men in dark blue suits were huffing and puffing, trying to catch their breath. One of the men held up his badge and said, "Hold on, ma'am. I'm Special Agent Christopher Frye of the FBI. What were you doing in that restroom?"

"What—I have to tell you what I did in the *bathroom*? That's creepy."

"Is there anyone else in there?"

"No, I don't think so. But I didn't check the other stall."

"You didn't speak with anyone in there?"

"Am I being detained for using a public restroom?"

"No, ma'am. You know perfectly well we're looking for your fiancé. If you've had any kind of communication with him, we need to know. Is there a phone in the restroom?"

"It's ex-fiancé. And you know, I didn't even notice. You want me to check?"

"No, thanks. We'll take care of that. So, you're saying if we find a pay phone in there, you didn't use it to make a call?"

Tabitha pulled her cell phone out of her purse and showed it to Agent Frye. "Why would I use a pay phone when I have this?"

"I'm the one asking the questions, ma'am. Please answer, did you use a pay phone inside the restroom?"

"No, I didn't. Now, can I go buy some groceries? Or am I not allowed to ask you that?"

"I wouldn't be so cocky if I were you. I'm this close to taking you in for further questioning." Frye held up his thumb and forefinger, a millimeter apart. "So enough with the attitude!"

"I'm sorry. But I just told Agent Falcone I haven't seen that dirtbag for more than two weeks. He's not my boyfriend anymore, and if I knew where he was, trust me, you'd be the first to know."

"All right, well, Agent Falcone will be here shortly. We're going to be checking for a pay phone, and if there is one, we're going to get the phone company's log of the numbers called. If you're not being up front with us, I suggest you tell me now before you regret it."

Tabitha had figured the FBI would examine the phone records. Her cousin worked for the phone company. When the agents got their logs, they would find a call was made to their generic number from that pay phone at about the time she was in the restroom. An operator had connected Tabitha to her cousin's extension. There were over three hundred people with desk telephones working in Tracy's building. The FBI would have a hell of a time trying to find which of them had received the call. Tracy's last name was not Freemont.

Tabitha responded to Agent Frye's question with confidence. "Go ahead and check. I've been straight with you."

* * *

For the longest time after her kidnapping, Annie was on constant alert, whether she was at work, running errands, or in the safety of her home. She still couldn't get used to the idea that her abductor was on the loose. For many months after her rescue, she would jerk to attention at the slightest noise or creak when alone in her apartment. Tonight, she didn't even notice the groaning sounds made by the settling of her building. Only by a supreme effort of will could she achieve some semblance of relaxation. The terror she had suffered at the hands of the serial murderer was enough to traumatize any human being for a lifetime. She wondered whether she was beginning to fall into a dangerous complacency. More than three and a half years had passed since anyone heard from the Nameless monster.

Part of the reason she was feeling more comfortable about life was her relationship with Daniel. Since their dinner at Capital Grille, they had been on two more dates. After he dropped her off at her apartment each time, he gave her a little longer kiss on the lips. Three days ago, he had accepted Annie's invitation to fix him supper at her apartment. The last time that happened, the results were disastrous. His acceptance was a good sign that his guilt over that night was finally dissipating.

Just as she put the last salad fork on the table to complete the setting, the buzzer rang—someone was calling from the intercom in the building's main entrance. Seeing Daniel's face on the monitor linked to the camera in the front portico, she buzzed him in. During the minute it took him to get to her penthouse apartment, Annie fidgeted like a teenage girl waiting for her prom date to arrive. For this special evening, she had chosen a red low-cut V-neck Christian Dior. The high hemline set off her athletic yet feminine legs. Daniel always used to tell her red was her color.

When she opened the door, she caught the way his eyes ran up and down her body. They greeted each other with a peck on the cheek. Once inside the apartment, Daniel handed to her a bottle of a cabernet sauvignon from Tamber Bey in Napa Valley—one of Annie's favorite California vineyards.

"That was sweet of you," she said. "You know me too well. Let me go get a corkscrew to let it breathe. It'll go perfectly with dinner. I decided to broil a couple of dry-rubbed fillets."

Daniel was definitely showing signs of moving on with his life. The idea that he was willing to share a bottle of wine with her at the apartment was hugely significant. It had to remind him of the night of their indiscretion, which ultimately led to Daniel's separation from Deborah.

Annie quickly turned away from him to hide that her eyes were welling up with tears. Daniel was a good man and deserved a full and happy life. It moved her to see he was finally taking a step toward putting the nightmare behind him. She left him standing in the dining room while she fetched the corkscrew from the kitchen drawer, opened the fine bottle of red, and set it on the countertop to breathe. By the time she rejoined him, she had regained her composure.

"There's something I need to talk to you about, Annie," said Daniel as they moved into the family room overlooking Fort Lauderdale Beach. "I'm going away for a while. I don't know exactly how long. We're moving the Domestic Terrorism Task Force up to Washington, D.C. I'm gonna be staying at one of the Bureau's apartments in the residential building at Quantico. I'll try to come home as often as possible. It probably won't be every weekend. My mother's agreed to come down and stay at my condo to take care of the kids while I'm gone. I was hoping you might check in on them every once in a while."

"I'd be happy to. I guess they're putting more pressure on you than ever to come up with results in the Fitch case, especially since the wave of attacks. You guys have any idea who's responsible? Has anyone taken credit for the bombings?"

"You know I can't talk about the investigation. I'll tell you this much, though. We've had the typical nutcases calling in, but we're following a few decent leads. These people are pros at disappearing and being evasive—especially your client's coworker, Andrew Lansbury. One lies, and the other swears to it."

"The file I gave you from the son's marijuana charges was no help?"

"The address he gave you was Tabitha Freemont's. He's long gone from there. I appreciate that you told me the story about your run-in with him. I know you had worries about attorney-client privilege. Anyway, it all fits. We have to be on the right track . . . Okay, enough shop talk. Let's enjoy the evening. How about a glass of that wine?"

"Do you mind if I save yours for dinner? I have a lovely white chilling in the refrigerator—not from Tamber Bey, but still very nice."

Annie and Daniel drank their sauvignon blanc aperitif and chatted about their families, friends, and future while they avoided talk of work or the Nameless killer, who was never far from their thoughts. After dinner, Daniel helped Annie with the dishes; then they returned to the family room, where she lit some candles. They continued their chat over another glass of wine. By that time, Annie noticed it was getting late.

"Daniel, it's almost eleven. Who did you get to babysit the boys?"

"Are you kicking me out? I don't usually get a babysitter anymore. Dale's fifteen now. This weekend, they're staying at their uncle's, so I don't have a curfew."

"Of course I'm not kicking you out. You can stay as long as you want. I'm not going into the office tomorrow until later. I have plenty of DVDs—wanna watch a movie?"

"That's not exactly what I had in mind." Annie and Daniel were sitting on the sofa, which faced the floor-to-ceiling picture windows. Outside, the night was calm and cloudless. The fronds of the palm trees lining Fort Lauderdale Beach were as still as a deer caught in the headlights of an oncoming car. A full moon hung high over the eastern horizon, creating its mirror image in the smooth, sleek Atlantic Ocean. Daniel slid over on the couch and tenderly kissed Annie on the lips. Though she had long hoped for it, she was a little taken aback by his move. Daniel took her surprise as disapproval and slid back to his place on the couch.

"Where are you going? Why'd you stop?"

"I thought you didn't want me to kiss you."

"Whatever gave you that idea?"

"It was kind of obvious. You jumped backwards when I moved toward you. Maybe you're not ready yet."

"I just wasn't expecting it."

Regardless of her deep love for Daniel, if he had made such a move on her even a few weeks ago, she would have rejected him for sure. It was a pleasant surprise that she felt comfortable with him kissing her. Annie slid over, put her arms around Daniel's neck, and kissed him sensually on the neck. For several minutes, they made out on the couch like two teenagers in love for the first time. When the passion reached a level that neither could contain, she stood up, grabbed his hand, and led him into the bedroom.

**Chapter 13**

The front lawn of Defense Secretary Brandon Atkins's mansion was blanketed with the colors of a beautiful autumn sunset. Red, yellow, and burnt-orange leaves from the Chanticleer flowering pear trees that lined the driveway did not leave a bit of the frozen ground uncovered. Winter seemed to be making an early appearance in the nation's capital and its environs. The trees were already bare, and temperatures had not made it up into the forties for the past week and a half. As Atkins raised his massive hulk from the backseat of his limousine and scanned the yard, he made a note to himself to have his wife hire someone to tidy up the clutter of leaves in the yard. He detested messes, and there seemed to be a few too many on his plate at the moment.

The president was making a monumental mess of things in the White House, and it wasn't just Atkins who thought so. Cooper's approval ratings had taken a nosedive over the past several weeks. It all started with his announcement in support of the passing of the Alvin Fitch immigration regulations. It was shortly thereafter that the series of domestic-terrorist attacks began. Two were obviously motivated by racism. The reasons for the bombing of the federal building in New York were still uncertain. As a consequence of the violence occurring throughout the country, the stock market was in just as bad a tailspin as the president's approval rating. Cooper had been scrambling ever since. He was putting a lot of pressure on Secretary of Homeland Security Logan and the FBI to beef up security and bring the culprits to justice.

The president had come to Atkins to ask for his recommendations on how to combat the outbreak of attacks. Atkins could barely conceal his annoyance when Cooper called him to the Oval Office for a private conversation.

The defense secretary still hadn't gotten over the president's blatant disregard of his suggestions for the immigration laws. Nothing would have pleased him more than to rub it in Cooper's face. Instead, Atkins had decided not to put much thought into it. He simply reiterated Daniel Falcone's recommendation to increase the law enforcement presence in minority neighborhoods of the major U.S. cities.

This upcoming week, Atkins was scheduled to meet with Border Patrol leaders from around the country at the president's request. Since the passing of the new immigration laws, activists were uniting their forces in Texas and California to form their own groups keeping watch over the Mexican border. Armed private citizens were recruited to prevent the entry of illegal immigrants. Mexican men, women, and children were being beaten and sometimes killed. The Mexican government was incensed and demanded that the U.S. government take action. The situation was getting out of hand and affecting the performance of the real Border Patrol. The president now expected Atkins to help clean up the mess. Cooper charged Atkins with the task of boosting the morale of the commanders of the U.S. Customs and Border Protection and inspiring them to work harder to prevent the activist renegades from taking the law into their own hands.

Atkins entered his home, greeted his wife, mentioned the front yard clutter, and went to his private office. Mrs. Atkins knew that when he retreated to that part of the house, he wasn't to be disturbed under any circumstances short of a full-blown emergency. The frigid weather had chilled Secretary Atkins to the bone. Before he got to the business at hand, he placed a couple of Duraflame logs in the fireplace and lit them. He stood in front of the fire, rubbing his hands together and considering the solution he had already initiated. Now was the time to make a major move separating himself from the president and his precipitous slide in the polls.

When the fire had warmed him a bit, he crossed the room and sat behind his huge polished cherrywood desk. He picked up the phone and dialed a District number. After ten minutes of conversation with the answering party, he sat back in his chair and finally relaxed. It wouldn't be long now before things went back to being neat and tidy.

\* \* \*

Tom Logan was seriously considering resigning his Cabinet post. A series of bad decisions by Benjamin Cooper were all but trashing his chances in the next presidential election. If Cooper had followed the counsel of his closest advisers in the first place, perhaps none of the craziness erupting around the country would have come about. Logan unequivocally refused to offer any support to the president in this time of need. To do so would be political suicide. It would intimate that Logan was taking partial responsibility for the screw-up—not a sacrifice he was willing to make. It pissed him off that Cooper expected his help.

To make matters infinitely worse, the president delivered a backhand blow at a Whitehouse press conference. He had the audacity to involve the responsibility and accountability of the secretary of homeland security. Cooper had made the unnecessary declaration that he had complete confidence in Secretary Logan's ability to address the problem of increasing violence. He promised the American people that Logan would take the necessary precautions to ensure that no further attacks occurred and to bring the terrorists to justice.

Logan refused to be the president's scapegoat. He had devoted a lot of time recently to reflecting on how to tender his resignation to the president. Taking that route came with a sizeable risk: he could be viewed as a quitter in tough times. Ultimately, he decided against that option. The other alternative he had pondered was even more dangerous and had already been set in motion. If he were ever to be exposed, it would destroy his career forever. In the end, though, he didn't have much of a choice. If he allowed events to take their natural course, his political life expectancy was probably nil anyway. The time to take action had been overdue regardless of the potentially disastrous consequences.

* * *

The indistinct chatter of people cavorting in the hallway brought Billy Ray to full consciousness after he had spent the past fifteen minutes or so in a state of half slumber. It was the first morning in many that he could sleep in, though it hadn't been the most restful of nights. He was up late after arriving in Washington on one of the last flights of the day. His trip to the nation's capital had been a last-minute arrangement after he got a call from the man he knew as Brody, requesting that he take the next available flight.

The hotel accommodations were spartan. They put him up on the outskirts of the city. Its clientele weren't people Billy Ray would ordinarily put himself in contact with. The thought of who might have slept in the bed before him kept him awake half the night. His idea to carry his own sheet from home to cover the hotel's linens hadn't helped. He didn't bother to use the blanket or comforter, so he was cold most of the night despite cranking the heat up to the highest possible setting. As he got out of bed and headed for the bathroom, he was happy his stay at the motel was nearly at an end.

Billy Ray was almost sorry he had let the D.C. contact become a part of the mission. If there had been a way to accomplish his goals without involving the bigwigs, he would have preferred it. Now it was too late. The Klan had accepted their money. True, the cash and information they provided were quite useful, if not essential, to the successful execution of the plan. Still, once you let politicians with deep pockets into the mix, they seemed to think that entitled them to pull all the strings. Billy Ray had no doubt that their benefactor was an extremely powerful person and that discretion was in order when interacting with him through Brody. The money spoke louder. It was the only reason he was willing to sleep in a dilapidated motel room where he was surely breathing the same air as the scum of the earth.

Though Billy Ray had no clue to the benefactor's identity, the agreement with the D.C. powerhouse to provide the necessary information was clear. At the time of the original contact with Brody, their backer had promised to let the Klan ultimately take credit for the plan. Brody assured him the man he represented was a devout believer in the organization's principles and tenets—a staunch conservative and a favorite to be a candidate in the next presidential election.

Initially, Brody's and his patron's contribution was supposed to be simple and for a limited purpose. Billy Ray had a feeling this meeting was a sign they wanted to get more involved. This wasn't an operation to get this unknown politician elected to the presidency—it was a revolution to take back the country that rightfully belonged to the Anglo-Saxon race. If any of their proposals didn't further that end, Billy Ray was going to tell them to shove it, no matter how powerful they were.

* * *

Four days after his meeting in D.C., Billy Ray checked the offshore account in a Belize bank, as instructed. Sure enough, twenty million dollars had been deposited in his name. With that kind of payoff, he could get a lot more excited about doing their dirty work. What they were hiring him to do was really a windfall, since it would help the Klan's cause tremendously. The cash would also be put to good use for other endeavors in the movement he was now calling the Klan's "neorevolution." No coup had ever been successful without funding, and the donor had promised that much more was available if he succeeded in completing Brody's work.

This enterprise was going to require an effort on a whole different level from the previous Klan endeavors. Fortunately for Billy Ray's sake, the timetable was not yet set. He would be getting more information from Brody in the very near future regarding when the deed was to be done. Meanwhile, Billy Ray had to keep the momentum rolling for his comprehensive mission.

They had hit the black community hard. That was just the first phase of his plan. The federal building in New York was the beginning of part two. This morning, he was returning to the Sunshine State. In the past, he would have made the fourteen-hour drive to the southern tip of Florida. This time, he had no choice. His overbooked schedule dictated that he opt for air travel. With money no longer an issue, he decided to reserve two seats for himself, to be sure he didn't rub elbows with any undesirables. Kyle and Keith were scheduled to meet him there later in the day. They were traveling separately.

An unsettled feeling twisted Billy Ray's stomach into a knot. Kyle Lansbury was getting to be something of a liability. Though he was a hard worker with a real passion for the cause, it wasn't a good thing that he was being investigated by the FBI. That was the last thing the Klan needed this early in the process: an inexperienced member trying to elude the authorities.

**Chapter 14**

The Jewish Community Relations Council of Greater Miami scheduled the celebration of Kristallnacht, otherwise known as the Night of the Broken Glass, for the first Sunday of the month. The event, commemorating the tragic night that foreshadowed the Nazi movement to exterminate the Jewish race, would take place at the Miami Beach Holocaust Memorial. During November 9 and 10, 1938, ninety-one Jews in Austria and Germany had been murdered in cold blood, and more than twenty-five thousand had been arrested and put in concentration camps. The Gestapo and S.S. attacked under the pretext of responding to the assassination of a German diplomat, Ernst vom Rath, by a German-born Polish Jew named Herschel Grynszpan. In fact, it was part of a much broader Nazi plan of anti-Semitism and genocide. Historians had long since agreed that this was the beginning of the "Final Solution," which led to the Holocaust.

Mimi Greenspan, along with three other survivors of the Nazi reign of terror, were to be special guests of honor at the event. Because of Mimi's scheduled hip replacement surgery in the fall and her importance to the celebration, its date had been advanced this year to September. Mimi was born in Vienna in 1921. Her husband, who had died more than twenty years ago, was a cousin of Herschel Grynszpan. On the night of November 9, 1938, she had watched as her mother, father, and two brothers were shot in the head at point-blank range. The same Gestapo officers who killed her family had brutally beaten and raped her, then placed her under arrest. Two days later, she found herself imprisoned in Dachau, in southern Germany, ten miles northwest of Munich. She would spend the next three years of her life in four different concentration camps, narrowly avoiding death by starvation, typhus, and execution.

182

Mimi Greenspan was a true survivor in every sense of the word. She had been on the brink of losing her life many times. For the first several months of her imprisonment, the only food she and her fellow prisoners got was a small piece of bread at midmorning and a glass of water. In a matter of weeks, many around her died of starvation and dehydration, while others succumbed to various diseases associated with malnutrition. Mimi, who was 17 years old when taken by the Nazis, had the resilience of a child, though the harsh treatment by the S.S. and the soldiers took its toll even on her youthful body. One morning, the unconscious, emaciated teenage girl was mistaken for dead and tossed on the pile of corpses in the prison's courtyard. She would have died there if not for one of the prisoners tasked with carting the bodies off for pit burial. When he picked her up, she was burning with fever. Avoiding detection by the guards, he carried her to his barracks, where he nursed her back to health.

What ultimately delivered her from certain death had nothing to do with enduring physical pain or eluding the gas chambers or a fatal infection. At the start of her third year of imprisonment, the officer in charge of her fourth and final concentration camp overheard her singing a German requiem while she was mopping the floor of his office. Under the ruse that he was interested in her talent, he asked her if she had any special training in music. When she told him she was studying to be a concert pianist before she was arrested, he hired her as a private music teacher for his three daughters. She remained employed in that capacity until Germany surrendered to the Allied forces in 1945.

The officer's true motives had nothing to do with his girls' education. Though she allowed it to happen in exchange for her life, he savagely raped her every day for four harrowing years. Mimi bore a hatred for this monster who had the gall to torture and murder her brethren and then force himself on her in the most intimate act between two human beings. At the time of Germany's surrender, before he released her, he professed his love for her and offered to provide a home and support if she continued to be his mistress. Without mentioning a word to him, she packed her meager worldly belongings and bought an ocean-liner ticket with money she got from pawning the few gifts of value he had given her. The next morning, she embarked to start a new life in the United States of America.

She soon learned that America's reputation as the land of opportunity was no hoax. To earn a living, she taught piano to the children in the Lower Manhattan neighborhood where she rented a room from a physician she had met on the ship. Within a year, she had more students than she could reasonably handle. Taking note of her success, the physician offered to invest in a building to help Mimi start her own private music school. With his assistance, she hired several more teachers. The school continued to grow over the years, and by the end of the 1950s, she had three of the finest music schools in the New York area.

Mimi met her husband ten months after arriving in America and married him two years later. Stanley Greenspan was successful in his own right, having started a retail clothing business in Manhattan. Together, they earned enough to enjoy a very comfortable lifestyle. When Stanley died suddenly of a heart attack, Mimi decided to live out the remainder of her years in the Florida sunshine. Since her children were married and pursuing their careers outside the state, she had no ties to New York. For the past twenty years, she had been living in the same condominium on Miami Beach. It touched her deeply that the Jewish people of the city honored her and her family annually and refused to let anyone forget the horrors inflicted by the Nazis before and during the Second World War.

184

* * *

Hundreds gathered around the statue designed and sculpted by Howard Treister to pay tribute to the six million Jewish victims of the Holocaust. As part of the program, Mimi Greenspan would be speaking as an eyewitness to Kristallnacht. There would be musical performances by the Sinai Aviv adult and youth choirs, and a candle-lighting ceremony. The entire event was scheduled to take place outdoors.

A stage was constructed for the guest speakers in the center of the large courtyard where the famous sculpture known as *Love and Anguish* had been erected. The forty-two-foot bronze forearm and hand rose into the sky as if beseeching the heavens for mercy. An Auschwitz number was branded on the forearm. One hundred thirty naked human figures in various attitudes of torment seemed to be climbing up the arm, trying to reach an unattainable summit.

On either side of the sculpture, risers were set up for the choir. A wall with black granite panels listing the names of the countless victims of Auschwitz enclosed the courtyard. Before taking her place on the stage, Mimi paid her respects by reading the names and saying a small prayer for those who had lost their lives during the Holocaust. As she made her way along the wall, she came across a sculpture of an emaciated, naked man and woman grasping each other's arms in a last good-bye. The memories this scene evoked always moved her to tears. She placed her knotted, arthritic fingers on the figures' smooth, cold shoulders and took a few moments to cry. After a while, she collected herself and finished her visit to the various sites of the memorial. By the time she completed her walk around the grounds, the supervisor in charge of the event approached her to let her know it was time to take her seat on the stage.

Rabbi Adam Fine was to open the ceremonies with a short prayer. Mimi's speech would follow. A young usher greeted her at the foot of the staircase, then helped her climb the steps up to the raised platform. She was slowly advancing toward her place to the right of Rabbi Fine when a bullet shattered the back of her skull, slinging blood and brain matter across her escort's face and the front of his suit jacket. He didn't have time to register what had happened in the split second before the next bullet ripped through his forehead. Bullets continued to spray across the stage, killing the rabbi and the other three survivors of the Holocaust who were scheduled to speak. Pandemonium broke loose. Screaming, panicked guests ran in all directions while others searched for anything that offered cover. Before the siege was over, twenty-five people were dead and fifteen more were gravely injured.

\* \* \*

The Mexican American Opportunity Foundation in Los Angeles was the largest Latino-oriented social service organization in the United States. It was established by Dr. Dionicio Morales in 1963, to aid underprivileged individuals and families in the Los Angeles County area. Since that time, it had grown into the largest social services institution in the country, having expanded its territory to include six other California counties. The services it provided included child care and development, assistance to senior and disabled persons, welfare-to work-counseling, a food bank, financial and computer-literacy education, and youth programs. The foundation had won a variety of awards for its humanitarian

186

efforts, most recently as the recipient of three Eureka awards for innovations in children's health care.

Estela Ruiz was a dedicated employee of MAOF. She had been working there since she got her high school diploma at the age of 18. For the past ten years, she had devoted herself to the child care and development program, which was one of the most important services offered by the foundation (at least, in her opinion). The projects it provided varied from infant and toddler care centers to BeSchoolReady lessons and parenting classes. Estela was a firm believer in the axiom that children are the future of the world.

From the time Estela was just 9 years old in Oaxaca, Mexico, she was essentially responsible for herself. Her father was killed in a drive-by shooting when she was just 5. Her mother, Juanita, was finding it impossible to support herself and her three children. The family was on the verge of starvation when she left her daughter and two sons with her aging mother and made the difficult decision to sneak across the border to America. Without the assistance of an experienced guide, she and two men from her village attempted the trek across the vast, searing Chihuahuan Desert. None of the three made it. Their dehydrated corpses were found two months later by a humanitarian group that provided the service of locating missing persons who had attempted the dangerous traverse.

At 9 years of age, Estela became the head of the household. Her grandmother was too old and feeble to earn the money to care for three young children. Just to put food in their mouths, she worked ten hours a day in the corn and strawberry fields on the outskirts of the city. At night, she would string beads into costume jewelry necklaces and bracelets in a factory that paid for piecework. There would be no childhood or education for the dogged young woman who was forced to grow up way before her time. For this reason, it became Estela's passion to help as many young people as she could to avoid the same fate. Only one dream in life mattered as much: she wanted to have children of her own.

For twelve long years of their marriage, Estela tried desperately to get pregnant. To make it happen, she and her husband took advantage of every method known in science and nature. When it became obvious they were spinning their wheels, they turned to a physician who specialized in fertility. The hopeful parents went through a battery of tests to determine if either of them was incapable of conception. The results proved quite the contrary—both were healthy and fertile. Being a young couple, they had few affordable options to assist them. Their first choice was the least expensive of therapies: a form of artificial insemination. After several unsuccessful attempts at four hundred dollars a pop, they abandoned that option.

For a while, they returned to the conventional method. In the meantime, Estela set aside every penny she could. Six years later, still without child, she had at last scraped together sufficient funds to afford in vitro fertilization. She was crushed when the doctor who performed the procedure informed her that the egg had not successfully attached to the uterine wall.

Even this didn't dampen her desire to have a child. As she and her husband advanced in their careers, they put the extra money they earned into the purchase of fertility drugs. Estela had been taking them faithfully for two years, with no better results.

Then, just a few weeks earlier, everything changed. Estela felt under the weather and was having a terrible time keeping food down. Unable to shake a constant underlying feeling of nausea, she vomited at least once a day. After all the disappointments, pregnancy was the last thing on her mind. Believing she

188

had a stomach virus, she went to see her family physician. He suspected that she was pregnant. But after all her disappointments over the issue, he didn't want to raise any false hopes. Without mentioning why, he drew blood for a pregnancy test. He would say nothing to her about it unless the results came back that she was indeed with child.

The headquarters for the Mexican American Opportunity Foundation was located on Garfield Avenue in East Los Angeles. Annexed to the building was a preschool with four separate classrooms of twenty-five students each. Normally, Estela's work was managerial in nature, so her office was located in the school's administration department. On this particular morning, she was substituting for a teacher who was taking time off for maternity leave. She arrived at the school an hour earlier than usual to prepare some activities for the kids. Keeping busy in the classroom helped her ignore the queasy stomach that continued to plague her.

After she had prepared for her class, she returned to her office to jot down a few notes, when her phone rang. She picked up the receiver and was surprised to hear her family physician's secretary ask her to hold for the doctor. It was unusual for him to call her so early in the morning, especially at work. Her first thoughts were that something was seriously wrong. To her delighted surprise, she got the best news of her life. The doctor explained to her that he hadn't told her the true reasons for the blood draw, to save her from another potential crushing disappointment.

Estela practically fell off her chair. Tears of joy smudged her eye makeup. She thanked her doctor profusely, hung up the phone, and felt like letting out a shriek of pure excitement. Since her colleague Mary Gutiérrez was in the very next office, she stifled the impulse. Mary had her 3-year-old boy, who attended the school, with her, and Estela didn't want to scare the child.

As happy as she was, she had to tell someone. Her husband was on a business trip, on a flight to San Francisco, so calling him was out of the question. Before she had the opportunity to make her way to her coworker's office to share her blessed news, a deafening blast shook the floor beneath her. In the school's basement, a bomb of ammonium nitrate and fuel oil, similar to the device that destroyed the Javits Federal Building in New York, exploded, bringing the ceiling crashing down on her and the woman and child next door. The initial impact didn't kill the two women, though the toddler died instantly.

Several seconds later, a second bomb detonated, engulfing the adjoining main building in flames. If Estela and Mary had not been trapped under the debris, they might have survived. They desperately tried to free themselves from the wreckage to no avail. Within minutes, they died of smoke inhalation.

Twelve people lost their lives as a result of the attack on the Mexican American Opportunity Foundation. Depending on one's definition of a human life, two others were lost that day. An autopsy would later reveal that Estela Ruiz was carrying twins.

**Chapter 15**

Boy Scout Troop 84 of Chatham County was having a campout at Skidaway State Reserve, just outside Savannah, Georgia. Ninety-three boys pitched their tents on two of the eighty-seven campsites available on the grounds. All kinds of fun-filled events were scheduled over a period of three days. This was 12-year-old Joey Campanella's first outing with his new pack, though he really didn't want to be there. His parents had made him come, hoping the trip would bring him out of his shell. His entire experience with first the Cub Scouts on Long Island in New York and now with the Boy Scouts in Savannah had been excruciatingly painful. Joey was overweight and not very athletic. The truth was, he hated sports. Having to go through all the physical challenges to advance through the ranks caused him nothing but humiliation and embarrassment. He was the butt of many of the other boys' jokes, and a victim of constant teasing.

Each of the scouts was assigned a tent mate, and of all the possible choices, Joey drew Cameron Hewitt, one of the biggest bullies in the troop. For the entire afternoon of the first day and evening, Cameron and his three sidekicks made Joey the target of endless slurs and insults. That night, he silently cried himself to sleep. He was terrified out of his wits, knowing he had to endure two more days of harassment. His anxiety and the unyielding stiffness of the cold ground made it impossible for him to stay asleep more than a couple of hours at a time. A few hours before daybreak, he decided on a course of action. He would take the coward's way out: first thing in the morning, he would feign illness and be sent home.

The adult Scout leaders were planning to wake the troop at seven to begin the day's activities. At 5:30, Joey finally drifted off to sleep, only to be

191

woken a half hour later by his tent mate, dragging him out of the shelter by his feet. Still disoriented from sleep, he looked up to see Cameron and his three kowtowers silently warning him to be quiet. Joey was alert enough to realize the dire consequences should he resist. The next thing he knew, he was being led deep into the woods.

Joey's tormentors were deliberately staying off the trails. When Cameron decided they had gone far enough, he ordered his accomplices to strip their victim naked. After a good laugh and a few disparaging remarks regarding certain of Joey's physical dimensions, Cameron warned his victim that if he told anyone who had done this to him, he would regret it for the rest of his life. Joey didn't doubt that the boys would follow through with the promise. He had every intention of doing as Cameron said. Before they left, Cameron told Joey to follow them back to the camp, or he would be lost in the woods. In return for their courteous invitation, Joey had to tell the troop leaders that he had decided to take a nature walk in the nude. One of the boys stuffed Joey's clothes into a knapsack, and they headed back toward camp.

Not only was Joey terrified, but the temperature was barely above fifty degrees. The stress and cool weather were making him shake uncontrollably. He willed himself not to cry—that would only make matters worse. He let the other boys get ahead of him, fairly certain he could find his way back. That way, he wouldn't have to listen to their snickering. When the sound of their voices was nothing more than a distant jumble of incomprehensible words, he stood up and started on his way back. It was going to take a while. His legs were trembling to the point that he was having difficulty placing one foot in front of the other. His pace was so slow, before long his aggressors were out of sight and earshot. Joey continued to advance in what he thought was the right direction. After fifteen minutes, a worry verging on terror began to take hold of him. At that point, he should have been close enough to the camp to hear the stream and the other Scouts' voices. Instead, he heard only his own footsteps.

Frightened, flustered, and freezing to the bone, he decided to turn around and head in the opposite direction. He walked for another ten minutes, listening intently for the sounds of rushing water. Focusing more on listening than watching where he was going, he didn't see the tree root lying across his path. Suddenly, he pitched face down on the forest floor. If the moss and leaf mold hadn't been fairly soft, he might have broken his nose.

After brushing off the leaves that stuck to his body, he looked behind him to see why he had lost his balance. What he saw horrified him more than being alone and naked in the woods. Rags were hanging off the bones of a decomposed human arm and hand protruding from beneath the dirt. Without realizing it, Joey screamed at the top of his lungs.

By that time, a search party had been organized by two of the adult scout leaders. Along with Cameron and his group of hooligans, they were combing the woods just 150 yards from where Joey lay on the ground in a state of shock. They rushed toward the sounds and found him huddled in a fetal position on a pile of oak leaves, rocking to and fro. The troop leader shucked off his jacket and placed it around the cold, hysterical boy. He looked up at the other members of the search party, intending to shout instructions. Not a sound came from his gaping mouth. The sight of the boys staring at the corpse's bony fingers, pointing at them in a macabre accusatory gesture, left him mute.

\* \* \*

Savannah-Chatham Metropolitan Police vehicles crowded the small parking lot of the Skidaway State Reserve Visitor Center. Detective Gray Clark was overseeing the work at the burial site. The department's crime scene analysis unit was probing the area around the hand. To avoid disturbing possible evidence, they had not yet dug to see what else might be buried there. A crew from a local funeral home was waiting for the word to begin the exhumation. So far, nothing of any significance could help identify the body or the perpetrator. By the looks of the arm and the report by the medical examiner at the scene, the corpse was at least a couple of months old. When Detective Clark got back to the office, he would look up missing-persons reports. It was pretty clear the body wouldn't be recognizable.

The CSI unit completed its inspection after two hours of taking pictures, bagging dirt samples, and searching the immediate and surrounding areas for trace evidence. Their job was not complete, however. They would stay for the exhumation in order to closely examine the body for fibers, hair, paint, or any other possible clue that could lead to the identification of the victim or his killer. Detective Clark didn't expect the digging to take very long. The grave looked shallow. He oversaw the diggers' work to be sure they didn't damage the body or any potential evidence. The corpse would be very brittle.

The excavation went off without a hitch. As expected, the body was in an advanced state of decomposition. The lead CSI officer took great care poring over the corpse with a magnifying glass. Much of the clothing was still intact, and the officer found several odd fibers and two hairs that didn't seem to match the victim's. When it came time to load the remains into the ambulance, four gloved men gently lifted the body onto a stretcher after deciding not to place it in a body bag, to avoid contamination and fragmentation. The ambulance would deliver the body to the medical examiner's office in Savannah, where the chief pathologist was waiting to conduct the autopsy. The pathologist at the scene documented postmortem changes before the unidentified victim was removed. Inconsistencies in those changes could later be used to determine whether the victim was moved by the perpetrator, and to validate or refute witness statements. It also helped in estimating the time of death.

Once the crime scene analysis was complete, Detective Clark dismissed the team and walked back to the visitor center, where his patrol car was parked. By then, they knew that the dead person was a male. The medical examiner estimated his age at 35 to 45, based on the incremental layers of cementum on the teeth. His hair color was black with some graying at the temples. Before the detective attached his seat belt, he called the squad secretary and asked him to check with the missing-persons unit for a male matching the minimal description they had so far. If it didn't render results, Clark instructed him to give the Atlanta field office of the FBI a call to request that they run a missing-persons search in the Chatham County area through ViCAP. Clark hoped to have the information by the time he arrived at the office. It would take him about a half hour to get there.

* * *

Daniel Falcone had just arrived in Washington, D.C., after what he considered a productive trip to the FBI's San Diego field office. As he merged onto I-95 south toward Quantico, his plan to head home for a change of clothes went up in flames. The San Diego special agent in charge had heard from a detective with the Savannah-Chatham Police Department that a body was discovered in a state reserve outside Savannah.

After his initial research, the detective had come to the conclusion that the victim could well be the missing FBI agent, John Christy. Harding was on his way to the airport to catch a flight from San Diego to Atlanta. He had a hunch that Daniel, as director of the Joint Terrorism Task Force, would want to meet him there. Over the past few days, it was becoming increasingly clear that the two agents were working toward a common goal. Both men were convinced that if they identified the culprits responsible for Christy's disappearance, it would lead to the resolution of the Alvin Fitch assassination and, perhaps, the hate crime attacks around the country.

At the San Diego field office, Daniel had copied and studied the files of each of the Ku Klux Klan members being investigated by John Christy. During the process, he found a few too many connections between the Lansburys and the Klan to chalk up to mere coincidence. A stack of photographs he had found in a file for the subject, Billy Ray Johnson, turned out to be of great interest. Christy had been focused on this son of a known Klan leader whose family had been the target of FBI investigations since the late 1930s. The undercover agent had kept a diary of his findings and thoughts during his operation. Daniel had it transcribed and filed.

Christy warned that Billy Ray was an up-and-coming force to be reckoned with in the Klan. For the past year, Christy had requested intermittent surveillance of Billy Ray's activities. On several occasions, he was photographed with Kyle and Andrew Lansbury and a third man, identified as Kyle's younger brother, Troy Lansbury. All the photographs were taken in Miami during the months immediately before the assassination.

196

The day he learned of the Johnson connection, Daniel had members of his task force doing everything in their power to locate Billy Ray for questioning. An agent from the Jackson division of the Bureau visited the Johnson estate, hoping to interview Billy Ray or at least determine his whereabouts from family or friends. His father said that Billy Ray had recently emigrated to Europe because he was disgusted with the leadership in America. Incredibly, Emmett Johnson didn't know what airline his son flew on, the date he left, or in which country he now lived. Billy Ray's mother and friends weren't any more accommodating.

It quickly became apparent that the people closest to Billy Ray were unwilling to cooperate, so Daniel was obliged to issue an APB. The bulletin specified that Billy Ray Johnson was wanted for questioning in connection with the Alvin Fitch assassination. In the highly improbable event that Billy Ray had left the country, Daniel filed the same report with Interpol.

The suspect's convenient disappearance only served to bolster Daniel's feeling that the Klan was involved in the more recent strikes on minority groups. Throughout the country and even the world, the panic was mounting as were the demands for results. Governors and the mayors of the major cities were getting in on the act. The media's finger-pointing and nonstop coverage were relentless. Their attempts to corner Daniel for updates and comments were just as determined. He was also getting daily calls from the president and the director of the FBI.

In response to the heavy pressure coming from all directions, Daniel had turned the task force into a well-oiled machine. Its members were approaching one thousand, including FBI agents, the CIA, and local police and sheriff's departments in the affected states. Daniel had ordered two of his lead investigators to apply pressure on Andrew Lansbury and Tabitha Freemont.

Christopher Frye was going to pay them daily visits and keep them under constant surveillance.

The circumstantial evidence was mounting against Andrew, although Daniel still didn't have what he needed to detain him on charges. Just last night, while completing his business in San Diego, Daniel had come up with an idea that could confirm the Klan's participation in Alvin Fitch's murder. As soon as he put on a fresh suit, he intended to meet with the Capitol police officers who had been protecting the senator the night he was killed. The discovery of Christy's body nixed those plans. With the permission of his SAC, Daniel had already reserved a Learjet for a flight back to the capital as soon as the business in Georgia was complete. He wanted to personally handle that interview.

John Christy's death had long become a foregone conclusion among the task force members assigned to investigate his disappearance. They were desperate for some real evidence to pin the murder on the Klan. According to the Savannah detective, some fibers and hairs found at the burial site could perhaps put the task force well on its way toward that objective. Though the final lab test results were not in yet, it was the medical examiner's preliminary opinion that the hairs did not belong to the victim. They were currently undergoing DNA analysis. The results would be entered into the FBI's Combined DNA Index System. If the perpetrator's genetic information was in the system, it could lead to his or her identification.

Daniel had no choice but to turn around and head straight back to the airport. He wanted to be there to assist with the crime scene analysis and other investigative procedures. A half hour later, he was boarding his field office's Learjet at Reagan International. They wouldn't be able to examine the crime scene tonight, but there was still plenty of other work to be done before they took

198

the trip out to Skidaway State Reserve. He planned to be at the burial site by sunrise.

\* \* \*

The Chatham County Coroner's Office was located directly across the street from Candler Hospital, where, just a few weeks earlier, Adalia Jones's best friend was treated for the injuries she suffered at the St. Christopher AIM Church carnival. After reviewing the investigative file and photographs accumulated thus far, Daniel Falcone and Ed Harding requested that Detective Gray take them to view the decomposed body found at Skidaway State Reserve. The victim was, in fact, John Christy, although they were still waiting for official identification via dental records. When the body was taken to the medical examiner's office and unclothed, they found, stuffed inside the crotch of the pants, the business card given to Christy by Agent Michael Gerard. Detective Gray was at the coroner's office when it was discovered, and he immediately contacted Gerard. At that point, the body's identity was no longer in question.

The card was examined for fingerprints, with no usable results. Someone had wiped it clean before placing it in Christy's pants. Daniel thought the perpetrators were either stupid or had no intention of being subtle. This was especially true since the burial site was just a half hour from a known Klan meeting place. These guys were on an aggressive campaign. Under such circumstances, mistakes were inevitable, and this was a major one.

While Daniel and Harding waited for the chief medical examiner to escort them in to view the body, they inspected the personal belongings found with it. If Christy had anything in his possession besides his clothing at the time of the murder, the perpetrators had taken it. The only things in the evidence bag were a pair of Levi's jeans with a thirty-two-inch waist and a thirty-two-inch inseam, a medium blue T-shirt, a pair of white socks, and size 11 Nike running shoes. Ed Harding had determined that these matched the sizes worn by John Christy.

When the doctor entered the room, Detective Gray introduced everyone, and the four men went to the examining room, where the body was still laid out on a gurney. The fetid odor of old death permeated the chamber. Though not as awful as the early stages of decomposition, it was still hard to bear. The corpse was severely decayed, and several generations of maggots had eaten away most of the flesh.

Having completed the autopsy just thirty minutes ago, the medical examiner had the results fresh in his mind. He gave a verbal report to the FBI agents. Based on the climate in Southern Georgia, it was his opinion that the body had far surpassed the first stages of decay, known as early and black putrefaction. The completion of that process usually required only a few days. The advanced state of mummification was solid evidence that it was underground for more than just a few weeks. Adipocere, commonly known as grave wax, had formed on the skin and flesh, giving it a dark, cheesy appearance. Some skin, bone, flesh, and most of the organs were lost, largely to insects, during the decomposition process. The coroner placed the time of death at right around the date Christy disappeared.

As soon as Daniel saw the body, he knew that the cause of death was strangulation. Despite the advanced decomp, there were clear signs of bruises and abrasions around the neck area. The coroner confirmed Daniel's suspicions, pointing out that when he performed the autopsy, he had found damage to the hyoid and thyroid processes, and a broken larynx. There was an ancillary fracture of the skull at the right temple, but the doc said the injury wasn't fatal. Before the strangulation, the perpetrator had hit the victim on the head with a blunt instrument.

The doctor had more difficulty explaining a second bone fracture. The femur of the left leg was broken in two. The unusual part was that the injury had been inflicted postmortem. He was stumped why the killer would do such a thing, which served no good purpose. Even more confusing was the type of break. It usually occurred as a result of a fall from a significant height, such as from a ladder or roof. As far as he knew, corpses weren't given to falling. No one present could come up with an explanation until Daniel offered his opinion.

"Ed, do you have any idea where Christy was when he was abducted?" Daniel asked.

"We can't say for sure. There was some evidence of smeared blood drops on the carpet of his hotel room. Why?"

"I'm just trying to make sense of the broken leg. Doctor, if he was thrown from a height, would it be consistent with this type of injury?"

The coroner replied, "It certainly is possible."

"John's hotel room at the Westin was on the second floor. And come to think of it, there was a balcony," said Harding.

Daniel asked, "Did your men check the area outside under the balcony?"

"I'd have to talk to the guys who were there that night. But I see where you're going. As soon as we're done here, I'll give Gerard a call and get a definite answer."

"It may be too late, but I'd give the grounds underneath the balcony another good going-over anyway. You never know what you might find."

**Chapter 16**

For as long as she could remember, Polly Flowers had dreamed of being an actress. Performing was her life, the theater her one true love. Never on God's good earth did she believe she would find herself employed in the oldest profession in the world. At 39, she was still a beautiful woman and had lasted several years longer than most high-end escorts. Still, her days were numbered. With no skills besides her talent for acting, she worried about what she would do once her Washington escort service let her go.

The work had been lucrative. Her annual income exceeded six figures, some years as high as a quarter-million dollars. On the downside, Polly was not very skillful with money management. Her mother would always say it burned a hole in her pocket. A good part of the problem was her fantasy that she was a member of the New York theater jet set, and she did her best to live as if it were true.

In her professional life, Polly rubbed elbows (and more) with some of the most powerful people in the world. She worked for one of the more exclusive secret escort services in the United States. The career opportunity had first presented itself when she was a struggling teenage actress living in New York City. Twenty years later, she was still stuck in this godforsaken business. She had met a lot of important people in the entertainment industry. Not one of them was willing to give her an opportunity. Other than her repeat customers, most of the men never wanted to see her again.

Now that she was nearing the end of her run, she didn't have much to show for it. She had refinanced her apartment until she owed more on it than it was worth. She owed astronomical amounts on her credit cards and didn't even own her seven-year-old Mercedes outright. She did have a lot of jewelry, but that would get her only so far. It had gotten to the point that she was sleep deprived over the thought of losing her source of income.

Polly had been seriously considering turning to medication for her anxiety when, just in the nick of time, she was offered the best role of her insignificant acting career. Her most loyal customer, a four-star general, was one of the most powerful military leaders in the country. For the past eight years, he had been working outside the Pentagon. At the time Polly met him, he had just lost his wife of forty-five years. The man was on the verge of a breakdown, completely devastated by her death. When he visited Polly for the first time, he had no intention of having sex. They spent the night until dawn talking about everything and anything. The general gave her a generous tip, and Polly thought she would never see him again. To her surprise, he returned a week later. Once again, his only requirement was her company and conversation. He told her she reminded him of his wife forty years ago, making her feel like the daughter he never had. Over the years, they became very close. After a while, Polly tried to reject his offers to pay for her company. Each time, he insisted on compensating her, always giving his best effort to convince her to quit the profession.

The job the general was proposing shocked Polly to the core. It seemed totally out of character. He admitted that he had great difficulty choosing her. He cherished her friendship so much, he had feared that asking her to engage in this underhanded scheme would devalue it. She was the only person he could trust with such an important task involving the utmost secrecy. He swore he had no choice but to go through with it. Believing he might be in some sort of trouble, she accepted the work. (It also happened to pay extremely well.) As a matter of fact, she probably would never have to sell her body again—if she could get her spending problem under control.

* * *

On a Tuesday afternoon, the week before Daniel's trip to San Diego, the presidential motorcade made its way from the Benito Juárez International Airport to the hotel in downtown Mexico City, where President Benjamin Cooper and Defense Secretary Brandon Atkins were spending the next two nights. An international economic conference was being held in the capital city. To smooth over relations with the Mexican government, President Cooper had decided to attend the summit himself. He and Atkins were also scheduled to have a private meeting with the Mexican president to discuss the Border Patrol issue. They were staying at the Four Seasons Hotel Mexico City, on the famous Paseo de la Reforma. The wide boulevard running in a straight line for twelve kilometers through the city center allowed for reasonably secure transportation for the president. His limousine was flanked by two motorcycle police officers, with two more directly in front and behind. Twenty-six other vehicles, loaded with up to five Secret Service agents and local police officers each, escorted the president to his destination.

Polly Flowers's trip to the Four Seasons Hotel did not consist of such pomp and circumstance. She sat alone in the back of an old green taxicab, waiting in traffic stalled by the president's motorcade. Normally, she wouldn't have been permitted to stay at the Four Seasons without an extensive background check. The general, with the assistance of some other very powerful men, had made sure that wasn't necessary. In fact, her room would be on the same floor as the president's.

The curtain for the first act of the show would go up this very evening. Polly felt as nervous as a leading actress performing her debut starring role on opening night, though not for the same reasons. The thought of being in the presence of the president of the United States was a dream come true. She hadn't exactly pictured herself meeting him in the manner planned, of course. She would have preferred being invited to the White House for a special event. Nonetheless, the idea that she would be touching him went beyond her wildest fantasies.

The airport was just seventeen kilometers from the hotel. With the traffic, it took Polly's taxi driver over an hour to get there. The day before she left Washington, a man in a dark suit had given her the hotel key and a map of all floors, with written directions. Instructed by the general not to stop at the front desk, she was to go straight to her room. She needn't worry about transporting her luggage; the general had told her to have her bags packed and give them to the man delivering the key. She was assured they would be waiting for her in the hotel room when she arrived.

As usual, the general did not disappoint her. When she entered her fifth-floor suite, her bags were already there and neatly put away. Her makeup and toiletries were arranged in perfect order in the opulent oversize bathroom. The dry-cleaned and pressed dress she would be wearing this evening was hanging in the closet. Even her more private articles of clothing were fastidiously placed in the drawers of the polished cherrywood chiffonier. Polly thought she could easily get used to this kind of service. The only hitch was quite a big one: she was not permitted to leave the hotel room for any reason. Her orders in that

206

regard were specific and inflexible. She wasn't to move until she got further instructions in the form of a call or text to a cell phone furnished to her.

Polly kicked off her shoes and tested the luxurious bed. Tired after the plane trip from D.C. and the extended ride from the airport, she decided to take a nap. It would help pass the time until she was called into action.

\* \* \*

Before joining the U.S. Secret Service, Thaddeus Raymond had been a career military man from the day after he received his high school diploma. For the last eight years of his duty in the Army Special Forces, he worked directly under Polly's general. During the assignment, he and the general had developed more than just a professional association. Theirs was a strong and close friendship— one that ordinarily would last a lifetime.

A specific incident that occurred shortly after Raymond's commission by the general was a significant catalyst to the evolution of their relationship. While visiting Afghanistan to attend a top secret military council, the general was mistakenly targeted by a Taliban assassin. Raymond was selected to provide protection for the general during his travels. The killer, a trained sharpshooter, was contracted by Taliban leaders to put a bullet in the head of the Afghan minister of defense, who was being escorted to the forum by the general and Raymond. The three men had been transported in a Sikorsky S-70 assault helicopter to the northwest limits of the Registan Desert in southern Afghanistan. An abandoned military base was to serve as the meeting site.

Raymond was the first to disembark when the chopper landed, then the general. As he stepped down, a shot rang out from a training bunker a hundred meters north of the landing pad. If Raymond had not caught the glint of the sun reflecting off the scope of the long-range Lobaev SVL sniper rifle a split second before it was fired, the bullet would have passed through the general's brain stem, killing him instantly. With lightning reflexes, Raymond tackled him to the ground. The round hurtled through the thin desert air, passing harmlessly through the empty space where the general's upper neck would have been if Raymond hadn't reacted in time.

Upon his retirement from the military, with the help of a glowing recommendation from the general, Raymond was hired as a Secret Service agent. Though that was ten years ago, this was Raymond's first assignment to the presidential detail. He was an addition to the team traveling with Cooper to Mexico. After reviewing the Secret Service's detailed scheme for covering the hotel, the director of the Secret Service, John Nash, suggested extra security. Recent tension between the United States and its neighbor to the south was cited as the reason. Raymond, who was fluent in Spanish, was assigned the post outside the door of the president's hotel room from the dinner hour through the following morning.

It was a frustrating hardship for Thaddeus Raymond to be away from home during what amounted to one of the most trying times of his life. He wouldn't have hesitated to reject this job if its reward weren't a promise to eliminate the source of his woes. Eight months ago, the love of his life had suffered a debilitating heart attack. The result was significant coronary muscle damage and severe congestive heart failure. Her prognosis was poor. Her cardiologist predicted that if she didn't have a heart transplant within six months, she would be dead.

Kendra Raymond was the perfect candidate for the procedure; that wasn't the issue. Thad's and Kendra's stubborn rebellion against formal institutions, namely marriage, had come back to haunt them. Because they weren't married and had temporarily separated when she became ill, his insurance wouldn't pay for the operation. Thaddeus made a desperate attempt to get her on his health coverage by marrying her at her hospital bedside. It was too late. The insurance company refused payment, citing the preexisting-condition exemption clause for a grandfathered health policy. The denial of coverage was confirmed when he filed suit against the insurer. The judge ruled against Thaddeus and his partner even though they had lived in the same household for almost ten years and had two children together.

This was a mission he would never in his wildest dreams have imagined himself doing. He had spent his life fighting for his country and protecting its leaders. Ultimately, it would most likely cost him his career. It didn't make for great job security when you took on the president of the United States. Fortunately, his employment would no longer be an issue. With the compensation he would be receiving through the general, he could pay for his wife's surgery three times over. As a major bonus, he was promised she would be moved straightaway to the top of the waiting list. Before he left the room to begin his duty, he tucked the vial given him by the general with his smartphone in his inside jacket pocket.

* * *

Polly was startled from her sleep by the ringing of her cell phone, indicating she had a text. She looked at the clock on the end table next to her king-size bed and

209

saw that she had slept more than four hours. It was already dark outside, and the sounds from the street below told her the city's nightlife was in full swing. As she glanced at the message, which included a page of instructions, she made her way to the bathroom to splash her face with cold water. Once she felt alert enough to comprehend, she picked up the cell phone and read the text from the beginning. The orders in bold type jolted her wide awake. She needed to be dressed and ready to leave the hotel room at a moment's notice anytime within the hour.

The text message reiterated the general's previous instructions that she appear to be an upscale prostitute—an easy ask since she had been living the life for the past twenty years. To save time and avoid worrying about creating a hairdo with what God had given her, she chose one of the wigs she had packed in her suitcase. She had decided on a Victoria Beckham chin-length brunette as most appropriate for the role. She affixed the wig to her head.

Her profession wasn't really so different from an actor's. It often required her to play different types of characters. It also demanded a certain degree of skill in costuming. She checked the final product in the mirror. Her reflection could very well have been a candidate for First Lady of the United States, and she had accomplished it all in just five minutes.

The dress chosen for her hugged her body closely but was not skin tight, and its conservative V neckline didn't show too much cleavage. As she struggled to pull it over her ample bosom without smearing her makeup, the cell phone rang a second time. With a final wriggle, she stretched the dress over her stomach. She hurried to read the brief text. In exactly six minutes, she was to leave her room and make her way to the presidential suite.

Polly looked at the watch—also issued for the job—then pulled the dress the rest of the way down over her waist and thighs. By the time she applied the final touches and made sure everything was on straight, she had only a minute to spare. She spent it concentrating on the role she was about to play. It would require a lot of physical effort. When the minute was up, she opened the door and stepped out into the corridor.

\* \* \*

The president's suite was located in an alcove not visible from the main hallway. Secret Service agents were posted in strategic positions on the T-shaped floor. The president's and Polly's rooms were located on either end of the top of the T. They were the only two rooms in that hallway. As far as anyone not in the know was concerned, the second room was vacant. Thaddeus Raymond and a government official had confirmed that for the rest of the team. The elevators were at the base of the T.

Nine agents could potentially see Polly on her way to Cooper's suite. Five of them were in designated positions along the main corridor, a second group of three were at the elevators, and the ninth was Thaddeus—the only agent assigned to the president's door. To get to Cooper's suite, Polly would have to cross the main hallway at the top of the T. It was while she was passing through that intersection that she would be within view of the other eight Secret Service agents—if they should look in her direction. The instructions required that when she left her room, she was to stop just before the intersection of the hallways. The agent posted at the president's door would motion her to pass when it was safe.

Twenty-five minutes before Polly was scheduled to leave her room, a drink was delivered to the presidential suite. Thaddeus didn't allow the runner to enter but accepted it at the door along with the complimentary fruit plate. After the waiter left, Thaddeus balanced the tray on his left palm, took a vial from his inside jacket pocket, emptied its contents—liquid oxytocin—into the hot drink, and entered the room. President Cooper, who was seated on the sofa reading the newspaper, instructed the Secret Service agent to place the tray on the coffee table. Thaddeus complied, pleading to God that Cooper not be in a talkative mood. His prayers answered, he quickly made his exit. Several minutes later, he reentered to find that the drug had done its job. Cooper appeared to be fast asleep. Thaddeus tried to rouse him without success. Satisfied that he was out cold, Thaddeus quickly removed all the president's clothing, then resumed his post outside the front door.

At exactly 11:00 p.m., the bell on the fifth floor rang, indicating the arrival of an elevator. The three agents posted in front of the elevator and all the agents in the main corridor turned toward the doors as they opened. Polly was waiting at the threshold just outside of her room. Thaddeus waved to her to continue across the hallway. She was unseen except by the occupant of the elevator—the same government official who had helped search Polly's room. He apologized to the Secret Service agents, claiming that he had accidentally pushed the wrong button on his way up to his room on the eighth floor.

In the meantime, Polly entered the presidential suite. The sound of voices at the elevators distracted the eight agents from any noise made as Thaddeus opened and closed the door quietly for her. She knew the layout from studying an online virtual tour of the room. A long hallway led to a large living area decorated with American Colonial furniture. After proceeding through the

212

entryway into the parlor, the first thing she noticed was the president of the United States, laying naked as a jaybird on the traditional mahogany wingback sofa. Though he appeared to be sleeping, Polly knew he had been drugged. She approached him and saw a cup with the remnants of what appeared to be hot chocolate, and an untouched plate of assorted fruits. Though she wasn't aware of this particular nugget of presidential trivia, it was well known by people who followed Cooper's life that he drank a cup of hot cocoa every night before he went to sleep.

Polly had a few moments before Thaddeus was supposed to rejoin her. She made her way to the bedroom to check out the setting that would be the final act of her performance. The king-size bed was made up with satin sheets and a thick handmade Belmont comforter that looked too beautiful to be the stage of what was planned. She figured the bedding alone probably cost upward of five thousand dollars. The room was furnished with gorgeous antique sofas and chairs, and the window dressings were fit for a royal palace. Before she could check out the bathroom, she heard the front door close and hurried back into the living area to find the Secret Service agent taking the empty cup and fruit plate to the kitchen.

\* \* \*

There wasn't much time. One of Thaddeus's jobs was to see this process done as quickly as possible. Whenever he entered or left the room, he was required to report the reason to one of his colleagues, who would then temporarily take up the post at the door. He had no intention of following that protocol. Considering the possibility that they could contact him over their earbud comm system for any number of reasons, the risk he and Polly were taking was substantial.

Both Thaddeus's and Polly's roles were scripted in as much detail as a Hollywood screenplay. They had rehearsed numerous times back home with a confederate acting as Cooper. Thaddeus returned to the living room, and together, he and Polly sat the president up, propping him against the sofa's arm. Polly removed her undergarments, sat next to Cooper, lifted his head, placed her lips on his, and feigned a passionate kiss. Thaddeus adjusted his position in front of the sofa until he could fit his two subjects on the screen of the digital camera while getting a good view of Polly's lack of undergarments. He snapped a few pictures, then laid the president in a prone position on the sofa while Polly disrobed. She wriggled out of the garment as quickly as was physically possible, then knelt at Cooper's side, placing his penis in her mouth. Thaddeus took several more photos from different angles. Over the next five minutes, they set the president up in various poses while Polly performed a variety of sexual acts. Thaddeus was able to rouse the president just long enough to get a single shot of him with his eyes open, though not enough for him to be aware of his surroundings.

The final pictures were taken in the bedroom. They managed to get a series of views with Cooper on top of Polly's naked body, then with her in an assortment of practiced poses on top. Before they could complete the job, Thaddeus had to take a status call from his fellow agents. Stepping outside the bedroom, he reported that all was well, and thanked his lucky stars that they believed he was still at his post. After signing off, he helped Polly get Cooper under the covers by lifting him and placing him back in the bed while she held back the sheets.

214

In order for Polly to leave the room, they would have to repeat the same process they had used to get her in. Thaddeus made a call on his cell phone. Five minutes later, he and Polly were waiting in the alcove for the elevator bell to ring. When the agents turned to greet Secretary of Defense Brandon Atkins, Polly made her way across the main hallway and into her room.

**Chapter 17**

The breaking story the following Wednesday morning set off an international media frenzy. Every major local, national, and foreign network sent their correspondents to D.C. to cover the sex scandal of the century. The first newspaper to reveal the details of the president's sexual escapade with a high-end escort was the most respected in the country: the *New York Times*. Though they were too politically correct to publish any of the scurrilous photographs, the reporter who wrote the story was sure to mention they existed and had been authenticated. They printed a picture of Polly Flowers, who became an overnight celebrity. She had not a single objection that her popularity was of the infamous sort. Enjoying every second of it, she was playing her role to the hilt. She had already appeared on *Anderson Cooper 360, The Tonight Show,* and David Letterman. Scott Pelley had contacted her to appear on *CBS Evening News* as soon as she could get to New York.

The *National Enquirer* wasn't as worried about its reputation as the *New York Times*. Its editors had no reservations about publishing the photographs of the president in all kinds of compromising positions, though they blurred out the portions of the pictures that would get them heavy fines from the Federal Communications Commission. *Playboy,* on the other hand, was excited to include the images in their entirety. The magazine had also made Polly a lucrative offer to pose naked for the centerfold. Opportunities were coming in more quickly than she could personally handle. Two days after the story went public, she hired an agent and manager to represent her and coordinate her growing schedule. In fact, she made the choice days before anyone knew of the scandal. The general gave her the name and number of one of the more

216

successful and controversial Hollywood agents—the same man who had represented Casey Anthony.

* * *

President Cooper categorically denied having any conscious sexual acts of any kind with Polly Flowers. In his initial address to the nation before a packed room of reporters, he expressed doubt the pictures were genuine. At the time, he didn't mention passing out the evening the episode allegedly occurred. Waking up the following morning, he had been in a state of total confusion. He had no recollection how he ever got into the bed. It wasn't typical for him suddenly to lose consciousness or fall asleep without trying. Normally, it required an effort. He didn't consider himself an insomniac, but he couldn't recall the last time he had fallen asleep without consciously getting in bed and lying still. Even more bizarre was the memory blackout.

By the next day, it didn't seem important enough to fret over. After getting confirmation from his press secretary that the photographs were not altered, he became very suspicious of the circumstances. He ordered his staff to do a thorough investigation of all Secret Service agents who were on duty that evening, to determine how it was possible for the woman to get into his room. Before waiting for the results, he made a public statement that he was set up.

Both professionally and personally, the president had taken a terrible hit. In her newspaper and television interviews, Polly Flowers was alleging that President Cooper originally contacted her shortly after he moved into the White House. She lied to the entire world about their relationship, the context of their first meeting, and that she had set up the camera to take the pictures, knowing

217

Cooper was too out of it to protest. She was quoted as saying that her purpose was to show America that its president was a pig.

In a follow-up story in the *New York Times,* Polly told the reporter that Cooper had called the number she gave online for escort services. Since their initial conversation, he had been paying her for sexual favors rendered at least once a month. Regarding Mexico City, she claimed that the president had invited her to spend several days at the Four Seasons Hotel and made arrangements for her room to be across the hall from his suite.

What truly floored Cooper was the statement by the Secret Service agent posted outside his hotel room door. Agent Raymond was corroborating the prostitute's story. It was becoming increasingly clear that he and Polly Flowers were part of an elaborate conspiracy. When he first heard of Raymond's statement, the president was confident he could successfully challenge the agent's credibility. Upon further investigation, he discovered that Raymond had an impeccable career record with the military and the Secret Service. That, combined with the indisputable legitimacy of the photographs, was not going to be easy to overcome.

Cooper's approval ratings had plummeted deep into the mud pits, and his home life wasn't going much better. Patricia was publicly supporting him. Behind closed doors, she couldn't hide her doubts. Even his closest allies in Washington seemed to be distancing themselves from him. Defense Secretary Atkins and Homeland Security Secretary Logan were rumored to be considering handing in their resignations. He expected the Republicans to be gleefully shredding him. He held out a glimmer of hope that the Democratic Party leaders would back him. Neither of his party's majority leaders in the Senate or the House of Representatives, nor any of the other more powerful Democratic members of Congress, extended a helping hand. Most of them were accepting the incident as true and condemning his behavior publicly in the media.

President Cooper was sure that if his personal investigation of the incident didn't yield any positive results, a move for impeachment was just around the corner. As an African American president, he had never doubted that he would have his detractors and enemies. He had always been prepared to suffer an array of slurs and insults. He had also predicted that he would have to respond to all kinds of lies and accusations. His main concern, though, was for his and his family's safety. Never had he imagined he would be trapped in a predicament such as this. He wasn't going to be able to resolve the matter on his own. Not only was he not a professional investigator, but also, his position precluded him from dedicating his time to anything but service to his country. He was going to have to hire the best, someone he could trust. Only one person came to mind who met those conditions and could get the job done.

\* \* \*

The final touches for Brandon Atkins's letter of resignation were complete. The only remaining task was to sign it and deliver it to the president. Though he had not yet scheduled an appointment with Cooper, he asked his secretary to arrange a press conference for the following day. Everything played out exactly as he planned it. To have abandoned the president for any other reason than his infidelity would have looked to the American public like quitting. But they would understand if he stepped down out of moral outrage.

Atkins wasn't pleased that he would have no official role in government for the moment. As a presidential hopeful for the 2020 election, he had to remain

219

in the public eye. His best option was to get started on his campaign as quickly as possible. He would wait several weeks to let the dust settle. Then he planned to announce his candidacy and hire the best campaign manager in the country. He knew he had a very powerful ally on his side to help him achieve his goals. When General Adam Montgomery spoke, Americans and legislators on both sides of the aisle listened.

He knew he could count on his closest friend and colleague of more than twenty years to execute the plan to bring Cooper down. Atkins leaned toward a conservative view on most issues, but compared to General Adam Montgomery, he was a practically a socialist. Montgomery was as far to the right as anyone he had ever known. The secretary of Defense was certain that his buddy, known as "the general" to his closest friends, had to be seething over the new liberal president's policies. Like many people in Atkins's circle, the general also owed him a favor or two. It was through Atkins's influence that he was ultimately appointed to the Joint Chiefs of Staff. Well aware of Montgomery's ultraconservative views, Atkins was confident he would agree when Atkins called in this most recent favor. Together, they had planned out every last detail of the Polly Flowers affair. The ultimate hope was that Congress would do the right thing and impeach the president. Neither Atkins nor the general had any confidence the moron could be trusted running the country for the remainder of his term.

* * *

Daniel Falcone's workload had kept him away from his children for far too long. He intended to take full advantage of his first day back in Hallandale in the past month and a half. He owed it to them, especially after bailing out on a Dolphins football game several weekends ago. He and the boys enjoyed a morning of tennis, then hit a movie matinee in the early afternoon. Tonight, there was important family business on the agenda. He would be revealing some special plans for the future and was quite stressed about it. The only time he could recall being more nervous was before the verdict at his trial for the murder of his wife and in-laws.

Dale and Timmy didn't know that their dad had been seeing Annie romantically for the past couple of months. Though they lived in the same county, they had been carrying on a long-distance relationship while Daniel was staying at the FBI facility at Quantico. On the rare occasions Daniel was in South Florida, he was making time to see Annie when the boys were either asleep or busy with school or soccer. Annie had taken several trips to Quantico to visit Daniel on the weekends he couldn't get home.

In defiance of the miles temporarily separating them, the past that all but precluded the rekindling of their relationship, and all the other reasons why it was such a crazy idea, they had decided to get more serious. They did not make the decision without hours of contemplation and conversation. Daniel's mind had changed many times during the process. Annie always knew that if the opportunity arose, she wouldn't make the same mistake twice. In the end, they both agreed that their love was too strong not to give it one more chance.

During the time of Daniel's estrangement from his wife, before her murder, Dale and Timmy were just 11 and 8 years old. They were too young to be told that Daniel's infidelity with Annie was the reason for their parents' separation. Even though this wasn't an issue, Daniel had been apprehensive about telling his sons he was in love with a woman who was not their mother. He

221

didn't want them to think he was trying to replace her. Daniel and Annie had debated whether she should be present when he broke the news. Annie thought it would go over better if he had a private family meeting with the boys. Daniel insisted that she participate. The final consensus was that Annie would come to dinner. When the meal was done, they would have a conversation together with the children. Daniel's mother was out of the picture for the evening, having agreed to make herself scarce until later.

They were barely ten minutes into the meal when work thwarted Daniel's big plans and interrupted his time with the boys again. To ease his guilt, he had been trying to convince himself that his jam-packed workload was just temporary. The inconsistency in that theory was starting to become as plain as the nose on his face. There was no end in sight. Something had to give. At the very minimum, his children deserved one present parent.

There was no consolation for repeatedly abandoning his boys. This unexpected call was from the president of the United States, and his request couldn't wait. The chief executive asked Daniel if he would take the first available flight to Washington. He didn't want to give any details over the telephone regarding the reason for the trip. He promised to explain fully as soon as Daniel arrived.

Daniel felt it would be unfair to lay the heavy news of his new relationship on his sons and then leave them to deal with it on their own. They already were going to be upset that he couldn't spend the rest of the weekend with them. He and Annie agreed that they should postpone the talk until the next time he was in town. Twenty minutes after they finished dinner, Daniel was on his way to Fort Lauderdale International Airport to catch the nine-o'clock flight to

D.C. He reached for the cell phone clipped to his belt, and called Christopher Frye.

"Hey, Chris. I'm on my way to D.C. I was wondering if you could do me a favor."

"What's up in D.C?"

"Forgive me, pal, but, I'm not at liberty to talk about it."

"What kinda bullshit is that? I'm your *partner.*"

"I know. I really am sorry. This has nothing to do with any of our cases. I just can't talk about it right now. Maybe later. Can I get you to do something for me?"

"Yeah, sure. What do you need?"

"While I'm up there, I want to reschedule that meeting with the Capitol Police officers assigned to Fitch the night he was killed. I was going to head straight back to D.C. from Savannah. Being so close to home, I thought I'd check on the boys first. Can you get that set up sometime tomorrow?"

"You got it, buddy. Good luck with that. I hope it pays off."

\* \* \*

Four men dressed in construction workers' garb scanned the empty hotel room / conference suite on the outskirts of Washington, D.C., for any type of surveillance equipment. A gentleman who introduced himself as Brody had given them the keys. It had been reserved under the false name John Jefferson for one night, though it would be occupied for less than an hour.

Once they completed the sweep, the leader of the four men contacted Brody to notify him the room was clean. One hour later, starting at eleven thirty p.m., four middle-aged men dressed in casual clothes, sunglasses, and ball caps entered the hotel room one at a time at fifteen-minute intervals. When all four were seated around the conference table, the man presiding over the meeting, who also happened to be a member of the president's Cabinet, addressed the group.

"Gentlemen, thank you for making yourselves available on such short notice. I know you all are on very tight schedules, so I'll make this as brief as possible. We all know the president was telling the truth when he claimed to be set up. Since the scandal, we've seen an unprecedented collapse in support for him. His approval ratings are the lowest in history for an incumbent president. Congress is seriously considering initiating impeachment proceedings. My opinion is, it will happen."

As an additional precautionary measure, the four men at the meeting had agreed not to use their real names. The man speaking pointed to the member of the U.S. House of Representatives and said, "The gentleman to my right would know more about what Congress has planned. If it becomes necessary, you can speak about that later. The question now is whether we want to go ahead with the plans Mr. Brody has so graciously set in motion for us."

"I don't see what the issue is," commented the third man in the room— the director of a governmental organization that possessed vital knowledge and power relevant to the group's goals. "There are no guarantees Congress is going to impeach the president, and then it's even less likely we'll succeed. It won't be easy to get the two-thirds majority required to pass. The president is like a cat: always seems to land on his feet. Thanks to our colleague here, we know he was set up. If the scam is exposed, Cooper comes out smelling like a rose. I see no reason to change our plans."

224

The fourth and final man participating in the meeting was one of the most influential men in American politics. He said, "Another thing we have to consider is, we've already involved people outside of Washington. These guys are extreme in their views, and I'm not so sure we could call them off at this point. They were making their own plans to do it before we ever approached them. Now they have our money."

"The Ku Klux Klan doesn't scare me," said the Cabinet member. "We can handle them. We control all the information they need to accomplish this mission. Any problems from them, and people can easily be eliminated. We're getting closer and closer to a position where we can win the next presidential election. I don't want to create a situation that'll cause the American public to feel sorry for Cooper or his party."

"Winning the presidential election isn't the only issue here," replied the member of the House of Representatives. "Already, this guy's liberal views are causing harm to our country. We all agree that the United States of America is our number one priority. We allow this guy to continue on his radical path, there may be no true America left for us to lead after the next election. I say we have no choice. For the sake of our forefathers and what they stood for, we must act without delay. We can't afford to wait for Congress to muddle its way through the impeachment process."

"Well, then, there seems to be a consensus," said the Cabinet member. "I agree. I wanted to be sure everyone was on the same page. Let's put this to a vote. All in favor of proceeding with the original plan, raise your right hand."

The decision was unanimous.

\* \* \*

The first snowstorm of the season had D.C. in complete gridlock, this time not of the political variety. Fifteen inches fell overnight on the nation's capital, breaking a mark for the earliest snowfall in recorded history. Travel was all but impossible. Both international airports had closed down, and the streets and highways were practically impassable. A multicar collision on Interstate 95, involving more than thirty vehicles, interrupted freeway access to the city from the north and south. Most schools and businesses had shut their doors.

For Special Agent Daniel Falcone, however, it was business as usual. He was lucky enough to make it to Washington before the blizzard stalled air traffic into Reagan International Airport. Getting to the White House could be a different story.

Cooper had invited Daniel to 1600 Pennsylvania Avenue for an especially early breakfast. He was due at the president's private dining room at five a.m. At four, a limousine was waiting for him under the porte cochere of his hotel, which was located just two-tenths of a mile from the White House. When Daniel walked out of the Hay-Adams Hotel, a Secret Service agent was standing at the rear passenger door, holding it open for him.

During the drive, Daniel couldn't help noticing that the roads from the hotel to the grounds of the presidential residence had been plowed as if specially for him. Sitting in the backseat of the limo, he racked his brain trying to figure out why Cooper was summoning him. He was supposed to receive a call from the president when he arrived at the hotel last evening. That never happened, because Daniel's flight was delayed and the president had retired for the night before it landed. An apology note from Cooper's chief of staff was waiting for him at the front desk, promising Daniel that everything would be explained at the five a.m. breakfast.

Daniel was admitted into the White House through an entrance not accessible to the general public, on the south end of the building. The Secret Service agent immediately escorted him to the president's residence, where a butler showed him to the parlor. It was only 4:35 a.m. by the time he was settled in a seat beside a baby grand piano in the large open area serving as a family room and dining area. The table was already set for two and adorned with an oversize centerpiece bowl of bright white amaryllis flowers. The walls were painted a butter cream color. Books, trophies, and various knickknacks decorated a series of white shelves built into the walls on either side of the room. An aroma of eggs and coffee drifted Daniel's way, making his stomach rumble. He could hear the barking of a dog from another part of the house. Ten minutes later, the butler reappeared, advising him that the president would be arriving in just a few minutes.

When Cooper entered the room, he extended his hand to Daniel and invited him to have a seat at the dining room table. The conversation started with pleasantries. After the waiter served them coffee and left the two men alone, Cooper addressed the reason for Daniel's trip.

"I'd like to get straight to the point, Agent Falcone. I invited you here to ask you a favor. There are a lot of people in Washington I could have turned to, but I chose you. I've been following your career for quite some time now. You're a man of great integrity and character. I'm an admirer. The bottom line is, I need your help. This sex scandal was a setup. We've tested the photographs, and unfortunately, I have to admit, they're authentic. Even though I have no recollection of anything that took place that night, I was evidently there. I have to

227

prove to the American public I was framed. Even more importantly, I have to prove it to my wife."

"Thank you for the kind words, sir. I assume that's where I come in?"

"Yes. You'll agree with me, there are several irrefutable facts. If I'm telling the truth, then Polly Flowers and Thaddeus Raymond are lying. They're the key to solving this puzzle. I don't think I have to tell you I have a lot of enemies in this city and around the country. I also don't think a Secret Service agent and a hooker are the masterminds of the plot to soil my name. Not only do I want Flowers and Raymond exposed, I want to know who's behind this."

"Mr. President, I'm flattered you chose me to help you. But I've got an overflowing caseload at the Bureau, not to mention I'm lead investigator on the Senator Fitch assassination, and heading the Joint Terrorism Task Force investigating the hate crimes. This kind of thing will take time, which, frankly, I don't have. I'm not going to lie: I don't particularly care to get involved in political matters."

"I've heard that you don't hesitate to speak your mind. I guess it applies even when your audience is the president of the United States. As it happens, I admire that in a person. It's the type of attitude that's going to get the job done. I can arrange things so you have the time. This is an extremely important matter, and I'm not just saying that from a personal standpoint. Obviously, I'd be lying if I said I don't have a selfish interest. But this country relies on its president. If I'm not trusted, nothing will get done. In the end, it will be America that suffers. The impeachment process, if the Congress chooses to take that route, will be a giant step backwards. I'm not saying resolution of the Fitch case and the hate crimes is not important, but I think you're skilled enough to work on all of it and get results.

I can't say that I didn't hope you might also identify with my predicament. I don't usually share issues about my marriage. It's at stake here as well."

"I do sympathize—totally understand what it's like to be accused of something you didn't do. But you knew that. Well played, Mr. President. If I say yes, what resources will I have at my disposal?"

"I don't want anyone to know you're doing this on my behalf, unless you talk to me about it first. It's to remain top secret. If there's anything you need, whether it's manpower or information, my staff will be available to you. I'll give you the card of the person you should contact. He'll give you what you need. I don't mind if you have your partner help—or any other agent you trust implicitly. Please restrict it to one, and let me know immediately who you've chosen. I won't sugarcoat things. Time is of the essence. The longer this goes on, the worse it is for me and for America."

Daniel didn't doubt that the president had selfish reasons for conducting this investigation. At the same time, he had always felt that Cooper had a deep love for his country and was a true civil servant in every sense of the word. The president cared about people. He wanted to create change not only for the less fortunate, but for all Americans.

No question, Cooper's ploy to suck Daniel in was a deft move. Daniel had never had any use for anyone who would resort to framing another human being. His personal experience only transformed those feelings into seething contempt. Even more importantly, he felt that Cooper was telling the truth. The people who had created this scandal deserved to be flushed out. It was dirty and underhanded, certainly unworthy of men in powerful positions.

Daniel was going to be busier than ever, and his children and Annie would suffer for it. But, this was the reason he had become an FBI agent: he wanted to make a difference. Hopefully, Dale and Timmy would understand one day. He knew that Annie would.

"All right, Mr. President, you have yourself a deal. One quick question: who do I report to?"

"I would prefer you report directly to me. I'll give you a secure line you can call. If I'm not available, you can contact my chief of staff. He'll also provide you with some very talented investigators. I'll be in touch with your supervisor so he's not on your back for your normal caseload. This is great, Agent Falcone. I had so hoped you would agree. I have every confidence you'll get the job done. I'll owe you a great debt of gratitude."

"For now, let's just take things one step at a time, sir. I promise I'll do everything in my power to get to the bottom of this. You know as well as I do there are no guarantees for any investigation. Is Thaddeus Raymond still employed with the Secret Service?"

"I understand. I'm still very thankful I have you on my side. If anyone can get results, it's you. And yes, Raymond still works for the Secret Service. Obviously, he's no longer on presidential detail. He's been reassigned to the Speaker of the House."

*No pressure,* Daniel thought to himself. Then out loud, he said, "Good. Then he's still here in Washington. We'll start with him. I have to warn you, I plan on taking a quick trip to Atlanta and then Mississippi. I should be back in Washington in three days. I hope that's not a problem."

"I'd prefer you got started right away, but I won't complain about a few days. It isn't going to make a significant difference in the grand scheme of things. Just please be sure to get started as soon as you get back."

"You have my word, Mr. President."

"Then what do you say we have some breakfast?"

* * *

As Daniel left the White House in the limousine provided by the president, he was feeling overwhelmed. A big break in the Fitch case could be the right medicine. It would certainly relieve a good bit of the pressure he was feeling. Knowing that Christopher Frye would already be on his way to the office at this early hour, Daniel called his cell phone to see if he had scheduled the meeting with U.S. Capitol Police Officers Joe Clerici and Ron Slater.

The news was good. Both men were in D.C. and would be available for a chat before their shift started at the U.S. Capitol Police Department on D Street Northeast. It would give Daniel barely enough time to get dropped off at his hotel, then grab a taxi to take him to their offices, located just over two miles from the White House. Instead of going through that exercise in futility, he asked Frye to confirm the meeting and the driver to turn around and drop him off at the U.S. Capitol Police Department. Fortunately, he had taken his briefcase containing the file and photos with him to the White House, and the roads had been plowed and salted.

Not ten minutes later, the presidential limousine pulled up to the curb at the entrance to a seven-story slate-gray concrete building. A passage had been shoveled from the curb to the doorway, and snow was piled at least four feet high on either side. Daniel pulled his coat tight around his neck as he made his way up the walkway and into the building, careful not to slip on the thin sheet of ice that lined his path. Just inside was a security post, manned by a pair of officers and equipped with a walk-through metal detector. Daniel immediately held his badge up to be examined and informed the officers that he was armed. He handed over his weapon, which was promptly returned after he passed through the metal detector.

The front welcoming counter was a few steps from the security post. Daniel approached, gave the greeting officer his badge and identification, and explained his business. The officer phoned Clerici and Slater straightaway to notify them of Daniel's arrival. Since both men were ready and available, they asked to have Daniel sent right up to the conference room on the second floor.

The two Capitol Police officers met him at the elevator, and escorted him to their meeting place. Daniel got to business as soon as they were seated.

"I have a few pictures I want to show you guys. If you don't mind, I would prefer to do this one at a time. Maybe one of you could step out; then we can switch?"

Slater volunteered to go first. After Clerici left, Daniel spread out on the table ten eight-by-six-inch photos of Billy Ray Johnson, Keith Peterson, Andrew Lansbury, the two Lansbury boys, and several confederates.

"I'm sure you know the drill. Please take your time to look at every photograph. Let me know if you recognize any of these men—more importantly, if you saw any one of them at any time during Senator Fitch's visit to Miami, whether at the hotel, Convention Center, or hospital."

Slater spent the next five minutes studying each face. When he was sure of his conclusion, he pointed at Billy Ray's photograph.

"This guy served at the banquet."

"You mean he was employed as a waiter to serve the meal?"

"Exactly."

Daniel could hardly hold back his excitement. He had to exercise all his self-control to stop himself from slamming the table with the flat of his palm.

"Are you absolutely sure?"

"No doubt about it. He was serving the senator's table."

"If he were so inclined, would he have had the opportunity to put a foreign substance, such as a drug, in Senator Fitch's food or drink?"

"I would imagine. As far as I recall, he was the only one who served anything to the senator. They brought it all from the kitchen. Anyone could have put something in his food or drink back there."

"Did you see him anywhere else besides the Convention Center?"

"Can't say as I did."

"Do you recognize any of these other guys?"

"No. Just the one."

"That's good enough for now. Would you mind sending your partner in? I know you must have questions. After he's done, we can all speak."

Slater complied with Daniel's request. Clerici entered the conference room seconds later and sat in the seat his colleague had vacated. Daniel repeated the same first question he had asked Slater. Clerici didn't need as much time to examine the pictures. When he spoke not long after he began to scan them, there was intensity behind his words.

"Holy shit! We questioned this guy." Joe Clerici was pointing to the picture of Billy Ray Johnson.

"What do you mean?"

"Crane saw him at the hotel the night we checked in. The next afternoon, we saw the guy standing in the lobby dressed like one of the waiters for the senator's dinner. Well, actually, Crane recognized him from the night before." Clerici continued his explanation of their interaction with Billy Ray Johnson that day. When he was done, he asked, "Who is this guy?"

Before answering Clerici's question, Daniel asked about the dinner and had the witness take a longer look at the other photographs in case he could identify anyone else. His responses confirmed what Daniel had already heard from Slater. After Daniel terminated the interview, Slater rejoined the meeting.

"The suspect's name is Billy Ray Johnson," said Daniel. "He's a known fanatical member of the Ku Klux Klan. In fact, we just put out a nationwide APB on him. I would appreciate if you guys didn't tell anyone about the information you have. The press is off limits. It's better that way for your own safety as well as for the investigation." Daniel looked at them with a quizzical expression on his face, wondering why they wouldn't have been aware of the all-points bulletin. Slater reacted after realizing what Daniel must be thinking.

"We don't deal with APBs. We both train rookie police officers. We only protect members of Congress when we're off duty, for extra cash."

"Yeah, if we had seen it, we would've gotten in touch with you right away. We want Crane's name cleared as much as anyone. He's a solid guy."

## Chapter 18

The only office on third floor of the FBI building in Quantico, Virginia, seeing any action was the one temporarily occupied by Special Agent Daniel Falcone. Most of his colleagues had left for the day hours ago. Lately, Daniel hadn't had much of an opportunity to get his office work done. Late at night, either at home or at the Bureau, was when he did some of his most creative thinking. There was so much going on in both the Alvin Fitch and John Christy murders that no one involved in either investigation got to spend much time anywhere but in the field. Now that Daniel had the president's special project on top of everything else, taking the time to separate himself from the chaos and reflect was imperative.

Hoping to confirm and bolster the statements of Clerici and Slater, he made a call to the Fitch task force coordinator immediately after leaving the police headquarters. He asked the coordinator to have several of the field investigators assigned to reanalyze the surveillance tapes they had obtained from the Ritz, Jackson Memorial Hospital, and the Miami Beach Convention Center. The project was greatly simplified now that they had a real suspect and a face to go with it.

The results were almost as good as Daniel had hoped. Billy Ray was recorded several times getting on and off the elevators and at the main entrance of the Ritz the day before and the day of the senator's assassination. He was also seen using a key card to gain access to a fourth-floor room. When the investigator called the hotel to determine who was staying in that room during that time, he was told it was vacant. The statement was not credible, leading Daniel to believe that either someone at the hotel was involved or Billy Ray had found a way to manipulate the records.

Convention Center cameras had captured Billy Ray getting out of a taxi and entering through the front doors, and also caught his interaction with the Capitol Police officers in the lobby. Inside banquet hall A, he was recorded serving dinner to Senator Fitch and filling and refilling his drinks over the course of the meal. Kitchen surveillance equipment marked Billy Ray performing a variety of activities, the most suspicious being a trip to the walk-in refrigerator. His departure from the Convention Center was no less suspect, because he left before any of the other servers were dismissed for the evening.

The hospital videos were the only disappointment. Due to concern for patient privacy, the corridors had no surveillance system. The only cameras were at the main, emergency, ICU, operating room, and outpatient entrances, and Billy Ray had not been recorded in any of those locations. Despite this setback, the team was very close to having enough for an indictment. The only evidence missing was the smoking gun—a connection linking Billy Ray to the medication that led to Fitch's death.

Daniel spent the rest of his day in his office at Quantico, communicating with his Fitch task force and arranging a full-throttle manhunt for Billy Ray Johnson. The first order of business was to place Billy Ray on the FBI's "Ten Most Wanted" list. Christopher Frye was disseminating photographs of Billy Ray to all the local and national news stations. They had agreed to broadcast the FBI's efforts to find him, specifying that he was wanted in connection with the assassination of Alvin Fitch. The same was requested of the major print news media, both newspaper and Internet.

Andrew, Kyle, and Troy Lansbury; Keith Simms; Richard Kraft; and Tabitha Freemont were all brought in for questioning. It was more than evident that some higher authority had given them the same instruction in the event they were contacted again by the authorities. The first words out of all six mouths contained the word "lawyer." At that point, no interviews could be conducted, nor could anyone be jailed. The evidence-gathering process regarding those subjects was still in its infancy. Though the case that Daniel was building against Billy Ray and his cohorts was gathering momentum by the day, the evidence against all concerned was purely circumstantial. For Billy Ray's possible coconspirators, the evidence wasn't enough to legally detain any of them. Once they exercised their Fifth Amendment rights, the agents were forced to release them all.

After completing the work generated by Clerici's identification of Billy Ray in the Fitch case, Daniel spent the rest of the night focusing on FBI agent John Christy's murder. Since the body found buried in Georgia was for all intents and purposes identified as Christy, the workload for that task force had doubled. Based on an obvious connection between the agent's and Fitch's murder and to create a better balance, Daniel and Ed Harding agreed to join forces. Both men were certain the Klan had a hand in Christy's murder. This was especially true in light of the latest discoveries.

Besides the photo lineup identification of Billy Ray Johnson, the most significant finding to date did not come from the hair and carpet fibers found at the burial site. Everyone on the investigative team ultimately agreed with Daniel's conclusion that Christy's body had been dropped from the balcony to the ground below. The vital evidence was found in the subsequent search of the bushes underneath the balcony of the Westin hotel room where Christy was staying. The lab managed to lift a partial print from a button that had detached from the victim's shirt. Kenny Jones was now locked up in a federal prison in Georgia and charged with first-degree murder of a federal agent. Neither Daniel nor Harding's men had convinced him to talk yet.

237

After reviewing the initial information gathered, Daniel believed that Jones had not acted alone or played a leading role in the murder. When first notified there was a fingerprint match, Daniel had expected a rap sheet for Jones with as many pages as a James Michener novel. He was surprised to find that not only was Jones clean, he was a practicing member of the Georgia Bar. It was through the Bar's fingerprint database that they made the comparison.

It was less of a shock that the suspect was a childhood friend of Billy Ray Johnson. Information uncovered by the research team revealed that Jones's parents were long-time members of the Klan who were still quite active in the organization. That discovery did not settle Daniel's questions regarding Jones's participation. By all accounts including those of Jones's friends, neighbors, and family, he had separated himself from his kin and their belief system at the time he left home to attend college. If it were just the blood relations and friends from Mississippi making such a claim, Daniel would have taken it with a pillar of salt, but that was not the case. Task force members interviewed former classmates from Mississippi State, along with Jones's friends and acquaintances in Savannah. Daniel had no reason to believe they weren't telling the truth. They all agreed that Jones abhorred the Klan and all the principles the racist organization supported. There was more to this relationship between Kenny Jones and Billy Ray Johnson than met the eye, and Daniel had every intention of getting to the bottom of it.

Daniel was leaning toward the theory that Billy Ray had at least played a role in the murder and was probably the mastermind. There was no known connection between Jones and any of the Klan members who were in Savannah that weekend, other than Billy Ray. Daniel's priority at the moment was to find out exactly how Jones fit into the puzzle. At a minimum, Jones had been present when the body was moved.

Based on the pattern of lividity, the medical examiner could say with reasonable certainty that the shallow grave was not the murder site. Microscopic examination of the carpet fiber by the FBI's Evidence Response Team revealed that it was a match to the carpets in the Westin Resort, lending credence to the argument that Christy was killed in his room.

Soon after Jones's arrest, the task force got a court order from a local judge requiring his saliva to be swabbed for genetic analysis. DNA test results from the hair found at the crime scene were compared to the genetic code of the saliva. They proved to be identical, putting Jones at the burial site as well.

Daniel planned to pay a visit to the federal prison in Florida where the only suspect in custody was currently incarcerated. This was his biggest lead since Tabitha Freemont and the recent photo ID in the effort to establish the Klan's participation in the Fitch assassination. Daniel was going to try to convince the federal prosecutor to offer some kind of deal for Jones's cooperation. A favorable plea negotiation could be what finally motivated him to talk.

There seemed to be something more to Jones's silence than merely protection of his rights. If Daniel could discover his true motivation, he could use it to the Bureau's advantage. He doubted that loyalty to the Klan was keeping Jones mum. The solution could lie in the reason for Kenny's apparent allegiance to Billy Ray Johnson.

Before leaving the office, Daniel called the United States Penitentiary in Coleman, near Wildwood, to notify them he would be there the next day to interview Kenny Jones. His flight to Orlando International Airport was scheduled to leave from Reagan Airport at eight in the morning. He set up the meeting with

Jones for one p.m., then called a rental car company to arrange for ground transportation. After all preparations for his trip were complete, he stuffed his personal travel files for the Alvin Fitch and John Christy murders in his briefcase, closed down his office, and headed for his temporary apartment at the opposite end of the FBI compound. If he was lucky, he might get five hours' sleep before his alarm woke him at an ungodly hour.

* * *

The Blue Ridge Mountains in Northern Georgia were the southern terminus of the Appalachian range. The maximum elevation south of the Carolina border was around 4,600 feet. Since the climate was not conducive to snow, there were no ski resorts, nor did that part of the state attract much tourism. Most of the towns in the Georgia highlands were sparsely populated, making them an ideal hiding place for Billy Ray Johnson and Kyle Lansbury. They chose the city of Dillard, population 198, at least half of whom were known to Billy Ray as members of the Ku Klux Klan. The remaining residents were ultraconservative and either family members or close friends of Klan affiliates. Fewer than a hundred occupied housing units stood on the heavily wooded area of 1.5 square miles at 2,100 feet above sea level. Billy Ray and Kyle were living in a 3,200-square-foot chalet owned under an alias by Keith Peterson's maternal grandparents. The house sat on five acres of forested mountainside overlooking the old Sky Valley Ski Resort. Keith Peterson's grandparents had bought it as a rental property for the ski season. Since the slopes had closed down, it stayed empty year round. When it became obvious that both Billy Ray and Kyle needed to go on the lam, Keith offered the chalet to them as a hideaway.

240

Most of the Klan members who owned homes in Dillard were originally from Jackson, Mississippi. Some lived in the small Georgia town year round. For others, their cabin or chalet was a summer home. For Billy Ray, it was the ideal site for the headquarters of a military installation. He and his family had invested in thirty acres of woodland southwest of Dillard under a fictitious name. From the time of its purchase, the property had been earmarked for construction of a guerrilla training camp. Clearing of the land was scheduled to begin within the next couple of months. Billy Ray was already in contact with underworld arms dealers and was planning to invest the money he had earned through Brody, to buy an arsenal of weapons fit to equip a small country's army. The construction project would begin as soon as he completed the mission with Brody.

Not being able to move about freely had been an annoying impediment. He had expected that sooner or later, the authorities might suspect the Klan and him specifically. It was inevitable that he would be forced to take advantage of one of the many suitable small Southern towns to hide and prepare for his next move. He just hadn't expected it to happen so soon. Mistakes had been made, and he would just have to learn from them. When all was said and done, he would be sure the Klan got the credit anyway. The time would come only when he was certain he had the upper hand.

The steps Billy Ray had taken to avoid being identified by the authorities had been for naught. Special Agent Daniel Falcone was proving to be a major thorn in his side. From what he understood from his inside sources in D.C., Falcone was leading the investigation. The FBI now had access to Kenny Jones. That was much more than just a passing concern. His former high school buddy was likely the loosest cannon he could think of. So far, he was keeping his mouth shut. Billy Ray wasn't overly confident it would last. He had gone over

241

several scenarios in his mind and with Keith Peterson. If the Feds offered Jones the right deal, he might sing like a bird. It was one thing to be sought for questioning when the FBI was dealing exclusively with circumstantial evidence. It was something altogether different when an accomplice pinned a murder rap on you—especially of a law enforcement agent. This wasn't a situation Billy Ray could afford to ignore.

* * *

The U.S. Penitentiary, Coleman near Wildwood, Florida, was a high-security facility for male prisoners convicted of noncapital or capital federal crimes. It also had a detention center for pretrial and holdover inmates, including those charged with murder. Kenny Jones was being housed in the detention center, which was in the southwest corner of the same building as the prison for permanent inmates. From the moment Kenny was placed behind bars, he feared for his life. He hoped keeping his mouth shut might be enough to keep him alive. Unless he was sequestered from the rest of the prison population, his chances of survival were not good.

The idea that his silence might not be enough to save his life gave him the incentive to play a more active role in assuring his well-being. No doubt, Billy Ray would be concerned that he might talk, and a scared Billy Ray Johnson was a very dangerous animal. Refusal to cooperate with the authorities would probably afford Kenny only a negligible advantage, perhaps none at all. Ronald Hill, Kenny's friend and lawyer told him that Agent Falcone was coming to pay a visit the next day. Kenny was seriously thinking about making a deal for his protection. Considering the desperate nature of his situation, it couldn't hurt. It

242

may even be possible to negotiate an agreement for his release. He had a lot of very good information he could share with the authorities—enough to put Billy Ray and a lot of his friends and family away for a long time. He would certainly keep open to that option.

\* \* \*

Prison Guard Trent Blake walked through the entrance at the Federal Penitentiary in Wildwood at exactly 6:45 p.m. to report for the evening shift, then went straight to the locker room of the main facility. He quickly changed out of his street clothes into his uniform, hoping for time to grab a cup of coffee before his shift started. He hadn't gotten his normal eight hours of sleep last night. Early yesterday morning, he had received an unexpected call from his cousin's Ku Klux Klan recruiter, Keith Peterson, asking for a favor.

Peterson wasn't Trent's favorite person in the world. They had met when Trent visited his cousin last month in New York. The guy was rude, cocky as hell, and didn't seem to have much use for Trent, who was also interested in joining the organization. A few weeks later, Trent had learned that his cousin warned Keith of a slew of Trent's vices that made him an unfit candidate for the Klan.

Ordinarily, Trent wouldn't even consider giving him the time of day, but what Keith was offering in payment was too good to refuse. The money he would receive for this job couldn't have come at a better time. He would be able to pay off a few gambling and drug debts that had become a major nuisance in his life, and still have a decent chunk of change left over. To be sure, some risk was involved. Luckily, he had some experience with this particular kind of request. It wouldn't be the first time he had orchestrated the murder of an inmate. Trent had been supplied the weapon at the time the deal was struck, along with a hefty down payment. Before leaving for the prison, he put the shiv in a backpack with the personal items he carried to work every day.

After fastening his belt and donning his prison guard jacket, Trent put his street clothes in his locker, securing it with a combination padlock. He proceeded to his scheduled work site, Cell Block C, went directly to the break room, and poured himself that cup of coffee he was craving.

His post was in one of the more dangerous sections of the prison. It was also where Jones was housed. Keith had been quite clear that he wanted the job done as quickly as possible. The inmates would be done with dinner, most likely playing cards, watching TV, making phone calls, or just relaxing in their cells. It was one of the more common times for a fight to break out among prisoners.

Trent had been employed by the Federal Bureau of Prisons for more than ten years. For most of that time, he was considered one of the best prison guards in the system. He had worked his way up the chain of command and had aspirations one day to become warden of his own penitentiary. Everything was going along according to schedule while Trent worked obsessively to achieve his goals—that is, until all his hopes and dreams were obliterated the day a fellow prison guard offered him his first Oxycodone pain pill.

Trent had been diagnosed with addictive personality disorder when he was an adolescent. He was in fourth grade and failing every subject when his parents discovered that he was spending most of his waking hours in front of a computer screen, playing video games. Until his introduction to Oxycodone, he had avoided addiction to more harmful substances or behaviors by following the instructions of his childhood therapist. Through the rest of his youth and part of his early adult life, he had done a damn good job directing his attention to productive and positive activities.

He couldn't have made a worse choice accepting his first Percocet. It was considered one of the most addictive of all the recreational narcotics. The feeling of euphoria and well-being it produced was an experience he had been chasing ever since his first high. Currently, he was either consuming orally, snorting, or shooting up fifteen or more thirty-milligram tablets of the pain medication per day. With the cost on the street up to twelve dollars per pill, it had become a more than one-thousand-dollar-a-week habit.

His salary as a prison guard was barely enough to pay for his monthly living expenses, much less his addiction. As a result, he was obliged to turn to other means of earning income, most of them illegal. He tried betting on football and baseball games. That just added to his mounting dependencies and debt. It put him into contact with loan sharks, from whom he had borrowed large sums of money for both gambling and drugs.

It was unavoidable that his disease should affect his job performance at the prison. He was eventually demoted to his former rank and placed on the evening shift. The demotion came with a salary cut, compounding his problems. To make up for the cut in pay, he became part of the elaborate prison drug-dealing enterprise. The same colleague who had introduced him to Oxycodone invited him to share in the profits of the world of corrupt prison guards.

He learned quickly that once you got involved in the sale of drugs in the corrections system, murder was an integral part of the process. Huge amounts of money were changing hands among hardened, violent career criminals. Eventually, the commerce was bound to lead to heightened tensions and loss of life. Trent had already arranged for the murder of two inmates who were stealing from his stash. It was fairly easy to get away with when you had fellow officers who would support your story and drug-addicted prisoners who had nothing to lose.

This particular murder was going to be different. There would be no witnesses or conspiracies. Trent was ordered to get it done on his own. That was a next-to-impossible feat considering all the cameras and surveillance at a prison facility. What Keith and his pals didn't know wouldn't hurt him. Trent wasn't willing to go to jail or give up the unbelievable amount of money they were offering. He knew exactly how he was going to handle the situation.

Paying an inmate to help would barely make a dent in his earnings. If he chose wisely, the perpetrator would never be a credible witness against him. He and his fellow officers had used prisoners on several occasions in the past to get their dirty work done, with no repercussions. They were a loyal bunch. Three of the lifers on Jones's cell block were Trent's customers. An offer of a month's worth of free stash ought to be more than enough.

All three were raving maniacs. Eightball was the logical choice. He had the cell next to Jones's. He was serving a life sentence for murdering eight federal employees in a random shooting. Later the same day, he shot his wife and her three children to death. His trial for the latter case was pending, with the government seeking the death penalty. The conviction and sentence were all but certain. Taking a human life for a month's supply of heroin would be a heaven-sent deal for a man without a future.

As Trent made his first patrol of the cell block, he noticed that Eightball was watching television in the rec room while Jones was lying in his cell, reading a book. After completing the run, Trent returned to the rec room and stepped inside. Eightball, who was due for a fix, looked up immediately, and Trent gave him the nod to follow. He led the way to the inmate gym, which at this time of night was never in use. Trent's back was to him when Eightball walked in twenty seconds later.

"I need you to do something for me, Eightball. It's big and I can pay you big."

"What you need, boss?"

"I need you to stick it to the new inmate, Jones. You know him?"

"He's the guy who offed the federal agent, right? He can't be all that bad."

"This is no jokin' matter. I want him to stop breathing."

"What's in it for me?"

"Two weeks of free dope."

"Bullshit. I ain't doin' it. That ain't nothin'"

"What the fuck, man? We're talking three thousand dollars' worth of heroin, easy."

"I don't give a shit. It ain't enough. Give me two months and I might think about it."

"Listen, asshole. I could cut you off completely. Besides, you know guys that would do it for less, and so do I. I'll give you a month's worth. And no coming back for more free shit when that's done. That's the deal, take it or leave it."

"All right, man, I'll do it. But I need some tonight."

"You'll get it right after it's done. You can do it right now. He's in his cell, reading a book. I'm going to put gloves on and act like I'm searching you for drugs. I'll slip an eight-inch shiv in your back pocket and cover it with your shirt. Make sure you stick him good. He's gotta die."

\* \* \*

Kenny Jones was drifting in and out of sleep while trying to read a science fiction novel he had borrowed from the prison library. It wasn't the story that had him nodding off every few lines. He hadn't gotten a good night's sleep since his arrest for the murder of the FBI agent—mostly because he was keeping an eye out for potential danger. A prison guard surreptitiously entering his cell in the middle of the night and slitting his throat was not out of the realm of possibility. Exhaustion was setting in, but for the moment, he preferred to stay wide awake and alert. Lights-out and lockdown were scheduled in fifteen minutes, maybe less. Prisoners were still roaming freely about the cell block.

He tossed the paperback under his bunk, stood up, and paced the floor of his little cage to get his blood flowing. Three short steps, then three short steps back. Plans for his scheduled interview with the FBI agent now dominated his thoughts. He had made the decision to share information with Falcone if it would save his life. The idea of convulsing and frothing at the mouth in a gas chamber sent shivers up his spine. He wasn't mentally equipped to deal with the prospect of dying. Though life in prison wasn't a great alternative, he could learn to manage. There were ways to stay alive. The chance that Billy Ray could end up behind bars also made the thought much more palatable. Kenny shouldn't have to take the whole rap without gaining some benefit. In the event they didn't release him for the information he was willing to provide, they could at least transfer him to a more secure location. In the meantime, he had to keep looking over his shoulder at all times.

Kenny returned to his bunk and slouched with his head and upper back propped up against the back wall. He laid the book aside. In this position, he could keep awake with an eye on his open cell door.

\* \* \*

Three minutes later, Jones's snores resounded in the hallway outside his cell, where Eightball was psyching himself up to enter. Eightball thought he might have a fight on his hands, and Kenny Jones could be a formidable foe. He was a big boy, at least six feet and about two hundred pounds, while Eightball was maybe five-six on his tippy-toes. What he lacked in height, he made up for in attitude and strength. Still, the less complicated the kill, the better. If he could make it to bunkside without waking Jones up, he could probably avoid a tussle. Unless Jones was faking the snores, he had to be in a fairly deep sleep.

Eightball had used up all the time he could afford. At any moment, a guard could pass by, and it would be a disaster if he couldn't get the job done before lockdown. Blake had made it crystal clear: do it tonight or no dope. Eightball walked the few feet to the doorway to Jones's cell and walked in. Two more steps, and he was at the head of the bunk, where Kenny continued snoring away. This was going to be a cinch. Eightball pulled the shiv from his hip pocket and eased closer to his sleeping victim. As he cocked his arm back to strike the fatal blow, suddenly and unexpectedly, Kenny Jones opened his eyes. It took steely resolve, but Eightball couldn't let surprise veer him off course, not if he wanted to get high tonight.

In the split second before the weapon penetrated Jones's throat, Eightball could tell that his victim recognized his fate. There was no time for a

249

defensive maneuver. The blade first cut through the Adam's apple and vocal chords, then tore open the carotid artery. That one blow would have been ample to bleed Jones to death. It wasn't enough for Eightball. He kept stabbing at Jones's throat until he was absolutely sure there was no chance for survival.

\* \* \*

Kenny tried to scream for help. The most he could muster was a raspy release of air. He finally tried to grab the shiv from Eightball's hand, but it was far too late. He barely had the strength to raise his arm. The realization that he had only seconds to live made him ignore the pain. It did nothing to abate his dread in the least. Each second that passed seemed like an hour of pure terror. Finally, as the blood slowed from a rhythmic spurting to a slow dribble, he drifted out of consciousness. Less than a minute later, he was dead.

**Chapter 19**

Daniel was livid when he learned of Kenny Jones's death and the way the prison authorities had handled it. The incompetence of the staff was almost beyond imagining. They had made many blunders, with sloppy treatment of the crime scene just the tip of the iceberg. Then there was another nagging matter: Daniel had worried that Jones's life could be in danger, without acting on it. He was just as angry with himself for not insisting on additional protection. What made it all the more exasperating was his feeling that he could have convinced Jones to cooperate.

Too many factors pointed at this being much more than a simple case of inmate conflict. One of the more obvious ones was the great *convenience* of Jones's death. He was a key witness to the murder of a federal agent, if not a coconspirator. The Ku Klux Klan had had too much to lose if he were to talk. The fact that prison guards trampled over vital evidence, got their fingerprints on the murder weapon, and failed to seal off the cell before the appropriate authorities could properly inspect the crime scene was suspicious in itself.

Delta's flight 1275 was making its final approach into Orlando International Airport as Daniel tried to let go of his frustration and prepare for a long and trying day. He was planning to spend the entire morning and afternoon at the prison. Depending on how things went, there was a significant chance he could be staying through tomorrow.

When he finished up in Florida, Daniel wouldn't be returning directly to D.C. Just yesterday, the task force research team had made an interesting discovery. He already had the squad secretary at Quantico book him an open-ended return flight to Jackson, valid through the following evening. It was time to

251

put even more pressure on Billy Ray Johnson's family. Daniel was particularly interested in speaking with his ex-wife. Former spouses were often a good source of information, especially if the marriage had ended poorly. Harding's team had never interviewed her, because they couldn't locate her. She had remarried and was now going by the name Sarah Thorpe in Ashland, Mississippi, a small town just south of the Tennessee line. Daniel planned to visit with Billy Ray's parents in Jackson, then drive the fifty-six miles north to Ashland to have a chat with Mrs. Thorpe.

The Boeing 767 touched down at 10:21 a.m., and by 10:35, Daniel was in his rented Lincoln Town Car, on his way to the federal penitentiary. The pen was just ten miles northeast of the airport, and he arrived less than fifteen minutes later. Ed Harding and the prison warden greeted him in the administration office. According to Harding, the Evidence Response Team was already conducting an inspection of the cell. Daniel asked the Warden if he could get a look, too, and the warden escorted him and Harding there personally.

As they approached, Daniel saw three FBI agents inside the cell, holding magnifying glasses and closely inspecting the walls, floor, and bed. He knew they would search every inch of every surface, looking for any trace evidence that might tell the story of Kenny Jones's violent and untimely death. So far, they had found human hairs on the floor, bed, and walls. Most of them were blond, the color of the victim's hair. They also discovered at least three other types of hair that did not belong to Jones. Though the identity of the murderer had been established beyond the shadow of a doubt, Harding and Daniel wanted to collect as much physical evidence as possible that might confirm or disprove others' involvement.

The prisoner known as Eightball had already confessed to the murder. The surveillance tapes showing him entering the cell just beforehand, then exiting covered in blood, confirmed his story. The FBI agents had every intention of conducting a thorough interrogation of the suspect and hoped to get him to admit he hadn't acted on his own.

There was no reason to delay the interview. So when the examination of the cell was complete, Daniel and Warren asked to be taken to Eightball. He had been transferred to solitary confinement immediately after he was cleaned of the blood from the incident. That was another of Daniel's frustrations. He and his team would never know what important evidence might have been washed down the drain as a result of the prison's poor judgment and hasty response. Now their most valuable source of information was a mass murderer—not a very encouraging prospect.

Eightball was well aware his actions would not give him much of a reprieve from solitary. He had orders from Trent Blake, who had been surreptitiously providing him with the promised heroin. The first words out of Eightball's mouth after he sat down across from the FBI agents in the warden's office were the last words they wanted to hear: "I want a lawyer." The conversation ended in the same moment it started.

For the next several hours, Daniel watched video of Kenny Jones's cell door and other parts of the prison where Kenny or Eightball might have been recorded. In the meantime, Harding and his men interviewed prison guards and inmates who might have information about the murder. As a favor to the San Diego agents, Daniel had volunteered to do the more tedious work, which was likely to take some time. Harding and his men were trying to get back home for a scheduled memorial service for Christy at their field office early the next morning.

253

Daniel was still watching video when all questioning had been completed and Harding and his men were already on their Learjet back to California. It was early evening when he witnessed the conversation between Trent Blake and Eightball in the prison gym. Twenty minutes later, after learning that it was Blake's day off, then obtaining his address from the administrative office, Daniel hopped into the Town Car and headed out to visit the prison guard.

Trent Blake's hometown, Fort White, population 564, was almost ninety miles northwest of the penitentiary. One of the prison guards who worked the C block had told Daniel that Blake didn't care much for Orlando, its suburbs, or any other populous area, for that matter. He was not a people person. It made no difference that his commute to work took more than an hour and a half; he would rather spend extra time on the road than fight the crowds every day.

Daniel could have a field day profiling such a personality. He chose not to call to schedule a meeting, preferring to pay Blake a surprise visit. The ninety-minute drive would give him too much time to prepare or even disappear. As a precaution, Daniel asked the staff at the prison not to warn their colleague of his imminent arrival. Daniel didn't know it, but he had caught a significant break. None of Blake's cohorts in crime were aware of Daniel's plans. After grabbing a bite to eat at a fast-food restaurant, Daniel merged onto I-75 and headed north.

* * *

The night was as quiet and peaceful as a library at three in the morning. A brisk, cold wind earlier in the evening had cleared the sky of clouds, unveiling a universe of brilliant heavenly bodies. Trent Blake sat on the front porch of his cabin, staring into the star-studded vault. It had a calming effect after the stress of the past eighteen hours. He hadn't gotten a wink of sleep since he left the prison yesterday evening. He was running on fumes and happy to have the next couple of nights off to catch up on some well-needed rest. If it hadn't been for his conversation with Keith Peterson earlier in the day, he might have dozed off hours ago.

Concerned that his stash of Oxycodone was getting low, Trent had called Keith, demanding payment for services rendered. His aggressiveness hadn't gone over well. Keith bluntly told him he would get his money when they were good and ready to deliver it. In rather brusque terms, Keith explained that discretion was absolutely essential in matters of this nature. Transfers of such large amounts of money must be done right to avoid traceability. That wasn't what Trent wanted to hear. He insisted on receiving his money immediately, or Keith and his group of friends would be sorry. Trent didn't know exactly what he was going to do. He only wanted the asshole to believe there would be trouble.

After making a series of phone calls, Keith agreed to send someone with the money that very evening, making sleep out of the question for Trent. The excitement of having all that cash was enough to keep him up for at least another couple of hours—or so he thought. Ten minutes later, he was sound asleep on his front porch. The two thirty-milligram Percocet pills he had taken before dinner were surely a contributing factor.

Trent woke suddenly when bright headlights coming up the dirt road to his cabin shone directly on his face. He had no idea how long he had dozed. His cold hands and toes were evidence he had probably slept for more than an hour. It seemed that the temperature had dropped at least ten degrees. Rubbing his hands together, he stood up from his chair to greet the approaching vehicle. As he stepped off the front porch, he felt a burning sensation searing through his left

255

triceps. A fraction of a second later, he heard a strange cracking noise. Before he could even check what could be causing the pain, another much louder blast came from the direction of the SUV coming up his driveway. The second bullet grazed across his right ear, making him scream out in terror. The realization he was being shot at came a second too late. In the time his thought processes sent the signal to his body to hit the dirt, a third bullet hit him in the center of his forehead, penetrating through the cerebrum and lodging itself in his brain stem.

* * *

Two men dressed in black stepped out of the SUV now parked directly in front of Trent Blake's cabin. The driver walked over to the body lying on its back and placed two fingers against a carotid artery.

"I'm pretty sure he's dead, Billy Ray," said Kyle Lansbury.

"Well, go get the bag out of the truck. Paul's still at least ten minutes away. We can't leave him out here." Paul Johnson was Billy Ray's first cousin and a lifelong member of the Klan. Coincidentally, he also drove a hearse for a funeral home in Roswell, Georgia. The plan was for Paul to meet Billy Ray and Kyle at Blake's cabin, then transport the body to his funeral home's crematorium—something they probably should have done with the FBI agent. In hindsight, Billy Ray had realized he should have taken the time to drive the several hours from Savannah.

Kyle opened the hatchback of the SUV and grabbed an extra-large gusseted poly bag. He walked over to Billy Ray, who was now standing over the body with a disgusted look on his face.

"There's brains and guts all over the place. Let's get him in the bag. We can bury whatever's left over when we're done."

The bag was eight feet long and could hold two or even three bodies if necessary. Billy Ray took it from Kyle and slipped the open end over Trent's feet, then dragged the bag up the length of his body, stopping just under the chin. "Hold his head up so I can pull the bag over it," Billy Ray commanded.

"I ain't touchin' that shit with my bare hands."

"Put on a pair of gloves, then, dumb-ass. Hurry up. Who knows who could have heard those shots. I don't want any nosy neighbors coming over here to check things out."

Kyle put on the pair of gloves he had in his jacket pocket. The smell of fecal matter expelled by the corpse, combined with having to raise a dead man's head covered with blood and gore, made him want to vomit. He fought it with all his might to avoid showing any weakness in front of Billy Ray. When he placed his hands on either side of the head, Kyle could feel the soft texture of brain matter underneath his gloved fingers. The sensation nearly cost him the battle. He clenched his teeth as Billy Ray lifted the bag over the head and tied a knot to seal it.

"I'll grab his feet; you get his shoulders," said Billy Ray. "Let's get him inside."

"Hold on. Let me get the door." Kyle stepped up onto the front porch and tried the door. As expected, it was unlocked. He opened it and placed a rock at its base to be sure it stayed that way. Together, the men carried the body into the house and laid it in the corner of the small living room.

"Go get the rifles from the car," Billy Ray barked. "And shut the door behind you. It's freezing in here."

Kyle grumbled under his breath but followed Billy Ray's orders. He walked up to the passenger's side of the vehicle and was about to open the door when, to his great surprise, a voice shouted from behind him.

"FBI. Don't move or I'll shoot."

\* \* \*

The lack of streetlights was making it very difficult for Special Agent Daniel Falcone to navigate the roads of the rural north Florida town. The poor marking of street names only compounded the problem. He was wishing he had asked one of the prison guards if they had a GPS device he could borrow. Considering the remoteness of the area, it might not have helped anyway. He wondered if half these streets were even on the map. Many of them weren't even paved. According to the directions he had punched up online, he should have come upon Trent Blake's street a mile or so back. He retraced his path several times, to no avail. After making a fourth U-turn, he noticed an old man on the side of the road, walking his Jack Russell terrier. He pulled off on the shoulder next to the man and rolled down the window.

"Excuse me, sir. Can you tell me if there's an Elm Street in the area?"

At first, the odd old man stared curiously at Daniel as if this were the first time he had seen another human being in his life. For several seconds, he inspected the stranger and his car without saying a word. Finally, just as Daniel was about to repeat his question, the man said, "What address you looking for?"

"Two-fifteen Elm Street. Do you know Trent Blake?"

As the man began to speak in response, the sound of gunfire came from what seemed a short distance away.

258

"That sounded like gunshots coming from his place," said the old man.

"How do I get there?"

"You know Mr. Blake?"

"Please, sir, I'm an FBI agent." Daniel showed him his badge. "I need to get there fast."

"There's a small dirt road a quarter mile west of here on the north side of the road. You'll need to turn around. It's easy to miss. There's a big boulder about my height on the swale just before the turn. Take a left on that road and it'll take you right up to his cabin."

Without saying another word, Daniel skidded off the road's shoulder and onto the main street and hooked a quick U-turn. He kept his eyes peeled for Blake's street. In the past twenty minutes, a bank of clouds had rolled in, blocking the light from the moon and stars and creating pitch-black conditions. At the last instant before he passed it, he caught sight of the boulder in his peripheral vision. He veered the car left so that the headlights illuminated the dirt road directly ahead. According to the MapQuest directions, Trent Blake's house should be .2 miles from the intersection.

Daniel was concerned his headlights could tip off his arrival. He considered extinguishing them, but it was so dark, he didn't dare. The canopy of trees overhead muted the little bit of light penetrating the overcast skies. Without headlights, he was bound to crash into a tree.

Proceeding slowly across the soft, dusty earth to make as little noise as possible, Daniel readied himself for a potential conflict. He removed his Sig Sauer 229 revolver from the holster vest inside his jacket. Holding it in his right hand while steering with his left, he continued at walking speed toward the cabin. He switched off his lights before breaking out of a patch of woods into a clearing.

A hundred yards ahead, through a less dense hammock of trees, he saw an SUV parked in front of the only house in the area. He parked his rental car on the side of the road and surveyed the yard. There appeared to be some commotion in front of the SUV. He slipped on a pair of gloves, switched the overhead light off to prevent it from turning on, then opened the door slowly.

The wind had picked up. With the moisture in the air, it felt to Daniel as though a snowstorm was imminent, even though this was Florida. A blast of chilly air swept across his face, stinging his eyes momentarily. In the distance, he could hear the mumbled conversation of at least two men. Due to the howling of the wind and rustling of leaves, he couldn't make out what they were saying. Using the trees as cover, he crept forward. By the time he reached the last line of evergreens at the edge of the cleared property line, the men were already inside the house.

Holding his gun out in front, arms outstretched, he came out from behind the tree and proceeded toward the house some fifty yards from where he stood. He kept his eyes trained on the front door and windows as he continued up the driveway. Moving silently and surreptitiously up to the SUV, he looked in through the passenger window to see two semiautomatic hunting rifles lying in between the seats. He was about to open the door to confiscate the weapons when he heard voices coming from inside the house. He quickly ducked behind the truck just in time to conceal himself from the man coming out of the cabin. He peeked around the rear bumper. The light from the cabin was enough for him to make out the man's face. It was Kyle Lansbury. As soon as Lansbury turned toward the passenger door and was about to open it, Daniel stepped out from behind the SUV with his gun drawn.

"FBI. Don't move or I'll shoot."

260

Kyle turned his head to see a man with a handgun trained on his chest. He thought about shouting out to Billy Ray, then reconsidered. The FBI agent seemed serious.

"Where's Trent Blake?" Daniel inquired.

"He's inside."

"Is there anyone else on the property besides you and Blake?"

"No, just the two of us."

"Put your hands up against the car and stand with your legs spread."

When Kyle complied, Daniel slowly approached him to pat him down, doing his best to keep an eye on the door and his subject. In the fraction of a second he spent turned toward Kyle to check for weapons, the front door swung open. Daniel turned toward the house to see Billy Ray aiming a handgun at his head.

"Drop the gun or I'll blow your head off," Billy Ray said.

"You don't want to do this, Billy Ray," said Daniel.

"Shut the fuck up and drop the gun now, or your dead." Billy Ray was both surprised and irate that Daniel had already identified him. He contemplated shooting him on the spot. After a moment, he thought better of it, deciding it might be a good idea to ask a few questions.

Hearing the maniacal tone of Billy Ray's voice, Daniel opted for discretion. "All right, all right. I'm putting it down." Daniel laid the gun on the ground in front of him.

"Now, kick it toward him," Billy Ray ordered, pointing at Kyle.

Once again, Daniel followed Billy Ray's instructions and pushed the gun with his foot in Kyle's direction. Kyle picked it up and immediately aimed it at Daniel's forehead.

"Now, hold on. Don't even think about shooting him. Maybe he can be useful." Turning to Daniel, Billy Ray asked, "How the hell do you know my name?"

"It doesn't matter how I know your name. You're in a whole lot of trouble. You're just going to make matters worse if you continue with this. If you turn yourself in and cooperate, this'll end a lot better."

"You're not the one in control here, asshole. If you don't want a bullet in the head, I suggest you start talking fast. And don't think I won't do it. I'm only gonna ask one more time. How do you know my name?"

"I'm an FBI agent. Your face has been all over the news for the last day or so. Listen, harming me will only make matters a lot worse. I can help you. If you cooperate, we can work something out."

"Fuck you and fuck the FBI. Who the fuck are y'all to say I've done anything wrong? Kyle, there's some twine in the tool box in the back of rig. Grab it. You"—he waved the gun at Daniel—"get inside."

Daniel started to say something, but Billy Ray cut him off with another threat. The deranged look in his eyes told Daniel that for the moment, it was probably best to do what he said. Billy Ray had the upper hand. Daniel had taken some courses in hostage negotiation, though he was far from an expert in the field. Offering Billy Ray leniency for cooperation was one of the most common strategies that negotiators used. Billy Ray was obviously not impressed. Daniel supposed he could count his blessings for still being alive. Now he had to figure out how to stay that way.

"What the fuck did you say my name for?" asked Kyle. "He might not a' known it."

"Didn't you hear what he said, you dumb fuck? My face isn't the only one that's been all over the news. He knows exactly who you are." Looking toward Daniel, Billy Ray asked, "By the way, what's your name?"

"Daniel Falcone."

* * *

Billy Ray couldn't believe his luck. This was the guy the people in Washington said was heading the investigation of the Alvin Fitch assassination. He was also the one who seemed to be making the most headway. "You're the asshole that's been harassing my family and friends. You haven't been that nice to Kyle's folks, either. We don't take kindly to people treating our kin like that, do we, Kyle?"

"Fuck no," Kyle replied, like the obedient pawn that he was.

"Let's get him tied up," said Billy Ray. "I know exactly what we're gonna do with this prick. You," he said to Daniel. "Don't even try anything stupid. It'll be the last move you make." Billy Ray drafted a plan in a matter of seconds. A bullet to the head was too easy a death for this guy. He wanted Special Agent Daniel Falcone to experience fear and suffering in the worst way imaginable.

Trent Blake's home was a small log cabin with four or five rooms, depending on whether you considered the dining area a separate room. The table where Trent Blake used to eat his meals was set in a large open space between the kitchen and living room. There was only one bedroom with an adjoining bathroom. The house was sparsely furnished; its few pieces were all wood.

Kyle sat Daniel in one of the dining room chairs on the far side of the table as Billy Ray closed the curtains of the window overlooking the front porch. While Kyle tied Daniel to the chair with the nylon mason's twine from the SUV, Billy Ray inspected the living room and kitchen areas. He was tweaking his plan based on what was available. He quickly pulled his cell phone from his jacket pocket and phoned Paul to call him off, at least for the time being. At this point, it was best not to have any other vehicles show up at the property. There were a few other houses in the area. Now that a law enforcement officer was involved, the less conspicuous they were, the better.

\* \* \*

Daniel didn't like what he was seeing. Billy Ray was spending an awfully long time behind the gas oven. The pipes would be connected to a propane tank somewhere on the property. After Billy Ray was through with his work in the kitchen, he made his way to the control mechanism that operated the gas fireplace in the living room. From where he sat, Daniel couldn't tell exactly what Billy Ray was doing. He suspected that the switch had a timing device.

Billy Ray's intentions were undeniable. Daniel's first thoughts were for his boys. They had already been through so much with the loss of their mother. The devastation they would suffer from his death would be tough to overcome. Knowing the type of evil he was dealing with, he didn't like his chances of survival. For the sake of his boys, Annie, and the rest of his family and loved ones, he had to give survival his best effort.

"Billy Ray, you really don't want to do this. There are other ways to make your voice heard. I can tell you're an intelligent and passionate man who loves his country. Your beliefs may be different, but we have the best system in the world for someone like you who wants to share his ideas with the world. You can do it without murdering hundreds of innocent people. I can help you get in touch with some of the most powerful people in our country."

Billy Ray had set the timer on the fireplace to ignite the flames ten minutes later. He apparently didn't have any desire to listen to Daniel's pleas for mercy.

"I don't need your fucked up advice. And I sure don't need your help. Let's get the fuck outta here, Kyle."

"Aren't you gonna put a bullet in his brain?" Kyle asked.

"I'm doing things my way. Can you think of a worse or more painful way to die?" Billy Ray was clearly speaking in a voice loud enough for Daniel to hear. A malevolent smile marred his otherwise handsome face.

Before Daniel had the chance to say another word, Billy Ray lit the pilot light with a match he found in a kitchen drawer and the two men were out the door. Daniel heard the fading sounds of footsteps, then the car engine as it moved away from the house and onto the main road. His heart was pounding. If Billy Ray wanted him to suffer, he had chosen the perfect means. Daniel had seen a person burn to death and its aftermath on many occasions. He would never forget the car chase for the wanted gang leader and the screams of the Fort Lauderdale detective engulfed in the flames of his smoldering police vehicle. It was the last way he wanted to die.

If he had any chance of surviving this, he couldn't let his fear blur his thought processes. He forced himself to think. The twine binding him to the chair was tied beyond tight. He expended every ounce of his strength to free himself, to no avail. He could already smell a faint odor of propane. He had only a few minutes before the fireplace ignited and set the cabin on fire.

**Chapter 20**

Sam Blackwell lived with Puddin', his Jack Russell terrier, in the log cabin he had erected with his own two hands more than ten years ago. He had built the house in the country for his wife, who was his world. For over thirty-five years of marriage, he had worshipped the ground she walked on. It was a terrible tragedy that Mrs. Blackwell never got the chance to enjoy the cabin she had dreamed of since she was a child. To live in the wilderness, away from the rat race of the big city, was an idea that had always fascinated her. Wildlife and living off the land were almost an obsession. She had fantasized about living in a secluded mountain cabin someday. Because her 55-year-old husband had been diagnosed with Raynaud's syndrome, a vascular-constricting disease exacerbated by the cold, she had settled for Fort White, Florida. Tragically, she would never cross her cabin's threshold. Just two weeks before they were to move in, she was run over while on her way to visit a neighbor. A driver of a van was typing a text message, veered off the road, jumped the curb and hit Mrs. Blackwell on the sidewalk.

To honor her memory, Mr. Blackwell had hopped on a plane and moved into the cabin the very day his wife was buried. He had been essentially living the life of a recluse ever since. With no children or family back in his home state of New York, he never set foot there again.

The only times he actually went beyond the boundaries of his property in Florida were to walk his dog and pick up supplies at the nearest shopping center, over twenty miles away. He was always sure to stock up as much as possible, to minimize the need to leave the house.

His nearest neighbor was Trent Blake. Sam made it a point to avoid any contact with the man. The only reason he even knew his name was because he had mistakenly received some of Blake's mail. Neither man had any interest in being friends.

Among the people who lived in the small town, Sam Blackwell was known as the "crazy hermit." As far as anyone knew, he never left his home to visit with other human beings, nor did he ever receive a guest. Adults didn't want anything to do with him, and children feared him. He was the villain of many an urban legend of murder and mayhem spread by kids and grown-ups alike. Of course, Sam couldn't care less what the people of his town thought of him. He had no use for them or anyone else. If he never had the company of another person for the remainder of his days, he would consider his life perfect. So long as the townspeople left him alone and minded their own business, he had no interest in getting involved in theirs.

Immediately after the FBI agent sped off in the direction of Blake's cabin, Sam headed straight back to his property. Other than the few people he was obligated to speak with while buying food and other necessities, the agent was the first person he had talked to in more years than he could remember. If Sam wanted to know what was happening on Blake's land, he could have hopped in his jeep and been there in less than five minutes, for the property was a half mile away as the crow flew. Sam knew no such curiosity. He had no desire to get caught up in anything Blake had gotten himself into. It wasn't until he heard a loud explosion coming from the direction of his house, then the distinct odor of fire, that he became mildly interested. Sam's land was full of very flammable pine trees, and his cabin was built entirely of wood. Since the passing of his wife, his dog, land, trees, and cabin were the only things in his meager world that he held close to his heart.

Sam grabbed the shotgun hanging over the hearth. Leaving the little dog behind, he walked out the front door into the dark night. The instant he stepped outside, the pungent smell of smoke assaulted his nostrils. Carrying the shotgun in his right hand, he jogged to the backyard to get a look at the sky over Blake's land. He could see at once that there was a raging fire on his neighbor's property. A gigantic plume of smoke rose into the air at the exact point where Blake's cabin was. Sam's first instinct was to call the Calhoun Fire Department. One major obstacle prevented him from doing so: he didn't own either a cell or landline phone. Even if he had, by the time they got their act together, the whole town would probably burn down. Evidently, no one else had called them, either. He could hear no sirens coming from any direction.

Being a recluse, Sam was prepared for just about every contingency that a man living alone could deal with. In an oversize storage shed directly behind his cabin, he kept a functional assortment of firefighting equipment. It included an Econoflow forestry fire hose with brass fittings, fireproof clothing, an ax, a gas mask, and a variety of fire extinguishers and repellants. He knew a bit about firefighting, having read books on the subject. His best option was to prevent the fire from spreading beyond its source.

He was reluctant to go to his neighbor's home and perhaps encounter people there. The alternative was to risk having his woods—and, even worse, his home—burn to cinders. After fetching his firefighting equipment from the shed and loading it into the back of his extended-bed Chevy Silverado truck, he hopped into the driver's seat. He floored the accelerator pedal, causing gravel to spew out from all four drive wheels. The truck lurched forward along the half-mile driveway that led from his cabin to the public roadway.

Three minutes later, he pulled into the driveway leading to Blake's place. After passing through the first stand of trees, he could see that three-quarters of the house was ablaze, the flames shooting high above the rooftop and into the night. Even with his truck windows raised, he could hear the crackling sounds of wood burning. The smell of smoke coming through the cab's air-conditioning vents had become significantly more acrid, and the sting in his eyes produced a steady stream of tears down his cheeks. In spite of his ailing eyes, Sam could see the car the FBI agent had driven, parked at the edge of the woods just before the clearing. The bright light generated by the flames illuminated the entire area around the town car, the yard, and the driveway leading to Blake's cabin. As Sam passed the agent's car, it appeared to be unoccupied.

Driving out of the hammock and into the clearing, he approached to within a hundred feet of the house. It was as close as he dared advance. The temperature inside his cab had already risen at least five degrees.

Before he hopped out of the truck, he directed his attention toward the large picture window that ran half the length of the cabin. The harrowing scene inside shocked him into action. The FBI agent he had met earlier was tied to a dining room chair, lying face down on the floor while a fiery inferno wreaked havoc all around him.

If the man was still alive, he must surely have been born under a lucky star. All four rooms in the house seemed to be furiously ablaze except for the dining room. His odds of still being alive in the dense smoke had to be slim.

Sam didn't think much of people. One thing he could not tolerate was a person who refused to help someone in need. His wife had believed that all life was precious and sacred. She wouldn't even harm a cockroach. She would be furious with him if he ignored the FBI agent's predicament. Refusing to acknowledge the extreme heat and smoke burning his throat and lungs, he jumped out of the truck. He threw on his fireproof jacket, hat, and gas mask, grabbed his ax and fire extinguisher, and sprinted toward the front door.

* * *

Before his captors left the cabin, Daniel was scanning the surrounding area, conceiving a plan of escape. He knew he wouldn't have much time after they were gone. Once the gas increased to a certain level, the pilot light alone would most likely cause an explosion. The industrial twine Lansbury had used to tie him to the chair was painfully sturdy, and Lansbury had done an efficient job binding him tightly, leaving barely any wiggle room. Even if he could shrug and wriggle his way along the wood floors to the kitchen utensil drawer, he couldn't use his hands to grab a knife. To exacerbate his predicament, he was trapped in a block oak dining room chair that seemed to weigh a ton. Panicked and rushed in his deliberation, he initially felt that his only option was to try somehow to use his strength and dexterity to free himself from the twine.

Within minutes of the time Billy Ray and Kenny walked out the front door, the smell of the propane gas escaping into the air was getting stronger. He prayed that the originating blast of fire wouldn't extend to the air around him. If that happened, he was doomed. If the heat produced by the discharge of flames didn't kill him instantly, he would endure a torturous death shortly thereafter. If

271

the highest concentration of the gas traveled away from the dining room, he had a sliver of hope. It might buy him some time, although it didn't solve the puzzle of how to liberate himself from the chair.

The longer Daniel analyzed the situation, the more impossibly desperate it seemed. No matter how frantically he tried to loosen the twine, he made no progress. To make matters worse, the dire circumstances caused him to waste precious time on concerned thoughts for his boys and Annie. His children would be destroyed beyond mending if they had to deal with another tragic death of a parent. Annie would probably spend the rest of her life in deep depression, maybe even be institutionalized. She had already been through so much. As he obsessed over all the catastrophic possibilities, he could feel the onset of a crushing headache and building nausea. The bitterness of bile rose from his stomach to assault his taste buds.

Daniel couldn't realize quickly enough that it wasn't going to serve his children, Annie, or him any good purpose to fret while the house burned down around him. Employing calming techniques he had learned during the FBI's survival training, he cleared his mind of all dark and unwanted images. He finally decided to try to scoot his way toward an exit. Just maybe, if could get there before the explosion, he could somehow throw himself toward the front door and open it. He didn't think Billy Ray or Kenny had locked it. They probably hadn't wasted the time to look for the keys, and Daniel hadn't heard or seen the locking mechanism engage. It was worth a try. At this point, he was running out of options, and three of the ten minutes set on the pilot light timer had elapsed.

To build some momentum with his first move, Daniel gathered every bit of strength he could muster to thrust his body up and forward. Instead of advancing in his intended direction, the chair rose up and teetered on its front

272

legs. As if in time-lapse photography, he could see in his mind's eye the unwieldy bulk of the wooden slab imprisoning his body tumble forward into oblivion. He watched the hardwood floor rise up to meet him, and the world went dark.

\* \* \*

Racing toward the cabin, struggling to carry the load of gear, Sam Blackwell kept an eye out for a water hydrant in case he had to use his industrial-size fire hose. His main concern was the FBI agent, though he wondered if anyone was else trapped inside. If that was the case, there was little chance of their being alive. The whole place was engulfed in flames except for the living and dining rooms. The agent was the only person visible in the area where the fire had not yet taken over completely. For all Sam knew, the man was already dead, but he had to try. Even with gas mask and goggles, it was hard to see in the smoke-filled cabin.

The window providing a view inside was in the living room on the northeast side of the cabin. The dining room where the agent had fallen was just behind it—part of one big space that included both rooms and an office with a desk and computer. The desk was already partly burned. Fire was spreading to different areas of the living room and had overtaken a wood rocking chair, coffee table, and large sofa. For the moment, the space around the dining room table had been spared, but the fire was moving fast. The flames were most prevalent toward the part of the living room closest to the window and bedroom on the northwest side.

Sam knew better than to try to open the front door using the latch. Though he had heat-resistant gloves on, the temperature of the metal handle could be well above a thousand degrees Fahrenheit. Nor did he want a burst of flames to envelop him upon opening the door. It was a much better idea to let the oxygen from outside enter the cabin gradually. He decided to use the ax to chop a few holes in the door, then break it down.

The first several blows seemed effortless. The adrenaline coursing through his veins gave him a boost of extra power to lift and swing the ax. After five or six strokes, he had smashed through the wood in several places. Contrary to what he had expected, it wasn't an explosion of fire. Flickers of flame rippled lazily through the open cracks. In the last two hours, the temperature had plummeted more than twenty degrees. The cold air, containing less oxygen, had suppressed the effect of exposing the house to it. Realizing that he needn't fear being incinerated by a rush of flames, he directed his next ax blow at the latch. He nearly fell forward, smashing his face into the solid wood as the door swung open and then violently sprang shut again. With the latch mechanism broken, it took just a push with the base of the ax handle to open the entryway to its limit.

Though most of Sam's clothes were fire and heat resistant, patches of skin on his neck and forehead were left uncovered. The heat assaulting those areas was almost more than he could bear. Initially, it forced him a few steps back.

Looking into the cabin, he took a few precious seconds to assess the situation in the area between the entrance and the dining room. The sofa facing the picture window was engulfed in flames. Unless he could leap over it and avoid the fire in the process, he would have to pass through a small space between it and the easternmost wall to get to the agent. The floor of the living room was burning toward the center and along the edges. Against the north wall, flames rose up toward the ceiling, licking the bare oak beams like a snake's

274

tongue testing the air for the scent of prey. Sam thought he could maneuver his way to the sofa, smothering any flames in his way with the fire extinguisher. The hard part would be getting through the narrow opening to the dining room without suffering serious burns to his neck and forehead.

Throwing caution to the winds, he dropped the ax and picked up the 15.5-pound Halotron I fire extinguisher, with a range of twelve to eighteen feet and an agent flow rate of 1.25 pounds. It was advertised to address fire risks in commercial and industrial applications. Sam prayed it would be enough to keep him safe as he stepped over the threshold, into the burning cabin.

Before he took a second step into the living room, he tested the device by spraying the argon gas at a burning section of floor. The product was expelled with such force, he almost lost his grip on the hose. Rather than reaching his desired target, the liquid repellant doused the edge of the coffee table, snuffing out the small swath of fire it contacted.

Concluding that it was safe enough to continue, Sam advanced into the house, spraying everything in his intended path toward the dining room. Perspiration poured down from his forehead into the gas mask and down the sides of his face. His legs felt as though he had stepped into a pot of boiling water. Even with the gas mask, breathing required major effort.

Ignoring his discomfort, he trudged farther into the cabin. The extinguisher was doing an adequate job of drowning any flames near Sam's body. As he advanced, he directed the spray full blast at the edge of the couch and floor where he would pass into the dining room. The chemicals worked their magic, allowing him to slip through the narrow space unharmed and work his way toward the man on the floor. When he was close enough to conduct a layman's examination, Sam dropped the equipment and knelt over the fallen agent's head.

275

He placed his index and middle finger on the left side of the man's throat. At that moment, a clamorous concussion from the kitchen threw Sam ten feet back toward the burning living room. His head struck the northeast partition wall. Half conscious, he slid down the drywall and landed on the hardwood floor in a seated position.

* * *

Special Agent Christopher Frye was at the point of barely controlled panic over a developing situation involving his colleague and close friend Daniel Falcone. From the North Miami field office, he was keeping in constant contact with Daniel, receiving hourly updates of the progress of his investigation in Wildwood. Aware of the murder of the witness Daniel meant to interview, Frye had recommended that Daniel wait to have an agent from the Jacksonville field office accompany him to the prison guard's cabin. Daniel ignored the suggestion. He didn't have the time to waste. There was no telling how long it would take to arrange backup. It could be as late as tomorrow. By that time, Trent Blake could disappear. In an attempt to appease Frye, Daniel had promised to keep him informed.

The last communication Frye had received was more than forty-five minutes ago. Daniel had requested assistance to find the prison guard's home in Fort White. Frye offered to check out some aerial photographs of the area. When he called Daniel back to report what he had found, there was no response. Agent Frye had tried Daniel's cell phone several times over the past twenty minutes with no success. Daniel may be hardheaded, but it wasn't his nature to renege on a promise to keep his colleague advised, or to ignore his calls. Even if he had lost service, he would have called from Blake's cabin by now. He would know that Frye would be forced to act under the circumstances.

There was no question in Frye's mind: it was time to alert the field office in Jacksonville that Daniel could be in trouble. Through shared investigations, Frye knew several agents based there. He had Special Agent Kent Denver's number saved on his cell phone. He clicked on the name to speed-dial the number.

"Hey, Kent, sorry to bother you so late. I think we might have a serious problem."

"What's up?"

Frye explained his concern for Daniel.

"We need to get somebody out there right away. I've called him at least five times in the last fifteen minutes. I left a message every time. It's not like him not to respond. I have to think he's in trouble. How fast can you guys get a chopper up there?" Frye gave him Blake's address.

"We're gonna have to get some guys together. I'll call the SAC; we'll get on it immediately."

"Do you have any idea what police department has jurisdiction in that area?"

"Columbia County Sheriff's Office, I believe."

"Okay, I'll look up their number online. I'm gonna ask them to send someone out to Blake's cabin right away."

"Do you want us to wait till they check things out before we head up there?"

"I'd rather not. I'm pretty sure Daniel needs help. Better safe than sorry."

"You got it, Chris. I'll keep you posted."

Frye hung up the phone, looked up the number of the Columbia County Sheriff's Department, and called. The sergeant in charge agreed to dispatch a deputy to the Blake cabin immediately. After Frye had done everything he possibly could, he tried Daniel's cell phone one more time. By then, more than an hour had passed since the first attempt to contact him. To Frye's immense surprise, it seemed as though his call was answered. He could hear muffled sounds in the background. An instant later, the phone went dead.

* * *

Sam Blackwell sat up against the wall, struggling to regain his senses. Fortunately, he never lost consciousness. He was aware enough to know that if he didn't get moving fast, the agent wasn't the only one who would die in the fire. Willing himself to clear his mind, he was ready to act in less than a minute after the second explosion.

The extinguisher had also been jettisoned through the air by the blast in the kitchen. It just missed hitting Sam, striking the wall inches from his head and landing innocuously on the floor within his reach. He set the extinguisher up on its base and saw that its sides had been crushed. Its only use now was for leverage to stand.

Once he was on his feet, he quickly assessed the progress of the fire since the last explosion. The kitchen behind the agent was engulfed, and the flames were advancing at an alarming pace toward the dining room. The back wall of the house, from the kitchen to the bedroom, was mostly obliterated. Sam could see the rear edges of the backyard, littered with logs. Small flames in the shape of teardrops spat upward from the burning wood. He felt lucky that the brunt of the blast had been directed toward that side of the house. If the opposite had occurred, both he and the agent would surely be dead. He could feel the concentrated heat of the fire through his pants and on parts of his face. The smoke seemed to be less of an issue, most of it flowing toward the open end of the house. The fire had progressed into the dining room, and some of the chairs and parts of the table were burning.

The agent was just feet away. Sam advanced cautiously toward the inert body. Removing the glove from his right hand, he bent over for a second time and placed his fingers over the left side of the agent's throat. He could feel the artery pulsing, though it was definitely weaker than his own, which he tested with his other hand.

Moving as fast as he could, he took a knife from the pocket of his fire jacket and cut the twine binding the agent to the chair. Then he stood up to appraise a means of escape. Though the entire back of the house had been blown out, the fire was raging from floor to ceiling in both the kitchen and the back bedroom, preventing him from using the missing wall for his exit. His only way out was back in the direction he had come in.

The sofa was burning again obstructing a direct route to the door. Sections of the floor were also in flames. Sam decided he would be able to get by the couch and could sidle his way through the rest of the living room to keep as far from the fire as possible. He could only pray that he would be strong and limber enough to do so while carrying the agent. By the looks of his muscled frame, he had to weigh at least two hundred pounds. Dragging him was not an option—with no protection for the agent's exposed skin, he would certainly suffer severe burns. Already, Sam was wasting precious time strategizing too much. One never knew. Another explosion could finish them both.

After Sam cut the twine, the body slithered forward and came to rest face down on the floor. Kneeling now, Sam pulled the agent's legs out from underneath the seat and turned him over on his back. Next, he bent the knees so he could slip his arm into the crook they made. He placed his other arm behind the agent's head and around his shoulders. Straining with the exertion of every muscle fiber, Sam raised the dead weight to chest level. Using the chair for support, he placed his elbow underneath the agent's head on the flat part of the seat and pushed himself up on one foot. Continuing to apply pressure against the chair, he thrust his body upward with all his might, laboring to bear his weight on the other foot and straighten to a standing position. Thanks to the adrenaline still flowing through his body, and perhaps a minor miracle to boot, he succeeded with his first attempt.

The moment he felt reasonably balanced, he shifted the agent into a fireman's carry, ran through the space leading to the living room, negotiated his way around the burning floor and furniture, then stumbled through the open front door. When he was finally outside, beyond his truck and more than forty yards from the cabin, he dropped the agent gently to the ground, on his back.

Free of his burden, Sam continued to pant heavily. It seemed as though he wasn't getting any oxygen. Sucking desperately for air, he finally realized he was still wearing the gas mask. He tore it off his face and threw it to the ground. Taking in the cold, crisp air was a welcome relief, though the heavy smell of smoke filled his nostrils. He sat on the hard ground next to the agent and willed himself to relax as he drew in deep breaths.

A frustrating thought crossed his mind as his respiration returned to a more functional rate. He had no idea what to do next. His knowledge of first aid was adequate, but this situation called for more than the items that came in a home kit. The agent needed immediate professional medical care, and the nearest hospital was more than an hour away. The only idea that came to mind was to get the agent into his truck. He just wasn't sure he had anything left in his personal energy tank to do it. To stand up on his own two feet was hard enough.

While thinking about giving it his best effort, he heard the chirp of a ringing cell phone coming from the area around the agent's waist. Sam looked down toward the sound to see a phone attached to the unconscious man's belt. As he fumbled to detach it, he accidentally hit the answer button. By the time he got the phone to his ear, the signal was lost. He tried to dial 911 with no success.

Sam threw the cell phone onto the dead grass in disgust. Now he had to reconsider lifting the agent and carrying him to his vehicle. He shot a glance at the man's abdomen and was unable to detect the up-and-down motion of the diaphragm. The temperature had dropped quite a bit in just the past fifteen minutes or so. He could see thick plumes of frozen vapor spouting from his own mouth when he exhaled. Seeing nothing coming from the agent's nose or mouth, he placed his fingers over the carotid artery, searching for a pulse. He felt nothing but the still, cool surface of the skin. The agent's heart had stopped beating.

Sam cursed his bad luck. After the risks he had taken to save the guy's life, he was damned if he would lose him now. He was going to have to do CPR. In theory, he should be able to execute it with no problem, having been a certified lifeguard when he was younger. If only this weren't his first time performing it since his failed attempt on his wife . . .

The first step was basic. Sam tilted the agent's head back and lifted his chin to create an open airway. Next, he pinched the nose shut, took a normal breath, covered the mouth with his, and blew air into the lungs until he saw the chest rise. After giving him a second breath, Sam placed the heels of both hands over the center of the agent's chest and pumped thirty times. The first round complete, he repeated the process, then checked to see if his patient was breathing. No vapor cloud was visible in the frigid air, but when Sam placed his ear against the man's mouth, he thought he detected a weak rush of air. He tested for a pulse and was relieved to find that the heart was beating—though far from robustly. He kept his fingers against the artery to keep track of the pulse.

Concentrating to count the beats, he heard the sweet sound of a siren in the distance. He waited several seconds, listening for the horn blasts of the emergency vehicles. Two minutes later, he could see the flashing red and blue emergency lights of a police cruiser through the trees. It turned onto the dirt road leading to the Blake property, then came at high speed.

Daniel was lying at the very edge of the driveway. Concerned that the police car might run them both over, Sam stood up and dragged the unconscious agent farther onto the front lawn. Then he turned to face the police car, waving both hands high above his head. Judging by the cruiser's speed just fifty yards away, at first Sam didn't think the driver could see him. The officer must have noticed him at the last moment, for he skidded to a halt fifteen yards beyond where Sam was standing.

Sam ran toward the police car as two officers got out. They immediately drew their guns and ordered him to lie face down on the driveway, with his hands behind his back. As one of them stepped over him and started to handcuff his wrists, Sam began to explain the situation.

282

"I'm not armed. I live down the road. I came over here when I saw the fire." He pointed in the direction of the injured man and said, "There's an FBI agent over there. He was trapped inside the house. He's near dead."

Deputy Gary Reed scanned the front lawn and saw Daniel lying still on his back about twenty feet from the driveway. He directed his partner's attention to the unconscious man, then made his way over to examine him while the other officer stayed with Sam. Deputy Reed felt the skin of Daniel's forehead with the flat of his palm. It was as cold as the ambient air. Like Sam earlier, he placed his fingers on Daniel's throat to check for a pulse. It was weak and abnormally slow. With his flashlight, he checked over Daniel's body for injuries but found nothing obvious other than a reddish cast to the skin of his face and hands.

On the way to the Blake cabin while responding to the call from the FBI's Miami field office, the two deputies had smelled the obvious odor of a major fire and immediately called the Alachua County Fire Department. Initially unaware of the exact site, they gave the captain approximate coordinates. After approaching the Blake cabin closely enough to identify that it was the structure on fire, they communicated with the already dispatched fire truck and ambulance to provide the address. They would be here soon.

In the meantime, Deputy Reed ran to the police car to retrieve several blankets that he kept in the trunk for the homeless and for missing persons found lost in the woods. He rushed back to Daniel and covered his body from the neck down. Then he radioed the department to determine the location of the ambulance. The dispatcher told him they were about five minutes from the Blake property.

Moments later, Deputy Reed heard the approaching sirens. While he and his partner waited for them to arrive, they questioned Sam about his involvement in the incident. He explained his meeting with the FBI agent on the main road, and his discovery of the fire not long thereafter. Based on Sam's age and his credible story, they assumed for the time being that he was telling the truth, and decided to treat him as a witness rather than a suspect. In another minute, two fire trucks and an ambulance arrived. While the firemen brought out their equipment to fight the fire, the EMTs worked to save Daniel's life.

**Chapter 21**

The whir and soft beeps of medical machinery filled the room in the intermediate care unit at Shands Hospital in Gainesville, Florida. Daniel Falcone was the only patient in a room that normally was furnished with two beds. After a rough night and a second bout of respiratory failure, Daniel had made it through the most critical point of the past twenty-four hours.

When he first arrived at the emergency room, the doctors were not optimistic with his prognosis. Daniel had inhaled a great deal of noxious smoke. Tests revealed that the carbon monoxide, cyanide, and methemoglobin levels in his blood were high enough to cause death. By nothing less than a miracle, intubation never became necessary. For most of the time after his admission to the hospital, he had been in a hyperbaric chamber, receiving concentrated amounts of oxygen to reduce the carbon monoxide level. He finally regained consciousness in the early hours of the morning after his ordeal. His doctors had agreed to transfer him to the intermediate care unit just an hour ago.

Already, Daniel had received calls from President Cooper, the director of the FBI, Assistant Director Howard Evans, Daniel's special agent in charge, and Annie. The nurses refused to let him take any of the calls except the one from the White House. In direct defiance of his doctors' recommendation that he remain in the hospital for the next couple of days, Daniel assured the president he would be back on the case later that afternoon. Even Cooper tried to convince him to stay an extra day or so. Daniel listened politely, then stubbornly insisted that he would be leaving the hospital within a few hours whether they discharged him officially or he walked out on his own.

Once Daniel deemed himself ready to hear the story of his rescue, Deputy Reed described it to him. An emergency medical technician and the Columbia County Sheriff's Department deputy had accompanied Daniel to Shands Hospital in the FBI helicopter that arrived on the scene twenty minutes after the EMTs started their treatment. Shands was the nearest hospital with a hyperbaric chamber. The chief EMT at the site insisted that Daniel be flown there immediately. Based on Sam Blackwell's estimation of the amount of time Daniel had been inhaling smoke, the chief felt that any lesser treatment wouldn't do.

In fact, several miraculous events had occurred, allowing Daniel to come through the ordeal alive. The first was the track of both explosions, dictated by the path of the gas as it flowed from the gas oven. If the full force of either blast had been directed toward Daniel, he would have been killed instantly. A second major stroke of luck may have been unintentional, yet it was no less significant. Daniel had fallen forward while trying to scoot his chair toward the front door. His nose and mouth ended up just an inch from the floor, where the concentration of smoke inside the cabin was lowest. Had he remained upright, he surely would have asphyxiated from smoke inhalation. Later, the doctors caring for him at Shands would confirm that his fall had saved his life. Christopher Frye's astute analysis of the situation and his quick response were just as important. Without the helicopter to fly Daniel thirty-three miles to the closest hospital with a hyperbaric chamber, the carbon monoxide poisoning would undoubtedly have done him in.

The man Daniel owed the largest debt of gratitude was Sam Blackwell. If not for his heroic efforts, all the other factors leading to Daniel's survival would not have been enough. The man described to Daniel as a recluse had saved his life. As he lay in his hospital bed thinking about all the work he had ahead of him,

Daniel promised himself he would take the time to give his savior a proper thank-you. Expressing appreciation to someone for saving his life was getting to be a habit. He already was indebted to Annie for rescuing him from the gas chamber. Though he was infinitely thankful, he didn't want that list to get any longer.

During their telephone conversation, Daniel assured President Cooper that he was feeling fine and that his health would not prevent him from continuing the investigation of the Polly Flowers affair. That wasn't the only issue on Daniel's mind. Billy Ray Johnson and Kyle Lansbury had just tried to burn him alive. Daniel was scheduled to meet with Ed Harding within the hour. When Harding heard about the incident, he immediately chartered the Bureau's Learjet and was currently on his way back to Florida. If there had been any doubt before that Billy Ray was directly involved in the murder of Special Agent John Christy, none remained.

\* \* \*

The bare trees of the Northern Georgia foothills seemed stripped of all life. The last shred of brilliant autumn color covering the landscape had disintegrated into the earth. Now the barren branches of hickory and maple stretched toward the clear blue sky like gnarled fingers from a children's fairy tale. The ground surrounding the Peterson mansion was as hard and impenetrable as the Appalachian granite bedrock to the north. Billy Ray and Keith Peterson had withdrawn from the rest of their group, who were still inside discussing the latest events and updates of the mission. Billy Ray had stormed out of the house, furious with his colleagues' admonitions that he exercise better judgment.

The people in Washington were not happy with Billy Ray's escapades at the Blake cabin. They were threatening to pull their funding. He had already incited the wrath of the FBI by killing one of their own. The Bureau would probably figure out Billy Ray's involvement in John Christy's murder. The attempted murder of a second agent would only serve to fortify their efforts to seek justice. Brody was warning them that the government's pursuit of the Klan would be relentless.

Billy Ray had argued to the elders attending the meeting via teleconference that he didn't have a choice. If he hadn't acted, both he and Kyle Lansbury would be behind bars right now, and all their hard work would be for naught. The elders weren't so much displeased with the ultimate action Billy Ray was forced to take as with his poor judgment leading up to that point. Hiring a known drug addict to silence Kenny Jones was just one example. It was the consensus among the elders and the sponsors in Washington that Billy Ray had a number of other options available to keep Jones quiet. They also felt that Blake's murder was recklessly executed. A single lookout posted at the entrance to the property could have warned Billy Ray and Kyle of Falcone's approach. If the Klan was going to be successful implementing the plan that Brody was funding, it would have to be done in an impeccably professional manner. Impulsive behavior and poor judgment were unacceptable and would surely prevent them from achieving their goal.

After Billy Ray and Kyle left the Blake cabin, they made their way back to the Northpoint Mall in Alpharetta, Georgia, where they had left Billy Ray's Mustang earlier in the evening. They had stolen the SUV they drove to the Blake property, from the mall's parking lot. To further confuse the police, before heading home, Kyle had driven the stolen vehicle to the Atlanta Hartsfield

288

International Airport while Billy Ray followed in his Mustang. They left the SUV in the airport's long-term parking lot and immediately headed back north to the Peterson family's place. By the time they arrived, news of the attempted murder of Daniel Falcone was already being broadcast on the national news channels. The first call from Brody followed soon thereafter, requesting the telephone conference.

One of Billy Ray's many character flaws was his inability to tolerate constructive criticism. It wasn't anyone's intention to remove him from his leadership role or to discount any of his accomplishments to that point. Billy Ray didn't see it that way. He reacted badly to Willis Zachary from Miami, the grand dragon from Massachusetts, and Brody, who were teleconferenced into the meeting. Red faced and screaming at the top of his lungs, Billy Ray reminded everyone that the mission was his idea in the first place. After a few choice words directed at everyone present, he stormed out. He was followed by his best buddy, Keith Peterson, who was used to taking on the role of calming Billy Ray and helping soothe his wounded ego. Keith was doing his best to convince Billy Ray that the elders were only offering advice. He didn't want his friend's attitude to get him into any more trouble. The elders knew Billy Ray and would forgive him. Keith was much more worried about the people in Washington. Not only were they very powerful, but at this point the Klan needed their cash. Alone with Keith, Billy Ray focused his anger on Brody and the Washington contingent, knowing full well they were more than just counseling him. They were pissed.

"I'm sick of those assholes trying to control everything," said Billy Ray. "This was my idea. I'm in charge. Who the hell are they to tell me I'm making bad decisions. Without me, we wouldn't be where we are right now."

"Preachin' to the choir, Billy Ray. I know better than anyone you're the mastermind behind it all. Unfortunately, we need those people, for the time being anyway. What we're doing costs big bucks. Look how much we've spent already with all the airline tickets, weapons, explosives, paying the people working for us, payoffs like the one we were supposed to give Blake. If we're gonna go all the way with your plan, it's gonna take a lot more money—a lot more than any of us have. Brody's people have an unlimited source of cash. We really can't afford to piss them off."

"I'll tell you what. I'm not gonna take them treating me like some kid who doesn't know what the fuck he's doing. They're gonna have to treat me with a lot more respect. If we lose them, I'll find a way. I always do. I'm not gonna let anyone talk to me that way."

Keith could tell he was making some progress. At least, Billy Ray seemed to be considering their financiers' continued involvement. Keith had seen Billy Ray tell people to fuck off, and never have anything to do with them again, for much less.

"Come on, Billy Ray," Keith pleaded. "For now, we really need them. They're acting like it was their idea. In the end, you'll get all the credit. I'm sure they know you're brilliant. You do your best with what you have to work with. They're just peeved Falcone didn't die."

"That's their problem. They just need to know who they're dealing with. I'm not gonna put up with that shit. I'll go back inside, but Brody better not talk to me that way again. If he does, they can go fuck themselves."

"I think you made that clear enough. You're not gonna have any more problems with him. He's got more information for us. Let's hear what he has to say. When it's all over, everybody will be listening to you, Billy Ray. Everybody. You'll be the hero."

* * *

It was midnight in the nation's capital. Brody was sitting on a bus station bench on Connecticut Avenue outside the Woodley Park Zoo. By his clothing, one would never know that the temperature was below freezing. He was wearing a light wool sweater with no protection for his bald head or bare hands. Brody was immune to cold weather. Having worked in both polar regions, he had spent twenty years of his life, on and off, in subzero temperatures. As part of an intelligence unit with the U.S. Marines, he conducted varied research experiments that would be considered controversial on home soil, most of them dealing with chemical warfare. He had weathered the extreme cold of the Antarctic Peninsula in winter. For him, any day above zero was a balmy one.

Without the least bit of discomfort, he had been waiting for the past fifteen minutes to be picked up by one of the group of men who had most recently engaged his services. It was stupid and messy to keep him waiting this long. Several of the group members were livid over the poor judgment exercised by the young Klan member. Brody felt that the pompous ass should have his partners in crime take a look in the mirror. All too often, the powerful people inside the Washington Beltway thought they were above criticism. It usually led to their downfall. It was a problem Brody was willing to overlook for the time being. He was getting paid really well, and all he could do was advise and educate. He had warned the secretary to be on time. There were many eyes in Washington, and sometimes, even the most secure precautions weren't enough.

Even though Brody was willing to overlook his employer's careless behavior, he couldn't go against thirty-five years of training and instinct. His eyes darted in all directions, keeping a lookout for anyone out of place. With the slightest turn of his head in one direction or the other, and his excellent peripheral vision, he could maintain a 360-degree field of vision. The people who knew him well often joked that he had eyes in the back of his head. So far, he had not detected anyone on foot in the vicinity, and only three cars had passed in the fifteen minutes he was waiting. Based on his experienced assessment of the cars' occupants, he didn't think anyone was watching. This time, they would probably get away with his employer's recklessness, but Brody's patience did have a limit. When it got to the point that he felt he was in danger from these careless acts, he would have to step down. For now, he would give the secretary another strongly worded warning.

In the distance, Brody could hear the sound of another approaching vehicle. Seconds later, he saw the headlights of a Cadillac limousine drawing near from the west. The car stopped directly in front of the bus stop bench, a back door opened, and Brody hopped in. The only passenger in the car was the secretary. The soundproof, opaque divider separating the driver's cab was up, and Brody already knew that the driver was the only person in the front seat—he had made note of that before he got in. The secretary and Brody had complete privacy for their conversation. Brody was first to speak.

"Mr. Secretary, I appreciate the work. But, if you're going to pay me to get things done the right way, I strongly recommend you take advantage of what you're paying for. When I make a suggestion, it's not because I like to hear myself talk. There's no wiggle room when it comes to the rules. You can't leave me out there waiting that long."

Like a typical politician, the secretary thought he could mollify Brody with a little charm. "I'm really sorry. The wife caught me sneaking out. She slowed me up a bit. You know how women can be. I promise it won't happen again."

"I don't need apologies or promises. Just please keep to the schedule. It's essential. That's the last time I'll discuss the issue."

The secretary was taken aback by Brody's abruptness. Brody knew that it was not so much the words as the emotion behind them that elicited the reaction. He wasn't one to show much in the way of feelings; indeed, he was as stoical as a sculptured bust. Tonight, he wanted the secretary to see that he was clearly miffed.

The secretary said, "Okay, I got it. Moving on, the reason I asked for this meeting is to discuss your participation in the mission. I know I initially hired you for planning and overseeing the operation. I'm thinking I might want you to play a more active role. The group has doubts about Billy Ray's and the Klan's reliability. I know it was my idea in the first place to use them. I don't want to make any changes, and the other guys know and understand that. We all would like to see you do more than manage."

"I'm not a mechanic. I'll tell you how to get it done. I'm not gonna pull the trigger, so to speak."

"That kid is making too many mistakes. I don't know if he can handle something this big."

"You should've thought about that before you decided to involve them. If you want the Klan to be a part of this, Billy Ray is going to be their man, I can tell you that much."

"The FBI agent they tried to kill has me worried, too. I know him well. He's not the kind of person you want on your case. He's going to be working double duty on this one. If you could be there with the young hothead, you could hold his hand; make sure he doesn't fuck up."

"No. I devise a plan, that's it. If he follows my instructions precisely, nothing should go wrong."

"That's exactly what we're worried about. If he can follow simple fuckin' directions."

"I'll see to it he's extremely well briefed. I'll have him practice until he's sick to death of it; then I'll make him practice some more. I guarantee, he'll be prepared and will know the plan like the back of his hand. Actually, I think the Johnson kid is pretty smart. Yeah, he's made mistakes, but he's the type of guy that learns from them. Sometimes, he lets his anger get in the way. I'll do what I can to help him with that as well. The guys he hangs out with, I'm not so sure of. I don't plan to give them anything important to do. I think that under the right tutelage, Billy Ray can get the job done."

"I hope you're right. I can't afford a screw-up. Falcone is persistent. Everything will have to go perfectly."

"Nothing'll go wrong. I'm not concerned about the agent. I've beaten the best around the world. When it's done, I'll be sure to tie up the few loose ends like you requested. It'll never come back to you. That's my job: to keep you safe. Failure isn't even in the picture."

\* \* \*

Against everyone's recommendation, including his doctor and nurse's, Daniel didn't spend his day in the hospital room convalescing. Not long after he heard the story of his rescue, he proclaimed himself fit to give his statement on his experience at the Blake cabin to the Jacksonville-based investigative team and the lead homicide detective for the Columbia County Sheriff's Department. Though his doctor had vehemently rejected his self-imposed prognosis at first, Daniel had negotiated cleverly. In exchange for agreeing to stay one more night in the hospital, submit to hourly blood analysis, and be monitored by the doctor's battery of machines, he was permitted to talk with his colleagues for a maximum of two hours in the morning and three hours that afternoon. He used most of the time responding to questions.

With the moments he had remaining, Daniel managed to collect a small amount of information on the investigation. The sheriff's CSI unit conducted the initial crime scene analysis. There was essentially no evidence that could help confirm Daniel's identification of the culprits, although the unit had made an exhaustive search. They found several charred bones belonging to the same person, scattered throughout the Blake residence. Daniel confirmed that he had seen a body there. The sheriff's department had submitted the bones for DNA testing. It would be several days before they had official results, though Daniel had no doubt the dead man was Trent Blake.

Once Daniel provided the make and model of the car the suspects were driving, along with the license plate number, an APB was issued throughout the southeastern United States. An NCIC report was immediately pulled, reflecting that the vehicle was stolen from the parking lot of a mall in Woodstock, Georgia, several hours before Blake's murder. Minutes after noon, a Fulton County police officer found the SUV abandoned at Hartsfield International Airport. No one thought the men had taken a flight—that would have made tracing their steps much too easy. Regardless, airport tapes were being collected for viewing. At day's end, there was no trace of either Billy Ray Johnson or Kyle Lansbury.

Shortly after sunrise the next morning, Daniel was harassing his nurse and anyone else who would listen, to get the discharge paperwork done. Sick of his constant badgering, the staff got the doc to write up the final orders and have Daniel released by eight a.m. A limousine, provided by the president of the United States, was waiting for him in the hospital's driveway at the main entrance. He instructed the driver to take him to Jacksonville, where he planned to join Ed Harding and the members of the Joint Terrorism Task Force who were working the murders of Kenny Jones and Trent Blake. Later that night, he planned to fly directly to Mississippi to show Billy Ray exactly what Special Agent Daniel Falcone's brand of family harassment was all about.

When Daniel arrived at his destination, Ed Harding was on the phone, trying to convince the sheriff's office in Columbia County to turn over jurisdiction to the FBI. It was the consensus at the Bureau that this was a federal crime. Any illegal activity committed by the Ku Klux Klan fell under that classification. A team of FBI experts had been working on this group of suspects for years, and their knowledge of the people involved and the team's resources were far superior to any available to the Columbia County Sheriff's Office or the Jacksonville FBI field office. Based on the volume of Harding's voice through the glass window of the SAC's office, and the intensity of his gestures, Daniel didn't think the conversation was going all that well.

At the end of the day, Daniel didn't think the sheriff would keep up the fight. From Harding's assistant, Daniel had learned that the department had a total of forty-two trained deputies, four of whom were detectives assigned to the homicide division. The number of murders in their jurisdiction rarely exceeded five per year, and most of those were followed by immediate arrests. Open cases requiring investigation were extremely rare, and dealing with a crime as complex as the Blake murder was way beyond their capacity. It wouldn't be long before they were forced to let the Bureau take over. Both Daniel and Harding wanted the transaction to be voluntary. If it didn't happen soon, they would exercise their power to take jurisdiction over the crime. At that point, getting cooperation from the locals would be next to impossible.

Before Daniel left Florida, he intended to read in detail the entire Blake investigative file of information collected while he was in the hospital. He wouldn't likely be able to pick up Billy Ray's trail. That didn't mean he wasn't going to give it a shot. At a minimum, he wanted to hear the results of the examination of the airport surveillance tapes. He wasn't optimistic that they would reveal any significant leads. If Billy Ray was smart enough to steal a car to avoid being tracked, he wouldn't be fool enough to escape on public transportation. He had to know that the airports, train stations, and bus terminals were monitored by video cameras and would be a priority on the authorities' to-do list. It was much more likely they had a second getaway car parked at or near the Atlanta airport. By now they could have traveled more than a thousand miles.

Daniel was absolutely positive about one thing: Billy Ray had just begun. If they didn't stop him soon, a lot more innocent people were going to die. He needed to talk to the Johnson family and especially Billy Ray's ex-wife. Although he didn't think he was going to get much cooperation from them, the more stress, tension, and turmoil he caused around Billy Ray, the better the chances that someone would make a mistake. The ex-wife could turn out to be his best opportunity to manufacture a lead. If Billy Ray's divorce had left behind any bad feelings, Daniel might collect some very valuable information.

Turning his thoughts to the president's case late in the day, Daniel had every intention of tracking down and interrogating Polly Flowers and Thaddeus Raymond. Finding them would be relatively easy. Nailing them down to a specific time for an interview might be the hard part, perhaps next to impossible. He had a plan to keep them from avoiding interrogation. Daniel grabbed his cell phone and accessed his menu of contacts, found the number he needed, and dialed it. Christopher Frye responded before the third ring.

"Chris, I need some help. Before I tell you what I need, you have to give me your solemn word to keep your mouth shut. No one can know what I'm asking you to do. Got it?"

"Sure, Daniel, what's up?"

Christopher Frye was one of the few people in the world Daniel trusted implicitly. In this particular instance, Daniel needed to be absolutely positive his partner understood the gravity of what he was about to share. "I mean it. No one. Not even your wife. This can't get out. If it does, it's my ass."

"Come on, Daniel, you know you can trust me. What's going on?"

"President Cooper has asked me to conduct a private investigation for him. He's allowed me to bring you in on it. Nothing major. I'll just need some help here and there. I'm heading up to D.C. in the next day or two. I need information on Polly Flowers and Thaddeus Raymond: their home address, where they work, anything you can find about their daily routines, et cetera. You think you can get something for me by tonight? I'd do it myself, but I'm on a really tight schedule and I don't know when I'll be able to get to a computer."

"Holy shit! *Cooper* came to you? Can't say I blame him. You'd be the first I'd go to if I was in deep shit."

"Yeah, well, I hope I can help. I'm gonna need someone to check on things for me every once in a while. The president offered his staff. Problem is if he's telling the truth, there are definitely people around him screwing him over. I don't want to share things with the wrong person. I'd rather have someone like you to turn to."

"Happy to help. This should be easy. I'll call you soon as I have something. I just . . . well . . . I was wondering, are you all right, Daniel? Do you think you should be getting back into it full steam already? Maybe you should have spent one more night in the hospital."

"You, too, Chris? Give me a fuckin' break! I appreciate the concern, but come on, I'm fine. I can't say I feel like a million bucks. I'll make it, though. I don't have time to be sick right now."

**Chapter 22**

Before his wife's illness, Thaddeus Raymond had never had trouble sleeping. The typical insomniac would have been jealous of his ability to catnap anytime, anywhere. He just closed his eyes, and seconds later he was in slumber land. He didn't even need a bed. According to Mrs. Raymond, he could fall asleep under any conditions, in just about any position. She swore that she had even caught him dozing off while standing.

Those days seemed to be over. Thaddeus hadn't gotten a good night's sleep in years. He thought perhaps he would recover his talent after his wife's surgery and full recovery. So far, it wasn't the case. It didn't take a rocket scientist to figure out why. Plotting against one's own government was high-pressure business. The rules were very similar to those of a street gang: once you were in, getting out was next to impossible.

Several weeks after the Polly Flowers affair, Thad got an offer he couldn't refuse, from a man known as Brody. Now Thad was embroiled in the middle of the biggest crime against the nation's leadership since Reagan got shot. He was offered a sum of cash that made the money he had earned in Mexico City seem like chump change. The names of very powerful people directing the conspiracy were revealed to him. An overwhelmingly heavy responsibility was placed directly on his shoulders. Thad was not so sure he was comfortable with his new role.

In fact, he would have done his part in the Polly Flowers affair all over again. To have his wife healthy was worth the burden he must bear for framing the president. To prevent anyone from discovering his payment from the general, he was telling the people close to him that his wife had made a miraculous recovery. He credited his prayers and those of the people of his church for the inexplicable cure. Like the Cooper incident itself, it was all a setup. The surgeons who performed the heart transplant, and the support medical staff were all hired by the general. The patient was given a false name so that no one would know that Thad had come up with the funds to pay for the operation. Later, false X-rays of her heart were substituted for those taken after the surgery by the cardiologist the general had hired for Mrs. Raymond's follow-up care. The doctor proclaimed that her turn-around was nothing short of a miracle. Conveniently, he never reported it to the medical community, and the media never got wind of the story. Mrs. Raymond had no further need for her pretransplant doctors, and the Raymonds were sworn to secrecy about the real cause for her renewed health.

After the Mexico City incident, Thad was transferred to a new detail, making it that much easier to avoid inquiring minds. His new colleagues didn't know him well, nor were they aware of his wife's prior heart problems. Thad wouldn't have to answer any inconvenient questions about her. He was already on the outs with most of his former coworkers—they didn't take kindly to his treatment of the president and wouldn't be in touch with him anytime soon. It was a pretty neat package, which, Thad was confident, would be closed and sealed from the public eye forever. That is, until Special Agent Daniel Falcone showed up on his doorstep.

\* \* \*

The information Daniel gathered in the days following his visit to Jacksonville hadn't turned up anything he didn't already know. As he had suspected, the inspection of the Hartsfield International Airport's surveillance tapes bore no fruit.

301

Billy Ray Johnson's and Kyle Lansbury's fingerprints were found all over the stolen vehicle, confirming what the investigators already knew based on Daniel's statement. After the airport, all trace of the suspects was lost. An APB for both men continued to be in effect for all law enforcement agencies around the country. The same applied to the photographs posted by the newspapers and the local and world news of each of the major networks. Many calls had come in, none of them resulting in any significant leads. Ed Harding's team was currently looking into Kenny Jones's life in greater detail. They hoped it might provide clues to Billy Ray's and Kyle's current whereabouts.

The trip to Mississippi was less productive than the few hours Daniel had spent in Jacksonville. He hadn't expected great results from Billy Ray's parents, and he didn't get them. Not only did they claim they had no idea where their son was, but Daniel's attempts at intimidation were a complete flop. Both the mother and father were cool as cucumbers. They even had the arrogance to play the Southern-hospitality card and invite him to stay for dinner. Seeing he was getting nowhere, Daniel declined.

Essentially empty handed, he left the Johnson estate and headed north toward the Tennessee line. His misplaced optimism that he would get some good information from Billy Ray's ex-wife was dashed the instant he arrived. She was a worse racist than Billy Ray. At first, Sarah Thorpe refused even to talk to Daniel. Eventually, he convinced her to answer some questions, employing his reliable threat that she could be arrested for obstructing justice. Her answers were no help whatever. Her attitude was even worse. She boldly told him she didn't know where Billy Ray was and that she would lie even if she did. Sarah Thorpe was a Billy Ray Johnson fan. She supported everything he was doing, and hoped that someday she would be able to help his cause.

Now that he was back in D.C., Daniel was ready to experience that good old rush he felt when he actually made some headway in an investigation. The number one item on his to-do list was not a likely contender to help him achieve that goal. Secret Service Agent Thaddeus Raymond was rock solid. Frye hadn't found a thing to impeach his credibility. Raymond's résumé was impressive. He had an impeccable record as a military man, Secret Service agent, and life partner. Based on everything Daniel had read about the guy, he seemed above reproach. While preparing, Daniel felt that it was going to take some serious ingenuity on his part if he meant to extract any useful information during the interview. It was exactly that sort of grunt work that ultimately led to an unexpected and significant discovery.

After hours of reading through pages of Secret Service personnel files and investigative reports provided by the president, including transcribed telephone conversations with Raymond's ex-colleagues, he had learned that his subject was a very devoted husband. When asked about Raymond's character, not one of the coworkers could deny his tireless fight to raise funds for his wife's critical heart transplant. He had spent all his savings on lawyers' fees in an attempt to force his health insurance company to accept coverage. When that failed, he tried everything he could think of to raise the money for the surgery, including starting up a charitable fund at his local church. At the same time, after his shift with the Secret Service he worked odd jobs every evening and, whenever possible, on his days off. To date, all his efforts had failed, at least as far as his former colleagues and Daniel were aware.

\* \* \*

Checking the monitor view outside his front door, Thaddeus Raymond felt the muscles of his neck tighten. He had had a top-of-the-line security system installed at his 1,700-square-foot three-bedroom, two-bath home in Alexandria, Virginia, including surveillance cameras placed in strategic areas around the property. Standing at his front door was Special Agent Daniel Falcone of the FBI. Thaddeus recognized him the moment he checked the monitor after the doorbell rang. He had seen Daniel on the news several times and read many newspaper stories about his nationally covered investigations. Only someone living in a cave could not know of Daniel's trial, conviction, and later exoneration for the murder of his wife and in-laws.

The cause of Thad's stress was what the general had told him about the agent. Falcone was known to be one of the best the FBI had to offer. What he was doing on Thad's doorstep was anyone's guess. Thad's overwhelming sense of guilt led him directly to the worst possible scenario. Somehow, they had discovered his involvement in setting up the president. Thad had never had much confidence in Polly Flowers. Could she possibly have confessed to the Bureau? Even more unthinkable-could Falcone be aware of Thad's most recent criminal activity?

Just recently, he and the general had talked about Daniel and his near-death experience at the Trent Blake cabin. They mostly talked casually about the incident, with the general commenting that Falcone seemed to have nine lives. Never did Thad expect to find the star FBI agent calling at his front door. The second ring of the doorbell gave him a start. Thad had been involved in many situations where many innocent lives, including his own, were in danger, and he always prided himself on his ability to maintain his composure. Moving quickly to avoid any suspicion created by his delay, he experienced an unfamiliar tension.

Guilt had never been a part of the equation before, and it had a way of changing one's behavior. Immediately upon opening the door, Thad greeted Falcone with a handshake and apologized for making him wait, offering the excuse that he was in the bathroom when the doorbell rang. Before Daniel could explain who he was and why he was here, Thad blurted out that he recognized his face from television. He introduced himself, then allowed Daniel to give him a brief explanation for his visit. He hoped he had succeeded in concealing his anxiety when Daniel announced that he had a few questions regarding the Polly Flowers affair. Thad put on his best smile and escorted his guest to the family room.

\* \* \*

In his preparations for this interview, Daniel had given much thought to what might incite a man of Raymond's caliber and professionalism to set up the president of the United States. Christopher Frye had come up with a lot of information, none of which helped answer the question. Revenge was one of Daniel's possible explanations. It was certainly a powerful motivator. He considered the angle that the president had committed some unforgivable offense against Thaddeus. Nothing that Daniel had uncovered so far confirmed the hypothesis. If there was any bad blood between the two, he doubted Raymond would admit it. Still, it wouldn't hurt to ask, and Daniel intended to do so eventually, though perhaps not in this initial meeting. The president had already said he didn't know of any reason why Raymond would have anything against him. The information, if it existed, would probably have to come from the people who knew Raymond best.

A second potential solution to the puzzle was Raymond's political views. Once again, the preliminary investigation was no help. It didn't turn up any reason to believe Raymond was an activist. Everything Daniel found in that regard could be used as evidence to the contrary. Secret Service agents were chosen based in part on their inclination to avoid choosing political sides. They were trained to refrain from developing opinions one way or the other about the people they protected. There was no evidence of his ever being a member of any political organization, nor was there evidence that he had any extreme views. This didn't seem a likely motive, though Daniel would keep it on the back burner and broach the subject in this interview.

The last and most compelling potential incentive considered by Daniel was personal gain. It would be a really good start if he could prove that Raymond had come into a large sum of cash. He intended to focus most of his questioning along those lines. If Raymond had been paid to frame the president, it wasn't obvious from the way he was living. He and his wife lived in a modest home. The family room was tastefully decorated and furnished with what Daniel considered appropriate for the income of a Secret Service agent. He had noted that the car parked in the driveway was a three-year-old Chrysler Sebring. Nothing he had seen up to that point would lead him to believe they were spending beyond their means.

\* \* \*

Thad offered Daniel a seat on the living room sofa, then sat on a lounge chair facing him.

"I didn't know the FBI had any interest in the president's scandal," Thad said.

"We're just investigating Ms. Flowers to be sure there wasn't any fraud involved."

"I've already given my statement to the Secret Service. I can get you a copy."

"That's okay, Agent Raymond. I already have it. I just have a few questions for you; then I'll be out of your hair. Mrs. Raymond isn't around, is she?"

"No, she's at the grocery store. She doesn't know anything about the incident."

"I know. I heard she was ill. I was just wondering how she's doing."

"I appreciate your concern. She's doing okay." Thad wasn't exactly sure how he intended to handle the issue of his wife if Falcone went more deeply into her health problems. It bothered him that Daniel seemed curious in the first place. A person's health was a private matter, after all. Thinking the issue through to its conclusion, he definitely didn't want to seem as though he was hiding anything. Falcone's claim that he was investigating Polly Flowers didn't sit well, either. Thad was fairly certain he himself might also be a subject of the investigation. It all could be complicated by the fact that Mrs. Raymond was coming home any minute. Lately, she had been the picture of health.

Kendra Raymond wasn't totally in the loop on how Thad ever came up with the money for the surgery. As a matter of fact, she knew nothing specific. She was aware that some strings had to be pulled to get her to the top of the list of heart recipients. Thad had told her some bald-faced lies. He claimed that some very powerful people he had close connections with were sympathetic to her story. They were willing to put up the money and arrange to have the operation done right away in repayment for the protection Thad had provided them. The only thing they asked for in return was to remain anonymous and that the operation be kept under the strictest secrecy. Though very grateful, Kendra was uncomfortable with all the mystery surrounding her surgery. Thad had warned her that she could never reveal to anyone, even family members, that she had heart transplant surgery. It had been especially difficult lying to her own parents, brother, and sisters.

For Thad, there was now a new and much more important concern. If Kendra showed up before the interview was over, she would have to lie to a law enforcement officer. As Daniel continued with the interrogation, Thad tried to multitask. He had to concentrate on the questions being posed, and his responses, while thinking about how he was going to get a word in with his wife before Daniel asked her any questions. It didn't seem likely that he would have the opportunity. He was going to have to rely on Kendra to abide by her promise to keep the surgery under tight wraps no matter who asked. The law was specifically mentioned as one of the categories that couldn't know.

"Did you know Ms. Flowers before that night in Mexico City?"

"No. That was the first time I ever met her."

"Did you speak with her?"

"The president introduced me to her. I shook her hand and said 'nice to meet you.' I don't think they were interested in talking to me."

"What did you do after the introduction?"

"Like it says in my statement, I went back to my post outside the door."

"Did you ever go back in the room before Ms. Flowers left?"

"No. The president asked me not to come in. He said that Ms. Flowers would be leaving within twenty minutes."

"Isn't that against Secret Service protocol? Aren't you supposed to check on him frequently until he goes to bed?"

"Yes, but we interpret that rule loosely. If the president wants privacy for a reasonable amount of time, we give it to him so long as we're not putting him in any danger. I checked the woman for weapons. She was clean. After she left and the president went to bed, I took my post in the living room of his suite, and another agent took over the front door."

"Do you know who took the pictures?"

"I assume Ms. Flowers set the camera to take them herself. That's what she said to the press. There was no one else in the room with them."

"So the president *allowed* her to take pictures. Is that what you're saying?"

"I'm not saying anything. I have no idea what happened in that room while Polly Flowers was in there. I let her in and I let her out, period. One thing I'd add is that the president seemed to have had a few cocktails. He was acting giddy. Whether he actually did or not before he got to his room, I can't say. It may explain how she got the pictures."

"You know that President Cooper is denying he knew Polly Flowers or let her in his room. Essentially, you're claiming he lied. Can I safely assume that?"

"All I can tell you is . . . uh . . . he told me to expect her and to let her in. You can make any inferences you want from that."

"I'd call that lying."

"Am I under investigation here? I'm getting the impression I'm being cross-examined."

"Not at all, Agent Raymond. I'm just trying to get to the bottom of this."

"I've given statement after statement about this affair. I've never changed my story. The president allowed Polly Flowers to come into his hotel room that night. What actually happened behind those closed doors, I can't be sure."

"Do you have an opinion?"

"It's not my job to have opinions. It's my job to protect. I'm not going to speculate."

"Fair enough. Let's move on, then. Do you have any idea how Ms. Flowers entered and left the president's room without being seen by any of the other Secret Service agents on the floor?"

"No. Your guess is as good as mine. You'd have to speak to them. The only thing I can think of is, maybe their attention was distracted. I heard the elevator arrive on the floor a couple of times."

Thad worried that Falcone would question the idea that the agents' focus on the presidential suite was diverted at the exact moment of Polly Flowers's ingress and egress. Even to Thad, it seemed a little too convenient to be coincidence.

"According to my file and what I've read, none of the other agents were ever aware that Polly Flowers was in the president's room. Aren't you supposed to report the entry and departure of guests?"

"Not necessarily. Not if it's in plain view of everyone. Also, the president asked me not to make any announcements through the earpiece about his guest."

"What kind of a relationship did you have with President Cooper?"

"I worked for him. What does that have to do with anything?"

Falcone's questions continued to be on the edge of accusatory. Thad was sure the agent was keeping a close eye on the specific words he chose for his responses and his reactive body language. Thad couldn't control his increasingly guarded and defensive behavior.

"Part of this investigation is to determine if the president is lying to the public. If he is, of course, it would mean Polly Flowers didn't commit any crimes. I was wondering if President Cooper felt comfortable enough to discuss the incident with you afterwards. Basically, I want to know if he asked you to keep things quiet."

"I had no contact with the president after that night except for a letter from his office dismissing me from any further presidential duty. He never said a word to me."

Thad was quite skeptical about Falcone's justification for the question, though he felt a slight bit of relief. The Bureau couldn't have any real proof he was involved in a setup, or Falcone would have taken a much more aggressive approach. The agent was letting him off the hook way too often. Thad's respite was to last only a few short seconds. The slamming of a car door coming from his driveway alerted him that Kendra was home. The stiffening of his body was surely noticed by Falcone.

"Is something wrong?" he asked.

"No, I'm okay. I just thought I heard a car door. Kendra might need some help."

Thad sprang up from his seat and headed straight for the front door. He managed to take only a couple of steps before it opened abruptly. Kendra burst through, overflowing with large bags and packages in both hands and held up against her chest. She greeted Thad with a broad smile, started to describe her purchases, then saw Daniel advancing toward her from behind her husband. Thad quickly grabbed several bags and escorted Kendra to the dining room table, where they set the bags down. Going back to the living room, Thad introduced her to Daniel, being sure to mention he was an FBI agent. Thad could see in her expression that she sensed his anxiety. It immediately wiped the smile off her face.

\* \* \*

Daniel was too clever to not detect the subtle changes in behavior. It didn't take as much ingenuity to be sure that her husband had been uptight throughout the interrogation. One other thing he couldn't help but recognize was the state of Mrs. Raymond's health. This did not seem to be a woman with a major disability.

At that point, Daniel had a decision to make: explore the issue or let it go for the moment? An interrogation of Mrs. Raymond about her heart condition would certainly reveal his true motivation for the visit. More importantly, he wanted to be prepared to address this major discovery. He was no expert on congestive heart failure. He had a general knowledge of the disease. That wasn't good enough to conduct an efficient and thorough interview. He decided to let it go for the time being. He would observe her behavior while he concluded his interrogation of Raymond. When he got back to his computer, he would educate himself on how Mrs. Raymond should be presenting in her supposed state of health.

\* \* \*

"What was that all about?" Kendra asked, closing the front door behind Daniel, who had just left.

"He says he's investigating the woman who slept with the president in Mexico . . . for fraud. He wanted to take my statement." Thad had to be careful about what he revealed. He didn't want to cause Kendra too much stress. It wasn't good for her during this time when her body was still getting used to the new heart. She had absolutely no idea her recovery was a direct result of that incident.

"You know, I always wondered about that woman. She seems like a flake to me. There's something fishy about the whole thing. I just don't know. Cooper did let her in his room, though. That part, I just don't understand. He seems like such a good family man to me. What do you think? You were there."

This was the first time Kendra ever broached the subject of that night. After it happened, she had been too sick to follow the story or even to care. By the time the operation was done and she was back to her normal daily activities, the hype had died down. Thad also intentionally gave her the sense he didn't want to talk about it. That was usually the case when it came to his work. There wasn't much about it he could reveal to her anyway. His best bet was not to go into any detail now, either. He would handle the stress for both of them. At least, he had felt a slight bit of relief after Falcone didn't seem interested in Kendra's illness. He wasn't going to start celebrating yet. It was nothing more than a good sign.

"Honey, I'm not paid to have an opinion. I just do what I'm told. I have no idea what their relationship was. I don't think I should talk about it, either."

"Yeah, I figured you'd say that. I like President Cooper. Hell, I voted for him. Sometimes, you need to let loose, you know. Break a rule or two just for the hell of it. You're too stuffy. Everything has to be just so. You could tell me a work secret or two. I am your wife, after all. You can trust me; I'm not going to say anything. You won't even tell me who you voted for in the last election, for Pete's sake!"

"You obviously have no problem letting loose. You were flitting around this place like the hostess of the year. I'm surprised you didn't invite him to stay and have dinner! You know people aren't supposed to know you had that operation."

"Is that what this mood is about? Am I supposed to act sick? 'Cause if that's the case, maybe I should have just kept the old heart."

Thad instantly felt bad about his comment. It was his job to make life easy for her, not make her feel bad. It wasn't her fault he was tense over the possibility of getting caught for the fraud he had committed. He had done it all for her in the first place.

"I'm sorry, honey. I don't know what got into me. Actually, I do like President Cooper. I voted for him, too. Now, that's between you and me. Does that get me some points? Does it qualify as letting loose?" Thad joked. "I feel bad about what Cooper's going through with this Polly Flowers bitch. Having to answer questions all over again reminded me of the situation. I wish I could help the president. Instead, I'm digging his hole deeper."

314

"You told them what you saw. That's all you can do, honey. But I understand. I know you'd help if you could. You're a good man. Thanks for sharing that with me."

\* \* \*

The minute Daniel hopped in his car, he dialed Christopher Frye's cell number. Instead of waiting for access to a computer, he decided to ask Frye to get him some facts on congestive heart failure. He was hoping to give the president a report this evening that would put a smile on his face. Even if he didn't get much out of Polly Flowers, his visit to Thaddeus Raymond could still prove fruitful.

Driving through the Virginia suburbs of D.C., Daniel was entering a much more upscale area than the Raymonds' neighborhood. According to his research, Polly Flowers had bought her new home just weeks after the incident with the president. Daniel would love to prove she had gotten the money for the five-thousand-square-foot, six-bedroom estate through a payoff for the scam she committed. Unfortunately, it wasn't going to be that easy. Since "Polly Flowers" became a household name, she had been making a lot of appearances on television talk shows. She was reported to have received a multimillion-dollar contract to tell her exclusive story to the *National Enquirer*. She was also rumored to have received a large payment from one of the Big Six publishing houses to write an autobiography. Flowers had let the world know that her dream was always to be a Hollywood actress. According to some newspaper articles Daniel had read, she was getting offers from producers to star in a movie about her own life.

A search of all Polly Flowers's bank accounts in the United States got Daniel nothing useful. He pored meticulously through hundreds of pages of statements and didn't find any deposits or expenditures out of the ordinary. He could legally account for every cent. Finding a suspicious deposit in any domestic bank was highly unlikely. If she had received a payoff, the money was certainly wired to an offshore institution.

Daniel had Frye helping with the financial research, too. He was comforted to be able to rely on his partner to do a good deal of the grunt work. Those accounts were notoriously difficult for law enforcement officers to pinpoint. The system was designed that way, especially for accounts created in Switzerland or the Caribbean islands. If anyone could decipher and uncover an anomaly, Chris was the man.

Polly Flowers lived in Mclean, Virginia, named by *Bloomberg Businessweek* as the most expensive suburb in the state and one of the richest in the country. The median home price was $789,000. Her neighborhood was considered one of the most exclusive in a city with a total population of less than forty thousand. Not a house on her block was valued at less than $2.5 million. Flowers had paid $4.5 million for her mansion. In order to gain access to her subdivision, Daniel had to pass through a guarded security station. He showed his badge to the officer and lied that he was investigating one of the residents for real estate fraud. The goal was to take Polly Flowers by surprise. He wanted to deny her even a second to prepare.

It was a little after nine p.m. He fully expected to find her at home. Daniel had read on the Internet that earlier in the day she had appeared on a local TV talk show and said she was glad to have a few days to spend at her new house. She wasn't scheduled to travel again until the end of the week, when she would be in Hollywood to meet with some heavyweight film producers.

He pulled his rented car into the driveway leading to the Flowers residence. An eight-foot brick wall surrounded the property, which covered more than two acres. Daniel had to stop at the locked gate, where a camera and talk box communicated with the housekeeping staff on the inside. His plan to show up unannounced was foiled.

His call was answered promptly by a butler staff member. Daniel held up his badge and explained that he had some questions to ask the owner of the house about recent burglaries in the neighborhood. After a slight delay, the gate opened, and Daniel rolled up the driveway toward the house. The winding pavement led through a thicket of trees and up to a circular drive. He parked in front of a flight of eight steps leading up to the front door.

Looking through the windows into the house, it appeared to be as black as the night sky except for some light coming from a corner room on the upper level. Daniel went to the door and rang the bell. The sound of chimes playing Michael Jackson's "I'm Going Hollywood" penetrated through the thick maplewood door. It had taken Daniel close to five minutes to get through the gate and up the driveway to where he parked his car. He waited two more for the butler to finally let him in.

Polly Flowers was nowhere to be seen. The butler had Daniel follow him into a library and study toward the back of the house, then announced that Miss Flowers would be down in just a few minutes. He asked Daniel to repeat his name, showed him to a seat on the sofa, and left the room.

Ten minutes later, Polly Flowers entered regally and quite dramatically. She carried herself with an exaggerated grace and sophistication. It was after nine in the evening, yet she was dressed to the nines in a long, flowing, red Versace evening gown with red stiletto heels. Hanging down the low neckline was a diamond-and-emerald necklace that had to have a total weight of more than six or seven carats, complemented by a three-carat diamond on the ring finger of her right hand, and an emerald tennis bracelet on her left wrist. To Daniel, she looked like a movie star. She was positively stunning.

* * *

Polly took one look at Daniel and had an instant crush on him. She had seen him on the news and in newspaper and magazine pictures, but it hadn't prepared her for the full impact in person. Playing opposite such a handsome man could only enhance her performance. Little did Daniel know, his plan to surprise her was thwarted long before he rang the buzzer at the front gate. The general had warned Polly weeks ago that the authorities could be paying her a visit in the very near future. Immediately after Daniel left the Raymond house, Thaddeus had phoned the general to tell him of Daniel's surprise appearance at his home in Alexandria. The moment that conversation was over, the general had called Polly.

Mainly, he wanted to remind her how she should handle the situation. The powers that be had left no stone unturned in preparation for this moment. They were under no illusions that Polly would avoid having to face a federal agent at some point. They had devoted an entire week of ten-hour days to her rehearsal. The plan had been determined, written out, and committed to memory until Polly could recite her lines in her sleep. Since any variance or conflict in her story could be disastrous, she was forbidden to stray from the script. So long as it stayed consistent, no one could prove she was lying. The same applied to her character. She would continue to present herself as the high-end prostitute introduced to the world in previous TV reports and newspaper articles.

The general had promised Polly that if she followed his instructions, everything would be fine. To relieve any worry she may have during the questioning, he assured her the FBI had no grounds to charge her with any crime. If they threatened to, it was just bluster and intimidation. Knowing it would pump her up for a brilliant performance, he told her this was truly her time to shine as an actress. Partly due to the role she was playing and also because she truly felt an attraction, Polly walked across the room toward Daniel, swinging her hips flirtatiously. She offered him her right hand, cleared her throat, and introduced herself, delivering her words like an aristocrat.

"Good evening, Agent Falcone. Can I offer you something to drink? Perhaps a cup of tea?"

"Ma'am, I'm not here on a social call." Daniel held up his badge and explained his position with the FBI. "I'm not here to investigate any burglaries either. The law requires me to warn you that you're being investigated for fraud involving the president of the United States—a felony that can carry up to twenty-five years in federal prison. I'm here to ask you a few questions about your night in Mexico City."

The general, well aware of the implications of a request for representation, had discussed with Polly the pros and cons of choosing not to cooperate. She certainly had the right to plead the Fifth Amendment and have a lawyer present if Falcone indicated she was being investigated for a crime. From the outset, it was decided that she would talk to the law if she was called in for questioning about the incident. Neither she nor her benefactor wanted to give the impression they had anything to hide. They would rely on Polly to adhere scrupulously to the script.

"That was very shrewd, Agent Falcone. But I have no problem answering your questions. I have nothing to hide."

* * *

With his notes at his side containing a list of all the statements Polly Flowers had made in her various interviews over the past week, Daniel interrogated her as if she were a hardened career criminal. To get the woman to slip up, to contradict one of her many previous allegations, he pulled out every stop and used every trick he had learned in his fifteen years as an FBI agent.

Everything about her reeked of deception. Her posture, her tone, her gestures, and her emotional tells were classic characteristics of someone who was lying. Nonetheless, when the last question was asked and answered, Daniel had absolutely nothing he could use to help prove that President Cooper was set up.

Though Daniel was fully expecting to come away with something of value from the interview, he refused to be disappointed. He had a pretty good feeling that he had stumbled on something big today, and was anxious to hear what Frye had learned about Kendra Raymond's heart disease.

**Chapter 23**

With a majority in both the House and the Senate, the Democratic Party was able to pass the Alvin Fitch Bill with relative ease and speed. A day after President Cooper signed it into law, lawsuits were filed in all fifty states challenging its constitutionality and citing a long list of other legal grounds for its repeal. Major coverage of the issue by every form of media, and the overwhelming interest by the American public, prompted the lawyers filing the individual cases to join forces in one class-action suit and retain the country's best federal attorney to oversee it.. Arguing that our nation's security was at risk, he got the U.S. Supreme Court to grant a writ of certiorari to hear arguments on its next docket.

While the army of lawyers was seeking to challenge the Fitch Act within the bounds of the law, others were employing much less conventional means to deal with the growing immigration concerns. Vigilante border protection resulting in cold-blooded murder had increased to an all-time high. Billy Ray and a carefully selected group of motivated young Klansmen were significant contributors to the record-breaking numbers. Border security, always an essential element of Billy Ray's overall plan, had been boosted to top priority in the past few weeks.

Shortly after the president announced he was supporting the Alvin Fitch bill, Billy Ray began recruiting existing members of the Klan from the four states bordering Mexico, to muster a paramilitary troop and prevent more immigrants from crossing illegally into the country. Fifty men were equipped with top-of-the-line M16A4 assault rifles and night-vision paraphernalia—the same used by the U.S. Marines. After several weeks of instruction overseen by former marines who were now members of the Klan, demonstrating how to use the equipment and perform nighttime operations, they were set loose to patrol the Mexican border in the states of California, Arizona, New Mexico, and Texas. Their orders were to shoot on sight any obviously suspicious individuals attempting to cross.

For Billy Ray, work under the cover of darkness was his sole means of physically contributing to the cause. He was rapidly becoming one of the most recognizable and infamous men in America. He couldn't open up a newspaper without seeing pictures of his face, from every possible angle, plastered all over one of the first few pages. It seemed that every time he turned on the news, whether local or world, there was a story about him, with more pictures and numbers to call for anyone with information that could lead to his capture. The same applied to the Internet.

Billy Ray was sure that Christy and his undercover men were responsible for all the face shots the media had at their disposal. Christy, at least, wouldn't be causing any more problems. Nonetheless, thanks to him and the FBI, it had been many weeks since Billy Ray could afford to go out in broad daylight without the very real risk of being recognized. This Mexican border gig was a perfect outlet for releasing his intense feelings of hate and participating in the execution of the plan that was his brainchild. At the very least, he would have something to do until the time was right to perform the ultimate deed—a job that would be relegated to someone else only over his dead body.

On this particular night, Billy Ray was intensely eager to prevent any undesirables from crossing the border. Being cooped up indoors all day was starting to grate on his nerves, especially with Thanksgiving and Christmas approaching. He wasn't a man who could easily sit still within the four walls of his house. The outdoors was his playground, above all during this time of the year.

It was hunting season. In the Johnson household, the turkey on the Thanksgiving table was never store bought. It was a family tradition to hunt and shoot the main course of every holiday meal, and the FBI- and media-imposed prohibition against enjoying these times with his kin was frustrating the hell out of him. Being prevented from taking advantage of the beautiful open spaces his country had to offer, while illegal aliens were given a free pass to citizenship, only embittered him all the more. Whoever tried to break into the U.S.A. under his watch was going to regret it.

It was a bitter cold night on the Texas border in the Chihuahuan Desert. At higher elevations than the Sonoran Desert to the west, the temperatures were much milder in summer and could be frigid in winter. Even in the fall, depending on the ferocity of the winds from the north, it could be downright Siberian. Tonight, there were gusts of up to fifty miles per hour, with sustained winds over thirty. The low for the night was predicted to dip into the teens. With the wind-chill factor, it would feel like well below zero. Billy Ray was appropriately dressed for the weather, with two sweaters over his flannel shirt, thermal underwear, a Chillwave parka, a thick wool scarf covering most of his face, and heavily insulated leather gloves. He had on two pairs of Chinook winter socks and Keen Summit boots—all products made in the good old U.S.A.

The Chihuahuan desert was normally a hot spot for smuggling illegal aliens into the United States by coyotes—men paid for their expertise and knowledge of the geography. The desolate, hilly terrain was ideal for surreptitious crossings. The past several weeks had seen a precipitous drop in the number of attempts at unlawful entry into the United States. Since the uptick in murders was reported in the U.S. and Mexican news, many hopeful emigrants were hesitant to put their lives at risk.

323

After a brief meeting of the nine Klansmen working this section of the desert, to determine the territory they would cover, they had split into teams of two, except for Billy Ray, who preferred to work alone. Over the past few nights, the only result he had managed to achieve was to freeze his ass off. In fact, not one of the men assigned to the Chihuahuan Desert had sighted any suspicious activity in the past week. Billy Ray was spoiling for some action.

The wind seemed to carry the stench of wetback in the air. Whether it was intuition, a truly acute sense of smell, or just dumb luck, Billy Ray was about to get his opportunity to do what he did best. Off in the distance, due south, he heard the rapid patter of Spanish conversation. He dropped to the ground, then quietly put the night-vision binoculars up to his face. It took a few moments for his vision to adjust after he put the cold plastic of the binoculars against his skin.

Peering through the lenses toward the sound of the voices, he focused on three people about 150 yards away, walking in his direction. The leader was a middle-aged woman whom Billy Ray guessed to be somewhere in her early forties. She had ample breasts and long, thick black hair that hung over the front of her shoulders. Her dark complexion and hair, round face, high cheekbones, and short stature pegged her for a Mexican Indian. Her tattered shawl with multicolored diamond and flower patterns, and the blanket coat she was wearing further confirmed her ethnicity. Just behind her, standing side by side, were two boys with similar features. One was a few inches taller than the woman. Billy Ray estimated his age at about 16. The other boy couldn't be more than 10.

Billy Ray waited patiently on the ground until the three had closed the distance to a few paces. All three let out a startled squeal when Billy Ray suddenly stood up, pointing his automatic rifle between the woman's eyes.

"Stop!" he shouted. Out of the corner of his eye, he saw the older of the two boys reach to his belt and pull out a hunting knife with an unusually long blade. Billy Ray didn't know whether to laugh or shoot the kid dead. Just like a spic to bring a knife to a gunfight. Knowing he might never get another opportunity like this anytime soon, he decided to have some fun.

"Drop the knife or I'll blow your mother's brains out," Billy Ray ordered.

"*No hablamos inglés. Por favor, no hiera a mis hijos,*" said the woman, holding her hands high in the air. She turned to pull her sons closer to her and noticed that the older one had pulled out his weapon. Without thinking twice, she grabbed its handle from his tight grip and threw it to the ground. Then she placed her hands together as if to pray and beg for the life of her children in her native language.

"I don't understand a word of that fuckin' gibberish. Now, shut the fuck up!"

\* \* \*

Flor Gómez was born to Zapotec Indians in Oaxaca, Mexico, thirty-seven years and two days before meeting with Billy Ray Johnson in the Chihuahuan Desert. She had lived the first fifteen years of her life in the northern mountains of the Sierra Madre. As the daughter of strict traditionalists regarding Mexican and Zapotec customs, Flor's role in the tribe and family was well defined. A woman's place was in the home, her responsibilities to cook, clean, and serve her man. A woman's sexual purity was highly valued in their culture and, undoubtedly, a vital part of their character in her father's eyes. It was instilled in her from a very young age that a woman's reputation was everything. There were certain expectations regarding her interactions with the opposite sex. As a child, she was permitted male playmates. When she reached adolescence, she was forbidden to walk the streets of her village without a proper escort.

To this day, Flor cringed when she thought about the moment her parents discovered that she was pregnant at just 15 years old. One evening, during the detention hour, in the janitor's closet of her school, one mistake with a boy who was 16 had changed the course of her life forever. She had thought she was in love with him since she first met him in *la escuela primaria,* the elementary school. But after the closet incident, he never spoke to her again.

In her 15 years, her father had never laid a hand on her. The smack she received across the face from his thick, callused hand left bruises for more than a week. She was kicked out of the house with the clothes on her back and a pillowcase full of personal items and possessions dear to her heart. It didn't amount to much: a bracelet given her by her grandmother, and a few books she had collected over the years.

Disowned by her parents and unable to seek refuge at the home of any local family member, she spent the first few nights of her forced independence on the streets of the City of Oaxaca. Even though it was becoming obvious that she was with child, she didn't escape the notice of several of the pimps who patrolled the city's streets in search of young runaways. Most chose not to deal with the situation. One man, old enough to be her grandfather, took particular interest in her.

At first, Flor thought that the old man was a godsend, a gift from above to care for her and her unborn child. She couldn't have been more mistaken. Shortly after taking her in, he began to show his true colors. For the remaining four months of her pregnancy, he forced her to perform all kinds of perverted

326

sexual acts with him. She tried to refuse only once. Despite his apparent age, the old man packed an amazing punch. A battered face and two black eyes were not something she wanted to experience a second time. Once she gave birth to her first son, the old man put her on a strict diet, then sent her out onto the streets to earn her keep. All the while, he continued to rape her several times a week.

The infant was a nuisance to the old man. He had two simple rules: keep the baby quiet and earn enough cash to make the annoyance worth his while. Perhaps it would have been better for Flor if she had been unsuccessful in the business. Then she would have been rid of the cruel, heartless pervert. To the contrary she was beautiful and had tremendous sex appeal, and she was his top-earning whore. He watched over her like a hawk, making sure she worked her territory for his maximum profit. Working so many hours, she got precious little time with her infant, so his other girls cared for the boy while Flor was out on the streets.

For a year and a half, she followed the old man's orders, enduring the violation of her body by his clients, and his bizarre perversions in bed. The night she came home to find her son missing from his crib was the final straw. She searched the obvious places. When the baby was nowhere to be found, she went to the kitchen, grabbed the biggest knife she could find, and entered the old man's room, bursting through the door without knocking. That alone was a courageous act, for his warning had been clear, the consequences well-defined: no one was permitted in his private room without an invitation.

Flor found the old degenerate naked, standing at the foot of his bed, masturbating while doing unspeakable things to her year-and-a-half-old baby. What she had feared most had come to pass. It sent her over the edge, and she ran at the old pervert.

327

"*¡Deja a mi hijo, cabrón!*" Flor shouted, lunging with the knife toward her nemesis. The old man jumped backward in an attempt to avoid her attack, but this only served to trap him between her and the wall. The adrenaline rushing through her body gave her the strength to knock him to the floor, onto his back. She was on top of him before he could make a move to defend himself. She stabbed him in the throat with such force, the blade penetrated flesh and bone and exited through the back of the neck. Crazed beyond reason by the rape of her son, she continued stabbing maniacally at his neck and face. Blood spewed from a severed carotid artery, soaking Flor's face, hair, and dress. By the time she regained her senses, the old man's face was an unrecognizable pulp.

She stood up calmly, almost in a trance, to find her child screaming hysterically. Aware of the blood covering her entire torso, she picked her baby up and carried him to the bathroom across the hall, holding him face forward with her arms extended in front of her. The child continued to wail as she placed him in the bathtub and removed all his clothing and hers, then stepped in and turned on the shower. She scrubbed her body as quickly as she could. Once she was satisfied she had removed all the blood and gore, she washed away the blood she had transferred to her child's underarms, back, and chest while carrying him. When the last of the red stream circled its way down the drain, she sat down in the tub and held her baby tight to her bosom until his sobs diminished and stopped.

The reality of what she had done finally struck her like a load of bricks. She shut off the shower and stepped out of the bathtub with her baby clinging to her shoulder. Turning her head away from him, she tried to hide her terror as she grabbed the towel hanging on a hook on the bathroom door. She had no choice but to run. One of the old pimp's other whores could be showing up at the house any minute. The stupid women who worked for him were actually jealous of Flor's moneymaking prowess, and they wouldn't hesitate an instant to report her to the police.

With the baby still in her arms, she ran to her bedroom, dried herself and him, dressed him in a fresh jumper, then sat him on the bed while she threw on a dress and a baby sling. She stuffed their meager possessions into two pillowcases, along with the money she had earned that night, and placed the boy in the sling. Before she left the house, she went back to the old man's bedroom. His pants were draped over the dresser located just inside the door. Flor reached into the back pocket, pulled out his wallet, and took all the cash. To avoid stepping in the pool of blood that had accumulated on the old shag carpet, she crawled over the bed to get to the closet on the other side. On the top shelf, behind a stack of shoe boxes, he kept a metal lockbox. Flor had seen him put money in it on several occasions. She didn't know where he kept the key, but she couldn't worry about that at the moment. She tossed the box into one of the pillowcases, climbed back across the bed, and went out to the kitchen, where she packed some food. Then she walked through the front door into the dark night.

Flor fled as far as she could on foot, traveling north of the city through the Valles Centrales toward Tehuacán. She made her way along the foothills of the Sierra Madre Oriental, trudging through the uneven terrain until the sun rose the following day. It was only her sheer determination and her love for her son that allowed her, three days later, to reach Tehuacán, the home of her brother from her father's first marriage. He took her in for a few days until she was forced to move on to avoid the authorities. Having had his own issues with the law, including two five-year stints in federal prison for credit card fraud and drug trafficking, he had his share of experience avoiding the police. He arranged for her to get a new identity with false documents and drove her to a shelter for single mothers in Mexico City.

With the shelter's help, Flor found a job sewing garments in a clothing factory on the outskirts of the capital. It was shortly after she moved into a small studio apartment the size of her bedroom at her parents' home that she discovered she was pregnant with her second child. She immediately dismissed from her thoughts the possibility that the old man could be the father. If she allowed herself to believe it, she wasn't sure she could be the mother the child deserved. The only way to ensure that she didn't reject the baby was to convince herself that the father was one of her countless johns.

For eleven years, she successfully avoided the police. She slowly advanced at the factory, ultimately earning a supervisory position. It certainly hadn't made her rich, but it, along with the money from the old man's lockbox, put a roof over her children's heads and food in their mouths while she set aside small amounts for their education. She had just begun to settle into a comfortable life when her past came back to haunt her.

Flor's ultimate undoing was the tenacity of a detective who refused to give up searching for the murderer of the old man. The case was one of two involving escaped killers, which marred his otherwise impeccable record. He was more than eager to travel to Mexico City after receiving an anonymous call from one of the victim's former prostitutes, who recognized Flor at a local market. The information eventually led him to the factory where Flor worked. His misfortune was making his move to arrest her on her day off. Her closest friend warned Flor of the detective's visit to the factory, and she had no choice but to flee once again. This time, she decided to find a way to cross the border to America, the land of opportunity. Ironically, if not for her friend, Flor would have been in a Mexican jail rather than facing a scary-looking gringo in the frozen, desolate American desert.

\* \* \*

"Get on the ground, facedown," Billy Ray ordered the older of the two boys, neither of whom spoke a word of English. Billy Ray chose to interpret his lack of comprehension as a refusal to obey the command, even though he was more than smart enough to figure out the real reason. In truth, he didn't need much to send him over the edge. The boy's noncompliance was enough. He aimed the gun at the boy's forehead and fired three shots in rapid succession. All three of them hit their mark.

The woman released a piercing scream of grief and rage. She lunged toward Billy Ray to prevent him from taking another shot. Her reaction wasn't nearly fast enough. Billy Ray calmly adjusted his aim a foot and a half to the left and several inches lower, firing a shot that entered Flor's skull at the bridge of her nose, right between the eyes. She fell to the ground on her back. He put two more bullets into her head for good measure, leaving the youngest child as the only living member of the family.

The boy, actually 12 years old, had grown up with the stigma of being much shorter than average for his age. Perhaps for that very reason, he had more courage than most grown men. Before Billy Ray could turn away from Flor, the boy was rushing toward him from behind at full speed. The raging child leaped onto his mother's killer's back, then reached with his right arm around Billy Ray's neck and began to squeeze. Billy Ray was surprised at the boy's response and the strength of his hold. Then a barrage of punches from a small fist crashed against his right temple.

Billy Ray had had enough. He reached behind him with his free hand, grabbed a fistful of the boy's thick black hair, and yanked him up and over his head. The boy flipped in a full somersault in the air and crashed to the ground on his back.

Ignoring the throbbing of his temple, Billy Ray lifted his leg and, with the full force of his fury behind it, stomped on the boy's face. Billy Ray could hear the facial bones cracking underfoot. The boy released a scream like that of an angry cougar. Paying no heed, Billy Ray continued stomping maniacally. Only fatigue and an increasing inability to breathe eventually forced him to stop several minutes later, though the boy was dead within the first fifteen seconds of the beating.

\* \* \*

"There's definitely something fishy going on, Daniel," said Christopher Frye through the speaker phone in his Chevy Impala. Frye was on his way to the North Miami field office from Fort Lauderdale International Airport. He had spent the day at Quantico, training rookie agents in the science of ballistics. While in Virginia, he had made the trip to Alexandria as a special favor to Daniel, to do a search of Kendra Raymond's medical records.

"How so?" said Daniel.

"There are no records to be found."

"You checked with all the doctors and hospitals on the list?"

Before Daniel had made his request to Frye, he had the president's team obtain a list of Kendra Raymond's doctors and treating hospitals, using claims filed by Thaddeus with his insurance company. Frye's plan was to use HIPAA regulations, which allowed the seizure of medical records from health care providers for national security and intelligence purposes.

"Of course. Her cardiologist claimed that all their record keeping was converted to paperless several years ago. Any actual written reports would have been more than five years old and destroyed. The office manager said that a few months ago, a major storm caused a blackout that erased many of their patients' records from the database, including Mrs. Raymond's."

"No fuckin' way."

"That's what they say. Obviously, you're gonna want to look into it more closely. It doesn't make a whole hell of a lot of sense that something as important as a person's medical records wouldn't have a major backup system."

Daniel groaned. "If I had a couple of clones, I'd get right to it."

"Wait. It gets way more suspicious. The cardiac surgeon she saw a few years ago, before the claim was denied, supposedly lost her records in a warehouse fire. Her family doctor is nowhere to be found. According to administration at one of the hospitals where he practiced, he closed up shop and moved out of the country."

"No shit? This is going to be a fuckin' nightmare."

"That's exactly what I was thinking. It would take people in very high places to accomplish a conspiracy of such magnitude, if that's what's happening."

"Or a whole lot of money. It takes cash to make things disappear and keep mouths shut. Then again, power and money go hand in hand. When you think about who would have a motive to bring down the president of the United States, countless factions come to mind. The obvious would be the opposing party. It's pathetic, but you have to add the fact that he's black to the mix. Then the list gets longer—way longer. Especially considering what's been going on all over the country. I just hope we're not dealing with powerful politicians. They're slippery bastards. Everything'll be sealed tight as a drum."

"If that's the case, I agree. We're gonna keep running into brick walls. Are you sure you're up to all this? A couple of days ago, your heart stopped beating twice."

"I'll survive. Can I count on you for more help if I need it?"

"You know I got your back. I'll do whatever I can. Just take care of you."

"I'll think about that after I catch the fuckers who tried to burn me alive."

**Chapter 24**

The landing gear of a privately chartered Gulfstream V jet touched down on runway 2 of the Baghdad International Airport, nineteen miles southwest of the city center. Plumes of whitish smoke rose from the black rubber tires and dissipated into the dry air. The only two passengers, Brody and Thaddeus Raymond, were on a thirty-six-hour mission to Mosul, in northern Iraq, to procure materials for the bomb to be detonated in Billy Ray's upcoming attack. Brody's benefactors had insisted on obtaining the explosives from a Muslim country. For the time being—meaning until after the next presidential election—they didn't want responsibility to attach to any domestic organization. History had proved that aggressive acts by the Ku Klux Klan had an adverse effect on the success of the more conservative political groups. They were not willing to take the chance that any remnants of the bomb could be connected with the recent domestic terrorism. Brody was setting things up to look like another offensive by al-Qaeda.

Brody and Thad would be meeting with one of the Muslim terrorist group's most notorious explosives experts. The leaders of al-Qaeda were more than happy to assist and even take blame for the incident that was scheduled to occur in less than two short weeks. It wasn't the first time they had conspired with American politicians to inflict terror and fear on the hearts of the American public. They were already well acquainted with the man named Brody.

Thad's involvement was necessary for the reason that Brody's benefactors recruited him in the first place. Muslim terrorist improvised explosive devices were his area of expertise in the Army Special Forces. During his tour in Iraq, he had diffused more than fifty bombs, saving hundreds of millions of dollars in military equipment and U.S. and allied installations. He was one of a handful of people in the United States with the knowledge to build one of the Islamist terrorists' bombs. During this trip, it was his responsibility to confirm all the necessary parts were obtained through al-Qaeda's black market.

To avoid detection at any of the airports, Brody had had Thad's appearance altered by a lifelong buddy—a retired CIA legend known for his masterful creation of disguises. Thad was no longer a fit, 42-year-old, fair-skinned, brown-haired Caucasian. He was a heavyset South Asian man in his sixties, with white hair, a large nose, and thick black-framed glasses magnifying his contact-lens-altered brown eyes.

As the aircraft came to a complete stop on the tarmac and the seat-belt sign went off, the two men rose from their seats and waited while a flight attendant opened the door. Two Arab men greeted them at the bottom of the steps. They whisked the Americans away in a terminal transport vehicle that took them to a separate part of the airport, where a hangar housing private aircraft was located. Inside the building, one of the Arab men blindfolded both Brody and Thad and helped them into their seats on a Russian built M-17 helicopter, while the other settled into the pilot's seat. The pilot pushed a button to activate the retractable roof. Once it was fully open, the chopper lifted into the desert air.

\* \* \*

Ten minutes later, the chopper was flying at an altitude low enough to avoid radar, on its way to a paramilitary camp in the mountains east of Mosul. This was not its maiden voyage from Baghdad to the base. They would fly across the eastern part of Iraq to avoid the more densely populated cities. The sun had long since set, allowing them to remain invisible from the ground. The engine was mechanically altered for silence to avoid auditory detection. Due to the indirect route, it took over an hour and a half to arrive at their destination.

The compound consisted of two residential barracks and a large concrete supply warehouse. Those structures were surrounded by three training sites. The pilot and his colleague helped the blindfolded pair step off the helicopter. They lifted and lowered Thad and Brody, then set them down where they were supported by two soldiers on the ground, who escorted them into the storage facility. Once they were inside, the blindfolds were removed.

The device Thaddeus had designed on paper for the impending attack was four times as powerful as the one used in the first attack on the World Trade Center. The most important ingredient he was after was 5,400 pounds of urea nitrate. The items Raymond had ordered were procured through the efforts of Mohammed Abdul Ashkani, the explosives expert who negotiated the purchases on the black market. Mohammed was waiting for the two Americans just inside the building. He took over for the soldiers and led Brody and Raymond to the double doors opposite the main entrance.

Mohammed was born in the Gilgit-Baltistan region of Pakistan, notable for being the home of K2, the second-highest mountain on the planet. An explosives expert himself, he was directly or indirectly responsible for seven terrorist attacks against American installations, and more than twenty-five bombings against various political entities. The death toll attributable to him alone exceeded one thousand. He was one of the most sought-after terrorists in the world by the United States and other governments.

Thad and Brody passed through the double doors with Mohammed, into a vast stockroom full of machines, vehicles, and living supplies. They continued to the far side of the room, to another door, which required a key to

337

enter. Mohammed pulled a key ring from his jacket pocket and unlocked three single-cylinder, grade 1 dead bolts. He stepped inside first, followed by Raymond and then Brody. The space, about half the size of the outer depository, housed an arsenal containing a wide variety of weaponry. Rows of shelving were marked with labels in Arabic. Raymond and Brody were led past the munitions area and into a fully furnished office. On top of a desk were two boxes and four large crates marked in English, "For Brody."

"Please feel free to look inside," said Mohammed. "It is all there. I check myself. Everything to make all five components of bomb."

Brody gestured to Thad to verify that everything was there. Thad spent the next half hour examining the boxes' contents to confirm that he had sufficient explosive and all the parts required to make a power supply, including Pakistani nine-volt batteries, initiator, switch, delay mechanism, and remote control. When he nodded, two men operating forklifts loaded the boxes onto the chopper. Then Brody and Raymond were blindfolded once more before leaving the building. They were taken directly to Baghdad airport, where they would immediately begin the thirteen-hour trip back home.

\* \* \*

In the past few weeks since his near-death experience, Daniel had not taken a moment for himself or his loved ones. His mind had even been distracted from the Nameless serial murderer. Every waking hour of his day had been devoted to the capture of Billy Ray Johnson and his cohorts, and the resolution of the president's predicament. On the Billy Ray front, Daniel was no closer to narrowing down his whereabouts than he had been for the weeks before the encounter in Georgia. If not for the progress he was making with President Cooper's assignment, he would have felt as if he were hitting his head against a brick wall.

Some of his more recent discoveries were the most significant to date. Initially, his efforts to obtain more information about Kendra Raymond were thwarted at every turn. Even Secret Service agents who were willing to talk about her illness before were now refusing to cooperate. Just two days ago, quite late in the evening, Daniel had received a call from a Secret Service agent who had protected the president during his campaign for the 2016 election.

"Agent Falcone here."

"Hi. This is André Green. I'm a United States Secret Service Agent. I got your number from an agent I work with. He said you were looking into the Polly Flowers matter . . . uh . . . asking about Thaddeus Raymond's wife. He really wants to help the president, but he can't afford to get involved. He knew I would."

André Green was the one of three black agents assigned to protect Cooper after he announced his intention to run for the presidency. Though Secret Service agents were expected to have no political party affiliations, Green considered himself Cooper's number one fan. After a year and a half on the campaign trail, Green had developed a great respect for the Democratic presidential candidate. An act of kindness on Cooper's part had played no small role in creating those feelings. He had stood up for Green when Secret Service management was issuing a reprimand that very well could have cost Green his job.

Green's wife, eight months pregnant with their first child, was rushed to the hospital the night of a Cooper campaign rally at Central Park in New York.

Tens of thousands of people were expected to attend. Cooper was in the room when Green was notified via cell phone that his spouse was in danger of losing the baby. Cooper insisted that Green be at his wife's side, and so Green went. The Secret Service brass didn't see it that way. As far as they were concerned, the only valid reason for abandoning an assignment was death or severe physical injury to the Secret Service agent. Not only was Green being pulled from Cooper's detail, he was to face suspension and possible termination. The Secret Service had no sympathy for Mrs. Green's predicament or the eventual birth of their child. President Cooper's insistence that André Green remain on his team ended all punitive proceedings, and André would be forever grateful.

The day he saw the news report about the Polly Flowers affair, he knew that it was bullshit. When his buddy, who was currently assigned to protect Cooper, called about helping Daniel Falcone with his investigation into Kendra Raymond's medical condition, Green was happy to step up.

"Do you have any information that would help prove that President Cooper was framed?" Falcone asked when he received the call from Green.

"I can tell you this: I worked with Thaddeus Raymond just before he was sent to Mexico City to help with the summit. I've been to his house several times. His wife was sick—near dead, if you ask me. Every time I was there, she was too weak to get out of bed. Raymond told me she needed a heart transplant or she wouldn't survive. Just a month or so ago, I ran into him at the hospital after Kendra had an operation, though I'm sure he didn't see me. My dad was in for triple bypass open-heart surgery. I was visiting him in the step-down unit. Kendra was being released."

"Which hospital?"

"George Washington University. I was standing outside my dad's room while his nurse gave him a bath. I couldn't help overhearing the conversation in the room next door. A doctor was talking to the patient. My ears perked up when I heard him call her Kendra—not that common a name. There was some discussion about a mistake with her name—something to that effect. I didn't get it all. Then he was giving her instructions about medications she would be taking for her new heart. A few minutes later, she was wheeled out of the room by Thad. I ducked back into my dad's room—had no desire to talk to him or his wife. The doctor came to see my father next. I remember his name because it was the same as mine. Dr. Green, Dr. Steven Green. His first name just came to me."

"Did you see Kendra Raymond in the wheelchair?"

"I saw both of their profiles: Kendra's and Thad's. I have no doubt it was them."

"Can I ask why you didn't want to talk to them?"

"I worked at President Cooper's side for almost two years. That man didn't cheat on his wife. Thad Raymond is a fraud and a fucking liar—pardon my French."

"You have any specific proof that he lied?"

"Just know it in my heart, man. I don't need more than that."

"We checked with George Washington University Hospital administration. They claimed that Mrs. Raymond was never a patient."

"They're fuckin' liars."

"Did you hear or see anything else regarding the Raymonds while you were there? Are you willing to testify to everything you just told me, under oath if it becomes necessary?"

"To your first question, no. To the second, absolutely."

\* \* \*

Dr. Steven Green was not Kendra Raymond's treating cardiologist. He had seen her on several occasions as a stand-in. On the day Agent André Green met Dr. Steven Green, Mrs. Raymond's cardiac surgeon was unavailable because he was performing an emergency angioplasty. When Kendra's nurse was having difficulty adjusting her temporary pacemaker, she requested assistance from Dr. Green, who was already in the unit.

The general was a man who usually left nothing to chance. He hadn't anticipated this sort of eventuality. Though Kendra was admitted under an alias, Dr. Green recognized her immediately. When he discussed the name mistake on the file with Kendra, she referred him to her cardiac surgeon for an explanation.

To satisfy his curiosity, Dr. Green called his colleague that evening. He was forced to leave a message after the connection went straight to voice mail. Instead of a return call, at ten p.m. he received a personal visit from two burly men in black suits on the doorstep of his home in Alexandria. It became obvious to Green rather quickly that his unexpected callers, who refused to identify themselves, were not the sort of people one argued with. They forced their way into the house, pushing past Green. Once they had his full attention, flipping open their jackets to reveal semiautomatic pistols holstered in their waistbands, one of the men made a proposition he called the "offer of a lifetime." It was clear that Green had no choice in the matter but to accept the astoundingly large sum of money. The spokesman explained in no uncertain terms that if Green were to reveal that he had treated Mrs. Raymond, he, his twin brother, and his brother's wife and children would die slowly.

342

Daniel Falcone's visit to George Washington University Hospital was nearly as horrifying for Dr. Green as his encounter with the men in black. The doctor wasn't accustomed to being questioned by FBI agents. The subject matter of the inquiry only made it that much more distressing.

After the terrifying experience at his home, Dr. Green had engaged in some serious reflection to sort out why his and his family's lives should be threatened over Kendra Raymond's medical condition. So far, he hadn't come up with much. Like the rest of the world, he knew that Mrs. Raymond's husband had a connection to the Polly Flowers affair. Dr. Green couldn't help but think that the president's political problems were somehow related.

The afternoon Daniel Falcone showed up unannounced at the hospital, he was waiting for Green as he came out of the cardiac intensive care unit. As soon as the doctor came through the unit's double doors, Falcone held up his badge.

"Dr. Green, I'm Special Agent Daniel Falcone. I'd like to ask you a few questions. Is there somewhere private we can meet?"

"You mean right now?"

"Yes, sir. Right now."

"Uh . . . I'm kinda busy. I am a doctor and this is a hospital, in case you haven't noticed."

"I just have a few questions about one of your former patients. It won't take long. I promise. Besides, I know you were heading back to your office. Your secretary gave me your schedule."

"Okay, but who is this about?"

"I think you might prefer to be out of earshot of your colleagues before we chat."

"Okay, follow me," said Dr. Green, with a grimace of reluctance.

He led Falcone down a long corridor to a bank of elevators. They took the first available to the fourth floor, then made their way to the east wing, which consisted mostly of doctors' offices, including Green's. After closing the door and offering Falcone a seat in front of his desk, Green sat in his chair.

"I'm not going to beat around the bush, Dr. Green. We suspect—no, we know—that the medical records of one of your former patients have been destroyed or tampered with. Her name is Kendra Raymond. Do you remember her?"

It had been made abundantly clear to Dr. Green that if asked, he was to deny ever having treated Mrs. Raymond. The thought of lying to an FBI agent conducting an official investigation was making him perspire. Wet stains were already growing in dark circles under his armpits. He couldn't imagine that he was going to be able to lie convincingly. He had never been good at it, and under the current circumstances, he didn't see any reason why that would miraculously change. If he opened his mouth, he was sure his voice would quiver.

He considered just telling the truth. Perhaps the FBI could protect him and his family. As quickly as he contemplated doing so, he changed his mind. Taking a deep breath to calm himself, he said, "That name doesn't sound familiar to me." He was relieved and surprised that the words seemed to come out evenly.

"I have information to the contrary."

Dr. Green stared at Falcone as if expecting him to continue. He just stared back.

"I don't know what you want me to say, Agent Falcone. I don't remember her."

344

"I think you do."

"What makes you think that? Why don't you tell me what information you have?"

"Because I don't answer questions—I ask them. I will tell you, though, it doesn't take an expert in lie detection to see that you're not telling the truth. You're nervous as hell. It must be seventy degrees in this room, and you're sweating. You can't sit still. I think you'd do yourself a favor if you'd just answer my question honestly."

Dr. Green didn't think that Falcone's comment could be farther from the truth. Perspiration was now trickling down his spine, leaving a snakelike trail of moisture down the back of his scrubs. The discoloration under his arms was increasing at an alarming rate. It had to be obvious to the agent. Green had performed delicate procedures, threading instruments through a patient's vascular system and into major arteries of the heart. Never had he experienced as much stress as at this moment.

His natural inclination had always been to do the right thing. He took the Hippocratic Oath seriously and was one of those true physicians, whose priority was to heal rather than get rich. During his childhood, his brother and peers had teased him mercilessly for being a teacher's pet and straight-laced kiss-ass. As an adult, he was a stickler for the rules. It went against every grain in his body to break them. Only self-preservation and concern for his brother and family were telling him to lie through his teeth.

As the seconds ticked away, he realized he had delayed much too long in responding. He was falling apart in front of his interrogator, and it was surely apparent.

"Doctor, I can see you're struggling. Let me help you. Tell me what's going on here."

Falcone's offer of assistance was all Dr. Green needed to hear. The truth spouted from him as if he had been injected with a serum.

"Kendra Raymond had heart transplant surgery under a false name. I was forced—"

The doctor never got the chance to complete his sentence. A bullet plinked through the window behind his desk, penetrated the back of his head, and burst through the occipital lobe of the brain, exiting through the nasal cavity past Daniel's right ear and finally lodging itself into the opposite wall.

\* \* \*

Former Special Forces lieutenant Jacob Briggs was lying flat on his stomach on the roof of the nine-story Jefferson House, located across the street from George Washington University Hospital. His M110 SASS sniper rifle was assembled and ready. At that very moment, he was peering through its scope directly into Dr. Green's office while in cell phone contact with the general. The receiver in his right ear was capturing any conversation between Dr. Green and Daniel Falcone. He was relating his observations to the general as the scene unfolded.

"We've got a problem. The subject is giving himself away."

General Adam Montgomery was thinking that he had made a huge mistake. He should never have let it get to this point. He had listened in on the bribe that his former special-ops men had dictated to the doctor, and there was something in Green's demeanor, a weakness, that led the general to believe there could be trouble. All the doctors who had been paid off were under

346

surveillance. Due to his uncertainty, the general had been keeping an extra-close eye on Dr. Green. As soon the general's man on the ground reported that Falcone had entered the hospital, Briggs had received the order to be prepared to act at a moment's notice.

"God damn it, I should have never let him live. I didn't want this job to get complicated. Fuckin' Falcone is everywhere. Son of a bitch!" the general bellowed.

"I can take care of that for you. I have a perfect shot right now."

"Has he revealed anything yet?"

"So far, he's denying he knows the patient. The back of his shirt is getting soaked from sweat. I can see it dripping down the side of his face."

"Let's give him a chance to do the right thing. We know he's very close to his brother. If he even speaks one syllable that makes you think he's squealing, put a bullet—"

Before the general finished his sentence, the report of the rifle reverberated through the receiver.

"Now get the fuck out of there."

\* \* \*

Daniel hit the deck as soon as he heard the sound of breaking glass and saw the doctor's head slump forward. He drew his pistol and called out Dr. Green's name. Getting no response, he hastily crawled around the desk, using it for cover. Rounding the corner, he stayed low, below the bottom edge of the window. When he made it to the other side of the desk, he could see that Green's arm was hanging down at his side. From a crouched position, with quick, efficient movements, Daniel reached up, grabbed the doctor's wrist, and checked for a pulse. There was none. Drops of blood spilled intermittently from the back of Green's head. He wanted to call out for help, but didn't want to put anyone in danger in case the sniper was still in position to shoot. It was probably too late for Green anyway.

Scooting on his stomach, Daniel moved as fast as he could to the wall. With his back against it, he shifted to a seated position, then looked up at the window to his left. He saw a small hole in the glass. Cracks spread out from its center like the strands of a spider's web. With a thrust from his legs, he slid his back up the wall until he was standing less than an inch from the window's edge. He shot a hurried glance toward the roof of the building across the street. A man carrying a canvas case large enough to hold a rifle was sprinting toward a door not ten feet in front of him.

Daniel had to make a snap decision. Did the circumstances warrant firing shots at the suspect? There was no way to open the window, and he couldn't order the fleeing suspect to halt—not through thick glass and across a street full of traffic noise. He decided he couldn't take the risk of using his weapon. For one thing, shooting a man in the back was rarely legal or acceptable. He did, however, feel safe enough to move out of the office.

While reaching for his cell phone to call for backup, he ran out the door to seek help for Dr. Green. Precious minutes passed as he searched for a hospital employee to inform about the doctor's predicament. He ran through the maze of hospital corridors until he finally notified a woman in scrubs coming out of an elevator. He took that same elevator to the first floor, then, running at top speed, followed the signs to the main entrance at Twenty-third Street Northwest.

A minute later, he was scanning the streets between the hospital and Jefferson House, looking for signs of the man he had seen on the roof. The scene before him was typical of any of thousands of university campuses around the country, with no fleeing criminals or suspiciously speeding cars. Young students, many with backpacks, walked along the street while others rode bicycles.

The D.C. FBI SWAT team, twenty police officers from the capital's Metropolitan Police, and as many University Police all showed up at the scene during the next four to ten minutes. A comprehensive manhunt began for the suspect, whom Daniel described as best he could. He was able to provide hair color, body type, and approximate height and weight, but not nearly enough to make a valid identification.

Dr. Green had died from the gunshot to his head. The local police department swept the roof of the Jefferson House and Dr. Green's office for evidence. Potential witnesses at both buildings were questioned. By the time the hunt was terminated hours later, several hospital employees said they had seen a man carrying a canvas case enter the hospital elevators at the main lobby. A thorough room-to-room search turned up nothing.

\* \* \*

A blast of cold late-autumn air hit Daniel in the face as he went out the automatic doors on the hospital's ground floor. The sting in his eyes and the shiver running through his body made him appreciate that he lived in sunny south Florida. For the moment, he had to put the discomfort from the weather out of his mind to concentrate on the business at hand. Although there were no clues to where Dr. Green's killer might be hiding, Daniel had made some interesting discoveries.

After his failed attempt to spot the suspect, he had rushed back to Green's office. He wanted to be able to search it for any kind of surveillance or bugging equipment before backup arrived. He would have waited for assistance from either the local FBI field office or the police to do a sweep with the array of devices they had at their disposal. This was not an official Bureau investigation, and more importantly, he simply didn't want the reason for his visit to Dr. Green to get around.

He donned a pair of latex gloves he kept in his briefcase, then started his search by checking the air-conditioning vents, the telephone receivers, and the underside of the desk. These were typical places where Military Intel, the CIA, and the FBI hid cameras, wires, or listening devices. The first place he looked yielded results. In the air-conditioning vent directly across from the desk, Daniel found what appeared to be a Sarnoff BLINC miniature camera—spyware typically used by the CIA, Special Ops and, at times, by the Bureau. Minutes later, he found a bug in the receiver of Dr. Green's phone, and an auditory recorder on the underside of the desk. As he received a call that the university police had arrived, he placed the equipment in his briefcase. If anyone discovered additional surveillance devices, it would be up to the investigating authority to make sense of it. Daniel later lied to his colleagues at the FBI and the local police that he was visiting Dr. Green to recruit him as an expert in the Fitch case, to describe the variety of drugs that could be used to cause chest pain.

**Chapter 25**

"I'm getting closer, Mr. President. Your suspicions were dead-on about the people who set you up. They're ruthless. They're professionals and they mean business. I'm pretty sure that CIA operatives are involved, if not the Bureau. Don't know if they're former agents or current. Let's hope it's not the military—that would pose all kinds of problems that I don't even need to tell you about. One thing is sure. These guys will stop at nothing."

After helping search for the suspect and spending another three hours giving his report to the D.C. Police detective assigned to the murder, Daniel had gone directly to the White House to meet with President Cooper.

"I can't tell you how much I appreciate your putting your life on the line for this mission. You can't be too careful, Daniel. I don't think any of us are safe at this point. Anyone going for the president of the United States using this kind of tactics has to have brass balls. You have any idea if more surveillance equipment was found anywhere else in Green's office or at the hospital?"

"When I left, they were finishing up the crime scene analysis. The lead detective had already done his sweep of the office. I don't think they were necessarily thinking to look for bugs or cameras. The theories I heard tossed around had nothing to do with top secret governmental operations. I must have gotten it all. Up to that point, they hadn't found anything."

"That's a good thing. Do you have any theories on how the guy got away?"

"I do. You know he was seen in the hospital, or at least, we're pretty sure of it. There's a possibility I just missed him coming in. I wasted too much time looking for someone to help Dr. Green. It could be, the unsub got rid of the weapon and blended in once he was in the medical center. It's unlikely but not impossible. Also, there is a helipad on the roof of the hospital. I couldn't see it from the street. I had everything sealed off right after I got back inside. If there was a chopper waiting for him, he might have had enough time to make it up there and get away before all means of escape were closed down. There was one student living in Jefferson House who said he saw a helicopter flying south away from the hospital as he exited his building right around the time the suspect would have lifted off."

* * *

Brody and each of his four benefactors were seated around an oval table in a dingy motel room in Northern Virginia, on what could aptly be described as the wrong side of the tracks. Like the previous meeting of the four highly placed political figures at the hotel on the outskirts of Washington, each of the four men was dressed in casual clothes, sunglasses, and a baseball cap. Following Brody's instructions, they had arrived at the motel room at fifteen-minute intervals.

Discretion was of the utmost importance. As high-profile bureaucrats, they were on the news of all major television networks just about every day. They had taken every precaution possible to prevent anyone from recognizing them. A new set of four men dressed in construction uniforms had swept the room for bugs just as Brody arrived. The president's cabinet member and self-appointed leader of the group spoke first.

"It's just days now until the big event. We're not talking about blowing up a church or a Jewish monument here. This is one of the most important things any of us will ever do in our lifetime. Not to be Captain Obvious, but what will happen in a few short days will go down in history. It's almost like divine intervention that they scheduled their event when they did. Brody here has made a suggestion that I want you all to hear. I, for one, am all for it. You have the floor, Brody."

"It's simple: I'd like to do away with Billy Ray right around the time the deed is done. I don't see any reason to wait. I know I've given him my support in the past, and I still think he's a smart kid. Now that we're at the brink of a major turning point, we can't afford to keep him around. We're all painfully aware that he doesn't know how to control his emotions. Mark my words: keeping him alive for any period of time will come back to haunt you."

"Listen, guys," said the congressman. "There's been a reason why we've wanted Billy Ray involved from the beginning. If things go wrong and they don't fall for the Muslim terrorist-attack ploy, with Billy Ray we have a backup scapegoat. If, by some outside chance, the authorities were to identify the bomber, the Klan becomes the focus. It's definitely not the scenario we prefer, but it deflects attention from us."

"That can still happen," Brody responded. "I can make sure he's the prime suspect if the feds don't go down the path we lead them on initially."

"Are you absolutely sure?"

"You have my guarantee, sir. It's infinitely riskier keeping him alive."

"Let's put this thing to a vote," said the Cabinet member. "All for Brody's plan, say 'aye.'"

"Aye," repeated every man in the room.

"Very well. The ayes have it, then. Everything is set for this weekend. It'll be the beginning of a new course that will set our country back on the right path. God bless you, and God bless America!"

\* \* \*

Kyle Lansbury was furious. Driving at breakneck speed south on I-95, he recalled his conversation with Billy Ray just three hours ago.

"What the fuck, Kyle? Seriously? You gave her this fuckin' address? You gotta be shittin' me. Is she on her way here now?"

"Yeah, man. I couldn't talk sense to her. She's pissed the doctor won't see her again until she pays her bill. She's obsessed with this fuckin' baby."

"I don't give a shit what's going on with you and her or the fuckin' baby. She shows up here and you're dead. You know that asshole Falcone has to have a tail on her. She'll lead 'em right to us. Are you fuckin' retarded, or what?"

"I tried to tell her I'd wire her money, but she doesn't trust me. Said they're not tailing her anymore."

"Listen to me good, dickhead. How the hell does she know if she's being tailed? We don't take chances. You get this thing straightened out, and I mean now. I don't care how you do it. Just get it done or you're fucked. And don't come back here after—you'll lead them right to our doorstep."

"Where should I go, then?"

"That's your fuckin' problem. Figure it out."

After his conversation with Billy Ray, Kyle had spent almost an hour on the phone with Tabitha, trying to talk her out of coming. Supposedly, she was already on the road. She needed to be back in south Florida the next morning for a sonogram. The doctor's office had told her not to show up if she didn't have the money to pay for it and her past-due balance. Her time constraints were the only reason Kyle could convince her to let him meet her at a motel halfway, in Jacksonville, Florida. She insisted that he pay her back for the room she intended to reserve. Little did she know, he had barely enough cash on him to pay for it, much less the thousands she had demanded for her medical bills. She warned him that if he didn't show up, she would be at their doorstep in Dillard, Georgia, by suppertime.

Before getting on the Interstate, Kyle had stopped at a liquor store to pick up a couple of six-packs. In the past hour of his trip, he had consumed one of them and was considering starting on the second. He was lucky to have already avoided two accidents and not crossed paths with any police. He suffered from the delusion that drinking calmed his nerves, though it often had the opposite effect. At the moment, his anger was reaching a peak. By the time he drove into the parking lot of the motel, he had worked himself up into a full-blown rage.

The liquor saturating his brain cells had caused him to throw caution to the winds. He pulled into a parking space directly in front of room 156—the number she had texted to him just fifteen minutes ago, after she checked in. He stumbled out of his car, lost his balance, regained it, then took a pratfall on the pavement. Swearing, he staggered up to the door and banged on it three times with his fist. Tabitha opened it almost immediately. She must have seen him arrive through the picture window facing the parking lot. She also must have seen him trip and wobble his way from the car to the room.

"You're wasted!" she snapped. "You fuckin' asshole. You drove all this way drunk."

She didn't get to say another word. He shoved her violently into the room and shut the door behind him. Tabitha opened her mouth probably to shout at him for pushing her. He never gave her the chance. He smacked her square in the mouth with his open palm, causing her to fall backward. The base of her skull smacked down on the thin carpet, which provided scant cushion from the concrete floor.

"Asshole, huh? Who's the asshole now, bitch?" Unaware that she had lost consciousness, he continued to speak.

"Who the fuck you think you're talking to? I'm not gonna take this shit from you anymore. You think you can tell me what the fuck to do just because you're pregnant. 'The baby this, the baby that.' I'm sick of the fuckin' baby. I'm sick of it all."

Kyle cocked his leg back and kicked Tabitha in the side of her belly, then did it again and again. The first blow connected directly with the head of the six-month-old fetus, killing it upon impact. Just seconds before the FBI special agents tailing Tabitha burst through the door, Kyle reached into the vest holster tucked inside his denim jacket, pulled out the .357 Magnum revolver he had stolen from the compound, put the muzzle in his mouth, and pulled the trigger.

* * *

The Joint Terrorism Task Force, which Daniel had put together, was in the final stages of filing the application for the indictment against Billy Ray Johnson for killing Senator Alvin Fitch. The federal grand jury had already indicted him and Kyle Lansbury for the murder of Trent Blake and the attempted murder of Daniel Falcone. Frye and a team of more than fifty agents had set a goal to establish

356

that Billy Ray was present at the Miami Beach Convention Center, the Ritz-Carlton, and Jackson Memorial Hospital on or near the night in question. After tedious weeks interviewing hundreds of witnesses from each of those venues, they were ready. Seven wait staff members working the Alvin Fitch dinner had confirmed Clerici's and Slater's observations by picking Johnson out of a photo lineup. Two people at the Ritz-Carlton had seen him the night before the assassination. One was a businesswoman staying on the same floor, who had passed him in the hallway the afternoon she checked in. The second was a Latino bellhop who asked to help Billy Ray with his luggage. He clearly remembered Billy Ray's rude refusal. Both successfully picked him out of the photo lineup.

The final piece of the puzzle, which may very well have sealed Billy Ray's fate, came from a hospital employee at Jackson Memorial. The photo chosen for the lineup was a bust shot. Consequently, when the mixed-race cleaning woman who crossed paths with him that evening picked him out of the lineup, she was not misled by the fat suit he was wearing. Once again, it was Billy Ray's demeanor that got him ID'd. Despite his efforts not to react, the disgusted look on his face, and his exaggerated maneuver to avoid her touch as she got off the elevator did not go unnoticed. Not only did she recognize him, but thanks to the unusual events that took place during her shift, she made the connection between her brush with Billy Ray and the night of Alvin Fitch's admission.

One final interesting task force find created a link between Billy Ray and at least one of the domestic terrorist attacks. Frank Hess was determined to be the driver of the Dodge Caravan that carried the bomb to the Javits Federal Building in New York. If not for the perseverance of his mother, the information might never have been discovered. Nothing was left of Frank's body to identify. After he went missing, Mrs. Hess conducted her own tireless investigation to find her son. She hung hundreds of pictures of him on trees and in public buildings in Brooklyn and Manhattan. One of the witnesses who had provided Frank's description for the composite drawing happened upon one of Mrs. Hess's photographs, posted in the lobby of the building where the witness worked. She immediately recognized the similarities and contacted the FBI. Through her identification and further digging by the terrorism task force, the connection between Frank Hess and Keith Peterson was uncovered. The fact that Peterson was Billy Ray's childhood best friend could not be a coincidence.

Once Peterson became part of the picture, the footprints found in a field across the street from Mary Magdalene Church in Alabama were compared to his known shoe size and those of Billy Ray Johnson and Kyle Lansbury. They matched. The circumstantial evidence wasn't enough to indict any of the three on those charges yet, though it was a great start.

Confident that the task force was in good hands, Daniel had spent the past couple of weeks at Quantico, working the Polly Flowers affair. He wanted to be with his team when the reports filed for application for the indictment were signed. Since the assassination had occurred in Florida, the paperwork would have to be filed in the federal court in Miami. He intended to have those documents in the prosecutor's hands by the following evening, which also happened to be the date of the re-creation of the Million Man March.

\* \* \*

In Alexandria, Virginia, it was a beautiful, balmy day. Though Kendra Raymond enjoyed fresh air as much as the next person, she looked forward to the cooler temperatures of November. There was nothing homier and more comforting than a log fire burning in the fireplace while she and her husband enjoyed their evening cup of decaf. She couldn't know that this evening would turn into one of the most dreadful of her entire life—even including the day her doctor notified her that she would die within twelve months if she didn't get a new heart.

She had just sat down on the family room sofa to wait for Thad, who was taking care of some business matters in his office. She still planned for them to have that cup of coffee despite the warm weather and watch her favorite reality show, *Dancing with the Stars*. When Thad came rushing out of his office looking as if he had just seen a ghost, Kendra was instantly on edge.

"What's wrong, honey?" she asked.

"The FBI agent's back. He's walking up to the front door as we speak."

\* \* \*

Thad had fully expected the agent to return at some point; he just hadn't thought it would be so soon. He had broached the subject of the operation again with Kendra the following day after Daniel's first visit but didn't want to get into anything specific at the time. He wanted to be certain that she knew she must never reveal anything about the transplant to Agent Falcone under any circumstances.

That conversation could have gone much better. Kendra was peeved about several issues. First, she didn't appreciate being ordered to commit a crime, namely, lying to a federal law enforcement agent. Second, his refusal to discuss it in any more detail was infuriating. Thad had told her he had every intention of doing so. It just wasn't the right moment. He conveniently omitted that he needed the time to think about exactly what he should disclose and what he needed to keep secret. If he had done a little soul-searching, he might have realized that he was stalling. Though the delay was unwise, he feared Kendra's response to the truth. And now it was too late. Falcone was about to ring their doorbell.

"Fantastic. I'm supposed to lie to this guy and I have no fucking idea why."

"Sweetheart, I'm sorry. I meant to talk to you about this. I didn't think he'd be back so soon. Please, baby, trust me. There's a vital reason why we can't tell him about the transplant. The consequences could be devastating. I have no time to explain now. Just please, don't say anything." Thad knew he was in big trouble. Kendra rarely used profanity.

The doorbell rang.

"Can't we act like we're not home? That'll give us a chance to talk. I'd really like to be a lot more prepared."

"Honey, the windows are open. The TV's blaring. The neighbors probably know what show we're watching. I'm sure he could hear it when he got out of his car. And just about every light in the house is on. Unfortunately, we have to do this. Let me do most of the talking."

"What if he asks me a question?"

"Just answer it with as few words as possible. I'll try to take over from there. I gotta get the door. You ready?"

"No."

Thad frowned, then cast a pleading look her way as he approached the door. It had to be obvious to Kendra that he was over the top with anxiety. She actually looked more stressed than he was, probably because her normally cool and collected husband was a mess. He opened the door and greeted Agent Falcone.

* * *

The instant Daniel walked into the Raymond home, he could sense the tension in the room. Kendra Raymond looked like a deer frozen in the headlights of an oncoming Mack truck. Thaddeus's hello had the faintest quiver. This would certainly work to Daniel's advantage. No Mr. Nice Guy tonight. As soon as everyone was seated, he began the questioning.

"I'm going to be direct. I'm sure you lied to me the other day, Mr. Raymond. I'm also pretty certain you know what the repercussions are for obstructing justice. I want to know exactly what you and Polly Flowers are up to—and no bullshit."

"I have no idea what you're talking about."

"Come on, you can do better than that. How much were you paid to set up the president?"

Daniel shot a glance at Mrs. Raymond after she released an audible squeal. He immediately turned to her.

"Are you in on this, Mrs. Raymond? And don't even try the 'I don't know what you're talking about' routine. It's not going to fly."

"Okay, that's enough!" Thaddeus shouted. "You're not going to speak to me or my wife like that in our home. Get out!"

"Sorry, pal. It's not gonna be that easy. I'd be glad to give you and your wife an escort to Quantico to answer my questions. It's your choice."

After a tense half minute of silence, Daniel repeated, "It's your choice. Make a decision, or I'll make it for you."

"Listen," Thad said, "I've told you and all the others everything I know. I'm telling the truth. My statement won't change. My wife has nothing to do with this. If you want to take anyone to Quantico, take me, and I'll answer all your questions again."

"That won't be possible. You know as well as I do that Mrs. Raymond is an integral part of all this." Daniel looked over at Kendra. The shock on her face was genuine. "It seems that she may not know it, but I do."

It was plain to see that Mrs. Raymond was on the cliff's end, on the ragged edge of failing at her attempt to maintain control. Daniel wondered if she was beginning to put two and two together. He could see her lips moving as if she were praying with as much fervor as she had ever mustered, that he wouldn't direct his next question to her. He was sure she was about to spill her guts.

Daniel continued, "Looks to me like she's not gonna be too pleased, either, when she's facing the gas chamber for treason."

The dam had broken. With tears streaming down her face, she turned to her husband. "Thad, what did you do?"

"Shut up, Kendra. We didn't do anything. And this interview is over. Take us to Quantico if you have to. We have nothing to say." Daniel was getting the distinct impression that Raymond was realizing much too late that he had made a huge mistake. With the information Daniel had now, he was sure Raymond had set up the president to save his wife. If only Raymond would admit it, something could be worked out. Unfortunately, it didn't seem likely to happen tonight. The husband held all the cards and he wasn't ready to talk.

"Are you saying you're pleading the Fifth?" Daniel said.

"Wouldn't you love that? I'm telling you we are done. Here or at Quantico, the results will be the same."

"How do you feel about that, Mrs. Raymond?"

"Kendra, don't you say a word. Now, you have a choice, Agent Falcone," Thad explained. "You want us to tell you nothing here, or at Quantico?"

Daniel had his answer. He may not get any admissions tonight, but he was sure that Raymond had been paid off. And Raymond knew that Daniel had the smoking gun. The next time he visited, he would take a different tack. The people Raymond had bargained with were obviously very dangerous. With permission from the president, an offer of amnesty and protection might just elicit a confession. Daniel would apply no more pressure tonight. Raymond and his wife had a lot to talk about.

**Chapter 26**

Ozzie Mills didn't have time to be excited about the event that had been her brainchild. Not only was the re-creation of the Million Man March her idea, but she had taken on the responsibility of coordinating the schedule of the speeches and entertainment.

For more than forty years, Ozzie had worked tirelessly as an advocate for civil rights. She was a former U.S. senator from California. She was a pioneer for the development of educational programs for young black women and men. Among African Americans, her face was just as recognizable as those of many sports figures and Hollywood celebrities. She had dedicated her life to public service, propelling her to become a leader in the community. The president of the United States also happened to be her brother.

She had chosen November 17 for a reason. Dr. Martin Luther King Jr. had been her idol since she was a young schoolgirl. There weren't many who knew more about that American icon than Ozzie Mills. On that date, Dr. King had delivered his famous "Love Your Enemies" speech at a Baptist church in Alabama. It was her favorite by far. The fact that it was delivered on her birthday pleased her. It had absolutely nothing to do with her preference. The subject matter of the sermon was an issue near and dear to Dr. King's heart, and one that would define him through history. Against his doctor's orders, he had risen from his sickbed to emphasize a tenet basic to him: to love and forgive one's persecutors. Ozzie believed with all her heart that Dr. King truly loved all people—even the murderer who would ultimately bring him down, if that were possible.

There would be no birthday parties today. Ozzie would be lucky to find time to eat, let alone to blow out the candles of a birthday cake. The meaning of the march and the symbolism behind it were enough of a celebration for her. When she first chose the date, she had worried about what the weather might be like in Washington, D.C. Dr. King must have been looking down on her and those who would be attending—it couldn't have been more perfect.

There weren't many people in the country who could have gathered the list of major celebrities and players booked to appear before the masses—some to speak, others to entertain. Thelma Brown was a big score. What a fine lady she was. She had taken the time out of her busy schedule to call Ozzie after accepting the president's invitation. Ozzie was ready to pay her a fee for her performance. Thelma refused to take a dime. She would be preceded by a slew of current black artists and highly placed politicians. The pièce de résistance, a speech by none other than her brother, the president of the United States, would cap off an incredible day. Ozzie had received hundreds of calls from top Hollywood actors and other celebrities of all races, requesting tickets that allowed access to the area closest to the stage. She had to be stingy with them without putting too many noses out of joint. It was going to be a veritable Who's Who in America.

\* \* \*

Tabitha Freemont had been in a state of severe depression for more than a week. She had spent most of that time in the Jacksonville hospital where the FBI agents took her. The first thought that came to mind when she regained consciousness on the day of her admission was for her unborn child. She had felt

365

her stomach—though still somewhat swollen from the pregnancy and the beating, it wasn't nearly as big as when she woke up that morning. Her screams for a doctor echoed throughout the entire ward.

The news she received was devastating: her baby boy had not survived the trauma. Tabitha's injuries were almost as serious. The emergency room doc told her she was lucky to be alive. By the way she felt, she wasn't so sure lucky was the way to describe it. The internal bleeding had been mostly contained within the uterus, which had suffered irreparable damage. Thus, the surgeon who performed the cesarean section to remove the baby had done a hysterectomy as well. Tabitha would never bear a child of her own.

For the first few days after her admission, her depression was so profound, she considered various plans for suicide. If she had had the means at her disposal, she very well might have gone through with it. By the fourth day, her injuries had healed to the point that discharge would have been appropriate, at least from a physical standpoint. Due to her state of mind, the doctors felt it best that she spend at least another few days in the psychiatric ward.

With medication and therapy, Tabitha was beginning to show signs of improvement. After a few short days, she was eating better and interacting with her therapists and fellow patients in group sessions. Actually, though, the depression was being replaced by a slowly simmering fury. She said nothing to the staff about her growing anger, for that would only delay her discharge. Soon, the low simmer grew to a raging boil. Her thoughts of ending it all turned to ideas involving the agonizing death of the men who had corrupted the father of her baby.

Tabitha had had big plans to rescue Kyle from the Klan. She was fairly certain the FBI tail had never been discontinued, even while she advised Kyle to the contrary. The sensation that she was being followed had been with her for weeks. She had held out the hope that when Kyle was arrested, she could convince him to snitch on the real culprits in exchange for his freedom. He might have been furious at first. In the end, he would have realized the wisdom of her strategy. More importantly, her baby would have a father.

At the moment, she had no sympathy for Kyle, whose corpse was decomposing six feet under. The bastard had gotten what he deserved. There was no way Billy Ray and his deranged gang of racists were going to get away with their part in the death of her baby. If it landed her in prison or the gas chamber, then so be it—the satisfaction she would get from their suffering would be well worth it.

The more she contemplated inflicting anguish and pain, the less satisfying the idea of murder appeared, for their misery would end with their death. Thoughts of how they would suffer behind bars generated a much more gratifying mental image. Billy Ray could never make it in a prison situation. Daily close proximity to blacks and Latinos would be a fate worse than death. She had enough information to put them all away, and she knew exactly how to make it happen.

\* \* \*

Kelly Olsen could feel the heat of the south Florida morning coming through her office window and warming her shoulders and back. She had specifically requested that Annie give her that space away from the air-conditioning vents and closer to the sun. Kelly was completely in love with Fort Lauderdale and everything about it, including the heat and humidity. At the moment, though, she was getting heated in rather a different way. The woman on the telephone was being a giant pain in her ass. This was the third time she had called in the past twenty minutes, insisting on talking to Annie.

The initial call had come in at eight a.m. on the dot—opening time for the law offices of Annie Bryan. Kelly told the woman she would have Annie call her back. Not five minutes later, she called again to complain that she hadn't heard from Annie yet. Kelly explained that her boss was a busy woman and would get back to her when she had the chance. That provoked a five-minute diatribe about the urgency of her issue. Kelly informed her that everyone requiring Ms. Bryan's services had a case that was urgent to them, but she would place the message in the "top priority" pile. That seemed to placate her for the moment, though Kelly had no intention of giving the call special attention.

This time, ten whole minutes passed before her number showed up again on the caller ID. Kelly considered letting it go to voice mail. At the last minute, she decided to answer so that she could demand that the lady stop tying up their lines. That didn't work, either. Now she was insisting that her case was a matter of life and death and that she would not hang up until she was connected with Ms. Bryan. The time had come to ask Annie how to deal with this lunatic. Kelly placed the caller on hold and rang Annie's office.

"I'm sorry to bother you with this, Annie. I can't get rid of this woman. She's called three times in twenty minutes, and now she's insisting it's a matter of life and death."

"Did you tell her to call the police?"

"I tried that. She said she wouldn't talk to them without representation."

"She didn't give you any idea who or what it's about?"

"No, she's just been a royal pain in the ass."

"Okay, I'll handle it. Put her through. What's her name?"

"Tabitha Freemont."

\* \* \*

The sound of Brody's voice had become like the nagging buzz of a gnat in his ear. This was the fifth time they had been over the detailed plan and schedule for the day. "Repetition is the key to success and the best way to prevent mistakes." If Billy Ray heard those words one more time, he was going to reach into Brody's mouth and tear out his voice box. He happened to agree with the statement, but enough was enough. He had disassembled and put together a replica of the bomb at least a hundred times in training sessions with Thad Raymond. He could do it in his sleep. Raymond had built the actual device in five days. Billy Ray would see it for the first time in another few hours.

The plan and schedule for this day had been devised more than a month ago. Billy Ray had even had a hand in it. He needed this time to himself to meditate, to prepare himself for one of the most important tasks of his lifetime. Children would be reading about it in textbooks for centuries to come.

If Brody and his people thought he was going to let the world think foreign terrorists were responsible, they were out of their minds. The time had come for the Ku Klux Klan to begin taking credit for its work. The nonwhite races, Jews, and Mexicans who were not welcome and had no place in the United States were about to see their world turned upside down. When the entire planet became aware of what the Klan could accomplish, the organization and the white race would earn a new respect. Membership would increase tenfold. He could begin to create a real army, an authentic American military that would reclaim the best country on earth.

\* \* \*

"This is Annie Bryan. How can I help you, Ms. Freemont?"

Tabitha's choice of attorney had been deliberate. This time, she had done some research. It would be another dagger in Billy Ray's and his friends' backs to see that she had enlisted the aid of a woman who was the product of the love between a black and a white parent.

"I need to see you right away."

"Ms. Freemont, all of my clients—"

"This is about the Ku Klux Klan. I know who's been bombing the churches. They have other plans, too. I need to talk to Agent Falcone right away."

Tabitha now had Annie's complete attention. "You should go directly to the FBI if you have that kind of information. You don't need me. I can get you in touch with Agent Falcone right now. How do you know him?"

"I *do* need you. Agent Falcone suspects me of helping a known criminal. I lied to him. I was protecting my dick of a boyfriend—him and all those evil bastards killing innocent people. No need for that anymore. I'm willing to tell him everything, but I need a guarantee. I don't want to go to jail."

"Miss Freemont, there are no guarantees in this business. I could stand by you and do everything in my power to get you the best deal possible. It might work. Especially considering the magnitude of the information you have.

370

Honestly, I can't be a hundred percent sure they won't charge you with something if you obstructed justice.

Second, if you know of plans to commit more crimes, and lives are in danger, it could put you in more trouble. Your best bet is to tell Agent Falcone everything you know, regardless of the consequences. By the way, what was your boyfriend's name?"

"I'd rather talk to you about the specifics in person." After a brief hesitation, Tabitha reconsidered. "Oh, what the hell. I can give you his name. You've met him: Kyle Lansbury."

Annie couldn't believe her ears. She would have liked to forget him, but the incident was all too fresh in her memory, especially with the recent news of his suicide. She asked, "Is that the same Kyle Lansbury who called me a 'nigger' and walked out of my office? Do you know anything about that?"

"Yes, ma'am. And I'm sorry. I'm the one who made the appointment with you. I didn't realize you were black, or I wouldn't have subjected you to that asshole. I'm not a racist."

"What made you choose me *this* time?"

"After he almost beat the crap out of me for making the appointment, I looked you up. I read a lot of stuff about you. I know you must be a great lawyer."

Annie wasn't so sure she was telling the truth, but this issue was far too important to ignore. "Okay, I'll help you. When can you get in here?"

"I can come right now. I could be there in fifteen minutes."

"I think you should do just that."

\* \* \*

The instant Daniel's flight touched ground at Fort Lauderdale-Hollywood International Airport, he turned on his phone to see that he had seven missed calls from Annie. Rather than listen to the messages she had left, he dialed her number. The first thought that came to mind was Damien Drysdale. Fear for his children made him sick at his stomach. The wait for Annie to pick up was all but intolerable.

"Hi, Annie. What's going on? Is everything okay? Are the boys all right?"

"Whoa, Daniel. Did you listen to any of my messages?"

"When I saw I had seven missed calls, I called right away. I assume it's an emergency."

"Everyone's fine. I'm sorry I scared you. What I called about is huge. Are you in Florida?"

"Yes, I just landed. We haven't even reached the gate yet."

"Can you come directly here? To my office?"

"You're starting to scare me again. What the hell is going on?"

"I have a client here who wants to talk to you. You're going to want to hear what she has to say."

"What does it involve? Who is this person?"

"Tabitha Freemont. Sound familiar?"

"How the hell did she end up in your office?"

"It's a long story. You need to hear it from the horse's mouth. She's told me some pretty incredible stuff."

"On my way."

"Daniel, before I let you talk to her, there's something we need to discuss."

372

"Are you going to start acting all defense lawyer on me? What do you want?"

"She wants full amnesty for any crimes she may have committed."

"How the hell can I guarantee you something like that without knowing what she knows and what she's done? Besides, I would have to run that by the federal prosecutor. It's not like I have the authority to make that decision. Can you throw me a bone? What do we have here?"

"I'm sorry, I can't give you any specifics. You know I wouldn't call you seven times and ask you to come right away if it wasn't important."

"Oh, well, that helps a great, steaming shitload."

"Listen, Daniel. I'm only trying to help here. And so is Tabitha. I have to represent my client, and I don't need attitude. What the prosecutor doesn't know won't hurt him. You control what you report. You don't have to tell him if she's withheld information. The only thing I'll say is that you might have her on obstructing justice, maybe accessory after the fact—nothing earth shattering—and I've already said too much. I'm as sure as I can be that she's telling the truth. This is big, Daniel. Humongous."

"Accessory after the fact isn't a minor offense."

"I know. It wasn't like she helped commit the crimes, though. Daniel, you really can't afford to dicker here. You know damn well you don't have to charge her with anything."

"All right, you have my word. I'll be there in twenty minutes."

\* \* \*

"I'm so glad you answered the phone, Mr. President," said Daniel. "You have a minute?"

"Not really. You got lucky. I was just taking two seconds to go to the restroom. I hope you have some good news."

"Well, not really. I'm calling to recommend that you cancel your appearance at the Million Man March this afternoon."

"What! Come again! Are you *serious*? Why?"

"I'm very serious, sir. I just spoke with a witness who was engaged to a Ku Klux Klan member working with Billy Ray Johnson. She told me that Johnson has been planning your assassination."

"Did she say how and when?"

"Well, no, sir. She doesn't have that information. But she tells me they've been taking lots of trips to Washington, D.C., lately. Today's event would be the perfect occasion for an assassination attempt. She gave me an address in Georgia where they've been hiding. I was hoping you would lay low until we arrest them. We're putting a team together right now to watch the house."

"How do you know this girl is telling the truth?"

"Other than my own assessment, I don't. But why take the chance? We could make an arrest within the next couple of days; then you could go back to business as usual."

"No offense, Daniel, but I live under the threat of assassination every day of my life. There have been thousands just since I took office. That's what the Secret Service is for. And they happen to be damn good at what they do. If I were to alter my behavior based on threats, I'd never get anything done. Bottom line: if she has no real—and I mean verified—evidence that there is a plot to assassinate me at the Million Man March this afternoon, I'm going to make my speech."

* * *

"He's not changing his plans, Chris." Daniel had made the call to the president on his way to meet with his partner at the Miami field office. He had given Frye a condensed update. Daniel had little doubt that Tabitha Freemont was telling the truth. Now he was facing a real dilemma: should he join the team being assembled to conduct surveillance on the Peterson house in Georgia, or head straight back to D.C.? He had a bad feeling about the march. It was the perfect scenario for an assassin. Millions of people would be milling about. This type of event was a nightmare for the Secret Service. The president was correct: they were good at their job. There would be tons of security, X-ray machines, rooftop snipers, local police, hundreds of Secret Service agents. Keeping track of a million people was still a herculean task.

"What are you gonna do?" asked Frye.

"I'm debating that right now. It's already eleven. If I left immediately, I wouldn't get to D.C. before two. The president is scheduled to give his speech at five. I'm going to have to see if the Learjet is available. If I decide to go back, I can't afford to waste any time. If Johnson does plan to act today, he obviously isn't going to be in Georgia."

"What does your gut tell you, Daniel?"

"I'm having a bad feeling. I think it could be today. No, let me rephrase that. I think it is likely to happen today. Johnson hasn't done anything major in a while now. He's due. But what can I do that the Secret Service can't?"

"You know damn well you're one of the best in the world at deciphering criminal minds. If someone were planning to kill me, I would pick you to protect me over the Secret Service any day of the week."

"Well, I appreciate your confidence, bud. But you are a little biased."

"Cut the shit, Daniel. You know you're good. You're wasting time. Get your ass out of here and go save the day."

\* \* \*

Thaddeus Raymond hadn't even bothered trying to get any sleep the night Daniel paid his most recent visit. Under the best of circumstances, he would have a hard time nodding off, and there was no way he would get any rest on the living room couch. As soon as Falcone left, Kendra had gotten up, stormed to the bedroom, and locked herself in. They hadn't spoken since. She finally emerged from her self-imposed isolation at about ten the next morning. She didn't even glance his way. Thad considered starting a conversation. He certainly owed her an explanation. Having had all night to think about it, he decided to come clean. At a minimum, he would tell her about the Polly Flowers affair and how he got the money to pay for her operation. She was his wife, life partner, and soul mate. She deserved to know.

Based on the sounds and smells coming from the kitchen, at least one of the reasons she had decided to spring herself from the locked bedroom was hunger. He could hear the sizzling of grease and smell the aroma of his favorite breakfast food: bacon. His stomach began to rumble, though he doubted she was cooking for two. Whether she was out of her funk or not, he had suffered about as much as he could handle. He rose from the couch, feeling a little stiff, and went into the kitchen. Kendra didn't turn away from what she was doing, though Thad had intentionally made a fair amount of noise pulling out a chair from the breakfast nook table. His discomfort with her attitude almost prompted him to get right back up and leave. The thought of how ridiculous and cowardly his escape would be quickly changed his mind. If he was brave enough to take a bullet for another man, he should be able to deal with a domestic situation in his own home. His tiptoe approach to starting the conversation wasn't exactly the embodiment of the fearless Secret Service agent.

"How are you feeling this morning, cupcake? I was going to fix breakfast for you."

Kendra had to smile at his chosen term of endearment, but she wasn't going to give him the satisfaction of letting him see it.

"Come on, honey, let's talk. I have a lot to say. I'm sorry. I've been an ass. I know I should be able to confide in you."

He had spoken the magic words. Kendra turned around, rolled her eyes, and finally spoke. "'Cupcake'? *Really?*"

"Aha! It got you to talk to me," Thad said, a big smile on his face.

"All right. I'll talk to you. You're lucky you apologized. But you have a lot of groveling to do. Actually, I take that back. No joking. This is too serious, Thad. I spent half the night thinking about this huge mess. If you can't tell me exactly what's going on here, I think maybe it's time we took a break."

"Don't say that, sweetie. I know I was wrong. I did it all for you."

"Bullshit, Thad. I want honesty. Isn't that what's most important in a relationship? Secrets don't work in a marriage. I understand there are times you can't tell me what's going on at work. But when it directly involves me, I want to know. I have a *right* to know. Even if it's something that has nothing to do with me, it would be nice to know you have the confidence in me to keep my mouth shut when you need me to, especially when you need someone to talk to. I want to be that person."

"I'm done keeping secrets, honey—unless it involves a national security issue, of course. You may want to finish your breakfast first. I'm not sure you'll still have an appetite when we're done."

Kendra took the frying pan from the burner and shut it off, then sat down at the table, across from Thad. "Go ahead. Let's get this over with."

"I've only been thinking about this for weeks, and definitely all night long. And it's still really hard to say. Uh, I was paid a lot of money to set up the president. I've been lying to you, the FBI, and the American public ever since. I did it for you. It was the only solution I saw for getting you a heart."

Thad had been looking directly into Kendra's eyes as he spoke. They gave away nothing. He hesitated before he spoke again.

"Are you going to say anything?"

"I'm not a stupid woman, Thad. Didn't you think I would know something was up? When this whole thing happened with the president, I had no reason to believe you weren't telling the truth. I've never known you to lie. It's not in your nature. But gimme a break, babe. No one gives away hundreds of thousands of dollars for nothing unless they're getting a tax deduction. The timing was pretty suspicious, too. At first, I didn't want to believe you would do such a thing. The man I fell in love with and have known for twenty years wouldn't be capable of doing something so dirty. When I finally accepted the truth, I figured you did it for me."

"So how long have you known?"

"What does it matter? I was waiting for you to tell me. I *needed* you to tell me."

"I really wanted to, baby. It was one of the conditions. It wasn't negotiable. They didn't want you to know."

"Who the hell are these people?"

"Sweetheart, you don't want to know. They're very powerful and ruthless. They would torture their own grandmothers to death to get ahead. It's too dangerous for you to have that information."

"I faced death every day of my life for more than a year. I'm lucky I'm here today. I'm not afraid of the bastards. Let me tell you, just because you did it for me doesn't make me happy. If I had known about all this beforehand—if you had let me in on the decision that basically had everything to do with me and my life—I would have told you not to do it. I'd rather be dead than get involved or be associated with people who are capable of such crooked and disgusting acts. I can't believe you did it. It's going to take me a while to get over it. Now, who are they?"

Thad cringed as Kendra spoke the words. Matters could be infinitely worse if she knew about his most recent doings. Even he had to admit to himself that if he had known he would be essentially blackmailed into building a bomb to kill thousands of people including the president of the United States, he might have thought twice about helping with the Polly Flowers affair. It wasn't outright extortion. Thad had known that once he agreed to frame the president, he could end up at the general's beck and call. But he could never have predicted this. The only reason why he put himself in that position in the first place was for the life of his wife. To hear her disapproval over just the Polly Flowers affair only magnified the poor decisions he had made, into a close-up of a very ugly picture.

"What difference does it make at this point?" he asked. "The only purpose it'll serve is to put your life right back in danger. I don't know if I can do that."

"Damn it, Thad! Haven't you learned a thing from all this. I'm your *wife*. I get to be involved in the decisions that affect us. You don't think these assholes will want more from you? You're their little pawn now, if you weren't already."

"What do you think you can do about it?"

"I don't know. Just maybe I can keep you from making any more really bad mistakes. Are you going to tell me?"

Thad had thought long and hard all night about what he was willing to reveal to Kendra to save his relationship. The Polly Flowers affair was obviously just the tip of the iceberg. Notwithstanding Thad's involvement, if Kendra knew what he knew, he doubted she would sit back and do nothing. When all hell broke loose, she could very well suspect that he was involved in the attack scheduled for later today. It could certainly be the end of their relationship.

There were several vital questions to answer. Would it make a difference to their marriage if he told her about the conspiracy and the bomb now? If so, was it worth it, given the potential consequences? When he told her, if the stress didn't kill her, Brody and his people would. In the end, the real issue was whether he was willing to do the right thing regardless of the end result. He had made a huge mess of things. After hours and hours of analysis, he decided the time had come to clean it up.

"It was the general, babe. He was asked by Secretary of Defense Atkins, an old military buddy of his, to help set up the Polly Flowers thing. I guess the general owed him a favor or two. The secretary wanted an excuse to separate himself from his close association with the president. Evidently, Atkins has hopes one day of being president himself. He paid for everything."

"Oh, my God, these politicians will stop at nothing for power. It's totally revolting. How many times have I told you there was something not right with the general? He's an asshole."

Thad took a deep breath, then dived in headfirst.

"Honey, that's not all. There's a plot to assassinate President Cooper."

"You're kidding, right?"

"I wouldn't joke about something like that."

"Oh, my God! Are you involved?"

* * *

She looked into her husband's sad eyes and knew the truth. All of a sudden, she felt light-headed. Her new heart was beating so fast, she could feel the pulse in her throat.

"Yes."

She cradled her head in her hands as she fought through waves of nausea. She managed to mutter, "When is this supposed to happen?"

Kendra looked up and could see the wheels spinning in her husband's head. It was as if she could read his mind. She was sure he was wondering if he was killing his wife right before his eyes.

"Honey, never mind. I'm going to take care of it."

From one second to the next, Kendra's demeanor made an about-face. The fury building inside her had given her strength.

"Tell me when!" she shouted.

"This afternoon."

Kendra sat there with her mouth wide open for half a minute. When the shock partially dissipated, she was yelling again.

"What! Oh, no, no, no, no! No way, Thad! Something has to be done. We can't let it happen. You were going to kill the *president*?"

"Wait a second. First, I have every intention of stopping it. I felt like my hands were tied. You don't know these people, honey. They wouldn't hesitate to kill both of us. I couldn't give a shit about myself. I was protecting you. I've made a huge pile of shit out of things."

"I don't give a damn what they do to me, either. I'm not going to sit back and let this happen. Either you pick up that phone right now and call someone who can prevent this, or I'm calling Agent Falcone."

"We can't use our phone. I told you. I'm gonna take care of this. I'll go across the street and ask if I can use Evan's cell phone."

\* \* \*

It was time. A driver hired by Brody had dropped Billy Ray off two blocks from his destination. Pedestrian traffic was far too heavy to get any closer. The streets of Washington in the vicinity of the Mall and Reflecting Pool were as crowded as downtown Manhattan during rush hour. Every way he turned, he saw an endless ocean of black skin. They were everywhere, as far as the eye could see. He could smell their stench in the air.

A set of credentials hanging on a cord around his neck allowed him access to the zone with the highest security restrictions for the Million Man March. He was dressed in the uniform provided to the men and women working on and around the main stage, at the base of the Washington Monument. The same man who had altered Thad Raymond's appearance for his trip to the Middle East had given Billy Ray a whole new look. He was now a middle-aged man with Mediterranean skin color, graying black hair, brown eyes, and a few extra pounds around his stomach. To get to his destination, he was going to have to make his way through the masses. Avoiding a bump here or a brush there would be impossible. His feet seemed glued to the blacktop at curbside where he had gotten out of the car. The blaring honk of a horn finally forced him to step up onto the sidewalk.

This was no time to freeze up. It wasn't as if he hadn't anticipated a capacity attendance. What he hadn't expected was the overwhelming intensity of the aversion he was experiencing. He had never been in such close proximity to so many vulgar, dirty subhumans in his entire life. It required a colossal effort to keep his last meal down. He tried to focus on the significance of his task, the magnitude of what he was about to accomplish, just to cope with being in the presence of such filth. If that didn't give him the motivation and strength to overcome this temporary stumbling block, nothing would.

Ten minutes later, Billy Ray found himself within twenty yards of the security checkpoint at the entrance to the restricted zone. For him to gain access, a Secret Service Agent would have to verify his badges, check to make sure he was on the typed list of approved volunteers, match his photo ID to the one next to his name, and have him pass through a full-body scanner. Every employee who had received similar credentials had been authorized access only after a two-month investigation by the Secret Service. Brody had given Billy Ray his only this morning.

He turned toward the Reflecting Pool to take a moment and calm himself. He had successfully negotiated his way through the crowd by centering his thoughts on the big prize, but not without a blow to his frame of mind. The stink had reached a saturation point that stung his nostrils. Too many black shoulders had grazed his, putting him in a state of high anxiety. The out-of-the-loop Secret Service agents patrolling the area would be trained to identify the slightest of suspicious behaviors. The man floating on the surface of the water, staring back at him, looked as though he had just escaped from an insane asylum. That wouldn't do. Billy Ray closed his eyes and painted a picture in his mind of what he projected to be the aftermath of the execution of his mission: a lot of dead black bodies. The tension in his chest, stomach, and shoulders began to ease. He stood up straight, turned away from the pool, and walked with renewed confidence toward the security checkpoint.

* * *

The FBI Learjet was speeding through the troposphere at more than five hundred miles per hour, heading north toward Washington, D.C. Daniel had commandeered the aircraft leased by the North Miami Field Office and normally reserved for use by the special agent in charge. His explanation to his superiors for his quick return to the nation's capital did not include his suspicion that the life of the president of the United States could be in danger. That would have set in motion a series of response measures involving a host of governmental agencies and scores of personnel. If he happened to be wrong, he would look like a complete idiot, especially in light of the president's rejection of his theory. To make such a proclamation would require much more concrete evidence than a gut feeling. Instead, Daniel explained to the special agent in charge that he had received information, from what he deemed a very reliable source, that Billy Ray Johnson was in Washington, D.C., at a specific location, and that an arrest was probable. It wasn't exactly accurate, but Daniel figured that the consequences of a failure on that count would be much more palatable than dealing with raising a false alarm regarding an attempt on Cooper's life.

Time was not on his side. The president was scheduled to speak at five p.m., immediately after the performance of pop star Thelma Brown. By the time Daniel had arranged for a pilot and could take off from Fort Lauderdale-Hollywood International Airport, the estimated time of arrival was 4:15 p.m. Fortunately, it was just a twelve-minute ride from Ronald Reagan Washington National Airport to the White House. That was under normal circumstances. With a million extra people marching around the city, the drive time could be easily twice that. Twenty minutes to save the president of the United States wasn't much of a window.

During their conversation, Daniel enlisted Chris Frye to travel with him and assist with whatever plan they developed. Frye had met him at the airport. After they took off, Daniel played the recording of his interview with Tabitha Freemont to bring his partner completely up to speed.

"Okay, Daniel, what's the plan?" Frye asked after the recording ended.

"I don't have much of one. The girl had no information about how they plan to assassinate Cooper. So far, it's been bombs and semiautomatic rifles. Shit, I'm not even sure it'll be Billy Ray who does the dirty work. Based on what Christy said in his reports, he's a guy who enjoys the limelight and getting attaboys from his peers. He's also a marksman. If he's the one who's going to do it, shooting might be his preference. Unless there's some major conspiracy going on with people on the inside involved, I can't imagine they could get a bomb close enough. What do you think?"

"How about alerting the Secret Service? Maybe they could do a better job of talking Cooper out of speaking at the event. They could at least be keeping an eye out."

"If the president rejected my warning, he may not appreciate me going behind his back. I just wish I had more to give them. Here's what I'm thinking. There's a really good chance the girl is telling the truth. I'm flying by the seat of my pants here, but I can't sit back and do nothing. I'm gonna get my ass out there and look for Johnson . . . or anything suspicious. Then, at least, if something does happen it won't be on my conscience."

* * *

Making it through security was a cinch, not that Billy Ray had any real concerns. He had to admit that Brody's men had set things up really well. Left to their own devices, the Klan wouldn't have been able to execute such a plan so easily. Truthfully, it would have been next to impossible. He was glad to get the benefit of having Brody on his side. That wasn't the same as being appreciative or thankful, though. Brody and whoever he represented were in for a big shock when he informed the media that the Ku Klux Klan was responsible for the president's death. Hopefully, Cooper would be joined in death by thousands of others.

At the moment, some famous, self-righteous Reverend Pig was delivering a speech to the crowd. Most of the stagehands were busy at their stations, handling whatever business was assigned to them.

386

Two trailers were set up behind the stage, abutting the Washington Monument. One of them was for the celebrities speaking or performing at the Million Man March. The other held equipment for the fireworks display to take place after sundown. According to the schedule, which was strictly enforced, no one was supposed to use the latter until a half hour before the fireworks began. The area behind the stage where the trailers were located had only one access point. Two Secret Service Agents were stationed there to ensure that only those authorized to enter one trailer or the other were permitted to pass.

After making it through that checkpoint, Billy Ray proceeded directly to the storage trailer. Hidden under a panel of flooring in the far corner, he would find the explosive, remote detonator and the separate pieces of the bomb he must assemble. He wasn't exactly sure how Brody had managed that particular trick especially considering that it included two and a half tons of urea nitrate. The trailer must have been built specifically for their purpose. Billy Ray didn't doubt that the man either had worked or was currently working for an agency such as the CIA. Their reach was far, maybe limitless. As long as everything was in its place as promised, Billy Ray couldn't give a shit how they accomplished it.

He climbed the steps leading to the front door, as if he owned the place. He used the key Brody had given him to gain entry. Once inside, he looked toward either end of the structure. Satisfied he was alone, he went straight to the designated cache. After countless rehearsals, Billy Ray's fastest time recorded for putting the brains of the bomb together and replacing it under the mock floorboard was a minute and thirty seconds. He was hoping to get everything done within three minutes. That would give him a whole minute and a half of leeway.

The floor of the trailer was made of cheap wood planks measuring six by twelve inches. The boxes of fireworks were stacked three high throughout the entire trailer. Billy Ray slid the boxes in the west corner about eighteen inches, until they no longer covered the pertinent plank. He got down on one knee, took a nail clipper from his trouser pocket, and used it to winkle up the floor board. Underneath, he found the components he needed as well as the massive amount of explosive running the length of the trailer's belly. The parts he would be working with were in separate sealed plastic bags. He removed each one, including the remote detonator, then went to work. He had the device together in record time. Following Raymond's instructions, he had saved the connection of the power source for last.

As he lowered the fully functional detonator into the empty compartment, he detected conversation just outside the door of the trailer. An instant later, he heard the distinct sound of a key being inserted and turned in the lock.

Billy Ray's next several moves would have to be fast and precise. He slipped the device into its space, replaced the plank, stood up, put the remote in his pocket, then pretended to be looking for something. The door swung open, and two black men stepped into the trailer. Billy whirled around as if startled.

The first to enter was genuinely surprised to find someone inside. "Oh, shit—sorry, man," he said. "We didn't know anyone was in here."

"You guys scared the crap out of me! What are you doing in here? I didn't see anyone else on the schedule."

"We got special permission to come in. My buddy lost his wallet. He thinks he might'a dropped it in here earlier this morning."

"Well, look out for a big-ass rat. I just saw one go underneath these boxes. I moved 'em, but he's gone."

"Hell, it better not come near me. I can't stand the nasty things," said the man who had lost his wallet.

"Well, have at it," said Billy Ray. "I'm done in here. He slid the boxes back in place and, being sure to keep a healthy distance from the two men, walked out, shutting the door behind him. He listened outside the trailer, pretending to read documents, as the men searched. Five minutes later, they appeared. The man who had lost his wallet was holding it in his hand, smiling and patting his companion on the back. As they walked off, Billy Ray was confident that the bomb was safe in its hiding place and that he had performed his task to perfection.

He couldn't have been more mistaken. As with many homemade bombs, Thad Raymond had designed a manual toggle as a backup to the remote-control detonation. In Billy Ray's rush to put the detonating mechanism into its cartridge, the switch to initiate the countdown skimmed against the edge of the adjacent board and was activated. The device was set to explode in twenty minutes.

\* \* \*

After Daniel's plane landed, he turned his cell phone on to find, for the second time that day, a string of missed calls from the same person. This time, it wasn't a number he recognized offhand. When he listened to the message, he recognized Thaddeus Raymond's voice immediately. Without saying a word to Christopher Frye, he pressed the callback button.

"Agent Falcone here. What's going on, Raymond? What do you know about the president being in danger?"

Frye perked up in his seat. Daniel placed the call on speaker phone.

"Thank God you called back. I've been calling my office. I was just about to try to get in touch with the director if you hadn't called just now."

"I don't have time for chitchat. Get to the point."

"There's a conspiracy to assassinate President Cooper. It's going to happen today when he gives his speech at the Million Man March. There's a bomb."

"And how do you know this?" Daniel remained calm. He had lots of questions, not the least of which was how Raymond knew about the plot and why he had waited until now to reveal it. There was precious little time to ask them, but he needed more to go on. The plane had landed ten minutes early, giving him a grand total of fifty-five minutes to make sure Cooper didn't take that stage.

"Please, just trust me. I'm telling the truth. I don't know the exact location of the bomb. I just know that they asked me a lot of safety questions about building a structure to support it. I'm sure it's got to be somewhere in the vicinity of the stage. You gotta get those people outta there."

"Thaddeus, I'm going to need some concrete proof for the president. How do you know about this?"

"There's a group of very highly placed and powerful men behind it all. One of them was like a father to me. His name is General Adam Montgomery. They've been working with the Ku Klux Klan. I designed and built the bomb."

Daniel had no time to be shocked or even mildly surprised. His senses were telling him that what he was hearing was the truth. He took another few minutes to ask some vital questions and get more information about the principals involved. There was a lot to do in very little time. The lives of the president of the United States and thousands of others depended on it.

*  *  *

While rising from his seat on the Learjet, Daniel couldn't click on his cell phone's listing of the president's private number fast enough. When there was no answer, he left a detailed message regarding the imminent attack. Next, he called the director of the FBI and advised him of the information he had obtained from Thaddeus Raymond. Director Ryan didn't hold matters up to question the situation. He also had no option but to take Daniel's message at face value. He said he would notify the top brass at the Secret Service, get a team of agents assembled right away, and do what he could to evacuate the crowd. Daniel hoped that Ryan would have more success reaching the Secret Service than he had trying to reach the president directly. There was a lot going on in Washington. Forty minutes' notice to clear out tens of thousands of people probably wasn't going to be enough. There was also no guarantee that Ryan's team would get to the president any faster than Daniel could. Now that the wheels had been set in motion, there wasn't much else he could do but get to the main stage himself. If it became necessary, he would deliver the message to Cooper personally.

Daniel had arranged for an FBI car to pick them up on the airport tarmac. He and Frye sprinted down the airstairs of the Learjet, then to the waiting Crown Victoria. As they hopped into the backseat, Daniel told the driver to do whatever it took to get them to the White House as fast as the engine would allow.

"Do you know what's going on in Washington today, guys?" the driver asked.

"Yes, we do," said Daniel. "And if you can't handle it, let one of us drive."

"What the hell is going on?"

"Just fucking drive and get us there fast. Your job might depend on it."

\* \* \*

Thelma Brown had just begun her set, which was scheduled to last twenty minutes. She planned to sing five songs in succession. Then she would have the honor of introducing the president. Several hours before taking the stage, she had met Cooper and his wife and three children at the White House. She was thrilled to hear that the first family intended to come out early to listen to at least part of her performance.

It had been quite a few years since she was nervous singing for a live audience. She could feel a tightness in her stomach as she stood offstage waiting for her cue. Halfway into the show, she still couldn't shake it off completely. It didn't help that when she took a peek toward the wings at the end of her third song, she saw the president and his family moving to the music.

\* \* \*

Backstage, the sounds of the beginning of the concert and cheers from the crowd were so loud, Billy Ray could hardly hear himself think. The stink had never totally disappeared from his consciousness. Now that the riskiest of his responsibilities were behind him, his awareness of his surroundings had returned. He headed directly for the stairway that would get him back to ground level and the exit from the restricted zone. There was no need to linger, and the earsplitting jungle music gave him that much more incentive to get out of here. He passed through the backstage area not visible to the audience, then turned left and found himself looking directly at the president of the United States, his wife and kids, and a group of Secret Service agents. They had arrived earlier than expected.

At the moment, Billy Ray's only purpose was to get back to a predetermined rendezvous point. From there, the same driver who had dropped him off would take him to a point far enough from the blast to be out of danger. He had to walk within feet of the president's covey, knowing he would be watched by at least the band of Secret Service agents. Crossing paths with his target on this day of supreme importance was just what Billy Ray needed to get him through the final stages. Looking directly at that black face and knowing that within the hour he would be dead gave Billy Ray the necessary emotional advantage. He proceeded past them without the slightest hesitation, descended the steps, passed through an alleyway, and emerged onto a walkway leading to the exit from the restricted zone.

The president's speech was scheduled to last twenty-five minutes. Once Billy Ray was shuttled to the safe zone—a McDonald's parking lot 3.8 miles from the Washington Monument, he would wait for a call from Brody to detonate the bomb. Two very important people, whom Brody refused to identify, would be in harm's way for part of the speech. A certain period of delay would be necessary to let them get far enough from the Washington Monument to avoid injury or death. Billy Ray couldn't give a rat's ass about whoever Brody wanted to

393

save from the blast. For now, he would follow their instructions. Soon enough, he would be the man in charge.

This time, the walk from the restricted zone to the rendezvous point with the chauffeur was not nearly as disturbing. The closer Billy Ray got to the final moments, the better he felt. His focus on the task at hand had become laser sharp. He barely noticed the people around him. The Town Car pulled up seconds after he arrived at the meeting place. When he hopped into the passenger seat and shut the door, the adrenaline coursing through his veins gave him the impression that he was indestructible.

Ten minutes later, after successfully negotiating through the heavy traffic, the driver pulled into the parking lot of a shopping center that Billy Ray didn't recognize.

"Where the fuck are you going?" Billy Ray asked.

"I need to take a piss. There are woods behind this shopping center. I'll be quick."

"Listen, shithead, you're not supposed to stray from the plan. Get your ass back on the road."

"What's your fuckin' problem, dude? We got plenty of time."

"I don't give a fuck how much time we have. You can't change the plan."

They had already made it behind the buildings by the time Billy Ray completed his last statement. The driver stopped the car, pulled a nine-millimeter pistol with a silencer from the space between his seat and the door, and pointed it at Billy Ray's forehead.

"I'm not."

He lowered the opaque passenger window and pulled the trigger until the pistol's action opened on an empty chamber. Billy Ray's body jolted as the first bullet slammed into his forehead, and then lay still.

When the shooting stopped, Billy Ray slumped forward, the right side of his head scrunched against the glove compartment.

The remote detonator was attached to a clip on his belt. The driver removed it, placed it on the seat between them, and waited for his next instructions.

\* \* \*

"Tom, I have some really bad news," said Director John Nash of the Secret Service. "I just got a call from Director Ryan at the Bureau. He says one of his agents has substantial evidence there will be an attempt on the president's life this afternoon. He wants me to get Cooper to call off his speech. He also asked me to do what I could to get the crowd evacuated."

"God damn it!" Tom Logan shouted into the cell phone "You gotta be fucking kidding me! Where did they get the information? What else does Ryan know?"

"The only information he shared with me was that there's a bomb planted somewhere around the stage that will explode during the president's speech. What did you want me to do? Give him the third degree? Anyway, Cooper is out there now, onstage. He went with his family to listen to the music. I could give the order for detonation right now."

"You out of your *mind*? Speaker White and I will be blown to bits with everyone else. We're backstage in one of the trailers."

"Sorry. How the hell was I supposed to know? I don't have a lot of fuckin' time, Tom. I've got to act, and fast. If I do nothing, Ryan is going to get suspicious. This is yours to call. What do you want to do? Can you make some excuse to get the hell outta there? When were you supposed to meet the president?"

"Five minutes before his speech is scheduled to start, which is in about five minutes or so. This could've all been avoided if the damn fool didn't want a photo op with us onstage. The liberal prick thinks he can convince the American public he's bipartisan. He's so far to the left, I'm surprised his skin's black and not red."

"Tom, we don't have time for a political discussion. You're preaching to the choir here. We gotta stop fucking around and make a decision. Either we detonate the bomb in the next few minutes, or we call it off."

"Son of a bitch. I can't believe this. We can't risk it, John. Call your man and tell him it's off. We can't risk it," Logan repeated as if to convince himself.

"Before you make a final decision, think about this. What if they know more? What if they know about *us*?"

"How could that be? And how would that change anything? If they know about us, it's best to call it off anyway."

"I don't trust Raymond. Never have. Never wanted the general to get him involved. You know he's been talking to Falcone?"

"If that's true, I want him dead."

Nash never had the opportunity to respond. From his office miles away, he could hear the explosion, and the line went dead.

* * *

As day faded into night, Daniel's ride raced north across the Potomac River on Interstate 395, toward the Washington Monument. Traffic on the freeway was relatively light, considering the number of people visiting the nation's capital. He figured that most of them were either at the march or at home watching it on TV. He wasn't complaining.

Once they got off the freeway, they would be able to take the special-events route reserved for official vehicles. They shouldn't be delayed at all. In just a few short minutes, they would be arriving at the White House. If Director Ryan hadn't already gotten the message through to the Secret Service and the president, Daniel was hoping to stop Cooper before he ever left his residence.

When they pulled up to the special gate Cooper had authorized him to use, the news couldn't have been worse: the president had already left the premises and was currently at the Mall.

"How close can you get me to the stage in this car?" Daniel asked the driver.

"I have no idea. I don't know what they've marked off between here and there." He looked up to the Secret Service agent in the booth for assistance.

"What's going on?" the agent asked. "What's the hurry?"

Daniel said, "The president's life is in danger."

"Go ahead and take the official vehicle route off East Street. It'll take you less than a minute. Anything I can do?"

"I assume there are security checkpoints along the way?" Daniel said.

"Right. I'll call ahead. You should have no problem."

"All right, then, let's move."

The driver pulled around the circle and floored the accelerator onto East Street. Six local police officers and at least four Secret Service agents were manning the checkpoint for entry onto the roadway limited to official use only. Evidently, the Secret Service agent at the White House had acted fast. They waved the Crown Vic through. Once again the driver pushed the engine to top speed. This road was designed to allow for high speeds as a quick escape route for the president. Thirty seconds later, the driver stopped in the area where the president's limo and other official vehicles accompanying him had parked.

Agents Falcone and Frye jumped out of the car as it was coming to a stop, and sprinted directly toward the stage. The music was deafening. The staircase leading up into the wings was yards from three monster speakers blaring out a dance beat. The two Secret Service agents manning the post blocked Daniel's and Christopher's access. Evidently, they hadn't gotten the memo. The entire area was packed to the gills with spectators. No one was being evacuated.

"Is the president on stage?" Daniel asked one of the agents, shouting as loudly as his vocal cords would allow.

"What?"

Communication was going to be next to impossible. Daniel decided to use a trick he had learned as a teenager to get another person to hear under similar circumstances. He reached up and pushed the tragus, the small flap opposite the ear canal, and slightly closed it off. Then he spoke into the agent's ear.

"I'm FBI Special Agent Daniel Falcone." He showed the agent his badge and had Christopher hold up his. "We have substantial evidence that there will be an attempt on the president's life. There's a bomb. We have to get him out of here."

No one else could be notified until the president was safely out of harm's way. The chaos caused by any announcements to clear the area could place his rescue in jeopardy.

The Secret Service agent heard every word Daniel had said, and acted swiftly. He spoke into his microphone as he raced up the stairs. Daniel and Christopher followed directly behind. The president and his family were about forty feet from the top step. They were already being quickly led by their personal Secret Service agents toward the exit. When Cooper saw Daniel, he stopped in his tracks. He said something, though not a word of it was audible. Daniel used the same maneuver with the president that he had with the Secret Service agent just moments earlier. One of Cooper's agents moved to stop him. The president waved him off.

"Sir, I know a lot more than I did earlier when I spoke to you from Florida. Please, just let us get you to safety."

Daniel's explanation was enough. The president allowed himself and his family to be escorted by eight Secret Service agents down the stairs and to his limousine at a half walking, half jogging pace. Once Daniel saw that Cooper was in his limousine and on his way out, he and Frye hopped into the backseat of their car and followed the president's motorcade through the escape route to be sure he was out of harm's way. It was their intention to turn back and help evacuate the crowd, but they never got the chance. At the exact moment the president's vehicle reached East Street, an earsplitting explosion rocked Daniel's car and blew out all the windows.

* * *

Hours after the blast, Daniel and Christopher sat in the outer room of the oval office, awaiting President Cooper's invitation to enter. Other than some minor cuts and scratches, Cooper and his family, the Secret Service agents accompanying him, and Daniel and Christopher had all escaped the attack unscathed. In the immediate aftermath, Daniel had seen the presidential limousine speed off in the direction of the White House. Figuring that the Secret Service had everything under control, he and Christopher jumped out of the car to head back toward the Mall, to help with the survivors. By the magnitude of the explosion, the vibration of the earth, and the black clouds of smoke climbing into the sky in every direction, Daniel knew that many had died.

The white obelisk that had stood in commemoration of the first president of the United States no longer soared 555 feet into the Washington sky. It had been obliterated. The stage was gone. On their way to ground zero, Daniel and Christopher had to avoid burning debris and foliage. The air was acrid with the smell of smoke and burned flesh. Sounds of screeching sirens seemed to be converging on the scene from every angle. They blended with screams from the people far enough from the epicenter to have survived.

When the two FBI agents arrived at what used to be the Washington Monument, the devastation was gut wrenching. Torsos, limbs, and strips and globs of gore were strewn across the grounds the entire length of the Reflecting Pool to the east. At least double the victims were strewn across the lawn to the west. No one within fifty yards of the stage on either side of the Monument had survived.

Many more people had been gathered on the west side because of the abundant space available in the field that extended more than a mile toward the Capitol Building, and because the stage was facing that direction. Both men headed that way, at a dead run toward the screams. They pulled bodies away from flaming grass and put out burning clothing with their jackets. Once the emergency vehicles began to arrive, they helped carry the injured and directed those who could move without assistance to tents set up for triage. It was the worst attack ever on the capital of the United States. Daniel was sure the death toll would far exceed that of the Pentagon on September 11, 2001. The lives of hundreds of very important American politicians, businesspeople, and celebrities were lost.

Four hours later, after they had done all they could, Daniel and Chris went back to the White House. There, they found that the president had been treated at George Washington University hospital for minor cuts and bruises. The doctors wanted to keep him overnight. Cooper refused and was back at the White House less an hour after his arrival at the emergency room. When he learned that Daniel and Christopher were there, he asked to have them brought to the Oval Office to meet with him.

The president himself opened the door to his office and asked the FBI agents to come in. He offered them seats across from his desk, then sat.

"First, thank you both for saving my family and me," said Cooper.

"Sir, I really didn't do much," Christopher interjected. "Daniel deserves all the credit."

"I know that, Agent Frye. You put your life in danger as well, and I owe you a great debt of gratitude. I guess I should have listened to you the first time around, Daniel. Maybe none of this would have happened."

"Sir, you did the right thing. It was a flip of the coin. All I had at the time was a gut feeling."

"Well, I won't ignore your gut feelings in the future. Now, can you tell me what you knew later that you didn't know when we first talked?"

"It seems there are people in this town who wanted you dead—people you might have called friends—or at least close colleagues."

"Are they in custody? Who are they?"

"I'll answer your second question first. There were four men, at least two of them politicians here in Washington, who conspired with the Ku Klux Klan to assassinate you. Secretary of Homeland Security Tom Logan, Speaker of the House Frank White, and the man known as the general, Adam Montgomery. There is a fourth individual who our informant could not identify, though he apparently holds some high position here in Washington. Billy Ray Johnson was given the so-called honor of detonating the bomb.

President Benjamin Cooper showed no outward reaction to the names. Daniel could see at least two emotions expressed in his eyes, however: sadness, then anger. He could not say whether the president was surprised.

"It was Thaddeus Raymond who spilled the beans," Daniel continued. "He was recruited by the general to take part in the conspiracy. He met with the three men he named. The fourth person in their group refused to have his identity revealed. Raymond designed and constructed the bomb. Immediately after my conversation with him, I called Director Ryan and told him everything. He took it from there. I got an update from him not too long before you called us in. He has reason to believe Tom Logan and Speaker White were killed in the explosion. After questioning both men's staffs and doing some further digging, we know that fifteen or twenty minutes before the explosion, Logan told his assistant he was heading down to the stage to meet with you. Several witnesses indicated they saw him on his way. They confirmed that Speaker White was with him. Even more convincing are photographs we were able to recover from a reporter from the *Washington Post,* who was taking pictures of the mall from the Capitol Building when Chris saw him. He shot a picture of Logan and White nearing the stage minutes before the explosion. Three separate surveillance cameras, set up by the Secret Service far enough from the explosion that they weren't damaged, confirmed the photographs taken by the reporter, and the times when they were taken. The general seems to have disappeared for the moment.

By the way, Raymond admitted that the Polly Flowers affair was all a setup. Secretary Atkins was the brains for that scheme. He supposedly had nothing to do with today's bombing. He went to the general to set you up. Evidently, some favors were owed. General Montgomery had his hand in a couple of pots. I'd say he wasn't a fan of yours."

"That's obviously the least of my concerns right now, though I'm glad to hear that the truth will come out. It seems like several of the people I surrounded myself with weren't fans. I've never understood, nor will I ever, how, even today, human beings exist who can hate so intensely simply because of the color of a person's skin. The acceptance of cultural differences and exchange of ideas is what has made our country so great. It was what the Constitution was based on, for God's sake! So many innocent and senseless deaths . . . children . . ."

The president bowed his head for a moment, then asked, "Your people really think Tom and Frank were killed in the explosion? That makes no sense. Why would they even be anywhere close to the Mall if they knew a bomb was going off?"

"We think something might have gone wrong—maybe a problem with the bomb. It could have exploded earlier than they expected. You weren't even supposed to be out there at the time, and it was meant for you. That's the only explanation I can think of."

"Or Thaddeus Raymond is lying."

"I don't think so, Mr. President."

"What about the Johnson kid?"

"I'll let Chris answer that for you, sir. He's been keeping up with that."

"Can I assume you know who Tabitha Freemont is, Mr. President?" Frye asked.

"The name's familiar. Refresh my memory."

"She's the woman who prompted Daniel to call you earlier today, to suggest that you cancel your speech. She gave us an address where Billy Ray and his coconspirators were hiding out. When Daniel called me about flying to D.C. with him, he also had me put together a team from the Senator Fitch task force to set up surveillance at the house in Georgia. There hasn't been any Billy Ray Johnson sighting. But three people staying at the house have been taken into custody. One of them, Andrew Lansbury, spilled his guts. He confirmed that Billy Ray was here in Washington to detonate the bomb. He also confessed that Billy Ray, one Keith Peterson, and Lansbury's son, Kyle, were responsible for all the other bombings around the country."

"It seems to me we have several suspects still at large. I'm not convinced that Logan and Frank White were victims of this attack, either. Maybe we should keep things quiet and see if they show up. Who else knows about this besides you guys and Director Ryan?"

"I'd say too many people at this point, Mr. President," replied Daniel. I don't know all the details. I'd assume the team that the director put together probably included at least fifty agents. I'm not sure what Director Ryan told Nash. If you ask me, sir, I think our only choice is to wait and see how things pan out. There are lots of dead bodies out there, most of them unidentifiable. I'm sure there will be some DNA testing. Eventually we could get some confirmation about Logan and White . . . uh, but it could take a while."

**Chapter 27**

"Nice going, General," said Secret Service Director John Nash. "I told you not to recruit Raymond. Motherfucker is straight as an arrow. I knew that Johnson kid would fuck things up, too. I warned you guys. What now, genius?"

Night had fallen in Old Town Alexandria, Virginia, where Nash lived in a four-million-dollar, five-bedroom Colonial brick house. He had spared no expense decorating his home. To the general, it looked as if it belonged in a magazine. A priceless crystal chandelier hung from the high ceiling in the foyer, and the art on the living room walls alone could support a family of five for a lifetime.

The director of the Secret Service was doing a piss poor job concealing he was furious that the general had shown up at his house. Nash's ulterior motives for offering some semblance of hospitality were more than transparent. He refrained from telling the general to "go to hell" only because he was one of the few people alive who knew that Nash was part of the assassination plot.

Neither man knew the identity of the snitch with any real certainty or exactly how much information had been revealed. Nash was making his opinions perfectly clear. If the Bureau had any names, it was Thaddeus Raymond who supplied them. As far as anyone knew, the general could be on the FBI's wanted list for the attack. Nash had good reason to doubt he himself was a suspect— Director Ryan wouldn't have contacted him and shared information if that were the case. And Raymond had no idea his boss was part of the conspiracy.

Brody, too, had died in the explosion. He was waiting on the west side of the Washington Monument for Logan and White to complete their appearance onstage with Cooper. After the three men made their escape from the scene and the deed was done, a substantial sum of money was to be transferred to an offshore account owned by Brody—a transaction that now would never take place.

"You better watch your tone with me, Nash. I'm not gonna take your shit. How do you know it was Thad? Why would I have missed calls from him? There are other Klan members who knew about the plot, how it was supposed to happen, and when. Besides, what the fuck are you worried about? No one knows you were part of it except me and the men you involved. Hell, it could've been one of your guys, for all you know."

The general had chosen to ignore Thad's calls until he could analyze the situation better. He wasn't so sure that Nash was wrong, although he preferred not to voice that opinion. In spite of his hunch, he couldn't help but come to Thad's defense. He had tried to be angry. At the moment, he was taking his frustrations out on Nash. The general had never been comfortable with Nash's involvement. Nash wasn't like the other three men. His motives were mostly, if not totally, self-serving, not based on any love or loyalty to his country. Nash loved money and power. It was more than obvious in his lifestyle and possessions. If not for the advantages provided by his position as director of the Secret Service, he might never have been included in the group of four.

"One more word about Thad, I'll take your head off. It was Logan who insisted on Johnson, and you know it. You weren't complaining too much when Zachary was supplying millions of dollars to fund us. What's done is done. Wasting time on that shit'll get us nowhere."

Willis Zachary, Ku Klux Klan grand dragon for the state of Florida, had secretly supported Tom Logan's political career since the beginning. It was Zachary who insisted that Logan and his men use the Johnson kid. That it was Billy Ray's brainchild to assassinate President Cooper hadn't really played into the decision at all. Zachary wanted the Johnsons ultimately out of the picture. With aspirations of his own to head the Ku Klux Klan into its promising future, he saw Billy Ray as a thorn in his side.

"Bullshit, General. You need to be thinking about Raymond. Your ass is on the line just as much as mine, if not more. Do you know where that fuck is?"

"I can find out easy enough. I could call him back."

"I see no harm in that. If he's working with the FBI, it's not like they can locate your secure cell phone. See what he wants."

The general considered Nash's suggestion. Perhaps he could get some indication of Thad's intentions from his voice. After all, there was no one in the world the general knew better. He decided to go for it. He grabbed his cell phone, punched the missed-call list, and dialed Thad's number.

* * *

Daniel and Thad had been over the scenario several times. An authentic performance was essential. Thad had no doubt that the general would see through any act that wasn't from the heart. Using Kendra as his source of inspiration, he just might be able to get the job done. He would probably never get to spend another night of his life with his beautiful wife, but it didn't change his motivation to make things right for her, to give her some peace. He didn't want her to believe that she was responsible for any part of the horrible tragedy. Perhaps bringing the guilty parties to justice would help in some small way.

At the moment, four FBI agents, including Daniel Falcone and Christopher Frye, were waiting with Kendra and Thad Raymond in a motel room in Woodbridge, Virginia. More agents were posted in strategic places in other

408

rooms and about the grounds in the event they managed to draw the general to their location. Taps were placed on the Raymonds' home and cell phones.

At the sound of Thad's ring tone, everyone in the room froze. He looked at the screen, then nodded to Daniel, indicating that it could be the general.

"Hello? General! Thank God!"

"Thad, you can imagine I'm in a very precarious situation. I'm not comfortable being on the phone with you right now. Why did you call?"

"Excuse me, sir? And I'm not? I would think it's obvious why I called. I'm at a dirtbag motel room with my wife. I was waiting to hear from you before I made any other moves."

"What are you talking about, Thad?"

"I assume you know the president was rescued?"

"Yes, I'm aware."

"I don't understand, General. I'm doing what I suspect you're doing: laying low. Why do you sound confused?"

"When did you find out things went wrong?"

"Harry Nelson contacted me from his post at the Capitol Building. He heard everything going on when the Secret Service agents were getting the president off the premises. He said he contacted you."

There were a handful of trusted Secret Service agents enlisted to get the bomb parts into the floor of the fireworks trailer at the Million Man March. One of those was Agent Harry Nelson, who was technically responsible for the canine unit at the event. It was no coincidence that he was also Logan's son-in-law.

Thad continued, "I immediately had Kendra get some stuff together. I did the same. We came straight here. I've tried to contact you several times. I need your help, General. I need to know what you want us to do. Do you know how they found out? Was it Billy Ray?"

* * *

With every fiber of his soul, the general wanted to believe what Thad was saying. He didn't want to think that the man he considered a son could be guilty of such betrayal. Though he preferred not to reveal his suspicions, now was no time to worry about hurt feelings. He had to hear how Thad reacted to being accused of informing.

"I'm going to be perfectly frank with you. There are very few people who knew about the assassination plot. I'm sorry, but I have to ask: did you warn the president?"

"Seriously, General, what the fuck? I'm busting my balls here. Kendra has no idea what is going on. It's all I can do to keep her from leaving or having a heart attack. I told her she can't know, for national security reasons. She's only going to believe that for so long. I made the fucking *bomb,* for Christ's sake! Do you think I want to go to death row?"

"Calm down, Thad. I had to ask. I get it. I believe you."

"All right. Well, what do I do now? I have no money. I can't get to my accounts."

"Just sit tight. I'll call you back."

* * *

"I think he's telling the truth, John," the general said. The question is, what do we do about it?"

"What makes you so sure?" Nash asked.

"Well, he has just as much to lose as any of us. These plans weren't contained well enough. Brody's hands were tied with Logan's commitment to Zachary. I think if we had done things Brody's way from the beginning, we would have pulled it off. There were too many hands in the pot. How do we know who Billy Ray told, and so forth and so on?

I wasn't sure about Thad, either. I knew he was cooperating with us against his will. With all the possible scenarios, it's just as likely, if not more so, that someone from the Klan was the snitch. It may ultimately get me in trouble." After a few seconds of hesitation he continued. "I'm going to give him the benefit of the doubt."

"What are you going to do? If it wasn't Thad, neither of us has anything to worry about. We really need to find out how much they know. It will dictate how we respond."

"I'm going to go meet him at the hotel. If I'm wrong, my life is fucked anyway. If it wasn't him, they won't know I was involved, and there's no need to panic."

"Where is he?"

"The Rodeway Inn in Woodbridge—the one on Jefferson Davis Highway. You know it?"

"Yep. You're looking at a death sentence if you're wrong. I expect you'll abide by our pact of secrecy?"

"Don't worry, John. I won't rat you out."

\* \* \*

The general was driving at a snail's pace, south on U.S. Highway 1 in Woodbridge in his six-year-old Cadillac Escalade. One more mile and he would arrive at the Rodeway Inn, where Thad and Kendra were supposedly hiding out. He had spoken to Thad twice since leaving Nash's home. Nothing in his old friend's voice suggested there was a major trap waiting at the motel. Still, an insecure feeling nagged at him. His senses were on high alert. Since the death of his wife, the general had three incentives to continue living: Polly, Thad, and the United States of America. The potential loss of all three had motivated him to take this risk. If Thad was working with the FBI, all would be lost.

On the spur of the moment, he decided to pull over onto the shoulder of the road. He pulled three items out of his glove compartment: a pen, an envelope, and his service pistol. He placed the pistol on the console beside him. On the envelope, he wrote a short note. After waiting for a man walking his Labrador retriever to step back onto the sidewalk, he merged back onto the road and continued at a faster pace toward the motel.

\* \* \*

A squad of twelve FBI agents had converged back at the Rodeway Inn. One of the agents had replaced the front desk clerk. The rest were in the room with Thad and Kendra or in one of the two adjoining rooms. A thirteenth and a fourteenth member of the team were undercover as pedestrians walking along the highway. One was disguised as a homeless woman pushing a shopping cart; the other was a man walking a dog. A fifteenth participant was waiting to leave

412

the parking lot in a Ford F-350 just in case the general had second thoughts and continued beyond the motel. Five other undercover agents were stationed in commercial parking areas south of the motel to cover that eventuality.

Daniel had received word from the agent on the street that the general was no more than a minute away. They could already have taken him down by shooting out his tires, but Daniel preferred to have a neat, clean arrest on the motel grounds. He ordered all agents to maintain their posts until the general turned into the parking lot. As soon as the subject passed through the entrance and continued on his way toward Thad's room, the truck "leaving" the motel would block the exit.

Forty-two seconds after Daniel received the report, the general's SUV approached the entrance and turned in.

* * *

General Adam Montgomery turned left into the parking lot of the Rodeway Inn. He was no longer disappointed, anxious, or angry over the day's events. A state of peace had taken over his psyche. He had come to terms with his inevitable fate. Neither the man walking the dog, the woman pushing the shopping cart, nor the Ford truck leaving the motel had fooled him. He witnessed the events that unfolded as if watching an instant replay of a television news report in accelerated motion. Peering in his rearview mirror, he saw the truck block the exit to the street, yet he continued to follow the directions given him by Thad, ultimately parking his car in the space next to Kendra's Jeep Compass. Agents spilled out of three rooms, surrounding his car, pointing their weapons, and shouting for him to put his hands over his head and step out of the car. The general calmly reached for the gun he had placed on the console. As he lifted it above the lower edge of the passenger window, several shots rang out from that side of the vehicle. Five bullets hit him. One of them pierced his heart, and two others passed through his brain, killing him instantly.

**Epilogue**

Daniel immediately felt a twinge of guilt after a series of congratulatory back slaps with his colleagues to celebrate the capture of the general and Secret Service Director John Nash. This really wasn't a day for any form of exultation. It had been Daniel's idea to use Thaddeus Raymond as a guinea pig to see if they could flush out any coconspirators in the plan to assassinate President Cooper. During his meeting with the president, he had gotten the call that the general had taken the bait. From there, it was a chaotic rush to get to the motel so that Daniel and Christopher could participate in the sting operation. Director Ryan had already assembled the team that spent the evening with Thad and Kendra at the motel. The Raymonds were present in the event the general called the motel directly to assure himself they were actually there.

Raymond wasn't happy that Kendra was a participant. He had no choice when she insisted. Before agreeing, he had made a halfhearted attempt to negotiate with Daniel for amnesty. The best Raymond could get was a promise to think about a recommendation for leniency. He wasn't expecting much. He had resigned himself to the fact that he must pay for his transgressions. He was directly responsible for the deaths of thousands of people. The least he could do was help bring all the guilty parties to justice.

Whether it was a stroke of luck, desperation, or stupidity, Daniel couldn't have hoped for better results. The general had left a suicide note of sorts, identifying John Nash as the fourth and final conspirator with the Ku Klux Klan to assassinate Cooper and implicating Willis Zachary as a major player. The director of the Secret Service did not go easily. He was not at his home in Alexandria when the team of more than twenty FBI agents showed up to arrest him. He might have gotten away if, after reading the general's note, Daniel had not immediately put out an APB requesting a special alert at airports and train and bus stations. TSA agents at Ronald Reagan International Airport recognized Nash through video surveillance. They took him into custody before he could board a privately chartered Gulfstream jet supposedly destined for Paris.

In his note, the general confirmed that Tom Logan and Frank White were killed in the explosion and implicated Willis Zachary as a major player in the racist attacks and assassination plot. The information regarding Logan and White couldn't be trusted 100 percent, though his claim did corroborate the many other much more reliable witnesses, photographs, and surveillance tapes. About two hours before the sting operation at the Rodeway Inn, a corpse was found in a Dumpster behind a strip shopping center a couple of miles from the National Mall. The body was subsequently identified as Billy Ray Johnson. Every one of the principals in the assassination plot was either dead or captured. Keith Peterson and Andrew Lansbury were arrested along with Troy Lansbury at the Georgia home where they had gathered for an anticipated celebration. In the next week, many arrests would follow for the attack on the Washington Mall, the other bombings elsewhere in the country, and the murder of Alvin Fitch.

It had been one of the most tragic days in U.S. history. Nevertheless, Daniel could not help feeling proud of his effort and those of his colleagues. They couldn't prevent the bomb from exploding, but they had saved the president and caught those responsible for the attempt on his life. In the coming days, major players in the Ku Klux Klan would be behind bars. The organization would suffer a significant blow.

As he bade his colleagues good night, Daniel thought about how much he was looking forward to finally sleeping in his own bed and resuming a normal life with his children and Annie in South Florida.

Printed in Great Britain
by Amazon